Other Books by Paul C. Colella

Patriots and Scoundrels: Charity's First Adventure

The Undefeated

Loyalty

—— and ——

Deceit

Paul C. Colella

iUniverse, Inc.
Bloomington

Loyalty and Deceit

Copyright © 2012 Paul C. Colella

iUniverse books may be ordered through booksellers or by contacting:

iUniverse
1663 Liberty Drive
Bloomington, IN 47403
www.iuniverse.com
1-800-Authors (1-800-288-4677)

ISBN: 978-1-4759-3214-0 (sc)
ISBN: 978-1-4759-3215-7 (e)

Printed in the United States of America

iUniverse rev. date: 6/13/2012

A masterful writer, Mr. Colella's compelling stories create intrigue, mystery and suspense. His ability to connect his characters and stories to his readers is unparalleled.

—Michael J. Freda, First Selectman of North Haven and former President and CEO of Corporate America

It is a traditional story with colorful characters, interlocking subplots, and rollercoaster cliffhangers. It's a definite page turner from start to finish.

—Mary Jo Cornwell, President of the Chatfield Book Club

Paul Colella has a natural gift for interweaving suspenseful storytelling with engaging characters that through his eye for detail become lifelike on the pages. His books offer a wholly rewarding reading experience.

—Kyle Swartz, Editorial Page Associate, the Record Journal

Loyalty is the constant effort to remain faithful to a cause, ideal, or relationship. Deceit is the deliberate misleading and deception of others to satisfy selfish or immoral acts. There is a thin line between loyalty and deceit, and the price sometimes paid for one's devotion is deception.

—Paul C. Colella

Dedication

In Memory of Mae Knobloch, a wonderful
person and a loyal reader.

And

For my Mom and Dad, I am blessed to have you as my parents.

To my niece Alyssa, and my nephew Philip,
Uncle Paul is proud of you.

To Ilona Sypniewski, I am grateful for your
honest opinions of my writing.

Acknowledgements

I want to thank my sister for her inspiration, support, and technical expertise during the writing of this book.

My appreciation also goes to Pamela Morello, Evelyn Auger, Frances Selmecki, and Irene and Rodger Salman whose encouragement and suggestions led to the creation of this book.

I am deeply appreciative to my former colleagues Elizabeth Bonvino, Rosemary Lauria, Grace Lineberry, Rose-Marie Lundell, Ed Monarca, Beth Pattivina, Paula Schwers, and Mary Shea for their support and friendship.

I also extend a special thank you to The Literary Lasses Book Club and The Friends of the North Haven Library.

Lastly, and certainly not least, I would like to express my gratitude to my relatives, friends, and faithful readers for their devoted support and loyalty.

Characters

Charity Chastine—a young girl who comes to America and befriends a gallery of patriots and scoundrels

Grace Collins—Charity's friend

David Cobb—a mill worker and Theodore Norton's friend

Theodore Norton—David Cobb's friend and Lydia Johnson's nephew

Elizabeth Higgins—Stanton Higgins' daughter and Mrs. Kensington's maid

Edmund Tate—Elizabeth Higgins' boyfriend and Colonel Parker's cousin

Mary Andrews—Jesse Andrews' mother and Charity's friend

Patience Wright—Charity's friend and guardian who lives in London

Constance Singleton Caruthers—William Singleton's daughter and Alexander's wife

William Singleton—Constance's father

Alexander Caruthers—Constance's husband

Benjamin Trumbull—a minister

The Marquis de Touvere—William Singleton's friend

Dr. Joseph Foote—the town physician

Stanton Higgins—Elizabeth's father

Joseph Pierpont—David Cobb and Theodore Norton's employer

Lydia Johnson—Theodore Norton's aunt and Stanton Higgins' neighbor

Monsieur Louis Monnerat--Laura Monnerat's husband and Philippe Monnerat's brother

Madame Laura Monnerat--Louis Monnerat's wife

Louise Bourget—a French revolutionist and Madame Monnerat's maid

Mrs. Singleton—Constance's mother

Colonel Benedict Parker—Charlotte Parker's husband and Mrs. Kensington's son-in-law

Charlotte Parker—Colonel Parker's wife and Mrs. Kensington's daughter

Jesse Andrews—Mary Andrews' son

Charles Parker—Colonel Parker's nephew

Mrs. Phoebe Kensington—Charlotte's mother and Colonel Parker's mother-in-law

Robespierre—French revolutionist leader

Dr. Mitchell Greenville—Mrs. Kensington's friend and physician

Lieutenant Michael Bradford—Mrs. Kensington's employee

Simon Blackwell—a former spy obsessed with Charlotte Parker

Hope Bradford—Lieutenant Bradford's sister

Colonel Ridgefield—Mrs. Ridgefield's husband

Mrs. Ridgefield—Colonel Ridgefield's wife

Jean-Luc Tessier—a French privateer and Louise Bourget's companion

Foster and Jennings—Mrs. Kensington's servants

Hastings—Judith Fairchild's servant

Honoria Noble—Ethan Fairchild's fiancée

Ethan Fairchild—Caleb and Judith Fairchild's son and Honoria Noble's fiancé

Evelyn Winchester—Judith Fairchild's sister and Ethan's aunt

Judith Fairchild—Ethan's mother and Caleb Fairchild's wife

Caleb Fairchild—Judith Fairchild's husband and Ethan's father

Mrs. Downey—Madame Laura Monnerat's assistant

Reverend Davenport—a minister and supporter of Madame Monnerat

Mrs. Holley and Mrs. King—members of Reverend Davenport's congregation

Seth—the little orphan boy

Lady Winfield—Lord Winfield's wife and Mrs. Kensington's friend

Lord Winfield—Lady Winfield's husband

King George III—the king of England and admirer of Mrs. Kensington

Monsieur Philippe Monnerat—Annabelle Monnerat's husband and Louis Monnerat's brother

Annabelle Monnerat—Philippe Monnerat's wife

Solomon Peabody—tavern owner

Caroline—Constance's maid

Nicholas Biddle—Charles' tutor and Mrs. Kensington's employee

Ebenezer Stiles—Charity's friend

Mr. Preston—an attorney

Book One

Chapter 1

Charity Chastine was born in the year 1773, a time when rebellion and revolution were brewing between England and her colonies. Her mother fell in love with a young man from one of England's prominent families. After a brief affair, he left Charity's mother and traveled to the colonies to make his fortune. Her mother was penniless and with child, so she took refuge at a workhouse on the east side of London, where nine months later Charity was born.

In 1775, after living at the workhouse for nearly two years and being subjected to poor living conditions and misery, they departed. They would have been left to the elements of the streets if it were not for the kindness and generosity of a woman named Patience Wright, a sculptor who owned a studio in London. Patience was a supporter of the American Revolution. She would pass on British military secrets to Patriot agents through toy dolls she fashioned out of putty and wax.

Charity grew up in the studio; she and her mother had their own quarters upstairs. Her mother and Patience taught her how to read and write and sew. When the Revolutionary War ended in 1783, America became its own country, free from the reign of England and its monarch King George III.

Six years later she celebrated her sixteenth birthday, and two weeks later her mother became stricken with fever. After a courageous fight to live, she died.

Charity decided to leave London and immigrate to America to start a new life. Patience understood her decision to leave, and she gave her some money and a finely dressed wooden doll with a brightly painted face. She told Charity to never misplace the doll, because one day it would save her life.

After a long and difficult sea voyage, Charity arrived at the port of New Haven, Connecticut, in the spring of 1790. Since she did not desire to stay in a city but longed for the surroundings of a small rural town, she embarked on a short journey by coach to North Haven. This small agricultural community that became incorporated as a town in 1786 by order of the General Assembly of New Haven was populated with people, some gracious and kind, some not so gracious and kind, with sorrows and joys, stories and secrets. She came to know these strangers and would eventually call them patriots and scoundrels.

The coach ride from New Haven to North Haven was bumpy and tiresome. The roads were lined with dirt and sand that created mounds of dust when the horses galloped by. Inside the coach was an elderly couple sleeping in an upright position against the soft upholstered seat. Across from Charity was a distinguished gentleman dressed in a black outfit, who engaged in polite conversation. He introduced himself as Reverend Benjamin Trumbull, a minister of the First Ecclesiastical Society. He was returning home to North Haven after attending a meeting for ministers in New Haven. Charity explained that she was looking for a place to stay in North Haven. He graciously recommended the Andrews' Tavern whose proprietor, Mary Andrews, was a charming hostess.

Reverend Trumbull also spoke of a woman by the name of Grace Collins, who worked as a hostess and server at the tavern. Her husband Samuel had been killed at Lake George in 1758 during the French and Indian War. Along with him was his good friend Moses Brockett Jr., a local resident.

When she asked Reverend Trumbull about the town of North Haven, he explained that the town had been incorporated as its own community free from the rule of New Haven, and its residents were farmers, mill workers, shopkeepers, tavern owners, and a small group who made up the privileged class.

"The tavern was originally owned by Timothy Andrews, but he died a few months back, and now his widow Mary is in charge of the establishment," said Reverend Trumbull. "Travelers and tradesmen stay at Andrews' Tavern or the home of the town physician, Dr. Joseph Foote."

Arriving in the center of town, Charity saw a meetinghouse, a Church of England, a few houses, and several barns that seemed to be in a shattered state. The roads were wide and sandy with no large public buildings or elegant shops, unlike what she had become familiar with in London.

When the coach made its stop at the tavern, Charity gathered her entrapments, thanked Reverend Trumbull for his kindness, and stood outside while the coach continued on its journey. She looked around. In her opinion, the town did not appear to be inviting.

"Hello there. Won't you come in and stay for a spell?" called a voice.

Charity looked up to see a short, stocky woman wearing a white, mop cap and an apron. She stood in a doorway holding a lantern. Charity accepted her invitation to come inside.

The tavern was spacious, with several tables and chairs, and a large stone fireplace slightly off the center of the room. The windows were small with no curtains. Had it not been for the English accents of the colonies and the somber dress of the men in the common room, Charity might have imagined herself back in England. The hickory fire burning in the hearth, the scrubbed pine tables, and even the sand on the floor reminded her of home. She placed her belongings on the dusty wooden planks of the floor and sat at a table.

The woman introduced herself as Grace Collins. Like the Reverend Trumbull had told Charity, Grace was a hostess and server at the tavern, helping out Mary Andrews. Grace brought Charity a large, steamy bowl of stew which she enjoyed very much.

While she was eating, Charity and Grace engaged in pleasant

conversation. Charity explained her situation to Grace who listened and then made a few recommendations. She suggested that Charity take up lodging in one of the rooms upstairs, and she offered her a job as a server at the tavern.

"I could really use the extra hands. Things get quite busy around here when travelers and tradesmen from Boston or New Haven make their way through," said Grace. "I'm certain Mrs. Andrews would not mind having a nice young lady like you at her fine establishment."

Charity had no place to go and no other offers, and Grace seemed genuinely kind. She decided to stay. While Grace went to speak to Mrs. Andrews, Charity sat in a large wooden chair in front of the stone fireplace to warm herself.

A few moments later, the door to the tavern swung open and in walked two men dressed in farm clothing. They both said hello to her while taking off their tricorn hats. The older man went to a table near the window while the younger one stood next to her by the fire warming his hands. As he stood by the fire, he took an interest in Charity's appearance. Against the chill of the evening, she wore no hat. Her hair, the golden brown color of honey, was cropped short, and David guessed she had probably sold the rest of it to buy food or lodgings. She stood in profile to him, and although the long cloak she wore hid the lines of her body, David could see hunger in the hollow of her cheek, and the line of her throat but she had the face of an angel. Her wide eyes were the azure blue of a summer sky, with all the innocence of a child. Yet her thick, dark lashes and soft, generous lips had all the seductiveness of a courtesan. Her features were delicate, and her flawless skin the color of cream. But it was her smile that fascinated him. At first there was silence between them. Then the young man made the first attempt to speak.

"My name is David Cobb, and that over yonder is Theodore Norton. We have just finished a hard day's work at the gristmill by Muddy River. Mr. Pierpont works us to the bone. And who might you be?"

"My name is Charity Chastine. I have just arrived in town. I have been offered lodging and a job here at the tavern by Grace Collins."

David was very gracious despite his unkempt appearance. He explained that Grace was a widow whose husband died during the French and Indian War. Charity thought it was a bit improper of him to engage in conversation with her, a person whom he did not know. But there was no place for her to go, and she did not want to be rude by leaving abruptly, so she stayed and listened.

David was infatuated with Charity's smile. It was a smile that could make a man abandon his ideals, forget his honor, and sell his soul. It was a smile that enslaved. It was magic. He continued to ramble on about some of the other residents to which Charity paid little mind. But then one story caught her attention. It was about Elizabeth Higgins, a local girl who fell in love with a Redcoat during the Revolutionary War. They were going to run away together to Canada, but they never made it. One night they met on the bridge over Muddy River, and the next day their bodies were found by workers at one of the gristmills on the banks of the river. Both had been shot. And just a few years before, three men who were searching for a hidden treasure in the nearby countryside mysteriously disappeared.

As David was about to continue, Grace interrupted.

"Are you telling tales out of your hat? Pay no mind to him," said Grace, with her hands on her hips. "Everything is all set. Come, my dear let me show you to your room."

Charity said good-night to David and followed Grace upstairs. After showing Charity her new dwelling place, Grace left her to settle in.

The room was cozy, with a bed, a chest for clothes, a washbasin on a table, and a chair in the corner. It reminded her of the room she shared with her mother above Patience's studio in London.

She opened the trunk and began to go through her belongings. She held the doll Patience had given to her. After hearing David's stories of the disappearance of those unfortunate treasure seekers and the deaths of the local girl and her lover, she was frightened. A terrible chill engulfed her body. She longed for her mother and Patience. She felt alone in a strange place surrounded by mystery, uncertainty, and a few kind faces that were still strangers to her.

Feeling exhausted from the long journey and the lateness of the hour, she undressed and went to bed. Before falling asleep, she tossed about for some time. She must have dozed off, because she was awakened suddenly by the wind blowing outside her window. She rose from her bed, and looked out the window. There was a full moon in the ebony sky, and by its light she thought she saw a man and woman walking into the woods. As she looked intently, the figures moved about in a confused manner. She thought, *perhaps they are in need of assistance.* So she wrapped a shawl around her and hurried outside. As she approached the edge of the woods, the man and woman disappeared. She called out to them, but no one answered. Suddenly, she heard footsteps and the snapping of branches from behind. As she tried to make her way back, she felt that someone or something was watching her. Then a body pressed up against her, a cold and clammy hand covered her mouth, and she fell into a state of terror.

She struggled to set herself free from whoever had her. The cold and clammy hand withdrew from her mouth, and a voice softly whispered, identifying himself as David Cobb. Charity's fear of panic dissipated upon hearing David's name.

"I'm sorry to have frightened you," said David. "What are you doing out here alone and vulnerable to the elements of the night?"

Charity thought quickly and told him that she needed a breath of fresh air. She did not tell him the truth for fear he would think she was mad. He escorted her back inside. While walking back to the tavern, she glanced over her shoulder at the entrance to the woods and saw nothing, but at the same time, she had the notion that whatever she had seen was not her imagination.

Once inside, she thanked David, and he went on his way. After shutting and bolting the tavern's large wooden door, she made her way upstairs. In her room, she held the doll that Patience had given her, and she burrowed under the quilt on her bed. By holding the doll, she felt as secure as if Patience was with her, and soon she fell asleep.

The next morning Charity met Mrs. Andrews, and she made her feel right at home. She reminded her of Patience, who was tall and bony with an angular face. But she also appeared to be a wise woman with a kind heart.

"I am glad you are here, my dear Charity. Since my husband's passing, I have taken ownership of the tavern, and I hope one day my son Jesse will take over," said Mrs. Andrews. "We are a small town with many kind people. Mrs. Collins and I will make it our duty to introduce you to them all."

Charity thanked Mrs. Andrews for her kindness and explained she came to the tavern upon the recommendation of Reverend Benjamin Trumbull who she met on the coach ride. Mrs. Andrews spoke highly of Reverend Trumbull and told Charity that he came to North Haven in 1760. He had been a schoolmaster, and was now the minister of the First Ecclesiastical Society, a very scholarly man with a magnificent collection of books in his library. He had joined the American forces during the Revolutionary War as a regimental chaplain, writing in his journal an account of the war by the loss of life he had witnessed.

"Reverend Benjamin Trumbull is a good man to have on your side," said Mrs. Andrews.

That afternoon Grace and Charity were tidying up the dining hall when a young woman dressed in a lovely blue gown with a lace cap entered. Grace introduced her as Constance Singleton, the daughter of William Singleton, a former ambassador to France and a member of the upper class residing in North Haven. Constance had recently returned from a several-month holiday in New York City. While in the city, she witnessed the swearing in of George Washington as the country's first president. She described the entire event to Grace and Charity telling them that Washington rode on a white horse as cheering crowds greeted him along the route. Townspeople built triumphal arches, and women in flowing white gowns spread flowers in his path, while local people rode their horses behind him. When he took the oath of office on the balcony of New York City's Federal Hall, the crowd roared, cannons boomed, and church bells clanged.

"It was a glorious event to witness," exclaimed Constance. "With Washington as our president, the days of the Revolutionary War and England's rule are behind us."

Constance and Charity seemed to make a connection. She was a young woman of good breeding and elegance, but also very polite and pleasant. Constance said that while in New York City she and her father heard talk about possible rebellion and revolution occurring in Paris. She explained that the peasants had grown very angry with King Louis XVI and his wife, Queen Marie Antoinette, blaming them for the poverty and suffering of the French people. The aristocrats were targets of angry mobs, she explained, and Paris was no longer safe for them.

"My father is afraid for his good friend, the Marquis de Touvere and his family. My father is hoping that he and his family will leave Paris before something terrible happens," said Constance in a troubled voice.

Constance stayed for quite some time and then left. After her departure, Grace and Charity began to get ready for the supper crowd.

Dr. Joseph Foote, who Charity remembered Reverend Trumbull mentioning, entered the tavern. He was a well dressed gentleman with a kind smile. Grace explained that the good doctor made it a habit to dine at the tavern as often as he could, because he enjoyed their delicious meal of veal cutlet and broiled chicken with green peas. Grace believed that the best way to keep a man happy was to satisfy his stomach.

"Let our men eat, drink, and be merry, and stay out from under the heels of us women," joked Grace with a smile.

The dining hall began to fill up quickly with dinner guests. David Cobb and his co-workers from the gristmill arrived to partake in a drink or two of ale. Lighted candles were on all the tables, and the lit fireplace gave off a warm glow that felt good on a chilly night. The room was filled with conversation and smiling faces. For the first time since her arrival, Charity felt at peace.

Unbeknownst to all at Andrews' Tavern, several thousand miles away, across the Atlantic Ocean, in the world renowned city of Paris, peace was fading rapidly. A sinister uprising was forming that threatened the welfare of countless individuals, mostly of the aristocracy.

The horses galloped down the cobble stone streets pulling the coach that carried the Marquis de Touvere, his wife Madame de Touvere, and his daughter Jacqueline. The Marquis and his family were fleeing Paris under the cover of darkness in an attempt to escape an impending and deadly disaster. He was exceedingly troubled, and his plan was to leave Paris and come to the United States to seek the assistance and generosity of his good friend, William Singleton.

The Marquis had been instrumental in aiding William Singleton, George Washington, and the patriots during the Revolutionary War. William Singleton was so grateful for the Marquis' assistance that he promised to one day return the favor. Now the Marquis was hoping to collect on that promise, because the lives of he and his family depended upon it. Their journey took them to a harbor where they boarded a ship bound for the United States.

At Andrews' Tavern, everyone was drinking and eating while Grace and Charity were busy attending to their patrons. Suddenly, a tall, lanky man wearing a hat entered. His hat and clothes appeared tattered, and he looked a fright. At first, he stood still like a statue while his grey eyes moved about the room. Then he took off his hat and placed it on a nearby table before making his way toward Charity. He stretched out his arms and spoke.

"Lizzie! My beloved Lizzie, where have you been? Why haven't you come home? I've been so worried about you," he said.

Charity was startled and confused by what he was saying. As he continued to come closer, David Cobb got in his way and grabbed his arm, but the stranger kept trying to reach Charity and continued to speak.

"Lizzie, why do you continue to ignore me? I know it is that scoundrel's doing. He's turned my beautiful daughter against me," he cried, his hands covering his face.

At that moment, David Cobb, Dr. Foote, and another man were able to escort the stranger out of the tavern. They said they were taking him home.

After they left, the remaining guests returned to eating and conversing. Grace went up to Charity and told her to pay no mind to what had just happened. She explained that the stranger was Stanton Higgins, the father of Elizabeth Higgins who died a terrible death some years ago. As soon as Grace mentioned the name, Charity instantly remembered the story that David had told her about Elizabeth and her Redcoat boyfriend who were killed near the bridge on Muddy River.

"He never accepted her death or the fact that she was in love with a Redcoat. Come to think of it, as I look closely at you, my dear Charity, you do bear some resemblance to her except that Elizabeth's hair was long and came below her shoulders," said Grace.

A strong feeling of uneasiness took hold of Charity. Suddenly, a gust of wind blew open the door to the tavern, but no one entered except a nasty cold breath of air ... and the presence of death.

Chapter 2

After Grace closed the tavern door, Charity still felt the presence of death in the room. She thought, *perhaps it is the cold chill of the night that blew in when the door opened. Or was it her encounter with Mr. Higgins? Or was it what Grace had said about her resemblance to Elizabeth? Or was her imagination getting the best of her?* She felt something was wrong and somehow she was unknowingly and unwillingly part of a town's dark secret.

The next morning the sun was shining and the birds were chirping in a tree outside the window of her chamber. She rose quickly, put on her Sunday dress, brushed her short, golden brown hair, and descended to the dining hall. Grace was waiting for her with a hot bowl of oatmeal, fresh fruit, and freshly made biscuits with honey.

"Come, my dear. Enjoy this delicious breakfast, and then we must make haste to church."

After enjoying the delicious meal, Charity helped Grace clear the table, and then they went to church service. Mrs. Andrews and her son Jesse attended the Congregational Church where Reverend Benjamin Trumbull was minister. Grace went to St. John's Episcopal Church across from the town green. Since Charity was an Episcopalian, she was glad to attend St. John's. The church had several wooden pews that faced a lovely hand carved wooden altar with a gold cross. The floor was made of stone and the stained glass windows added a colorful luster and peaceful presence inside.

Before the service began, Grace explained to Charity in a soft voice that when the Revolutionary War ended there were only fourteen

Episcopal clergymen left in Connecticut; one of them was Samuel Andrews, no relation to Mrs. Andrews, who had served Wallingford, North Haven, Cheshire, and Meriden since 1762. Unfortunately, Andrews was a Loyalist throughout the Revolution and had for a time been under house arrest in Wallingford. Since strong feelings of mistrust and contempt were held against him, Andrews resigned from all his parishes in 1785 and immigrated to New Brunswick, Canada.

"After Andrews left, St. John's had no rector for a few years, but we were held together by Joseph Pierpont, owner of the gristmill where David Cobb and Theodore Norton work. Pierpont was assisted by Titus Frost, who is married to Mabel Stiles, granddaughter of the Reverend Isaac Stiles," explained Grace. "The parish has survived the war and some new families have joined us." A few moments later Grace stopped talking because the service had begun.

Charity enjoyed the Sunday service at St. John's. It reminded her of the church she went to in England with her mother and Patience. While they were walking back to the tavern, David Cobb rode up to them on horseback. He dutifully tipped his hat to them and wanted to talk. Grace abruptly told him that they had no time to talk and needed to be on their way. She took hold of Charity's soft hand and they hurried back to the tavern.

Upon their return, Grace stayed outside to gather some wood for the fireplace, and Charity began to sweep the floor. A few minutes later, the tavern door opened, and in walked a woman Charity had not yet met. She was short and masculine in appearance with short dark hair and a pale, condescending look upon her face. As she entered, Charity politely told her that they were not serving anyone until the evening. The woman said she was not there for food and drink but was on a mission to find a hat that belonged to a friend. She introduced herself as Lydia Johnson, a friend and neighbor of Stanton Higgins. Upon hearing that name, Charity dropped the broom and stood still.

"Oh, my dear, are you feeling well? I hope I'm not disturbing you.

Mr. Higgins was here last night, and he forgot to take his hat, so I am here to retrieve it," she said.

Charity helped her search the room for the hat. While they searched, Lydia and Charity engaged in simple and brief conversation. While they were talking, Grace returned, and Charity could see she was not happy to see Lydia Johnson. She threw the bundle of wood that she was carrying down on the floor and spoke to Lydia in a harsh tone.

"What are you doing here? The devil's servant is not welcome here," uttered Grace.

Lydia pleasantly explained that she was looking for Mr. Higgins' hat and apologized for the intrusion. Grace told her that if the hat were found, she would return it. Then she ordered the woman to leave. Before Lydia departed, she turned to Charity and with a devilish look in her eye said, "My dear Charity, we shall meet again soon."

Grace was agitated by Lydia's visit. Charity's curiosity got the better of her, so she asked Grace what was the matter. As far as she was concerned, Lydia was a bit foreboding in appearance and talkative, but she seemed harmless.

"Stay away from that woman. She is nothing but trouble," said Grace adamantly. "Lydia Johnson caused trouble between Elizabeth Higgins and her father Mr. Higgins."

When Charity asked Grace to explain further, she excused herself by going into the back room and shutting the door. Charity had terrible feelings of loneliness and confusion taking control of her. All at once she did not know whom to trust, and she questioned whether North Haven was the place for her. Little did she realize while she was standing alone in the main room that someone was watching her from outside the window of the tavern.

Several thousand miles away in Paris, turmoil was erupting in the streets. Looking out of the window of his apartment, Monsieur

Louis Monnerat observed the chaos occurring below. He was very disturbed by what he saw, but his train of thought was interrupted by his wife Laura.

"My dear Sir, I have just learned from my maid Louise that the Marquis de Touvere and his family have left Paris for good. They have left the country and have gone to America to seek the assistance of his friend William Singleton," explained Laura. "Louise encountered one of the Marquis' servants at the marketplace, and he told her that the Marquis dismissed them all, closed up his chateau, and the family took their personal belongings and left last night, never to return."

Monsieur Monnerat became enraged. He threw down the glass he was holding and stomped on the broken pieces. The Marquis had something very valuable that Monsieur Monnerat wanted, and he was determined to possess it. He thought for a moment while curling his black moustache, and then he instructed his beloved Laura to have the servants pack their trunks and personal belongings immediately. He told his wife they were leaving for America.

"Paris is not a very safe or healthy place to be these days," said Monsieur Monnerat. "Let us follow the Marquis' example and go to America. If I'm not mistaken, the Marquis would have gone to see his friend Singleton somewhere in Connecticut, and that's where we shall go. It will be a reunion of old friends, and one to die for."

He then took his wife's hand, both of them laughing wickedly as they left the room.

Charity had finished her chores at hand and decided to go for a walk. She hoped that some exercise in the warm sunshine would do her good. She walked down the dirt road, taking in the scenery and listening to the birds chirping in the blossoming trees. Some time passed, and she came near a river. She could see several mills not far in the distance, but since it was Sunday, they were deserted.

She saw a bridge nearby and began to walk across it. When she reached the center of the bridge, she stopped and stood still. A cool breeze began to blow. She felt a nasty chill come upon her, and she wrapped her shawl tightly around her upper body. With the exception of the wind blowing, all was silent, until suddenly the silence was broken by a loud voice calling from behind her.

"There you are, my Lizzie. Get away from that scoundrel and come home with me at once!" shouted the voice.

Charity turned to see who was yelling and saw that it was Mr. Higgins. He was running toward her. Her legs froze under her, and she could not move. Soon he was upon her, and she tried desperately to escape. She pushed and shoved, but he continued to come at her. She finally got her legs to move, but instead of going forward, she moved backward. As Mr. Higgins tried to grab her, she lost her balance and went over the railing, screaming in terror.

Her body was dangling from the bridge, and she could hear the water of the river down below. The wind was now blowing fiercely, as she tried desperately to hold onto the planks of the bridge. Her heart was pounding rapidly, her mind was racing in panic, and her grip was slipping away. She could do nothing but scream as she got closer to taking a dreadful plunge into the river.

Just as she was about to let go, strong and steady hands tightly grabbed her wrists, and she heard a familiar voice call out to her.

"I got you. Don't let go. I will pull you up. Just don't let go," shouted the voice.

With a giant tug, Charity was lifted miraculously up and over the railing. As she came over the railing, she fell upon the person who had courageously saved her. It was David Cobb.

Charity was shaking profusely from the fear of her ordeal. David got her to her feet and embraced her. His strong arms around her made her feel at ease.

"You are safe, my dear Charity," said David as he stared into her blue eyes. "Come. I will take you back to the tavern."

As they walked off the bridge, Mr. Higgins was sitting on the ground sobbing and calling out to his beloved Lizzie. Charity looked at him with pity, but David held her tight with his strong hands and hurried her along. Walking away, they were unaware of the presence of Lydia Johnson watching their every move in a nearby bush. As they continued on their way, Charity was certain that she heard a hideous laughter coming from somewhere in the distance.

When they returned to the tavern, both Grace and Mrs. Andrews were waiting for them. They were relieved to see them—mostly Charity. Mrs. Andrews went to make some tea for Charity while David and Grace escorted her upstairs to her room.

"Thank God you are safe, my dear," exclaimed Grace. "What possessed you, child? Wandering about without a chaperone? I am never letting you out of my sight again."

Entering the room, Charity collapsed on the bed and sighed with great relief. Grace thanked David for his assistance and then firmly instructed him to leave. He looked at Charity with a smile, bowed, and departed. Grace closed the door and helped Charity into bed after taking off her shawl and shoes. She told her to rest and said she would return momentarily with a cup of hot tea.

After she left, Charity reached for her doll and held it tightly. Her body was finally in a state of calm, and she felt secure so she closed her eyes and began to think of pleasant things.

Two days passed since the ordeal on the bridge, and Charity had not left the tavern. Grace made sure that she was in sight of her watchful eyes.

While they were folding the linens, Constance Singleton arrived at the tavern. She apologized for her unannounced visit, but she came to inform them that her father was giving a ball at Singleton Lodge, and they were all invited to attend. Constance explained that the gathering was to welcome his friend, the Marquis de Touvere, and his family to town.

"The Marquis and his family arrived yesterday. My father is

so happy that they are here and safe from the danger in Paris," said Constance. "My father wants his friends from Paris to become acquainted with the residents of North Haven, and what better way to do it than by giving a ball?"

Grace and Charity accepted the invitation, and Constance stayed for a brief time and had a cup of tea with them. Before she departed, Constance left an invitation to the ball for Mrs. Andrews and Jesse with Grace. Charity admitted to Grace that she longed to go to a ball, but she had nothing to wear. Grace assured her that she would take care of the attire, and that they were certainly going and would have a wonderful time.

The night of the ball finally arrived. Mrs. Andrews sent for the carriage, and she, her son Jesse, Grace, and Charity rode in it to Singleton Lodge, located near the High Ridge Mountains on the outskirts of town.

Grace had told Charity earlier that William Singleton had been involved in shipbuilding before he was appointed ambassador to France. He had the honor to know and work with Benjamin Franklin in Paris during the Revolutionary War. The Singletons' large fortunes had been handed down through the generations.

"William Singleton is a man of good breeding and generosity," she said. "Even though he is from fine lineage, he makes it a point to associate with everyone. He adores country people and finds country manners to be most charming."

Some time later the coachman reined in the four horses pulling the carriage beside a wrought iron gate bounded by two enormous limestone gate piers. Atop each pier capital stood a giant eagle, its wings spread impressively, as if to guard the property. After conversing with the gatekeeper, the driver drove up the short gravel carriageway. Upon their arrival at Singleton Lodge, footmen helped the passengers out of the carriage. Jesse escorted his mother inside, and Grace and

Charity followed behind. Servants took their wraps. They stood in a reception line where Constance and her parents were graciously greeting their guests. After the introductions, they proceeded into the great hall where many of the guests were already assembled. Some of them were standing, drinking wine and conversing; others were sitting down observing the activities in the room, and some were dancing to the music provided by the musicians at the far end. Large and elegant chandeliers with lit candles hung from the ceiling and illuminated the entire room.

Once all the guests had arrived, the Singletons entered the reception hall. The musicians stopped playing, and Mr. Singleton began to speak. He thanked everyone for attending, and he introduced the Marquis de Touvere, his wife, and his daughter who entered the room with all eyes upon them. The Marquis was good looking and gentleman-like with a pleasant appearance, and he had easy, unaffected manners. His wife and daughter were lovely, dressed in beautiful gowns with elegant lace. Their fine features and noble appearance drew the attention and admiration of everyone in the room.

The Marquis soon acquainted himself with all the principal people who were present. He was lively and unreserved, dancing every dance while his wife and daughter sat at the other end of the room with Mrs. Singleton.

Constance went over to Grace and Charity and kept them company, pointing out certain guests and providing them with information about each one. She introduced them to Colonel Benedict Parker and his wife Charlotte. The colonel was a man of fine fortune who had fought alongside George Washington at Saratoga. Charlotte came from a notable and respected New Haven family now residing in Wallingford, Connecticut.

While the ball was taking place, a ship entered New Haven harbor. On board were Monsieur and Madame Monnerat. The captain gave orders for disembarking, and the ship hands brought the passengers' trunks and other entrapments ashore. Monsieur and Madame Monnerat hailed a carriage, instructing the driver to take them to the finest lodging establishments in the city. While riding in the carriage, they discussed their plan of action.

"Tomorrow, I will make inquiries as to the whereabouts of William Singleton," said Monsieur Monnerat. "Once we find him, we will find our dear friend the Marquis and his family, and our reunion will commence."

Madame Monnerat was very pleased with her husband's plan, or perhaps she was more pleased with herself. She was the kind of woman who fancied herself superior to all other women. Her husband believed himself to be devious and artful, as well as cunning and dangerous. They were described by their acquaintances as having souls as black as night and hearts as hard as stones.

———————————

At Singleton Lodge, the guests had enjoyed an exquisite dinner and were returning to the great hall for more music and dancing. Constance excused herself and went upstairs to her room to change her gown, because she had spilled punch on it during dinner. Mrs. Andrews and Jesse were engaged in conversation with Dr. Foote and Reverend Trumbull, both good friends of the Singletons. As Grace was conversing with Mrs. Singleton and Madame de Touvere and her daughter, Charity amused herself by walking the hallway of the first floor. Singleton Lodge was a grand place with magnificent decorations and furnishings.

At the far end of the hallway, she entered a room that was the library. To her astonishment it was filled with shelves containing countless numbers of books. Elegant furniture was arranged throughout the room, portraits hung on the walls, and red velvet drapes hung from the tall, narrow windows. Charity remembered

Constance telling her that her father was a collector of books; many of them he acquired while in Europe.

Feeling a bit flushed, Charity opened the doors that led out to the terrace. As she stood outside enjoying the cool night air, her solace was suddenly interrupted when her eyes caught a glimpse of what appeared to be a young couple moving about in the distance.

Studying them further, she realized they were the same couple she had seen entering the woods near the tavern several nights ago. They had a ghost-like appearance.

Her concentration on the couple was interrupted by a conversation in the library. While she was out on the terrace, Mr. Singleton and Colonel Parker had entered the library, and were engaged in a heated discussion about a priceless missing diamond being sought after by the monarchs of England and France. Mr. Singleton accused Colonel Parker of purloining it, and the colonel accused Mr. Singleton of the same.

Meanwhile Constance had gone upstairs to change her gown and was descending the stairs to rejoin the guests when she tripped on the trail of her gown and fell down the stairs. Her maid screamed in fright.

The maid's scream distracted Mr. Singleton and Colonel Parker. And as Mr. Singleton turned his back and attempted to leave the room, Colonel Parker picked up a silver candlestick holder and hit him on the head, knocking him to the floor.

Witnessing this vicious act, Charity was filled with terror and accidentally knocked over a statue that fell and broke into pieces. The falling statue alerted the colonel, and with the candlestick in his hand, he made his way out onto the terrace.

Chapter 3

Charity managed to kneel down with her head between her knees and her body pinned up against one of the terrace doors. She held her breath and prayed that Parker would not see her. The colonel came out onto the terrace and stood still, looking straight ahead.

His stare was interrupted by a knock at the door. He calmly and quickly walked back into the room.

Charity mustered up the courage to quietly move out from behind the door and, with her head down, peeked carefully into the library. She saw the colonel put back the candlestick and drag Mr. Singleton's body behind the large sofa. Upon doing this, he called out to whoever was knocking at the door.

"One moment, please. I will be right there," shouted the colonel.

When the colonel opened the door, his wife Charlotte appeared. She explained in a frantic voice that Constance had fallen down the stairs and Mrs. Singleton needed her husband. Colonel Parker pretended that he did not know of Mr. Singleton's whereabouts and then hurried Charlotte out of the room, closing the door behind them.

Once they were gone, Charity emerged from her hiding place and went to see Mr. Singleton. He was lying still but appeared to be breathing. She placed a pillow under his head. He groaned a bit and then was silent again. Charity was in a panic. She didn't know whether to go for help or stay with Mr. Singleton. If she left the library, would the colonel see her? What if someone else saw her? Would she be blamed for what had happened?

While she was trying to figure out what to do, she heard voices coming down the hall.

She quickly ran back out to the terrace in an effort to conceal herself. The voices soon gave way to silence. She realized that she had to get out of the library and rejoin the other guests in the great hall. She felt terrible leaving Mr. Singleton, but it was the only logical thing to do. She hurried down the hallway and made her way back to the party.

The guests were all talking about poor Constance. As Charity was trying to compose herself, Grace came up to her.

"Where have you been, Charity, my dear? Dear Constance took a nasty fall down the stairs," exclaimed Grace. "Two of the servants carried her up to her bedroom, and Dr. Foote is examining her as we speak."

Charity fibbed and told Grace that she had taken a walk down the hallway when she heard a scream. She expressed concern for Constance's condition.

Their conversation was interrupted by Reverend Trumbull who announced to everyone that Constance had a bump on her head and a sprained ankle, but Dr. Foote was confident that she would make a full recovery. Charity was relieved to hear the news about Constance, but now her thoughts were focused on Mr. Singleton.

The Marquis took charge of the ball. He told those present that Mrs. Singleton wanted her guests to continue to partake in music and dancing, but she would remain with her daughter. The music began to play, and the Marquis, without a care in the world, gathered together a handful of ladies and gentlemen and started to dance.

Mrs. Andrews and Grace decided it was time to depart. Jesse instructed one of the servants to send for the carriage. Colonel Parker and his wife left at the same time. As she was getting into the carriage, Charity heard Mrs. Parker expressing her concern for Mr. Singleton. Her husband told her not to worry, saying he must be taking a walk around the grounds and he would soon return. Charity thought *if only that were the truth.*

That entire night Charity tossed and turned in bed. Every time she closed her eyes she saw Colonel Parker striking Mr. Singleton with the candlestick again and again. Then she pictured herself running away from Singleton Lodge with the colonel chasing her. As she looked over her shoulder, he became Mr. Higgins and was calling her *Lizzie.* Then she found herself on the bridge at Muddy River, and Lydia Johnson pushed her over the railing, laughing wickedly.

Charity sat up in bed trembling with fear and held on tight to her doll in an attempt to find comfort. It was then that she wished she had never left London or her beloved Patience.

The next day Monsieur Monnerat kept his promise to his wife by making inquiries about Mr. Singleton. Since the Singletons were a respected and well-known family, it was easy to find someone who could tell Monsieur Monnerat of the location of Singleton Lodge. He decided to travel to North Haven and pay a call to the Singleton family. Unbeknownst to Monsieur Monnerat, he would learn some tragic news when making his visit to Singleton Lodge.

Back at the tavern, Grace, Mrs. Andrews, Jesse, and Charity were busy attending to the patrons. The dining room was filled with many tradesmen returning from Boston. Some were on their way to New Haven to sell their wares to local shopkeepers, and others were on their way to New York. All the patrons were eating, drinking, and conversing. Theodore Norton and David Cobb had stopped by with a delivery for Mrs. Andrews. Charity was glad to see David, and he gave her a jovial greeting. Grace made certain that their encounter was short lived.

"We have many patrons to attend to. There's no time to talk," she said. "Come, Charity. Get back to work."

David agreed graciously, but gave Charity a smile and a wink of the eye before leaving. David and Theodore went into the back room with Jesse Andrews. While Charity was occupied with waiting on tables, Colonel Parker and two other officers entered, but she did not see them. A few minutes later Lydia Johnson came in. She went right up to Mrs. Andrews and began speaking in a loud voice. Everyone in the room turned their attention to her.

"My dear Mrs. Andrews, I have just returned from Singleton Lodge with terrible news to report," announced Lydia. "I went to see Mrs. Singleton, who, the day before last, requested me to tailor one of her gowns. I was greeted by the housekeeper who told me that Mr. Singleton was dead!"

Everyone in the room fell silent. Mrs. Andrews held her hand over her mouth, Grace had a shocked look on her face, and David and Theodore, coming from the back room with Jesse, were stunned by the news.

"How could this be?" inquired Grace. "We saw him last night at the ball! He was very much full of life."

Lydia Johnson explained, "After the ball had concluded, Mr. Singleton could not be found. Mrs. Singleton had the servants search the entire place from top to bottom. They eventually found the poor man lying on the floor in the library with a large wound to the back of his head." She continued, "The authorities from New Haven went to Singleton Lodge to investigate. They suspected that he was the victim of a robbery, because the doors leading out to the terrace were found wide open, and there was a broken statue outside on the terrace. The most puzzling part was the pillow placed under Mr. Singleton's head."

At that moment, Charity was paralyzed with fear and dropped the tray she was holding. Its contents fell to the floor with a crash. As she bent down to clean up the mess, two muscular hands grabbed the broken dishes, and she heard a voice speak to her.

"Allow me to assist you, my sweet and lovely Charity."

She lifted her head, and to her surprise, she saw that it was Colonel Parker. He was dressed in his army uniform with shiny black boots, and there she was in a mop cap and apron that covered her dress. When she glanced upon him, all she could envision was what she witnessed him do to Mr. Singleton, and chills ran down her spine. She could not speak as she found herself looking into the dark eyes of a murderer.

The colonel was very gracious and kindly helped Charity clean the debris from the floor. He then insisted that she sit for a spell and collect her thoughts. She went along with him and did not reveal a single thing about what she knew. Lydia's news had created a somber feeling throughout the tavern.

David went over to see Charity but was interrupted by the colonel who returned to the table with a glass of water for her. He appeared to be benevolent and charming on the outside, concealing his malevolent and dangerous nature. With David by her side, Charity felt secure.

A few moments later Theodore Norton came to get David and told him that they were needed back at the mill. They left, and Lydia Johnson followed behind them.

Mrs. Andrews waited for the majority of the crowd to leave, and then told Grace that she and Jesse were going to Singleton Lodge to pay their condolences. Grace was in charge.

Seeing that she was herself again, the colonel excused himself to join his fellow officers at another table. Charity rose to her feet and returned to her task at hand.

While she was working, she felt that the colonel was watching her closely. After some time, he and the other officers finished their meal and departed. Before leaving, Colonel Parker thanked Grace and Charity for their hospitality, and as he walked out the door, he turned and spoke to Charity.

"Take care, my dear Charity. Take very good care and be safe," uttered the colonel.

Charity was so relieved after he left. Grace was very sad about what had happened to Mr. Singleton. She was also disturbed that a terrible crime could happen in such a small town where everyone knew one another.

"Evil knows no boundaries, and we must always be on our guard, for the Devil is always at work," said Grace.

———

At the Grand Inn in New Haven, Madame Monnerat was sitting in her private suite enjoying a cup of coffee when her husband entered the room. He told her what he had found out at Singleton Lodge. Both of them were more disappointed than sorry that William Singleton was dead. They were curious about who killed him.

"William Singleton was our only link to the Marquis. I wonder if whoever killed him wanted what we are searching for, or did this person find it and kill to keep it?" speculated Monsieur Monnerat.

His wife shared the same thoughts. Their conversation was interrupted by Madame Monnerat's maid Louise who came into the room to tell her employers of alarming news that she had just heard from people in the main hall. Louise said, "Rumors have it that in Paris an angry mob stormed the Bastille, murdered the head jailer and the guards, and freed the prisoners. Another mob went to the palace at Versailles and brought the king and queen by force back to Paris where they remained under house arrest."

Madame Monnerat dropped the cup she was holding. Monsieur Monnerat instructed Louise to return to the main hall to find out more information on the matter. The Monnerats were disturbed by what they were told, but not surprised. They realized that leaving Paris was a very wise thing to do. They now knew they could not return to their beloved city; the United States would be their new home. They were more determined than ever to find the Marquis at any cost.

———

The next day Grace and Charity went to pay a call to Singleton Lodge, but when they arrived the housekeeper told them that Mrs. Singleton and Constance were not receiving visitors. At the same time, Dr. Foote was on his way out after paying Constance a house call. He said that she would heal physically, but he knew he could not heal her grieving and broken heart over her father's untimely demise. He also said that the Marquis and his family left Singleton Lodge at Mrs. Singleton's request and took up lodging at a place. He did not know where. Charity thought it quite odd for Mrs. Singleton to ask her husband's friends to leave, especially at a time like this, but she kept her thoughts to herself.

Upon returning to the tavern, Charity went outside to sweep the dust and dirt from the stoop. She wished that David would stop by for a visit, but she was certain he was busy at the mill.

While she was toiling away, a grand barouche pulled up to the tavern. Charlotte Parker got out and greeted Charity before going in to see Grace. Charity saw a little boy get out of the carriage and walk into the road. He was dressed in satin breeches with silk stockings and shoes with silver buckles. He bent down and was sketching in the dirt with a stick.

Just then she heard the galloping of horses. She looked to the right and saw a wagon drawn by two horses rapidly heading their way. She ran as fast as she could, screaming at the top of her lungs. The little boy stood up as the wagon drew near, but she managed to push him out of the way, both of them falling to the ground. They narrowly escaped being trampled by the horses and the wagon wheels.

Hearing the commotion, Grace, Jesse, and Mrs. Parker came running out of the tavern. Jesse helped Charity and the boy to their feet. They were covered with dirt and sand, and the little boy was crying but seemed unharmed. Jesse carried him inside with Mrs. Parker behind them and Grace holding Charity's hand. Mrs. Parker was so grateful for what Charity had done that she embraced her, with tears in her eyes.

"Thank you so much. You are truly a guardian angel," she cried. "You saved the colonel's nephew, the son of his late brother and his wife. How can we ever repay you?"

At that moment, the door of the tavern swung open, and in

walked Lydia Johnson. She went over to Charlotte and Charity and apologized for what had happened. She explained that she and Mr. Higgins had been returning from New Haven, and as they came into North Haven, the horses began to gallop out of control. She claimed she had no way of stopping them.

Mrs. Parker and Charity accepted her apology, grateful that no one had been hurt. Grace was not so forgiving and told Lydia to leave.

Going out the door, Lydia turned her head and glanced at Charity with such a hideous smirk on her face that it gave her the chills.

Mrs. Parker took the colonel's nephew home, and Charity was so drained from the experience that she went upstairs to bed. Grace brought her a hot cup of tea and told her to stay in bed and not to worry about helping with the supper crowd, because Jesse and Mrs. Andrews would be on hand to assist her. Charity did exactly as Grace instructed.

She must have fallen asleep for a while; when she awoke the room was dark except for the light that was coming in through the window. She got out of bed and looked out the window. It was then that she saw the young couple moving about in the dark. This was the third time she had seen these apparitions. They soon entered the woods and disappeared. She felt a chill engulf her body and she quickly went back to bed.

She tossed about for some time, listening to the voices downstairs in the dining room. She was beginning to fall asleep when the door to her room opened and Grace walked in. She had come to check up on her and see if she needed anything. Charity told her she was feeling a bit hungry and would like something to eat. "I shall return with a nice meal," said Grace.

Grace left the door slightly open, but Charity paid no mind, knowing that Grace was returning soon. She closed her eyes and began to think about the young couple, trying to convince herself that they were only shadows in the night. She was slowly drifting off to sleep again when she heard footsteps coming up the stairs and assumed it was Grace returning.

She had her eyes closed, the quilt pulled up to her neck to keep warm, and she felt relaxed and at ease. The door creaked open, and as she opened her eyes, expecting to see Grace, to her horror a pillow came down upon her face. She struggled to breathe as the pillow pressed more and more on her face. She was in a state of panic while the breath of life was being snuffed out of her.

Chapter 4

Just as she was about to succumb, Grace entered the room and interrupted the heinous act in progress. She screamed in terror while dropping the tray, and then hit the assailant with her fists.

"Oh, my good gracious, there's a demon from hell trying to harm my precious Charity!" screamed Grace. "Please, help us!"

As Grace was yelling and hitting the intruder, the pillow was lifted from Charity's face. She was desperately gasping for the breath of life. The intruder pushed Grace out of the way, and she fell upon the bed. She turned to Charity while the attacker ran out of the room. The people in the dining hall heard Grace's screams for help and started climbing the stairs.

As the intruder tried desperately to escape, he lost his balance, fell down the stairs, and lay motionless at the bottom. Dr. Foote and Jesse examined the body. Dr. Foote pulled off a pillow casing the attacker had used to conceal his face. He then checked for a pulse that was not there and shook his head sadly, indicating the person was dead. The fall had caused the attacker to break his neck.

Dr. Foote and Jesse looked at the dead man's face, and to everyone's shock, it was Theodore Norton. And on the floor next to Theodore's body were several silver coins that must have fallen out his pocket as he fell down the stairs. Jesse and two other men removed Theodore's body from the tavern and placed it in the barn.

Dr. Foote came upstairs and gave Charity a quick examination. Grace brought her a glass of cold water as she tried to recover from another horrible experience. Everyone was kind and attentive to her, especially Mrs. Andrews, who kept inquiring about her well being.

David Cobb had arrived at the tavern and was shocked by what he was told. He couldn't believe what Theodore had tried to do to Charity. He ran up the stairs, tripping over his feet, and raced into her room. He nearly pushed Grace and Mrs. Andrews out of the way. David embraced Charity, wrapping his strong, muscular arms around her. His embrace made her feel safe and was well appreciated.

"Thank God you are all right," cried David. "You have been through a terrible ordeal. I can't believe that Theodore Norton would do such a thing!"

"We are all shocked and baffled by Theodore's act and his motive," said Charity. "I only knew him as a patron at the tavern, and our encounters had always been pleasant. Why would he want to harm me?"

"I do not know," said David shaking his head. "And I am afraid we may never learn the truth."

Dr. Foote instructed Charity to return to bed, and Grace volunteered to stay and watch over her. Charity wanted David to stay, but she knew Grace would never allow it.

David said, "I will call on you in the morning." Then he went with Dr. Foote to tell Lydia Johnson, who was Theodore's aunt and only living relative, what had happened.

As Charity remained in bed, Grace told her that Theodore's father had been killed fighting a battle in the Revolutionary War, and two years later his mother died from yellow fever, leaving him in the care of his mother's sister, Lydia Johnson. Charity snuggled under the quilt, and with Grace stroking her head gently, she eventually fell asleep holding her doll.

Two days later Grace and Charity attended William Singleton's funeral along with Mrs. Andrews, Jesse, and several townspeople.

The service was somber and took place as a raw wind blew across the cemetery. It lashed at black-clad mourners, whipping somber bonnets and tricorn hats and beating at bared heads. Mrs. Singleton, with a poker-straight face, was careful not to show any emotion, but Constance cried excessively for her and her mother. When the minister had finished his sermon with a prayer, the caretakers had begun to methodically shovel the muddy clumps of earth onto the coffin. When the grave was filled and mounded, bedraggled bouquets of flowers were placed upon it. Then the mourners gathered around a grieving Constance and her mother to say a last comforting word. Afterward, Grace and Charity went up to Constance, and she thanked them for attending.

Constance told them that her father had been a wonderful man, but unfortunately had gone into debt unbeknownst to her and her mother. In order to pay off the debt, Mrs. Singleton intended to sell Singleton Lodge, and she and Constance were planning to move to Virginia and live with Mrs. Singleton's cousin, Jeffrey Wilmot.

Mr. Wilmot owned a large, beautiful plantation with many slaves. Although Constance and her mother did not approve of slavery and disliked the heat and mosquitoes, they were at the mercy of their cousin's generosity due to their precarious situation.

Constance further explained that Singleton Lodge would be purchased by a Frenchman named Monsieur Monnerat, and he and his wife would be taking possession within a week. She also told Grace and Charity that she would miss them, and she promised to write often. As the mourners were leaving, Constance stared a few moments of looking down at the mound covered with flowers. She whispered a final farewell to her father, and then slowly walked away. With her face turned away from the biting wind, she made her way to the horse drawn carriage by the edge of the road. The driver opened the door and Constance climbed inside. She rested her head against the upholstered seat. Her mother remained silent and stared out the window of the carriage. The driver snapped his whip and they trailed a long line of assorted rigs and carriages down the deeply mudded road from the cemetery.

After returning to the tavern from the funeral, Grace and Charity got busy in the back room preparing the meal for the afternoon crowd. They talked about how odd it was that the Marquis and his family were not present at the funeral.

A messenger interrupted their conversation and their task with a letter for Charity. It was from Phoebe Kensington, a wealthy widow from Wallingford, inviting Charity to tea at her home. Charity did not know her, but Grace explained that she was Charlotte Parker's mother.

"Mrs. Kensington is extending you this invitation as a thank you for saving the little boy's life," said Grace. "Whatever her intentions are, you must go and make the most of it."

With Grace poking and prodding Charity, she had no choice but to go. She put on her Sunday dress and green bonnet, and was driven to Kensington Hall in Mrs. Kensington's personal carriage.

On the ride through Wallingford, Charity observed that the town seemed more affluent and populated than North Haven. She recalled a story that Jesse Andrews had told her of George Washington, coming through North Haven on his way to Wallingford to acquire gun powder and ammunition for his soldiers, and staying overnight at Kensington Hall. When the carriage passed through the main gates, Charity peeked her head out the window and she saw that Kensington Hall was a beautiful place and much larger in size than Singleton Lodge. The mansion was constructed of stone and wood and had several brick chimneys and tall windows with large black shutters. The lovely gardens and manicured grounds complemented the mansion.

When she arrived, a footman helped her out of the carriage and escorted her into the mansion. After she had entered the large front door and stepped into the long hallway, the housekeeper showed Charity to the parlor where Mrs. Kensington was waiting for her. She was a short woman. The gently rounded figure that had once made her seem doll-like had thickened into solid matronly lines. She moved with a quick, light step and from under her lace cap silvery ringlets lined her forehead giving her a disarmingly youthful look. Charity felt that her appearance was like a beggar in comparison to her gracious and elegant hostess who was dressed in a green gown with lace and a strikingly beautiful necklace around her neck.

Mrs. Kensington went across the room and went up to Charity. "I am delighted to meet you, my dear," she said as both women bowed to each other. "Please, come and sit next to me on the divan. I shall ring the bell for tea."

Even though they were strangers, Charity and Mrs. Kensington had a delightful conversation. Mrs. Kensington expressed her gratitude and complimented Charity for her bravery the other day.

"My daughter Charlotte, her husband, and I are in your debt for saving our precious boy, Charles," said Mrs. Kensington. "He is the sole heir to the Kensington fortune, and that makes him very special to us."

At that moment, Charlotte Parker and her nephew entered the room. Charles ran to Charity and embraced her with a jolly smile. Mrs. Parker gave Charity a gracious greeting and expressed how delighted she was to see her. Charity engaged in pleasant talk with both women while Charles played with his toys in the corner.

After some time had passed, Mrs. Kensington instructed her daughter to take Charity on a tour of their home. Charles stayed with Mrs. Kensington while Mrs. Parker, or Charlotte, as she asked Charity to call her, toured the beautiful mansion. After seeing several rooms, Charlotte took her into the conservatory, which Charity thought was the grandest room of all. It was filled with ornate furniture from England, with lovely red velvet drapes on the windows. In the corner of the room, there was a magnificent pianoforte. Beautifully colored rugs from the Far East covered the floors, and a large chandelier with white candles hung from the ceiling in the center of the room. On the walls were portraits of Kensington family members.

The tour came to an end when a servant came in and told Charlotte that her assistance was needed in the kitchen. Charlotte looked at

Charity and said, "Please, stay and look around the room. I shall return momentarily." In her absence, Charity admired the elegant furniture and the magnificent portraits hanging on the walls.

A few minutes later her pleasure was abruptly interrupted by the sound of a door slamming shut. When she turned around, to her surprise she saw Colonel Parker standing in the room. He walked toward her. She tried to avoid him, but he grabbed her arm, and she could not break free. Then he looked right into her blue eyes and spoke with a cunning tone in his voice.

"It is so good to see you again, my dear Charity. I must thank you for saving my nephew's life. For that I will always be in your debt. There is no need to fear me. I mean you no harm. I would like to become good friends with you."

Chills ran down her spine as she heard his words. She was unwillingly being befriended by a devious and dangerous scoundrel who also was a killer, and he was indebted to her for saving his nephew's life. For all she knew, he may have had deadly intentions for her as well.

Colonel Parker's invitation of friendship greatly disturbed her, and she found herself at a loss for words. Luckily, at that moment, the door to the room opened, and Charlotte entered. She apologized for leaving Charity and was a bit surprised to see her husband. The colonel craftily explained to his wife that he stumbled upon their guest quite by accident and was so pleased to see Charity. He further told her that he insisted on them becoming friends. Charity played along with the colonel by smiling pleasantly.

Charity did not want to overstay her welcome, so she told the colonel and Charlotte that she had to be on her way. Before leaving, she said farewell to Mrs. Kensington and thanked her for her hospitality. The colonel helped Charity into the carriage and whispered in her ear, "Remember what I told you, my lovely Charity. We must become good friends."

As the carriage drove away, Charity looked back and waved to Charlotte and Charles while the colonel stood tall with a sly smirk upon his face. She was relieved to be heading back to Andrews' Tavern. She kept asking herself the dreaded question of how much longer she could keep what she knew about Mr. Singleton's death a secret before someone would find out—if that person didn't already know.

When she arrived back at the tavern, Grace and two officers from the constable's office were waiting for her. Grace introduced them to Charity and explained that they were investigating Theodore Norton's attempt on her life. Grace stayed by Charity's side the entire time while the men asked her questions. They told Grace and Charity that they suspected Theodore of killing Mr. Singleton and stealing money from him and that they were puzzled about his motive for trying to take Charity's life.

Charity told them she was as shocked and baffled as they were by the attack. She wanted so much to expose Colonel Parker as the real culprit, but something inside her kept her from doing so. After some time had passed, the two men thanked her for her indulgence and cooperation, and departed.

When they had gone, Grace put her arms around Charity, and with a deep look of concern in her eyes she said, "Charity, my dear, I am so worried about you. I feel it in my bones and in my heart that someone means you harm. Theodore Norton was acting on behalf of the real guilty person. I cannot understand why someone would want to commit a heinous act like murder upon a beautiful and loving young girl like you."

Charity froze for a few seconds, and then told Grace that everything would be all right. Grace collected her thoughts, and returned to the back room to prepare for supper. She did not ask Charity about her visit to Kensington Hall for she seemed preoccupied, so Charity did not say a word.

That night Charity tossed and turned in bed for several hours. Every time she closed her eyes to try to fall asleep, terrible images flooded her mind. She saw the colonel hitting Mr. Singleton with the candlestick while Theodore Norton and Lydia Johnson laughed at his evil deed. Then she saw someone falling down the stairs, and when she looked at the person's face, it was Mr. Higgins. The most terrifying image was that of Grace and David sitting at a table in the tavern with their throats cut and Mrs. Kensington standing next to them with a bloody knife in her hand.

The next morning she could barely get out of bed from lack of sleep. The tavern was crowded with several tradesmen and merchants on their way to Boston. They were discussing the horrific events taking place in Paris. A radical by the name of Robespierre had taken control and formed a new government. He and his associates were ordering the arrests, imprisonments, and executions of hundreds of French aristocrats. They also spoke of the sad illness of Benjamin Franklin who was loved by many Americans and the French.

With all this talk about death and revolution, Charity went outside for a breath of fresh air. A few minutes later, a fancy carriage pulled up to the tavern, and a well dressed, distinguished looking gentleman with a black moustache emerged. He greeted Charity with a slight bow, and then he asked to see the proprietor. Charity took him inside and introduced him to Mrs. Andrews. He said he was Monsieur Louis Monnerat, and he and his wife were the new occupants of Singleton Lodge.

While he was speaking, Charity remembered that Constance had told Grace and her at her father's funeral about Monsieur Monnerat. His polished manner and charm mesmerized Mrs. Andrews and Charity. He explained that after he and his wife were settled, they intended to host an assembly as a way to meet the people of North Haven, and he asked Mrs. Andrews for her assistance. Mrs. Andrews was flattered by the man's request and gladly offered her assistance.

A short while later, Monsieur Monnerat as well as many of the tradesmen and merchants left. Mrs. Andrews and Charity were tidying up, and Charity asked her where Grace was, because it was not like her not to be absent, especially when there was a crowd at the tavern. Mrs. Andrews replied that Grace was very troubled and had something personal to attend to.

The women's conversation was interrupted by Jesse who told his mother he had to go to the mill to pick up a delivery and asked Charity to accompany him. Seeing that things were quiet, Mrs. Andrews let her go. When they went outside, Grace was returning to the tavern.

Upon seeing Charity, she began to cry as she embraced her and spoke. "My beautiful Charity, promise me that you will be safe and live the happy life that you so richly deserve."

Her words struck Charity as very odd. Charity hugged her friend and told her not to worry. As Charity and Jesse pulled away in the wagon, Charity watched Grace enter the tavern, and for a moment she got an uneasy feeling that this was the last time she would see her.

At Kensington Hall, Colonel Parker and Charlotte were taking a walk in the blossoming gardens under the watchful eyes of Mrs. Kensington who was spying on them from the window in the drawing room.

The housekeeper, announcing the arrival of a visitor, interrupted her tenacious guard duty. Mrs. Kensington was delighted to see that it was Dr. Greenville, a physician and close friend. She instructed the housekeeper that they were not to be disturbed and to close the door behind her.

The two friends greeted each other and started talking.

"Is everything going according to plan?" asked Mrs. Kensington. "There will be no tolerance for any mistakes."

"I assure you, my dear lady, everything is the way you have requested it," replied Dr. Greenville. "I have enlisted the help of Lieutenant Michael Bradford, a soldier of fortune, who was very eager to accompany your special guest to Kensington Hall tomorrow afternoon. I must also tell you that I have it on good authority that Monsieur and Madame Monnerat have arrived in town and also the

Marquis de Touvere and his family are now residing at the Grand Inn."

"It's convenient and coincidental that they are all within my reach," said Mrs. Kensington. "They are all pathetic, weak, and insolent fools just like my son-in-law, the so-called honorable Colonel Benedict Parker," she sneered.

Then she walked over to the desk and took out a crown jewel box that she showed to Dr. Greenville. She told him the story about how the people she just mentioned, including her husband, were involved in a robbery plot to steal a priceless diamond called the Winfield diamond that belonged to England's royal family. She explained that she and her husband shortly after the war, had attended a masquerade ball hosted by the King, during which the diamond was stolen. After the robbery, the men foolishly went to celebrate at a tavern in London, and the tavern caught fire while they were there, and in the commotion the men were separated. The diamond was assumed to be lost, or perhaps taken by one of them. The men were also seeking a treasure map that had belonged to Monsieur Monnerat's cousin who had been a pirate some time before.

Mrs. Kensington opened the box. Inside was the diamond, sparkling magnificently.

She poured two glasses of sherry, and a very pleased and astonished Dr. Greenville proposed a toast: "To us, two cleverly disguised Loyalists who are indeed masters of the game."

Jesse and Charity returned to the tavern with David, who was hoping to get a hot meal. As they approached the front stoop, the door swung open and Mr. Higgins came running out, shaking his fists and shouting, "Don't go in there, my dear Lizzie. It's not safe. Come with me."

When he tried to grab Charity's arm, David pushed him away. The three of them went inside and found the dining hall empty except for Grace who was sitting in a chair by the fireplace. Charity called out to her, but she did not answer. Charity approached her and shook her shoulders, but she slumped forward. They saw blood coming out of her nose, and she was clutching Charity's doll in her hand.

Chapter 5

At that moment, Mrs. Andrews returned from visiting a sick neighbor. Upon seeing Grace's condition, Mrs. Andrews ordered Jesse to get Dr. Foote. David carried Grace upstairs to her room as Mrs. Andrews and Charity followed. He put Grace in bed, and Mrs. Andrews placed a wet cloth on her forehead. Grace's eyes were open and looking up at the ceiling, but she did not speak a word. The doll was still in her hand. Mrs. Andrews told David and Charity that she thought Grace had a stroke.

Dr. Foote arrived, examined Grace, and confirmed Mrs. Andrews' impression that Grace had a stroke. The left side of her face was paralyzed into a crooked expression. Charity began to weep. David comforted her, embracing her with his strong arms. Mrs. Andrews told Charity to have faith and keep good thoughts about Grace's recovery. Dr. Foote suggested they watch her closely during the night, and if possible, they would move her to his home the next day where he and his wife could care for her.

David offered to stay and assist Mrs. Andrews and Jesse with the supper crowd.

Charity sat in a chair next to Grace's bed and watched over her, trying her best to keep from crying but water leaked from her eyes and rolled down her cheeks from time to time. Grace's present condition reminded her of when she sat by her mother's bedside when she was sick with the fever, helplessly watching the life drain out of her.

While she was attending to Grace, unbeknownst to her, Mr.

Higgins was hiding in the woods behind the tavern, just watching and waiting in the shadows of the night.

The next morning they took Grace by wagon to Dr. Foote's home. Charity did not want to leave her, but Mrs. Andrews assured her that Grace was in good hands. Dr. Foote's house was a more appropriate place for her to be than upstairs from the tavern where noise and commotion could hinder her recovery. Charity told Dr. Foote that she would visit every day, and he assured her that the door would always be open.

When they returned to the tavern, Mrs. Andrews and Charity went inside while Jesse unhitched the team and brought the horses to the barn. Charity went straight to her room and sat on the bed in complete silence.

A few minutes later she heard Mrs. Andrews. "Charity, please come down here. You have visitors waiting to see you," she called.

She hurried down the stairs, and to her surprise, standing in the dining hall was Mrs. Kensington and a gentleman dressed in a green suit with gold buttons with whom she was not acquainted. Mrs. Kensington was dressed in a beautiful blue gown with elegant lace and a matching bonnet.

"My dear Charity, let me introduce you to my close and dear friend, Dr. Mitchell Greenville," she said.

They engaged in conversation, and Charity found Dr. Greenville to be very charming. Mrs. Andrews told them about Grace, and they expressed their concern that seemed genuine. Dr. Greenville affirmed that she was in good hands with Dr. Foote, because he knew of Dr. Foote's impeccable reputation as a physician. Mrs. Kensington then extended an invitation to Charity to accompany Charlotte, Charles, and Colonel Parker to a fair in New Haven.

Charity thanked her for thinking of her, but politely declined the invitation by saying that Mrs. Andrews needed help with the noonday crowd. Mrs. Andrews replied that she was not expecting a large turnout and insisted that Charity go because it would do her a world of good. Since she no longer had a legitimate excuse, she agreed to attend the fair. Mrs. Kensington said that she and Dr. Greenville had to return to Kensington Hall, because she was expecting the arrival of a special guest. But Charlotte, Charles, and the colonel were waiting for her outside. Moments later, Charity was riding in a fancy carriage on her way to a fair with Charlotte Parker, her adorable nephew, and her villainous husband.

At Singleton Lodge, Monsieur and Madame Monnerat were settling in to their new home. Monsieur Monnerat was attending to the task of making sure that the wine cellar was carefully stocked with the finest wines and champagne. Madame Monnerat was trying to get accustomed to her new surroundings which were somewhat disappointing compared to her beloved home in Paris. Although she longed to return there, she knew that if she and her husband did, it would lead them to their tombs.

Madame Monnerat was becoming increasingly agitated by her husband's slow efforts in locating the Marquis de Touvere and his family. She longed for the day when she could hold the Winfield diamond in one hand and the treasure map in the other.

While indulging in an afternoon cup of tea, her solitude was interrupted by Louise who announced the arrival of a visitor. The visitor was Lydia Johnson. At first Madame Monnerat was not pleased or impressed to be visited by a commoner, especially a woman who was dressed in farm attire, but her opinion soon changed when Lydia explained the purpose of her visit.

She told Madame Monnerat that she was a longtime resident of North Haven, very well acquainted with practically everyone in town, and also familiar with several people from New Haven. Madame Monnerat's interest in her visitor was growing. She offered Lydia a cup of tea and then they talked. Madame Monnerat learned that Lydia was a farmer's wife, a midwife, and a seamstress. Monsieur Monnerat soon joined them and was as pleased as his wife was to make Lydia's acquaintance. After hearing her story, he suggested that his wife hire Lydia as her personal seamstress.

When the offer was made, Lydia did not hesitate to accept it. She assured her new employers that they would be pleased with her labor, and that this was the perfect distraction she needed to take her mind off her nephew Theodore's death.

After Lydia finished her tea and left, Monsieur Monnerat commented that although Lydia was not in their social class, she was much like them in many other ways. Madame Monnerat agreed and speculated that her new seamstress would be very useful. Then they both laughed wickedly, contemplating their next move in finding the diamond and treasure map they both avariciously longed to possess.

Charity honestly enjoyed the afternoon at the fair. She not only had the opportunity to see several sights in New Haven, but also spent some time with Charlotte, Charles, and the colonel. She had to say that the colonel was very attentive and enjoyable to be with. There were several times that she had to keep reminding herself that he was a man of wicked character.

It was nearly suppertime and Charlotte insisted that Charity dine with them at Kensington Hall. Outnumbered three to one, she accepted the offer. When they arrived at Kensington Hall, Charlotte went upstairs to change for dinner. The colonel went to tell the servants to set another place at the table, and Charles and Charity engaged in a game of hide and seek. Charity counted while Charles went to hide, and when she had finished counting, she moved about the hallway and entered the drawing room, where she eavesdropped on conversation that she heard coming from the adjacent room.

Mrs. Kensington and Colonel Parker were having a heated discussion.

"How foolish it was of you to bring Mr. Kensington here. Once Charlotte finds out that her dead father is alive, she will be very angry at her mother dearest," said Colonel Parker with a sarcastic tone in his voice.

"Charlotte will never learn the truth about her father. It is for the best that she does not see him in his terrible condition. The fire has taken its toll upon him," replied Mrs. Kensington.

She reminded the colonel of how disgusted she was by the crime that he, the Marquis, Monsieur Monnerat, William Singleton, and her husband had committed. She also expressed contempt for their uncouth and vulgar behavior at a disreputable tavern in London which ended in disaster with the loss of a priceless diamond and treasure map. Mrs. Kensington warned the colonel that if Charlotte learned the truth, he would be very sorry.

Then Mrs. Kensington abruptly left the room. Charity did not want her presence known, but she sneezed, and the colonel came in the room. He grabbed her and shoved her in a chair, clutching her wrists tightly while placing his boots heavily upon her feet so that she could not escape.

As he got closer to her face, Charity suddenly saw two hands come from behind the colonel, grabbing him and throwing him to the floor. She glanced up, and found herself looking at a dashing stranger with very broad shoulders, long dark hair tied neatly with a ribbon behind his neck, and crystal blue eyes that were most attractive. The stranger pressed his foot upon the colonel's throat and then spoke to her.

"Are you all right, Miss?" he asked.

Before she could answer, Mrs. Kensington returned to the room, and with a look of vexation upon her face she demanded an explanation for what was taking place. Suddenly, Charity felt like a fly trapped in a spider's web. However, this web had been spun out of deceit, deception, and treachery.

Before the stranger or the colonel could speak, Charity quickly came up with a story that was fictitious, and she prayed it would satisfy those who were inquiring. She explained that she and Charles were playing hide and seek, and she startled the colonel when he unexpectedly came upon her hiding place. She further said that she was not in harm's way and that the colonel's sudden and irrational reaction made the outcome seem more serious than it actually was.

Mrs. Kensington instructed the stranger to release Colonel Parker. The colonel, feeling embarrassed, angry, and somewhat relieved, got up, giving a nasty look to the stranger. He then grabbed a carafe of wine and a glass and went into the next room, shutting the door behind him.

Mrs. Kensington had a solemn expression on her face, but introduced Charity to the stranger.

"Charity Chastine, please meet Lieutenant Michael Bradford. Lieutenant Michael Bradford, this is Charity Chastine."

After the introductions, the lieutenant was very charming while still maintaining a tough appearance. He apologized for acting too swiftly, but from what he had observed, he assumed that Charity was in need of assistance. While he was speaking, Charity could not stop looking at his fine blue eyes. Mrs. Kensington told Lieutenant Bradford that Dr. Greenville was in need of his assistance. He gave Charity a modest smile, told her that it was a pleasure to have made her acquaintance, bowed slightly, and then he left.

Charles came running into the room with his arms open wide to embrace Charity. His embrace made her feel happy and helped her to forget about the predicament she just had been in minutes before. Charlotte followed Charles, and she announced that dinner was being served in the dining room. Mrs. Kensington told them to go ahead to the supper table, and she would join them momentarily.

Mrs. Kensington sought out the colonel who was in the next room drinking excessively.

"Filling your belly with wine and getting into a drunken state," she said. "How typical and pathetic that is of you. I must warn you that I do not accept Charity's story, and I know that she is concealing the truth to protect you, or she's afraid of you. Whatever the reason is, I order you to leave her alone or next time I will have Lieutenant Bradford finish what he started."

The colonel retaliated by saying, "Before the lieutenant could get a hold of me, I shall tell Charlotte the truth about her father, and then I will inform the authorities and your friends and neighbors that you dear mother-in-law are a devoted Loyalist in disguise, who, if had your way, would want King George III to regain control of the former colonies. And do not forget what happened to several of your neighbors who swore loyalty to England. They were exposed and fled to save their lives while their properties were confiscated."

Mrs. Kensington listened, her face poker straight and her eyes filled with contempt. "It will be over your dead body," she replied. "I must leave your presence for your face and arrogance offends me."

She left the room to join the others in the dining room. The colonel retreated to a private area where he found comfort with a bottle of wine.

After dinner, Charlotte excused herself to put Charles to bed while Mrs. Kensington and Charity returned to the drawing room. Mrs. Kensington, in her forthright manner, offered Charity a position as Charles' governess. She told her that Charles was very fond of her, and from what she had observed, she knew she would be very attentive to him. She also expressed concern for her work at the tavern, saying it wasn't a proper position for a young girl like her. She offered a handsome wage with lodging at Kensington Hall. Although her offer was very attractive, Charity had reservations about accepting it, especially as the thought of being under the same roof with the colonel was not tempting. She told Mrs. Kensington that she needed time to ponder the decision, but it would be forthcoming.

After tea with her lovely hostess, Charity departed. On the way back to Andrews' Tavern, Charity kept thinking about the strange occurrences and shocking conversations she had witnessed at Kensington Hall. She also thought about her intriguing encounter with the lieutenant, which pleased her very much despite the circumstances of their meeting.

When she arrived at the tavern, Mrs. Andrews and David were there. Mrs. Andrews had seen Grace earlier in the evening and gave

Charity a report on her health. Then she and Jesse went to visit a neighbor, leaving David and Charity alone. When David inquired about Charity's afternoon at the fair and her visit at Kensington Hall, she told him that it was enjoyable, but she didn't reveal the whole story. She also told him of Mrs. Kensington's offer, which he was not very pleased to hear.

"Are you going to accept the position? Don't forget you are needed here, especially now that Grace is ill and cannot be of assistance," said David.

Charity got the impression David did not want her to work at Kensington Hall and told him that she needed time to decide.

It was getting late, so he decided to leave for home. Charity walked him outside and waved good-bye as he slowly disappeared into the distance.

As she was about to go inside, a cool breeze began to blow. She looked over her shoulder and saw the ghostly couple making their way into the woods. She shut her eyes for a moment, hoping that her mind was playing tricks on her. When she opened them, the couple was gone. Feeling a bit uneasy about being alone, she hurried inside and closed the door behind her. Then she went upstairs to get ready for bed.

On the other side of town, Monsieur and Madame Monnerat were enjoying a game of cards, when an unexpected visitor stopped at Singleton Lodge. As the maid announced the arrival of Colonel Benedict Parker, Monsieur Monnerat dropped the cards he was holding and rose immediately from his chair. Both he and his wife were surprised to see the colonel, who entered the room in a drunken condition and collapsed on the sofa. He informed them that he had it on good authority that Mr. Kensington was alive, residing in secrecy under his wife's orders at Kensington Hall. The Monnerats wanted more details. They listened attentively while the colonel babbled on about how his mother-in-law had hired a soldier of fortune by the name of Lieutenant Bradford to watch over her husband, who was not in good health as a result of the fire.

"Lady Kensington is always one step ahead of us. We must unveil her devious plan and put our efforts to the task of finding the Marquis, the diamond, and the treasure map before someone else does, or we will be left with nothing," replied Monsieur Monnerat. "Let us form an alliance among the three of us and we shall do battle with Mrs. Kensington." Colonel Parker agreed by shaking hands with Monsieur Monnerat, and then collapsed on the sofa.

At the tavern, someone was shaking Charity, calling her Lizzie. She opened her eyes and was shocked to see Mr. Higgins standing by her bed. She immediately rose from her bed and tried to get away from him. She called out to Mrs. Andrews and Jesse, but they did not answer.

"Come, Lizzie, we must get out of here. There is a fire downstairs. We must hurry! Take my hand!" shouted Mr. Higgins.

Charity pushed him aside and ran down the stairs. To her horror, the dining hall was engulfed in flames. Mr. Higgins followed her, and they tried to make their way to the front door. They tried desperately to open it, but it would not budge. The smoke and flames were getting to them, and they started choking and gasping for breath. As they headed toward the back room, Charity glanced up to see a burning beam coming down on them. She screamed in terror as Mr. Higgins and she stumbled into each other and fell to the floor, helplessly trapped surrounded by a fire from hell.

Chapter 6

The fire was all around them; flames were consuming everything. Charity felt trapped in hell and believed for certain that they would succumb to their deaths. She began to lose consciousness, and someone grabbed her arms and began to drag her body into the back room and out the back door. She was coughing profusely, but the night air felt good. When she looked up to see who her rescuer was, to her grateful surprise it was Mr. Higgins.

"No need to worry, my Lizzie. You are safe and, I will protect you from the demon who means you harm," said Mr. Higgins.

By now, several neighbors who had seen the fire were at the tavern offering their assistance to put out the flames, but sadly the fire had a head start consuming the fine establishment.

Mrs. Andrews and Jesse arrived and were shocked by what they saw. Jesse joined the others in their efforts to extinguish the powerful blaze. Mrs. Andrews came to Charity's side, inquired about her health, and then asked what had happened.

Charity told her that after David had left, she had gone to bed, and before she went upstairs she made certain that there was no fire in the fireplace and no lit candles. She told her she remembered waking up with Mr. Higgins standing by her bed and telling her that the place was on fire. She also told her that Mr. Higgins saved her life.

David Cobb arrived and interrupted Charity's statements to Mrs. Andrews. He was very worried about her well being. When he saw Mr. Higgins standing by her, he went into a rage and began attacking the poor man by accusing him of causing the fire. Charity instantly came to her rescuer's defense, but David would not listen to her.

"You killed your daughter and her lover, and now you tried to kill Charity!" shouted David. "Thank God you did not complete your evil task!"

Frightened by David's anger and accusations, Mr. Higgins ran off into the woods. David wanted to pursue him, but Jesse begged him to assist with the fire.

After several hours of tedious and tenacious efforts on everyone's part, the fire was put out, but by then Andrews' Tavern had been reduced to ruins and ashes. Mrs. Andrews stood silently staring at the ruins. She was devastated to see what had become of her late husband's dream and years of hard work. Charity was grateful to be alive, but she was very sad for the Andrews who had lost not only their home, but also their livelihood. She felt that it was her fault. She had also come to a shocking revelation that someone wanted her dead. This person had failed twice, but what if he or she tried again and succeeded? Since the Andrews and she had no place to go, Reverend Trumbull kindly offered them lodging at his humble abode.

The word of what had happened spread quickly throughout the town, and the next day, concerned neighbors descended on the Trumbull residence, offering condolences and assistance.

Charity went with Mrs. Andrews and Jesse back to the tavern to see what they could salvage. While they were shifting through the ruins, Mrs. Kensington and Charlotte arrived. They were upset to hear what had happened, and Mrs. Kensington took Jesse and Mrs. Andrews aside and spoke privately with them while Charlotte stayed with Charity.

"I am so glad that you are alive. "You have been through a horrible ordeal!" cried Charlotte, embracing her.

"Yes, it was a terrible ordeal but I am grateful to be alive. Thank you for your concern. I am very upset for Mrs. Andrews and Jesse. I wish there was something I could do for them in their time of need," said a sad Charity.

A few minutes later Mrs. Andrews took Charity's hand and asked her to take a walk with her. As they walked, she explained to her that Mrs. Kensington generously offered to financially assist Jesse and her with the rebuilding of the tavern. Mrs. Andrews told Charity that she and Jesse would reside with Reverend Trumbull and his family while it was in her best interest, and for her protection, to accept Mrs. Kensington's offer to be Charles' governess and to live at Kensington Hall. She was very persistent, reminding Charity that there was nothing for her at the tavern any longer so Charity decided that Kensington Hall would now become her new home.

———————

At Singleton Lodge, Madame Monnerat was sitting at her desk in the drawing room, writing a note. When she finished, she rang for one of the servants and instructed him to deliver the note to Charlotte Parker at Kensington Hall. As the servant left to carry out Madame Monnerat's task, her husband entered. Getting the feeling that his wife was up to something devious, he inquired about her thoughts.

She cunningly told him that what she was doing would benefit their cause and she would reveal the truth all in good time. She asked about Colonel Parker, and her husband told her that he was still asleep in the guest bedroom. Madame Monnerat informed her husband that it was time to find the Marquis, and she suggested they hire someone who had expertise in locating individuals. He liked the idea and wasted no time putting his wife's suggestion into action. They believed that the Marquis was the one who most likely knew the whereabouts of the diamond and the treasure map.

———————

Before they went to Kensington Hall, Charity asked Mrs. Kensington if her driver would take them to Dr. Foote's home so that she could visit Grace, and Mrs. Kensington graciously honored the request.

When they arrived at the doctor's residence, Dr. Foote informed Charity that there was no change in Grace's condition. She went into the room where Grace was lying in bed, and Dr. Foote's wife was attending to her.

Upon seeing Grace, Charity began to weep. She prayed that Grace would get out of bed and hug her and speak to her, but her prayers went unanswered. She noticed the doll on a chair in the corner of the room. She gave Grace a kiss on the forehead and took the doll with her—it was the only remembrance of her life in London with her mother and Patience.

When they arrived at Kensington Hall, Mrs. Kensington and a servant showed Charity to her new quarters while Charlotte read a note that had just been delivered to her. She became very agitated but kept the contents of the note to herself. She later went to Charity's room and helped her get settled into her new surroundings.

In the afternoon, Charity had tea with Charlotte, Dr. Greenville, and Mrs. Kensington. Charlotte remained quiet but cast suspicious glares at her mother. When they had finished their tea, Mrs. Kensington and Dr. Greenville retreated to the drawing room, and Charlotte confided in Charity. She showed her a note that read:

My dear Charlotte, your mother is hiding someone from you. If you go to the east wing of Kensington Hall, you will find this person, and your discovery will no doubt shock you, but you need to know the truth.

There was no signature, but whoever had sent the note had certainly succeeded in arousing Charlotte's curiosity as Charity's.

Charlotte told Charity that she was going to find out whom her mother was hiding in the east wing and she enlisted her assistance. Charlotte trusted her and wanted her to accompany her on her mission. Charity wanted to assist her friend, and was curious herself, so she agreed to go with her. Charles was taking a nap, the colonel wasn't home, and Mrs. Kensington and Dr. Greenville were preoccupied, so they went on their journey to search for the truth.

They entered the east wing. All the drapes on the windows were drawn; very little light peeked through. Charlotte and Charity looked around, and then suddenly heard the sound of someone crying. It seemed to be coming from a room down the hall. They came to the room, and as Charlotte opened the door, the crying stopped. All was silent for a few seconds, and then to their shocked surprise, a man wrapped in bandages came from out of the shadows and grabbed Charlotte. Charity tried to free her, but the man shoved her out of the way, and she fell to the floor. He put his hands around Charlotte's throat and began choking her. Their search had led them into the clutches of a mad man, and there was no one to save them!

Just as they were to become the mad man's victims, Lieutenant Bradford burst into the room and wrenched the man off Charlotte. He then shouted at them to leave immediately and to close the door behind them.

Charity grabbed hold of Charlotte, who was gasping for breath, trying to recover from the frightful experience, and they did what the lieutenant instructed them to do.

As they stood outside the closed door, they could hear a scuffle and the sound of furniture being thrown about the room. Eventually, there was silence, and Lieutenant Bradford emerged from the room.

"Ladies, you are safe now. You do not belong here, so please, for your well-being, leave now," insisted the lieutenant.

When Charlotte began asking questions about the man wrapped in bandages, the lieutenant made no response and abruptly went back into the room, locking the door behind him. Although he was rude, they were grateful for his assistance—and his blue eyes were just as captivating as when Charity had first encountered him.

They left the east wing and hurried to the drawing room. Charlotte stormed in and, in an excitable and insolent voice, began questioning her mother about the stranger. Dr. Greenville tried to calm her, but she was relentless and would not stop until she had some answers.

Mrs. Kensington was very disturbed when she heard they ventured to the east wing and found her special guest. After Charlotte explained about their unpleasant encounter, Dr. Greenville excused himself and went to see if the lieutenant needed assistance.

"Who is the man wrapped in bandages, and why are you hiding him? He tried to strangle me," ranted Charlotte. "I want the truth, and you cannot put me off!"

Mrs. Kensington told them that the stranger was a patient of Dr. Greenville who'd had an unfortunate accident and was in need of care and shelter.

Before she could finish her explanation, Charlotte revealed the note to her mother. Mrs. Kensington became infuriated and told her daughter to forget the entire matter, and then she tore up the piece of paper.

Getting no satisfaction from her mother, Charlotte left the room in tears. Mrs. Kensington closed the door and asked, "Charity, how did my daughter acquire this obscene note?" Charity responded, "A servant had given Charlotte the note, and she asked me to accompany her to the east wing. I went out of concern for Mrs. Parker."

Mrs. Kensington thanked Charity for her consideration for her daughter, but instructed her to remain silent about the matter, and then she dismissed her. Charity did what her employer asked and decided to go outside for some fresh air.

While Charity was outside, Mrs. Kensington assembled the entire household staff in the great hall where she inquired about the delivery of the infamous note. Upon learning the truth, she instructed the servants to return to their tasks while she and Lieutenant Bradford embarked on a visit to Singleton Lodge.

Charlotte had taken to her room, and Charles was still napping, so Charity went for a walk in the beautiful gardens. The flowers and bushes were in full bloom and the lush green lawns resembled a carpet. The surroundings were picturesque and tranquil. But when she stared toward the east wing, chills ran down her spine. All of a sudden, she needed to get away from Kensington Hall.

She asked two of the servants, Foster and Jennings, if she could accompany them on their errand. They were heading to Pierpont's mills to get supplies, and they agreed that she could go with them.

When they arrived at the mills, the servants told her that they would be a while, so she decided to take a walk down the road that took her to the ruins of Andrews' Tavern.

At Singleton Lodge, Monsieur and Madame Monnerat, along with Colonel Parker, were having a wonderful time playing cards and drinking wine from crystal glasses. Their pleasure was interrupted when Louise announced the arrival of Mrs. Kensington and Lieutenant Bradford.

When they entered the room, Mrs. Kensington was startled when she saw the colonel, and then she became furious. She demanded an explanation as to why Madame Monnerat sent the vile note to her daughter. Madame Monnerat rose from her chair and, with a ghoulish grin, spoke.

"My dear Mrs. Kensington, I believed your daughter needed to know the truth. Secrets can be very harmful to family relationships," said Madame Monnerat.

Before she could continue, Mrs. Kensington boldly commanded her and her husband to mind their own affairs.

Looking at Madame Monnerat, Mrs. Kensington noticed a brooch she was wearing. "Where did you get that brooch?" asked Mrs. Kensington. Madame Monnerat boasted that she won it in a card game with Colonel Parker. This response vexed Mrs. Kensington greatly.

"That is my property. I gave that brooch to a dear girl who was in my employ. When she died tragically, the brooch was missing. I demand you return it to me this instant."

When Madame Monnerat refused to do so, Mrs. Kensington informed her that she would have charges of thievery brought against her. Not wanting any trouble, Monsieur Monnerat firmly told his wife to give the brooch to Mrs. Kensington, which she did begrudgingly. After the brooch was in her possession, Mrs. Kensington instructed Lieutenant Bradford to escort her son-in-law to her carriage and wait for her there.

After the men had left, Mrs. Kensington warned Monsieur and Madame Monnerat to stay away from everyone at Kensington Hall, and to never again trespass against her, or they would be very sorry. She departed, leaving her trespassers concerned, and wondering at her insolent threats.

When they returned to Kensington Hall, Lieutenant Bradford went to the east wing while Mrs. Kensington and the colonel went into the library. Mrs. Kensington stood near a desk, her back to her son-in-law, and then she spoke in a rigid manner.

"I know that you were the one who told Monsieur and Madame Monnerat about Charlotte's father, and they wasted no time in tormenting my daughter with that pathetic note. I cannot believe you had the brooch that I gave to Elizabeth Higgins the night she was leaving to go to Canada with your cousin Edmund Tate. When she and your cousin were found murdered the next day, the brooch was missing. Since you had the brooch, I can only make the horrific assumption that you killed them."

The colonel denied the allegations, but Mrs. Kensington ignored him. She continued to accuse him of squandering his family's fortune, and being a thief, a drunk, a womanizer, and now a murderer. While the colonel tried to retaliate with harsh allegations against his mother-in-law, Mrs. Kensington turned and faced him with a pistol in her hands.

Charlotte was walking by the library, heard the argument, and rushed in. When she saw her mother aiming a pistol at the colonel, she shouted and pushed her husband out of the way just as Mrs. Kensington fired the weapon.

Back in North Haven, Charity was standing by the ruins of Andrews' Tavern, remembering the first time she arrived in town and the people she had met. Grace was like a mother to her. Her thoughts were interrupted when she saw someone enter the barn, so she went to see who it was. When she entered, the barn was empty except for Mr. Higgins, who was sitting in a pile of hay. Upon seeing her, he rose, embraced her, and then spoke.

"I'm glad to see you, my dear Lizzie. I need to protect you from that scoundrel who means you harm."

He spoke with kindness and concern in his voice and for the first time Charity was not afraid of him. She thanked him for saving her from the fire and gave him a kiss on the cheek. His eyes filled with tears, and then he took her hand and told her that they had to leave quickly.

They started to depart, but were startled by the sound of the barn door suddenly shutting. Charity looked straight ahead, and to her surprise, David Cobb was standing in their path. He stood with a demonic countenance upon his face while pointing a pitchfork at Charity and Mr. Higgins.

Chapter 7

Charity did not know what to make of David's actions, but before she could react, Mr. Higgins kicked him in the knees and threw hay in his face. As David fell to the ground, they opened the barn door, and fled.

"We must flee from here, my dear Lizzie. Let's run to the mills and get some assistance," shouted Mr. Higgins.

After their escape, Lydia Johnson found David, recovering from Mr. Higgins' attack. Upon seeing him, Lydia handed David a loaded musket, instructing him to go after them.

"Go and kill that foolish old man and that witch Charity Chastine! Kill them! Avenge my nephew Theodore, your good friend. Do to them like you and Theodore did to those traitors Elizabeth Higgins and Edmund Tate. This time they must not escape like they did from the fire I started in the tavern," proclaimed Lydia.

Overcome by the evil in his heart, David took hold of the musket and went to carry out Lydia's heinous deed.

When they arrived at the bridge by Muddy River, Mr. Higgins was short of breath so they rested. Charity could see the mills in the distance with several men working and moving about outside, so she felt somewhat safe. Mr. Higgins, who was feeling melancholy, began to recall the events of that terrible night.

"Elizabeth fell in love with two men," he said. "The first time she was only fifteen, and she had a brief affair with an army officer of high rank. After he defiled her, he left my Lizzie for a young lady of high society and my daughter was left with a broken heart and with child. Not to disgrace either one of us, she became a recluse in our cabin where she stayed until the child was born. Upon the child's entry into this life, my Lizzie made the heart-wrenching choice to give the baby away. She lived with great sorrow and emptiness for nearly two years until she came to the assistance of a wounded Redcoat officer shortly before the Revolutionary War ended, nearly six years ago. She was hiding him, nursing him back to health in a cave near Indian Lookout when I discovered them. After I disowned my daughter, she and her Redcoat lover found sympathy and assistance from an influential and wealthy woman from Wallingford. When I learned of their impending elopement and journey to Canada from Lydia Johnson, I became enraged and confronted them. Our confrontation did not end well. I begged her to leave him but she refused to listen to reason.

She pleaded, ' "The war has ended. Edmund and I are going to live in Canada where we will not be judged. I beg of you to wish us well.'

Edmund implored, ' "I love your daughter and will protect her with my life. Please give us your blessing.' "

"Not in this lifetime," I told her. "Be gone from my sight! I hope you suffer for breaking my heart. From this moment on, you are dead to me!"

"They left me and I never saw them alive again. The next day their bodies were found on the banks of this river with bullet wounds to their heads. I buried them on my property under an oak tree, and I still tend to their graves every day."

"The first time I saw you at the tavern, I thought you were my Lizzie who came back to me, and I've been watching over you ever since. I know now you are not Lizzie because she is resting in her grave. Forgive me, Lizzie, forgive me," wept Mr. Higgins.

Feeling sorry for the poor man, Charity embraced him and told him that his daughter forgave him.

Then David Cobb interrupted their moment of solace. He

had found them and was pointing a musket at them with deadly intentions.

Monsieur and Madame Monnerat arrived at the North Star Inn in New Haven where they met a man by the name of Simon Blackwell who had served as a spy for the Continental Army during the war. Disguised as a woman, Blackwell successfully smuggled important papers and documents out of British camps. After the war, he received public recognition from George Washington and John Adams for his bravery and patriotism.

Since the war's end, Blackwell earned his living seeking hidden treasures and people who were assumed missing or in deliberate concealment. He was highly recommended to Monsieur Monnerat, and he was about to earn his worthiness.

When they entered the inn, the crude, simple furniture revolted Madame Monnerat. After meeting Simon Blackwell, Monsieur and Madame Monnerat followed him upstairs to a room down the hall. When they opened the door, they found the Marquis in a compromising position with a young girl. Caught by surprise and embarrassed by the intrusion, the young girl ran to hide behind a screen while the Marquis hastily put on his clothes.

Monsieur Monnerat informed the Marquis that after he was decent, he was to come downstairs where they would be waiting for him. He reminded the Marquis that escape was impossible. They closed the door, and Simon Blackwell stood watch while Monsieur Monnerat and his wife waited downstairs. They now had the Marquis in their clutches.

Both Monsieur and Madame Monnerat believed they would soon have the diamond and the treasure map in their possession, and perhaps Mr. Blackwell would be of some assistance dealing with their irritating nemesis, Mrs. Kensington.

At Kensington Hall, Mrs. Kensington fired the pistol, the bullet narrowly missing Charlotte.

The sound of the pistol firing alerted some of the servants, who came running into the library. Mrs. Kensington remained calm, and with a solemn expression she told the servants the pistol accidentally went off while she was showing it to her daughter and the colonel.

After the servants had gone, Charlotte retaliated by telling Mrs. Kensington that she was as crazy as the man in the east wing, and if she ever tried to harm the colonel again they would take Charles and leave Kensington Hall forever. Then she and her husband, his face in a smirk, left the old woman's presence.

Mrs. Kensington dismissed her daughter's threat as petty. She busied herself by putting the pistol back in the desk and taking out the crown jewel box that contained the diamond.

"My pathetic son-in-law," she said to herself. "You may think you have triumphed over me, but only for a brief moment. You may claim to be innocent of the murders of Elizabeth and Edmund, and that may be so; however, I know you are guilty of other sins from your past. I will deal with you and the others in due time," she declared holding the diamond, and then she broke into nefarious laughter.

Back on the bridge, David Cobb was determined to kill Mr. Higgins and Charity. When Charity begged him not to harm them, he went into a rage and ranted that they were traitors just like Elizabeth and Edmund, and they had to die. He said they should have died in the fire, and that would have ended it all. As David Cobb was about to fire the musket, Mr. Higgins jumped up and lunged at him pushing him against the railing of the bridge. While they fought, David lost his balance, fell over the railing, and plunged into the river below.

Mr. Higgins embraced Charity and told her that they were now safe. As they looked down at the river, they could not see any sign of David's body. Then suddenly the wind began to blow fiercely, and they could hear the sound of footsteps on the planks of the bridge. As they turned their heads, they saw what it was.

A tall, lanky man dressed in farm attire with a tricorn hat on his head, a pipe in his mouth, and a dog by his side was in their midst. He removed the pipe from his lips and spoke to them.

"Are you folks having a bit of trouble? Let me be of some assistance if I may. Don't mind my dog Pogo. His bark is worse than his bite. Please forgive my manners and let me introduce myself. My name is Ebenezer Stiles, and I do not live far from here."

Mr. Higgins and Charity were relieved to see Mr. Stiles and glad that it was not David Cobb. They told the stranger of their ordeal. When they were finished, he shook his head and said he knew David and thought many of his actions were suspicious.

A few minutes later, some of the workers from Pierpont's mills came to the bridge. When Charity and Mr. Higgins told them what had happened, they volunteered to go below the bridge and search for David's body along the riverbanks. Mr. Higgins went with them, leaving Charity on the bridge with Mr. Stiles and Pogo.

Pogo took a liking to Charity, and Mr. Stiles remarked that his dog was very particular when it came to meeting strangers. He recalled that Pogo was very fond of another young girl who died some time ago on this very same bridge. When he mentioned Elizabeth's name, a terrible chill engulfed Charity's bones and she felt the wind blowing against her cheeks. Mr. Stiles told her that sometimes at night he could see apparitions that resembled a young couple moving about in the woods. He was convinced that the couple was Elizabeth and Edmund.

"When I told my neighbors of what I've seen, they told me that my mind was playing tricks on me, but I know better. Since Elizabeth and Edmund were murdered, their spirits cannot find peace, so they roam around aimlessly in the shadows of the night," explained Mr. Stiles.

After he told Charity of his sightings, she knew what she had been seeing was not her imagination either.

The search for David's body proved futile, so they departed and went to inform the constable of what had happened. As they left, unbeknownst to them, Lydia Johnson was hiding in the nearby brush. Enraged by the outcome of the situation, she kept her presence hidden until they had gone, and then like a snake, she slithered away, taking the sense of evil with her.

At Kensington Hall, the colonel was sitting on a bench watching Charlotte play with Charles. The colonel stared at his wife, admiring her beauty and goodness. She reminded him so much of Elizabeth Higgins, Mrs. Kensington's personal maid, who he had a fancy for. The colonel's mind wandered back in time to the night that Elizabeth and Edmund died. He remembered walking down the hallway and hearing voices coming from the library. When he peered in, he saw Mrs. Kensington and Elizabeth talking. Mrs. Kensington gave Elizabeth a brooch, and then embraced her and told her that she and Edmund would have a new beginning in Canada. She also told Elizabeth that she would be by their side if they ever needed assistance. After Elizabeth left the library, the colonel followed her out to the garden where he begged her not to go.

"My beloved Elizabeth, I implore you not to go to Canada with my cousin Edmund. Stay here with me. We are meant to be together. Love conquers all."

"I do not love you," she said. "What we had was a brief indulgence to satisfy a lustful desire, and it was a sin that I regret. I love Edmund, and he loves me as a human being and a partner, not as a trophy or possession like you do. Charlotte and you are engaged and you need her, or perhaps you need her good family's name and fortune more than her love. You love no one except yourself," replied Elizabeth.

The colonel became angry at her response and tried to stop her from leaving. When he grabbed her shoulder, she slapped him and pushed him away. As she broke free, the colonel pulled off the brooch she was wearing. The colonel stood alone holding the brooch in his hand, weeping bitterly as she ran into the distance. Then Charlotte called to him and asked him to join her and Charles for a stroll, which he did, and his memories slowly faded as he became occupied with them.

In the drawing room, Mrs. Kensington and Dr. Greenville were playing a game of chess, Mrs. Kensington's favorite game. When visiting Philadelphia before the war, she had the distinct pleasure of playing chess with Benjamin Franklin who taught her some of his fancy skills that he learned while playing the game in the salons of Paris.

The present game was interrupted by a servant who gave an envelope to Mrs. Kensington. Inside was an invitation from Monsieur and Madame Monnerat for Mrs. Kensington and guests to attend a ball they were hosting at Singleton Lodge the following week.

"How very intriguing it is of them to invite us to a ball," said Mrs. Kensington. "They are no doubt up to something. By all means, I will accept their invitation and pretend that it is an olive branch that I will break in half once I expose their true intentions. I am always not one, but two steps ahead of my adversaries. Checkmate, my dear doctor," she said, taking the king from her opponent.

"Well done as usual, my dear Phoebe. You are still master of the game and the fairest one of all," said Dr. Greenville.

In the east wing, Lieutenant Bradford was returning to his post after having a meal in the kitchen. When he came to the room where Mrs. Kensington's special guest was residing, the door was wide open, and the male servant who was keeping watch was lying on the floor unconscious. The lieutenant frantically searched the room as well as the entire east wing, but the man he sought could not be found.

At the constable's office, Mr. Higgins and Charity gave their statement to the authorities. Charity had an uneasy feeling that somehow David had survived the fall off the bridge, but that perhaps something else had happened to him. Her feelings would prove valid momentarily.

Just as they had finished their business, Jesse Andrews came bursting into the office. While trying to catch his breath, he exclaimed that they had to go to the barn next to Andrews' Tavern to see the shocking discovery he and his mother had made.

When they arrived at the barn, Mrs. Andrews and some neighbors were waiting outside. She explained that she, her son, and some workers from the mill were putting lumber to rebuild the tavern in the barn for storage when they made a horrible finding.

Mr. Higgins, the constable, and Charity followed Jesse into the barn while Mrs. Andrews waited outside with the others. Charity screamed in fright, for they saw David Cobb lying in a pile of hay with a pitchfork in his back. Scrawled in the dirt next to his body was the word "Judas." Outside, not far away, someone wicked was watching and waiting.

Back at Kensington Hall, Lieutenant Bradford, with the assistance of Dr. Greenville and a handful of servants, searched intensely for the missing man. Mrs. Kensington remained in the drawing room and waited. To herself, she cursed William Singleton, the Marquis, the colonel, and Monsieur Monnerat for getting her husband involved in the devious plot to steal the diamond from the royal family. She wished they all had perished in the fire at the tavern in London for their crime.

"I will make them all pay for corrupting my husband and attempting to bring disgrace to the respectable name of Kensington," vowed Mrs. Kensington to herself as she knocked over the pieces to the chess game.

Outside in the gardens, Charlotte, Charles, and the colonel were having a wonderful time. Charles was ahead of Charlotte and the colonel. Kicking a red ball that rolled into the bushes, Charles approached to retrieve the ball when two hideous looking hands emerged from the bushes, ready to grab the little boy and hold him captive—in the clutches of a mad man.

Chapter 8

Just as the hands reached out to grab an unsuspecting Charles, Lieutenant Bradford came from behind and took a solid hold of the man, saving the little boy from his abductor. Dr. Greenville and the servants assisted the lieutenant in escorting the man back to the east wing while Charles, never suspecting a thing, recovered the ball and joined Charlotte and the colonel as they continued their stroll about the beautiful grounds.

It was early in the evening when Charity finally arrived at Kensington Hall. A servant informed her that Mrs. Kensington wanted to see her, so she went to the drawing room and waited. A few minutes later, Mrs. Kensington came in.

"Oh, my dear Charity, Foster and Jennings told me what you and Mr. Higgins have been through! I am so relieved you are safe and that villain David Cobb has been brought to justice. From this moment on, I will not allow you to leave Kensington Hall without a proper escort," she insisted.

Charity told her that she need not worry about her. Mrs. Kensington interjected by saying, "You are a special and appreciated addition to the Kensington household." Charity thanked her for her kind words, and then asked for permission to take her leave and go to her room to rest before supper.

After Charity had gone, Mrs. Kensington rang the bell and called for Lieutenant Bradford. The lieutenant secured the situation in the east wing and then joined his employer in an intense conversation. Mrs. Kensington praised him for his swift and effective actions dealing with her husband, expressing approval of his discretion and loyalty, which she held in high esteem.

Then she asked a favor.

"I would be pleased if you would escort Charity to the ball. I have the suspicion that you both have a fancy for each other, which I commend. It is my opinion that you and Charity would make wonderful companions, and perhaps later on, a delightful couple," said Mrs. Kensington with an approving smile.

The lieutenant admitted to his employer that he admired Charity's spirit, courage, and beauty. He also explained that she reminded him of his sister Hope, who had been taken prisoner by an Indian tribe some years before the war.

"The men from our town, including my father and me, were away on a hunting expedition when an Iroquois tribe attacked the town and took my sister prisoner along with several women and children. After two months, the Indians released them in exchange for weapons and supplies. Hope never returned home. While she was captive she became involved with a young Indian brave and chose to remain with him and his tribe," recalled the lieutenant with sadness in his voice. He went on to say that her actions devastated the entire family. Just before his father died, he uttered Hope's name three times and then closed his eyes forever. The lieutenant blamed himself for not protecting his sister. Then the lieutenant told Mrs. Kensington he would carry out her request which pleased her very much.

For the next several days, Charity stayed at Kensington Hall, devoting her time to taking care of Charles and spending time with Lieutenant Bradford, which Mrs. Kensington cleverly orchestrated, and Charity had no objection. She reflected on the heinous actions of David Cobb and his friend Theodore Norton, the fire at the tavern that nearly killed Mr. Higgins and her, poor Grace who suffered a stroke, the action of Colonel Parker upon William Singleton, and the man wrapped in bandages residing in the east wing. Above all, she could not stop thinking about Elizabeth and Edmund being killed by David Cobb who also met his end with a pitchfork in his back. Mystery, grief, and death had plagued this quaint town.

The night of the ball finally arrived, and Charlotte and her mother saw to it that Charity was dressed elegantly in a gown lined with lace, and beautiful pearls to match. The lieutenant looked very handsome in his tailored suit, and Charlotte and the colonel made a good looking couple. Mrs. Kensington and her escort Dr. Greenville also looked well. As they rode by carriage to Singleton Lodge, Charity felt like a princess in a fairy tale.

Upon arriving at Singleton Lodge, footmen helped the ladies out of the carriage, and inside Monsieur and Madame Monnerat graciously greeted their guests. Those in attendance were Dr. Foote, Reverend Trumbull, Jesse and Mrs. Andrews, the Marquis, Mr. and Mrs. Pierpont, and many others with whom Charity was not yet acquainted.

The lieutenant was a perfect escort. He introduced Charity to Colonel Ridgefield and his wife, and a man by the name of Simon Blackwell whom the lieutenant served with during the war. Colonel Ridgefield told them that he and his regiment were stationed in New Haven and his men were in need of a great deal of training as well as the hospitality of a good society.

He went on to say that President Washington was committed to building up the country's army. The president was troubled by both the recent war between England and France and the revolution in Paris, but since the United States was in financial debt from the Revolutionary War, and the army was weak, the country had to stay neutral.

During the course of the evening, Charity had the pleasure of dancing with the lieutenant, the Marquis, and Colonel Ridgefield who were all wonderful partners. The Marquis' wife and daughter were not present, and he indulged himself by dancing with many of the young ladies in the room. After they had danced the minuet, Monsieur and Madame Monnerat proposed a toast honoring the people of North Haven. When the toast was finished, the music played, and the dance floor filled with elegant ladies dressed in flowing gowns and refined gentlemen dressed in fine suits.

Meanwhile, Charlotte went out to the terrace for some fresh air. Simon Blackwell interrupted her solace and started chatting with her. Blackwell boldly began to express his admiration for her beauty while insulting her husband and recalling the past.

"Benedict does not love you. He loves only himself and your mother's money. He has wronged you, my lovely Charlotte, with his immoral endeavors, especially fathering the child of one of your mother's servants and then claiming the little boy to be his nephew. How could you love and honor a man of such deceitful character?" ranted Simon.

Before Charlotte could respond, a jealous and enraged Colonel Parker, who had overheard Simon's words, grabbed hold of him and began punching him repeatedly, causing Simon to fall. The colonel bent over him, but Simon jumped up and shoved him into a corner. While Charlotte begged them to stop fighting, Simon continued to strike the colonel without mercy.

Unaware of what was taking place outside, all those inside, including Charity, were having a splendid time. Mrs. Kensington, however, with crocodile eyes, kept a close watch on the host and hostess. As the ball continued, a carriage pulled up to Singleton Lodge, and a woman with no escort emerged and entered.

When she came in to the great hall, the musicians stopped playing, and all eyes were fixed upon her stunning, elegant appearance. As she stared into the crowd, there were looks of shock and dismay upon everyone's faces except for the Marquis and Monsieur and Madame Monnerat. Overcome by curiosity, Charity asked Mrs. Kensington who the woman was.

"Oh, good gracious, it cannot be. Unless my eyes and the eyes of everyone present are deceiving us, the woman standing before us is Elizabeth Higgins," cried a bewildered Mrs. Kensington.

Complete silence fell upon the entire room. Monsieur and Madame Monnerat and the Marquis, grinning ghoulishly, were very pleased to see the lovely and mysterious guest whose sudden appearance turned a grand evening into a shocking and sinister moment.

As Charlotte pleaded with Simon to stop striking her husband, Lieutenant Bradford appeared and intervened by grabbing hold of Simon and saving the colonel from any further attacks. Charlotte went to be with her battered husband and helped him to his feet while the lieutenant escorted an enraged Simon Blackwell inside.

"What in Hades were you thinking? You were beating the man relentlessly to the point of death!" shouted Lieutenant Bradford.

"I would have succeeded if you had not interfered," responded an unremorseful Simon.

Their conversation came to an abrupt end as Charlotte and the colonel walked past them. The colonel was leaning on his wife, his lip bloody and blood streaming from his left nostril. He stared at Simon, and then spoke.

"Stay away from my wife and me, and keep your outrageous tales and lies to yourself, or I promise that you will live to regret your actions," threatened the colonel.

Simon advanced toward the colonel, but Lieutenant Bradford stopped him. Charlotte and Colonel Parker left as Lieutenant Bradford instructed his friend to compose himself and let what had transpired to be done with. Then both men returned to the great hall, although Simon was not yet finished with the colonel.

In the great hall, all the guests were still in shock by the arrival of the lovely mystery woman who, according to Mrs. Kensington, had an uncanny resemblance to the late Elizabeth Higgins.

Monsieur and Madame Monnerat wasted no time in approaching the woman and greeting her. Madame Monnerat embraced her, and then Monsieur Monnerat took the woman's hand and introduced her to the guests.

Mrs. Kensington made her way through the crowd, and without an introduction from Monsieur Monnerat, introduced herself and inquired about the woman's identity and her family's name.

"My name is Honoria Noble, and I am the daughter of Randolph and Eugenia Noble from Pennsylvania," replied the lovely lady with a gracious smile.

When Mrs. Kensington pressed for more details, Monsieur Monnerat politely told her that he needed to introduce Honoria to his other guests and they excused themselves. As they walked away, Mrs. Kensington caught a glimpse of Madame Monnerat who had a devious smirk on her face.

"I have not yet figured out what game you and your husband are playing, but I must warn you both that once I figure it out, I will expose you by winning the final round," promised Mrs. Kensington.

As she walked away, Madame Monnerat laughed. Then she enjoyed a drink with the Marquis who seemed to be enjoying himself immensely, watching Honoria Noble as she made her acquaintance with the guests at the ball.

In the meantime, the lieutenant went to Charity, and said that Mrs. Kensington wanted them to leave at once, and so they did. On their return to Kensington Hall, no one uttered a word, and Charity felt as if the carriage ride home was the calm before the coming of a terrible storm.

The next day Charity went to visit Grace at Dr. Foote's home. The lieutenant went with her at Mrs. Kensington's request. When they arrived, Dr. Foote informed Charity that Grace had been agitated the last two days. She went over to Grace's bed, and stroked her head gently, saying, "Grace, it is Charity." Hearing Charity's name, she opened her eyes and tried desperately to speak. Charity got closer, and she uttered these words.

"Charity, you take good care, and trust no one. Hold on to the doll and never surrender it," she said. Then she closed her eyes and was silent.

Charity stayed for a short time, and then the lieutenant and she departed. On their way back to Kensington Hall, Lieutenant

Bradford felt that Charity needed a distraction, so they stopped at the Rising Sun Tavern for a light meal. The tavern owner was a chubby man with rosy cheeks and a jolly laugh. They were treated with hospitality, and the food was delicious. The lieutenant's company was most enjoyable. He helped Charity to relax and take her mind off her visit with Grace.

At Kensington Hall, Madame Monnerat came without an invitation to call on Mrs. Kensington. While she waited in the drawing room, Madame Monnerat occupied herself by admiring the fine furnishings.

"Are you looking to purloin something? Or are you here to tell me more about your guest Honoria Noble? She made quite an impression at last night's ball," said Mrs. Kensington sarcastically.

Madame Monnerat turned about and greeted her hostess dutifully before sitting on the sofa. Mrs. Kensington told her uninvited guest not to make herself comfortable because her stay was to be brief.

Madame Monnerat inquired about why Mrs. Kensington and her party departed so early. Mrs. Kensington ignored the question and demanded to know more about Honoria. Madame Monnerat avoided the subject by asking about Charlotte and the colonel. Then she angered Mrs. Kensington when she inquired about Mr. Kensington.

"You do not fool me with your petty inquiries, Laura Monnerat. You and your husband may have impressed your guests last night, but you failed to win my approval. As far as I am concerned, you and your husband have no good name or title and are outcasts from your own country. All of your motives are fraudulent, just like your mysterious Honoria Noble," replied Mrs. Kensington.

Madame Monnerat cunningly tried to play the dumb fox game. Mrs. Kensington retaliated by informing her that she was very well acquainted with the families of Philadelphia's fine society, and there were no persons by the names of Randolph and Eugenia Noble and daughter Honoria. She blatantly accused Madame Monnerat, her husband, and the Marquis of playing a game of deception which she was going to put to an end. Madame Monnerat, who was unaffected by the old woman's threats, defied her by laughing wickedly. Her laughter irritated Mrs. Kensington so greatly that she slapped Madame Monnerat in the face. Charlotte had entered the room and was shocked by her mother's uncouth action.

Lieutenant Bradford and Charity arrived back at Kensington Hall. He escorted her to her room and expressed that he enjoyed their visit to the tavern. When he departed, Charity felt elated by the strong affections she had for him.

After entering her room, she remembered Grace's words concerning the doll, so she went to retrieve it. However, the doll was no longer in the place where she had left it. She searched the entire room and came up empty handed. Unbeknownst to her, as she pondered where the doll could be, someone was standing outside her door in the hallway holding the doll in his hands.

When Lieutenant Bradford returned to the east wing, he encountered a frantic Dr. Greenville, who explained that Mr. Kensington had once again managed to escape. Without wasting any time, the lieutenant, Dr. Greenville, and some servants began to search for Mr. Kensington.

In the drawing room, Charlotte apologized to Madame Monnerat for her mother's outrageous behavior. Mrs. Kensington, showing no remorse for what she had done, ordered Madame Monnerat to leave at once. Madame Monnerat appeared to take her leave, but she stayed behind and eavesdropped on Charlotte and her mother.

Charlotte demanded an explanation from her mother while insinuating that she was keeping secrets that were causing irrational outbursts and unacceptable behavior. Mrs. Kensington responded by accusing her daughter of disrespecting her while allowing the colonel to poison her mind against her own mother. She also informed Charlotte that the people she was defending were scoundrels who had no place in any decent society.

Suddenly, a man wrapped in bandages came crashing through the terrace doors of the drawing room. Charlotte screamed in fright as the man fell to the floor. He looked up at Mrs. Kensington and spoke.

"Phoebe, why are you keeping me a prisoner in my own home? What have you done with the diamond and treasure map? Give them to me!" he shrieked.

Then the man lost consciousness, leaving Charlotte and Mrs. Kensington staring at him. After hearing all this, Madame Monnerat was attempting to leave when Colonel Parker suddenly appeared unexpectedly. He grabbed hold of her and ushered her forcefully into a nearby room, and then locked the door behind them.

Chapter 9

"How dare you treat me in this vile manner? I demand that you release me at once. If my husband knew about this, he would not hesitate to take you to task," cried Madame Monnerat in an agitated state.

The colonel stared at his beautiful captive and smiled with a devious grin. He then told her to compose herself and listen to what he was about to say. Realizing that she had no other option, Madame Monnerat did as the colonel instructed.

"My lovely Laura, I know you overheard some information that cannot leave this place. Since we have similar goals, I believe that it is in both our interests to assist one another by forming an alliance between us, excluding your husband and the Marquis," said the colonel.

"I am not interested in becoming involved with you for any reason," responded Madame Monnerat.

She explained that her loyalty was to her husband, who would be very pleased when she told him what she learned from her visit to Kensington Hall.

The colonel laughed, saying, "Your husband has no great love for you. He revealed to me on numerous occasions that you are an expensive nuisance who has not given him a child. His lack of love for you gives him roaming eyes for other women," said the colonel hurtfully.

Then he told Madame Monnerat that it was upon her husband's recommendation that he, the colonel, William Singleton, the Marquis, and Mr. Kensington go to the tavern in London the night they stole the diamond, and it was Monsieur Monnerat's careless flirting with a young tavern maid that started a fight between him and two other men. The altercation knocked over several candles, creating a deadly fire that nearly killed all those present. Several people were burned, including Mr. Kensington, whom many people presumed had died.

Madame Monnerat accused the colonel of telling tall tales, and he simply responded by saying, "I have witnesses including the Marquis to corroborate my story."

Madame Monnerat became infuriated, but then began to listen to the colonel's proposal. He charmingly convinced her that he had a plan to retrieve the diamond and the treasure map from his mother-in-law, and that once he accomplished that, he intended to leave Charlotte and share the spoils of a good fortune with a woman he truly desired.

"Charlotte was stricken with small pox when she was a child," he explained. "She miraculously survived, but the disease left her barren. Charlotte is not very desirable as a wife, especially to gentlemen of high society. I only married her for her family's good name and fortune. You, my beloved Laura, would make me a very happy man, because we are so much alike," confided the colonel, touching her cheek gently.

Feeling a bit flustered, and overwhelmed by the colonel's offer, Laura wanted to leave his presence immediately. "I will remain silent about what I know," promised Madame Monnerat. "I need some time to consider your proposal." Seemingly pleased with her response, the colonel let her go. On her way back to Singleton Lodge, Madame Monnerat contemplated life as the wife of a colonel, and was intrigued by the possibilities.

Mr. Kensington was returned to the east wing, and Lieutenant Bradford and Dr. Greenville made provisions so that he could not escape in the near future.

Charlotte relentlessly demanded answers from her mother about the man's identity and his mention of a diamond and treasure map. As usual, Mrs. Kensington was very crafty and evasive in her responses. Charlotte became frustrated and angry and abruptly left the room.

Once Charlotte had gone, Mrs. Kensington sent for Charity. She took Charity into her confidence and told her of the incident, deliberately leaving out some of the facts. She then asked if Charity would speak to Charlotte to convince her that her mother's actions and treatment of the man in the east wing were justifiable for his own welfare and all those residing at Kensington Hall. Charity reluctantly agreed to Mrs. Kensington's request in the hope that she would learn the truth and help to ease some of Charlotte's agonies.

When Charity went to Charlotte's room, she was not there. A servant informed her that Charlotte left to visit friends in New Haven.

Charity made her way back to her room, but as she was walking down the hall, she had the feeling that someone was following her. Yet, every time she glanced over her shoulder, no one was there. When she reached her room, she entered and closed the door quickly. She knelt down and looked through the keyhole, and she saw the shadow of someone pass by. She became frightened and decided to remain in her room for the time being.

When Madame Monnerat returned home, she went to the library, but before entering the room she overheard Monsieur Monnerat and the Marquis engaging in an inappropriate conversation while drinking and playing cards. Revolted by what she heard, Madame Monnerat did not make her presence known. She informed Louise that she was going to New Haven and would return later.

When Madame Monnerat arrived in New Haven, it was late afternoon and the streets were crowded with many townspeople, including several officers dressed in uniforms. When the carriage came to the milliner's shop, Madame Monnerat ordered the driver to stop. She descended from the carriage and began walking down the street. Then Madame Monnerat soon came upon Charlotte Parker conversing with Colonel and Mrs. Ridgefield. Madame Monnerat spent some time with them, but suddenly saw someone she recognized in the near distance. She excused herself and went in pursuit of this person.

Some time later, a loud scream was heard, from the direction in which Madame Monnerat had gone. Upon hearing the scream, Charlotte, Colonel and Mrs. Ridgefield, several officers, and a handful of townspeople hurried to see what had happened. In an alley behind the shops they found an unconscious Madame Monnerat lying on the ground.

Colonel Ridgefield was the first to approach her. He saw that Madame Monnerat had a pale complexion and a puncture wound on her neck.

Charity finally mustered up the courage to leave her room at Kensington Hall. She went downstairs into the library to get a book to read. Perhaps reading would calm her nerves, so she selected a book and sat in a chair, opening to the first page. After barely finishing the first sentence, she heard a noise from the hall, so she went to investigate who or what was making the disturbance. To her surprise, she saw Mr. Higgins making his way to the front entrance.

When she called out to him, he turned. In his arms he was holding a sleeping Charles wrapped in a blanket. Startled by her appearance, he quickly hurried into the drawing room while muttering something about protecting someone's grandchild. Suddenly, Colonel Parker stepped into his path, holding a pistol to his head and thwarting his escape.

"Give the boy to Charity and I will not harm you," shouted the colonel.

"He is my Lizzie's flesh and blood, and I am saving him from the people in this house. My Lizzie would want it this way," cried Mr. Higgins.

"Your daughter Elizabeth has been dead for several years. The boy is mine and shall remain here with me at Kensington Hall. For the last time, give him to Charity or meet my wrath," ordered the colonel.

With the pistol held at his head and no means of escape, Mr. Higgins, with sadness in his eyes, reluctantly placed Charles in Charity's arms. He kissed the sleeping boy on his forehead and whispered to him that he loved him.

At that moment, Mrs. Kensington and Lieutenant Bradford entered the drawing room, shocked to see what was taking place. Mrs. Kensington instructed the lieutenant to assist Charity in taking Charles back to his room.

After they went upstairs, Mrs. Kensington took charge of the situation by ordering her son-in-law to put down the pistol, and then she demanded an explanation from Mr. Higgins concerning his unthinkable, inappropriate actions.

The old man explained that he had no intention of harming Charles, but was going to take him to live with him in his cabin in the woods.

"I want my grandson to get to know his grandfather. You can provide him with material possessions, respectability, and the advantages of high society, but I can give him love and tell him stories about his mother that will keep her memory alive," cried a pitiful Mr. Higgins.

The colonel became enraged and was about to strike Mr. Higgins, but Mrs. Kensington ordered Mr. Higgins to leave her home at once. She also promised him that no charges of kidnapping would be brought against him.

Recognizing the fact that he had been defeated, Mr. Higgins departed, alone with his sad and heavy heart.

When Mr. Higgins was out of their presence, Mrs. Kensington reprimanded the colonel for his insolent behavior and reminded him that violence was unacceptable and unbecoming to any member of the Kensington family.

Colonel Parker boldly reminded her that it was his efforts that prevented Mr. Higgins from taking Charles. He mocked his mother-in-law's speech about proper conduct and accused her of being a hypocrite by keeping her own deranged husband a prisoner in the east wing. Then he revealed that he knew she had the diamond and the treasure map, and attempted to make a deal with her. He said he would quietly divorce Charlotte, give legal guardianship of Charles to her so he could be raised a Kensington, and then he would leave town to pursue a new life of exploration in the Ohio Valley, if she would surrender the diamond and the treasure map to him.

Mrs. Kensington denied that she was in possession of the items he sought, but told the colonel that he was free to take his leave at any time and Charles would remain with her.

Colonel Parker told her to take some time to consider his request and reminded her that she had more to lose than he did, because he knew secrets about her that would destroy her and the fine Kensington legacy.

Taking pleasure in taunting his mother-in-law, he took his leave while Mrs. Kensington, who did not feel at all vanquished, studied the pieces to the chess game displayed on the table and carefully plotted her next move.

The townspeople of New Haven were trying to make sense of the vicious attack upon Madame Monnerat who suffered a loss of blood from the puncture wound. Two physicians carefully examined her; they believed she was the victim of a wild animal roaming the alleys in search of food. They concluded that Madame Monnerat's catatonic state was due to shock from the beastly attack.

When Monsieur Monnerat learned of what had happened to his

wife, he made arrangements to have her brought back to Singleton Lodge, and he hired Lydia Johnson to tend to her.

———————

At Kensington Hall, Charlotte, who had been one of the witnesses who found Madame Monnerat, gave a firsthand account of the incident. Charlotte's story troubled everyone, especially the colonel, who was very agitated upon hearing the details.

During the next few days, Charity gave full attention to Charles with the assistance of Lieutenant Bradford. Charlotte spent her days visiting Mrs. Ridgefield in New Haven, and Mrs. Kensington and Dr. Greenville spent much of their time in the drawing room behind closed doors. Colonel Parker, unbeknownst to his wife and the others, was spending his time at Singleton Lodge.

One evening after supper, Mrs. Kensington informed Charity that she and Dr. Greenville were going to pay a call to a sick neighbor. Charlotte and the colonel were not at home, but the lieutenant and the servants would be present if she needed assistance, especially if Mr. Higgins were to make a return appearance.

After they had gone, Charity went to the kitchen to get a glass of water and then went upstairs. Before returning to her room, she peeked in on Charles who was sleeping like an angel. When she returned to her room, she placed the candle she was carrying on the table and was about to take a sip of water when suddenly, a cold, clammy hand covered her mouth. She dropped the glass in fright. Then she turned and saw it was Mr. Higgins.

The poor man apologized for sneaking up on her, and then he begged her to allow him to see Charles. Before she could respond, there came a knock at the door. It was Lieutenant Bradford, who had heard the glass breaking, and was concerned. Charity did not want him to discover her surprise visitor, so she tried desperately to hide Mr. Higgins as an impatient Lieutenant Bradford cautiously began to open the door to make his way inside.

At Singleton Lodge, Monsieur Monnerat, the Marquis, and Colonel Parker were waiting anxiously for Mrs. Kensington who demanded a meeting with all three of them. When she and Dr. Greenville arrived, Mrs. Kensington wasted no time in getting down to business. She informed them that she was tired and no longer amused by their pathetic efforts to disturb her about the diamond and the treasure map. Monsieur Monnerat assured her that they would continue relentlessly until they had what they wanted. She boasted that she had what they were so tirelessly searching for, and she was willing to make a deal.

The Marquis told her that a deal was unacceptable, but the colonel instructed him to be silent and let his devious mother-in-law have her say. Mrs. Kensington told the terrible trio that she was going to keep the diamond as a reminder of her connection to her beloved England and its royal family, and as compensation for the tragedy that had befallen her husband. Mr. Kensington had had the diamond concealed in his coat pocket; it was discovered after he returned to her care following the fire. She then gave them an old journal written by a surveyor in 1740 describing the landscape of the nearby countryside, and a parchment of paper with a treasure map sketched on it.

"If you follow this map carefully and read the journal, you will find a fortune beyond your wildest dreams. I must warn you; legend has it that the treasure is cursed and the last unfortunate souls to search for it were never seen or heard from again," said Mrs. Kensington.

Unconcerned about the legend, the men agreed to Mrs. Kensington's terms and were very pleased when she gave them the journal and the map. Then they all made a pact to keep their little meeting a secret.

Unbeknownst to the unscrupulous group, Lydia Johnson was listening from the hallway. An even more dangerous and mysterious stranger wearing black boots listened in hiding outside on the terrace while furiously clutching Charity's doll in his hands.

Chapter 10

Monsieur Monnerat escorted Mrs. Kensington and Dr. Greenville to the main entrance while Colonel Parker and the Marquis remained behind examining the journal and the treasure map. Both men were wondering where the treasure they so desperately were looking for was buried.

When Monsieur Monnerat returned, he informed his partners that they needed to begin their search immediately. While they discussed their plan of action, the mysterious black-booted spy left the terrace. In another part of Singleton Lodge, Lydia Johnson was devising a plan of her own that would enable her to acquire a portion of the treasure.

On the carriage ride back to Kensington Hall, Dr. Greenville commended Mrs. Kensington on her clever and successful plot of retaining the diamond while surrendering the treasure map and the journal to her adversaries. When he expressed concern that the colonel and his companions might end up with the better half of the deal, Mrs. Kensington reassured him that the diamond was worth ten times more than the treasure. She also told him that her son-in-law, the Marquis, and Monsieur Monnerat would make spectacles of themselves spending their time and resources searching endlessly for a treasure that was nowhere to be found except in the annals of legend.

Charity was desperately trying to conceal Mr. Higgins from Lieutenant Bradford who kept knocking at the door, determined to enter the room. She quickly managed to hide Mr. Higgins under the bed and then went to open the door.

"I beg your pardon, but it is highly improper for a gentleman to persist on entering a lady's room without a proper invitation," Charity said in an effort to distract the lieutenant.

"I apologize for my lack of manners, but I heard the sound of breaking glass and I assumed that you may be in trouble. My actions may seem a bit hasty and inappropriate, but they are genuinely out of concern for you," responded the lieutenant.

His sincerity along with his mesmerizing blue eyes made for a perfect apology, which she wholeheartedly accepted. After she explained that she had dropped a glass by accident and there was nothing to fear, Lieutenant Bradford said good night and departed. Once he was gone, Mr. Higgins came out from under the bed and thanked Charity for not giving him away. She told him that she could not be his accomplice in his scheme to see Charles, and he had to leave at once. Before Mr. Higgins left, Charity asked him how he was able to enter Kensington Hall without detection. He explained that there was a secret passage in the library that led to a hidden tunnel under the mansion, and its passageway led directly outside to the gardens. His daughter Elizabeth had told him about the secret entrance several years ago.

After he left her room, Charity's curiosity got the best of her so she decided to follow him. She got downstairs and was about to enter the library when Mrs. Kensington and Dr. Greenville arrived. Mrs. Kensington inquired about Charles, and after Charity told her he was sleeping peacefully in his room and all was quiet at Kensington Hall, she and Dr. Greenville retreated to the drawing room. Charity then hurried to the library to catch up with Mr. Higgins, but when she entered, there was no sign of him. It was as if the many shelves of books had swallowed him up.

The next day Charlotte invited everyone to attend an event in New

Haven where several veterans from the Revolutionary War along with explorers and mountain men were giving speeches about settlement in the Ohio Valley. Mrs. Kensington and Dr. Greenville declined the invitation, because they were expecting a visitor. The colonel was not at home, so the lieutenant and Charity accompanied Charlotte. Crowds gathered on the town green and listened with interest to the speakers who told stories of adventure and vast and beautiful lands with unlimited resources that awaited settlers in the new territories of the Ohio Valley. While many of the spectators were intrigued by what they heard, Lieutenant Bradford reminded Charlotte and Charity about Indian attacks, famine, disease, and other unknown dangers that awaited unsuspecting newcomers in a frontier.

After listening to the lieutenant, Charity's enthusiastic opinion of exploration and expansion was dampened by fear and disapproval.

They met Colonel and Mrs. Ridgefield at the event and they seemed to be very good friends with Charlotte. It was late in the afternoon when the speeches concluded, and Colonel Ridgefield and his wife graciously invited them to attend a gathering at an assembly hall not far from the town green. Not wanting to disappoint Charlotte, who had her heart set on attending, Lieutenant Bradford and Charity agreed to attend.

There were many people at the assembly hall, including the officers from Colonel Ridgefield's regiment, who were eating, drinking, talking, and laughing, seemingly without a worry on their minds. While Lieutenant Bradford engaged in conversation with Colonel Ridgefield and some of the officers, Charlotte excused herself and went outside for some air while Charity walked about the hall.

She had a brief conversation with a serving girl named Hannah. She was very polite and had a fair complexion and nice smile.

They were interrupted by the proprietor of the establishment, who asked Hannah to go outside and get some firewood. She left to carry out her task, and Charity joined the lieutenant.

The entire place was filled with many faces and much laughter and commotion.

A few minutes later, the guests heard a loud scream, and a group of them rushed outside to see what had happened. Lying on the ground next to a neatly stacked pile of wood was young Hannah. The poor girl's complexion was pale white, and she bore a wound on her neck similar to the one Madame Monnerat had on her neck when she was found. Unfortunately, unlike Madame Monnerat, Hannah was dead.

In the meantime, an unsuspecting Charlotte was taking a leisurely stroll, enjoying the evening air, when suddenly she heard footsteps from behind. When she glanced over her shoulder, there was no one there. Feeling a bit nervous, she began to walk quickly.

She stopped for a moment to catch her breath and wipe her face with a dainty handkerchief when she heard a howling sound in the nearby distance. Then, without warning, someone grabbed her from behind. Charlotte fainted from fright, and her black-booted abductor carried her away, leaving the handkerchief on the ground.

At Kensington Hall, Mrs. Kensington and Dr. Greenville were visited by Honoria Noble, whom Mrs. Kensington had summoned. Mrs. Kensington was determined to find out more about the young woman who had created quite a stir at the Monnerat's ball.

Honoria was very cautious in her responses to her host's inquiries. She maintained her family's lineage from Philadelphia and explained that her parents were old acquaintances of Monsieur and Madame Monnerat whom they met some years ago while on holiday in Paris.

Mrs. Kensington played the dumb fox game for some time, and then she made her calculated move. Two of her servants brought a large portrait covered with a bed sheet into the drawing room. When the servants left, Mrs. Kensington rose from her chair and unveiled the portrait.

Honoria stared at the painting with a false expression of bewilderment that vexed Mrs. Kensington. Then she politely asked who the young woman was in the painting. Mrs. Kensington said it was one of Honoria's ancestors, Rebecca Noble, from Salem, who in 1693 was accused of witchcraft and was executed.

Honoria denied any relation to the woman in the painting and cursed Mrs. Kensington and her family for her wicked allegations. Mrs. Kensington accused Honoria of being a fraud, and she said that she had proof to substantiate her accusations. Honoria continued to curse, when suddenly a fierce gust of wind blew open the terrace doors, filling the room with a terrible, chilling sensation of evil.

Monsieur Monnerat was returning to join his partners after checking in on his wife, and found an unconscious Marquis lying on the floor. Monsieur Monnerat revived the Marquis, and the man told him someone had hit him over the head while he and the colonel were studying the map.

Then Monsieur Monnerat, with the help of a few servants, searched the lodge and the grounds for the colonel. However, their search was futile. It was quite evident to an enraged Monsieur Monnerat that the colonel had fled, taking with him the journal and the treasure map. Watching nearby, the colonel's accomplice, Lydia Johnson, was laughing wickedly to herself while Colonel Parker escaped.

Darkness, confusion, fear, and death permeated the assembly hall. A young woman no more than twenty years of age was dead; another young woman had fallen into the clutches of a despicable creature; and a third woman was forced to face the painful and scandalous past of her ancestor. A merry gathering of local townspeople, commoners and privileged alike, had turned into a night of fright.

The authorities quickly arrived to investigate poor Hannah's demise. People were frantic and upset, horrified and shocked by what had occurred. Colonel Ridgefield tried to keep order and offered assistance to the constables while they questioned the guests.

After Lieutenant Bradford and Charity gave their statements, they noticed that Charlotte was missing. With the help of some of Colonel Ridgefield's officers, the lieutenant and Charity took to the streets to look for their missing friend. They searched frantically but diligently. Charity could feel the terrible chill of the night air on her face, and she heard an awful howling in the distance that made her take a tight hold of the lieutenant's arm.

They did not find Charlotte, but they discovered a handkerchief embroidered with her initials lying on the ground. Their minds raced with fear, and the haunting question on all their minds was *what happened to Charlotte?* Little did they know that she was not far from them with someone who was deliberately keeping her hidden and against her will.

Dr. Greenville hurried to close the terrace doors in Kensington Hall that had suddenly blown open, letting in the chilly night air. Honoria was very angry and upset over Mrs. Kensington's accusations that she was a descendent of Rebecca Noble, the woman in the portrait, a condemned witch from Salem. Mrs. Kensington kept her poker face, unaffected by Honoria's cursing. She challenged Honoria's sanity by continuing relentlessly with her accusations.

Finally, Honoria could no longer withstand the mental torment, and she broke down. She admitted the truth, confessing to Mrs. Kensington that she had cruelly succeeded by exposing her fraudulent lineage and her connections to a seventeenth century witch. A sobbing Honoria told Mrs. Kensington and Dr. Greenville that Monsieur

Monnerat and his wife had caught her in a compromising position with the Marquis.

In an effort to protect her reputation and that of her family, she reluctantly entered into a scheme of deception. She would portray the so-called twin of a dead young woman named Elizabeth Higgins as a means to disturb Mrs. Kensington. She explained how her appearance at the ball was planned to shock the guests while serving as a distraction for the Marquis, the Monnerats, and Colonel Parker, who plotted to retrieve a diamond and a treasure map from Mrs. Kensington, whom they believed possessed these items.

When she had finished her confession, an exhausted Honoria sat down on the sofa and tried desperately to regain her composure. Feeling triumphant, Mrs. Kensington sat down next to Honoria, took her hand, and gently caressed it. With her crocodile eyes, she gazed into the young woman's eyes and spoke.

"My lovely and deceitful young lady, I must compliment you on a tremendous performance. Although you have failed, I bear you no ill feelings or harm, because I know you were a pawn used by a group of loathsome connivers whom I shall take delight in dealing with later on. As for you, I admire your craftiness as well as your deviousness, and I would like us to become friends, for I believe we shall mutually benefit from our newly established friendship," replied Mrs. Kensington with a ghoulish grin.

Realizing that she was at the mercy of a mighty opponent, Honoria agreed to join Mrs. Kensington in her devilish crusade against Monsieur Monnerat and his conspirators. Pleased with Honoria's decision, Mrs. Kensington and Dr. Greenville drank a toast with their newly acquired companion. While they sipped sherry from crystal glasses, Honoria stared at the captivating portrait of Rebecca Noble. Suddenly, she heard a hideous laughter echoing in her ears that did not seem to be heard by Mrs. Kensington or Dr. Greenville.

At Singleton Lodge, an enraged Monsieur Monnerat was pacing the library floor while the Marquis sat in a chair recovering from being hit on the head. Monsieur Monnerat cursed Colonel Parker and promised his friend the Marquis that they would reclaim the journal and the treasure map, and then even the score with the colonel. He reminded the Marquis that once they found the buried treasure, their lives would be filled with magnificent riches, and they would live in abundance till the end of their days. Lurking in the shadows outside the library, Lydia Johnson was envisioning what her life would be like with her share of the treasure promised to her by her accomplice Colonel Parker.

Thousands of miles away in a city engulfed in turmoil, chaos, and revolution, the heinous plan of a ruthless leader was about to unfold. It would ultimately shatter the dreams of certain greedy individuals. Looking out a window of his quarters, Robespierre, the revolutionary leader of the new government of France, was watching with evil delight while several carts carried members of the French aristocracy to the guillotine. He was interrupted by a muscular young man with dark hair and devilish eyes, entering the room in an arrogant manner.

The man's name was Jean-Luc Tessier, a former pirate turned soldier of fortune, with a charming but dangerous reputation. He had a talent for luring his victims into his web of doom by taking them into his confidence with his good manners and false kindness before revealing his insidious side. He once captured the undivided attention of three brutish pirates whom he then outwitted by stealing their gold and putting a bullet between the eyes of each one. Rumor had it that only the wrath of God could stop Jean-Luc and this made him the perfect person to carry out Robespierre's bastardly plot.

The revolution's leader's plan was for Jean-Luc to go to the United States and, with the assistance of Madame Monnerat's maid, Louise

Bourget, a strong supporter of the French Revolution, recover the Winfield diamond that had been stolen from England's monarch, as well as to find a hidden treasure believed to be buried somewhere in the mountains of Connecticut. The diamond and the treasure would help to finance the revolution.

Robespierre assured Jean-Luc that he would be rewarded handsomely for his efforts. Intrigued by the offer, Jean-Luc accepted the challenge. He promised to take care of Robespierre's enemies, Monsieur and Madame Monnerat and the Marquis and his family, for eluding their appointment with Madame Guillotine. This overjoyed Robespierre, and the two men shook hands before Jean-Luc departed for America.

In New Haven, Lieutenant Bradford and Charity, along with their search party, with lanterns in their hands, continued to walk the streets looking for Charlotte. While they searched, an unconscious Charlotte was lying on a bed, not far away in an abandoned shop in the back of an alley. Someone wearing black boots and holding a doll in his hands was sitting in a chair keeping a close watch on his elegant captive.

Soon Charlotte began to stir, moving her body and groaning a bit. The stranger rose from his chair and went to the bed. He gently stroked her head and softly whispered pleasant words in her ear. Hearing the stranger's soothing, enchanting voice, Charlotte opened her eyes and, to her astonishment, found herself staring at the face of an old friend.

Chapter 11

As Charlotte was about to call out his name, she lost consciousness. He continued to stroke her head gently and then placed the doll in her hand. A few minutes later, an elegantly dressed woman accompanied by a tall, male servant entered. The stranger instructed the woman and her servant to take good care of Charlotte. Then the servant took Charlotte into his arms and carried her outside to a carriage waiting in the alley. The stranger gave the woman a letter and instructed her to personally deliver it to Mrs. Kensington the next day. And then they went separate ways.

The search for Charlotte went into the early hours of the next morning. Colonel Ridgefield looked up at the pale pink streaks that had begun to lighten the dawn sky. He politely insisted that Lieutenant Bradford and Charity take lodging at a local inn while he sent word of what had happened by a post rider to Kensington Hall.

The next day Colonel and Mrs. Ridgefield had breakfast with the lieutenant and Charity. While they dined, it became unpleasantly apparent to Charity and the lieutenant that the colonel and his wife were not very troubled by Hannah's death or Charlotte's disappearance. Conversation focused on expansion and settlement in the Ohio Valley, and the French Revolution. After they had finished their meal, Colonel Ridgefield told Charity and Lieutenant Bradford there was nothing more they could do except hope for the best and return to Kensington Hall to lend support to Charlotte's family.

When they arrived at Kensington Hall, the lieutenant and Charity were surprised to find a calm and complacent Mrs. Kensington playing chess with her faithful companion, Dr. Greenville. They stopped playing the game when Charity and the lieutenant came in. Mrs. Kensington expressed her gratitude for their concern and assistance in searching for her daughter. She then told them that she had received a letter from Charlotte early in the morning in which she wrote of her safety, and that she had spontaneously decided to stay for an indefinite period of time with friends who lived by the shore. Lieutenant Bradford and Charity were relieved but shocked by the news. They began to ask questions, but Dr. Greenville told the lieutenant that his assistance was needed in the east wing, and Mrs. Kensington told Charity to attend to Charles, who was asking for her. They did as they were told, but both Lieutenant Bradford and Charity were puzzled by the entire situation.

Several weeks passed, and there were no answers to the vicious and mysterious attacks on Madame Monnerat and Hannah, nor had Charlotte returned home. Her absence did not seem to affect her mother, but Charles missed her greatly, and so did Charity. Colonel Parker had not been seen or heard from for quite some time as well.

Then one afternoon two visitors came to Kensington Hall, and each one's presence would coincidentally set off a chain of shocking events.

Mrs. Kensington was in the library when Honoria Noble arrived. Honoria seemed agitated. She confided in Mrs. Kensington that ever since seeing the portrait of her ancestor Rebecca Noble, she had been tormented by a hideous laughter that would not leave her head. She insisted that the portrait was sinister and should be destroyed, but Mrs. Kensington laughed, assuring her new friend that there was nothing to fear from a very old portrait.

Their conversation was interrupted by the arrival of yet another visitor. Not wanting to be seen, Honoria took refuge in the room adjacent to the library.

The visitor, who was wearing black boots and a gold ring on his finger, was announced as Simon Blackwell. He greeted Mrs. Kensington in a gentleman-like manner, but then shocked her by his conversation. Simon revealed to Mrs. Kensington that he and his friends, Colonel and Mrs. Ridgefield, were taking very good care of Charlotte, and that she was happily residing at the Ridgefield's home. He reminded Mrs. Kensington of their agreement, which angered her greatly, but she responded to him calmly.

"I assure you that I will continue to honor our agreement, even though I have made a deal with the son of Satan. My daughter and the Kensington legacy are very precious to me, and I will do anything to protect them both. I must compliment you and Colonel and Mrs. Ridgefield on your devious and well executed plot to lure my Charlotte into your bosom of false friendship, and then to snatch her in the shadows of the night! Now you hold her for ransom and diabolically blackmail her mother."

"My dear Mrs. Kensington, your secrets, especially your Loyalist connections are safe with me and my companions. We will not harm Charlotte. Once Colonel Parker has been taken care of, Charlotte and I, with your blessing, will be together. I have loved your daughter for a long time. She deserves someone much better than that inferior being, your son-in-law," replied Simon, with a look of delight upon his face.

He explained to Mrs. Kensington that her son-in-law would soon be apprehended by the authorities for the attack upon Madame Monnerat and for the murders of William Singleton and the serving girl Hannah. The colonel would face his doom at the gallows. The plan would succeed, and in the end everyone would get what he or she deserved. Mrs. Kensington warned Simon that she was not a woman to be trifled with. Simon agreed, but laughed before taking his leave.

Honoria came back in from the other room, frantically warning Mrs. Kensington that Simon Blackwell was a foul fiend and that she must find a way to stop him and save her daughter. While Mrs.

Kensington tried to calm Honoria, the poor girl heard the hideous laughter again. She covered her ears, but it would not subside, and she left the room abruptly. In the hall, she caught a glimpse of Rebecca's portrait. The laughter became more incisive, causing Honoria great discomfort. She hurried outside in a panic and collapsed on the ground.

In the library, an angry Mrs. Kensington walked over to the chess game, stared at it, then knocked off the pieces, by chance leaving only the queen remaining in place. She took the queen into her hands, reminding herself that it was the most powerful piece of the game. She, therefore, was and would remain the master of the game.

While Mrs. Kensington was distracted by her thoughts, Mr. Higgins emerged from the hidden passage in the wall, and quietly made his way past Mrs. Kensington. He crept upstairs to retrieve Charles to take him away. This time he was determined to let no one stand in his way.

Monsieur Monnerat and the Marquis had left on a mission to find Colonel Parker and get the treasure map from him. Monnerat left Lydia Johnson in charge of the servants and the household.

Jean-Luc, Robespierre's agent, had arrived in the port of New Haven the day before, and upon learning the whereabouts of Monsieur Monnerat's residence, paid a call to Singleton Lodge. Louise Bourget greeted him, and was enchanted by him. After he revealed the secret code to her, Louise took Jean-Luc out into the gardens.

Jean-Luc told Louise his purpose, and she pledged her full cooperation. Unbeknownst to either of them, Lydia Johnson, who was attending to Madame Monnerat, had crept out onto the balcony above to eavesdrop, and overheard their conversation.

Madame Monnerat began to stir, uttering Colonel Parker's name. Before Jean-Luc and Louise had finished speaking, the evil Lydia gave a push and managed to send a large stone statue crashing down upon an unsuspecting Jean-Luc and Louise. Lydia looked down from the balcony, staring at her heinous deed, but was taken aback by something she had not expected to see.

Near the outskirts of town, a coach carrying tradesmen stopped at the Rising Sun Tavern. The tradesmen went in for food and rest while the coachmen attended to the horses and then went for a walk around the building.

As they approached the back of the tavern, they saw what appeared to be a pair of boots protruding from a group of bushes. They investigated and to their shock and dismay, found an unconscious Colonel Parker lying on the ground with several long strands of hair clutched in his fist.

Charity was in her room in Kensington Hall reading a letter she had received from her friend Constance Singleton who to her surprise, had gotten engaged to a wealthy plantation owner. Charity was disturbed to learn of her engagement to a slave owner, because she knew that Constance despised slavery and believed it to be a sin.

Her train of thought was interrupted by the sound of voices outside her room. When she opened the door, she saw Mr. Higgins talking to Charles and holding him by the hand, as they made their way to the stairs. While she tried to catch up with them, she saw that the man wrapped in bandages had once again escaped from the east wing, and came out from the shadows and attacked a startled Mr. Higgins.

Charity quickly grabbed hold of a frightened Charles. Then Lieutenant Bradford came from behind the man wrapped in bandages and tried to subdue him, but his efforts failed.

Suddenly, the man grabbed the stunned Mr. Higgins, whom the lieutenant tried to save by tackling the man, but the lieutenant's push was so forceful that all three of them fell violently down the stairs. They remained still at the bottom of the stairs while a sobbing Charles and Charity looked on in horror.

While holding a sobbing Charles, Charity stared at the three men who remained still at the bottom of the stairs. A few seconds later, Dr. Greenville appeared and hurried down the stairs to offer his assistance as Mrs. Kensington emerged from the library, her face startled. She shouted for assistance, and several servants came into the hall.

"Good gracious! What has happened to these men?" exclaimed Mrs. Kensington.

"It was a terrible accident," Charity said. "Mr. Higgins and Charles were making their way to the stairs when the man in bandages came out of the shadows and attacked Mr. Higgins. I grabbed Charles. Then Lieutenant Bradford appeared and tried desperately to save Mr. Higgins, but they all started struggling, and within seconds all three of them fell down the stairs."

Lieutenant Bradford began to stir, as did the bandaged man, but Mr. Higgins did not move. Dr. Greenville hastily instructed the servants to take the bandaged man into one of the rooms on the first floor. Then he examined the lieutenant who rose to his feet, appearing stunned by the ordeal, but did not seem to be injured.

Mrs. Kensington instructed one of the servants to assist the lieutenant into the library, and then she insisted that Charity take Charles to his room and remain there with him. Dr. Greenville attended to Mr. Higgins. Charity had a terrible feeling that he was not as fortunate as the others. Mrs. Kensington went into the library and closed the door.

Lydia Johnson was dismayed that she did not see the crushed bodies of Jean-Luc and Louise lying on the ground among the shattered pieces of the statue toppled over the balcony. Angered and disappointed by the failure of her evil deed, she retreated into Madame

Monnerat's room. She heard Madame Monnerat softly but distinctly utter Colonel Parker's name. As she went closer, Madame Monnerat without warning opened her eyes, but remained stationary.

Lydia removed the extra pillow from behind Madame Monnerat's head. As she held the pillow in both her hands and was about to cover Madame Monnerat's face, a voice shouted at her from the entrance of the room.

"What are you doing to my mistress?"

A surprised Lydia turned about and saw that it was Louise Bourget standing in the room. Although she was fuming inside to see Louise alive, she skillfully hid her emotions and solemnly explained that she was attempting to make Madame Monnerat more comfortable.

In an effort to get Lydia to leave, Louise informed her that a visitor named Jean-Luc Tessier had arrived, and he wished to speak to the person in charge during the absence of Monsieur Monnerat. Lydia put down the pillow and left the room, smiling at Louise with a devilish look in her eyes.

Outside Kensington Hall, a lovely Honoria Noble was lying on the ground trying to ignore the painful sounds of hideous laughter echoing in her head. As she tried to get up, a well manicured, strong hand reached out to her. Honoria grasped the hand and found she was staring at a tall, well dressed gentleman with dark hair and sideburns.

"Let me help you to your feet, my dear lady. My name is Ethan Fairchild. I was on my way to pay a call to Mrs. Kensington when I saw you lying on the ground."

Honoria rose to her feet and thanked the gentleman for his assistance. Then she told him her name and begged him not to enter Kensington Hall. She became restless with fright and asked if he would take her away. Feeling sympathy and concern for the lovely lady he had just become acquainted with, Ethan escorted Honoria to his carriage and instructed his driver to leave.

Inside Kensington Hall, Charity had managed to put a shaken Charles to bed. When he fell asleep, she went to the window and saw Foster and Jennings carrying Mr. Higgins' body to the stables. Mrs. Kensington came into the room and whispered to Charity to step out into the hall. She calmly explained that Mr. Higgins did not survive the fall, and that she considered his death an unfortunate accident brought on by his own carelessness. She informed Charity that Lieutenant Bradford and the other man were recovering nicely, and she had sent word to the authorities of what had happened.

Charity's eyes filled with tears as sorrow overcame her. Mrs. Kensington told her not to mourn for Mr. Higgins and to remain complacent for Charles' sake.

"Mr. Higgins was a guilt ridden and tormented old man who never forgave himself for his ill treatment of his daughter Elizabeth," said Mrs. Kensington. "Now he is at peace, and we will no longer be troubled by his attempts to abduct our precious Charles. Now my dear, you must go to the library to see Lieutenant Bradford. He has been asking for you." After wiping her tears, Charity went downstairs.

After she had left, Mrs. Kensington quietly tiptoed to Charles' bedside where she watched him sleep. She whispered in his ear that he was the heir to the Kensington fortune, and she would teach him how to become the master of the game.

———

Lydia went into the drawing room at Singleton Lodge, and came face to face with Jean-Luc Tessier, the man she had tried to kill just a short while ago. Jean-Luc introduced himself and inquired about Monsieur Monnerat. Lydia explained that he was not at home, and she was in charge of the household during his absence. Jean-Luc was charming and cunning, as was Lydia. They engaged in petty conversation and did not mention the fallen statue.

Their encounter was interrupted suddenly by Monsieur Monnerat's arrival home. Monsieur Monnerat called out to Lydia who turned her back on Jean-Luc to greet her employer. When Monsieur Monnerat entered the drawing room, Lydia smiled at him, as a calm and calculating Jean-Luc stood tall, holding a dagger behind his back.

Lieutenant Bradford was upset about Mr. Higgins' demise and blamed himself. He confided in Charity that Mr. Higgins reminded him of his own father in that they both lost their daughters to unforeseen and tragic circumstances and, in the end, they both died with broken hearts. As Charity tried to offer comfort with some kind words, Lieutenant Bradford excused himself and went for a solitary walk in the gardens.

Feeling a bit unwanted, Charity returned to her room where she found a note on the bedside table. It read: *You must leave Kensington Hall immediately for there are danger and death residing here. If you remain, you shall end up like old man Higgins. Dead!*

Panic and fear enveloped her. She fled from her room and hurried to find Mrs. Kensington. A servant said she was in the library waiting for the authorities to arrive. As Charity approached the library, the door was slightly open. She peeked in and could see Mrs. Kensington speaking to Simon Blackwell whom she remembered meeting at the Monnerat's ball. She knew it was improper to eavesdrop, but their conversation intrigued her.

"My dear Mrs. Kensington, I have returned to inform you that at this very moment your son-in-law, Colonel Benedict Parker, is being apprehended and will be charged for the attack upon Madame Monnerat and the murders of William Singleton and the tavern maid, Hannah," declared Simon with great satisfaction.

"As much as I despise my son-in-law for his many indiscretions, insults, and injuries upon my family and me, he is not a murderer. His conviction and execution will blacken the good name of Kensington while you, the true murdering villain, elude justice and take my daughter Charlotte as your prize!" replied Mrs. Kensington in disgust and vexation. "I believe I made a grave judgment in error when making this deal with you."

Simon laughed and ridiculed Mrs. Kensington for her weak moment of compassion for the colonel. He reminded her of Charlotte's well being while vindictively dangling Charity's doll in her face.

Chapter 12

Charity was shocked to see Simon Blackwell in possession of her doll. He was taking great pleasure in tormenting Mrs. Kensington, and their conversation was most alarming. Charity continued to listen, and the details became even more disturbing as Mrs. Kensington said, "That doll is the property of Charles' governess, Charity Chastine! How did you acquire it? I despise you! You are using my daughter as a bargaining piece in your plan!"

Simon Blackwell appeared to be very pleased in believing he was in control of the situation, and he boasted to Mrs. Kensington about his wicked deeds. "I followed Mr. Higgins, who didn't suspect a thing, through the secret passage under the mansion and into the library. I purloined the doll from Miss Chastine's room, because when I saw it the doll reminded me of Charlotte. I have a fancy for disguising myself in women's clothing, which served me well when I was a spy for the Continental Army," replied Simon.

"You are vile, and I want you gone from my sight immediately!" exclaimed Mrs. Kensington.

Simon ignored Mrs. Kensington and wickedly continued to reveal details of his heinous behavior. To Charity's shock, Simon began to recount the night William Singleton had died, but it was not at the hands of Colonel Parker, as she had believed it to be all those months.

Simon explained that he had attended the ball at Singleton Lodge, disguised as a woman, keeping a very close eye on William Singleton, and waiting for the right moment to make his move. He said that his opportunity came when he was hiding in the library and saw Colonel Parker strike William Singleton on the head with a candlestick, and that Charity tried to offer the injured man comfort by placing a pillow under his head before leaving the room. Then Simon emerged, and with another pillow snuffed the life out of a defenseless Mr. Singleton.

When Mrs. Kensington asked Simon why he had committed the murder, he smugly explained that he was fulfilling the task that Mrs. Singleton had hired him to perform. He said that she wanted her husband to pay for his numerous indiscretions. Then Blackwell continued, confessing to the attack on Madame Monnerat who had the misfortune to recognize him in the alley, and on Hannah who was a victim of circumstance, used to provide a distraction to Charlotte's abduction. He showed no remorse for his crimes and went so far as to say that when satisfying one's greed and lustful desires, there were no limits or concern for mercy and human life.

After hearing Simon Blackwell's horrible story, Charity truly believed that Charlotte was in the clutches of the devil's disciple, and Mrs. Kensington had succumbed to a deadly opponent. She started to leave to find Lieutenant Bradford, but Dr. Greenville came to her. Putting his index finger to his lips, he motioned her to follow him outside.

While Charity was outside with Dr. Greenville, the authorities had arrived to investigate what had happened to Mr. Higgins. In the meantime, Simon Blackwell left a shaken Mrs. Kensington who composed herself and dealt with the authorities. After telling them that Mr. Higgins' death was an accident and supplying them with specific details, she told them that she would take charge of his burial. Satisfied with her story and familiar with her position and reputation in society, the officers felt no need to investigate further. At Mrs. Kensington's request, they took Mr. Higgins' corpse from the stables and brought it to an icehouse near the center of town where it would remain until the funeral.

Dr. Greenville and Charity found Lieutenant Bradford, who was still roaming about alone. Dr. Greenville confided in them about Simon's intentions for Charlotte while Charity revealed what she had overheard him tell Mrs. Kensington. They agreed that Charlotte was in grave danger and needed to be rescued. Dr. Greenville knew of Charlotte's location and offered to escort them there while enlisting their assistance in his rescue plan.

After they agreed to help Dr. Greenville, he informed Mrs. Kensington that he was going to New Haven to acquire medicine for the bandaged man. He told her that the lieutenant and Charity were accompanying him and they would all return home by nightfall.

To their surprise, Mrs. Kensington gave them leave. Unbeknownst to them, she was preoccupied with other matters, pondering why the authorities did not mention the arrest of the colonel as Simon had promised.

When they left for New Haven, Mrs. Kensington was keeping a close watch on Charles while Foster and Jennings did the same for the bandaged man in the east wing.

Monsieur Monnerat returned home to find a stranger by the name of Jean-Luc Tessier waiting for him. Lydia introduced the two men and then excused herself and went to attend to Madame Monnerat. Monsieur Monnerat offered a glass of wine as Jean-Luc stood holding a dagger behind his back.

When Monsieur Monnerat inquired about the purpose for Jean-Luc's visit, Jean-Luc wasted no time in revealing who he was, and he told Monsieur Monnerat that Robespierre sent his regards.

Upon hearing this, Monsieur Monnerat became very upset, and he approached Jean-Luc and, grinning ghoulishly, threw the glass of wine in his face. He tried to run out of the room as Jean-Luc threw the dagger, which narrowly missed him. Jean-Luc sprang like a wild beast, toppled Monsieur Monnerat to the floor, and the two men fought violently.

Upstairs in Madame Monnerat's bedroom, Madame Monnerat was calling out Colonel Parker's name. Angered from hearing the colonel's name, Lydia put her hands around Madame Monnerat's throat and began to choke her. Louise Bourget was just returning to the room, and when she saw Lydia choking Madame Monnerat, she tried desperately to stop her.

The women engaged in a terrible fight, hitting each other and pulling hair. Lydia screamed that she despised the French and the English. Unremorsefully, she bragged that she had coerced her nephew Theodore and his friend David Cobb to kill Elizabeth Higgins and her Redcoat boyfriend Edmund Tate. Between gasps, she said she had ordered them to kill Charity and Elizabeth's father. Lydia bemoaned their failed attempts that consequently led to their own demises.

"I believe that all traitors to this country must die!" shrieked Lydia. "Madame Monnerat is betraying her husband by calling out the name of another man! She must be punished, and you will not stop me! That statue should have crushed you and that Jean-Luc for plotting against my employer, Monsieur Monnerat. All of you must die!"

As they wrestled, a candle was knocked off a table next to Madame Monnerat's bed. Within seconds the drapes were on fire and the room was engulfed in flames. Lydia managed to shove Louise against the wall and quickly made her escape into the dark hall, like a demon in the night. Louise grabbed hold of a helpless Madame Monnerat and tried to drag her out of bed, but her efforts were futile. She screamed for help while the flames surrounded them.

In the drawing room, Jean-Luc had managed to overcome Monsieur Monnerat by knocking him unconscious. He heard Louise's cries for help and hurried upstairs where he found the two women trapped by the fire. Quickly grabbing Madame Monnerat, he carried her in his arms out of the blaze, with Louise behind them.

Somewhere by the sea on the outskirts of New Haven, they arrived at the place where Simon was keeping Charlotte. Lieutenant Bradford and Charity were surprised to learn that it was the residence of Colonel and Mrs. Ridgefield. A doorman told them that the colonel and his wife were attending an assembly in town. Recognizing Dr. Greenville, the servant let them in, but they did not see Charlotte. Instead Simon Blackwell, who had been waiting for their arrival, greeted them.

After entering the place where Charlotte was captive, Charity felt overcome by a terrible feeling and took hold of Lieutenant Bradford's hand. Dr. Greenville's behavior was very clever but cautious as he explained that they had come to inquire about Charlotte's health.

As they had rehearsed the plan during the carriage ride over, Dr. Greenville, the lieutenant, and Charity played their roles, trying to persuade Simon that they had turned their alliance away from Mrs. Kensington and now wholeheartedly supported his intentions for Charlotte by offering their assistance and friendship. They explained that they had witnessed the ill treatment Charlotte had received from her husband and her mother, and they believed Simon was Charlotte's knight in shining armor come to save her.

They were unaware that Simon saw through their charade, and he was pretending to go along with them. He invited them to stay for tea and said that Charlotte was resting but would join them soon. After some small talk, Simon had a servant bring the tea, and he told his guests he was going to get Charlotte, but they should go ahead and have their tea while it was hot.

Charity dutifully poured the tea and served it to Lieutenant Bradford and Dr. Greenville. Since the lieutenant was well acquainted with Simon from serving with him during the war, he was troubled by Simon's gracious behavior and his suspiciously quick departure. As they were about to sip their tea, the lieutenant threw his cup to the floor and quickly shouted, "Do not drink the tea. It's been poisoned! Simon has seen through our plot, and I fear that we now have spoiled our chance to save Charlotte from her lunatic captor. We have to find them!" exclaimed the frantic lieutenant.

Then the lieutenant looked out the window and caught a glimpse of Simon and Charlotte hurrying along the beach. He banged on the window and shouted loudly, but his efforts were in vain. He ran out of the house and onto the beach to pursue them. Dr. Greenville and Charity followed behind, but Lieutenant Bradford was much faster than they were, gaining a lead on Simon and Charlotte. They hurried along the shore as the waves crashed upon the sandy beach.

The pursuit led them to the top of a cliff that Dr. Greenville called Widow's Bluff, where, according to legend, widows who had lost their husbands to the sea would stand on the edge lamenting before leaping to their deaths. The lieutenant was the first to come upon Simon and Charlotte who were dangerously close to the edge of the cliff.

Lieutenant Bradford attempted to call out to Charlotte, but Simon got in front of her and ordered her not to listen to him. Instead he filled her head with lies about the lieutenant's intentions. Simon and Lieutenant Bradford began to argue just as Dr. Greenville and Charity arrived. When Charlotte saw Charity, she cried out joyfully and tried to come toward her, but Simon pulled her back to him, causing her to lose her balance.

To their shock and horror, Charlotte stumbled backward and lost her footing and fell off the cliff, screaming in terror. A horrified and devastated Simon looked down below at the raging, fierce waves of the sea swallowing up his beloved helpless Charlotte. He turned back to the others with a wicked, hideous look, shouting out in great anguish.

"It was your meddling and interference that has caused the death of my precious Charlotte! I curse you and all the days you shall walk on this earth!" ranted Simon.

Then he joined Charlotte by throwing himself into the sea. The lieutenant hurried to the edge of the cliff and, looking down, the only sign he saw of either of them was Charlotte's lace cap lying on the jagged rocks below. Dr. Greenville bowed his head in sorrow and wept bitterly. Charity cried on the shoulders of Lieutenant Bradford while her ears were plagued by the piercing sound of waves crashing down on the shore beneath Widow's Bluff.

Jean-Luc, with Louise's assistance, carried Madame Monnerat outside the lodge. Gently placing her on the ground, Jean-Luc stared intently at Madame Monnerat's face, Jean-Luc realizing that he had known her some years before.

He remembered a brief, but powerful encounter with Madame Monnerat in a marketplace in Paris, five years earlier. He recalled they both had their eyes on the same basket of fruit, and after a charming conversation, Madame Monnerat managed to acquire the basket, leaving Jean-Luc empty handed. However, she the image of a beautiful young woman etched in his memory, to emerge upon their unexpected reunion.

The servants came running out of Singleton Lodge carrying some belongings. When they asked about Monsieur Monnerat, Louise looked at Jean-Luc and begged him to go into the burning lodge to get him. At first Jean-Luc hesitated, but gazing at Madame Monnerat, he told Louise to watch over the lovely woman as he went in to retrieve her husband.

When he entered the drawing room, he looked about thoroughly, but Monsieur Monnerat was nowhere to be found. He searched the entire lower floor and still found no one.

As the smoke began to get to him, he made a quick departure. When he got back outside, Louise informed him that one of the servants told her that Monsieur Monnerat was seen on a horse galloping down the road from Singleton Lodge.

Jean-Luc stood tall, anger in his eyes, and stared down the road, making a silent vow that Monsieur Monnerat and he would soon meet again.

A few miles away at Winchester Park, Ethan Fairchild brought a frightened Honoria Noble to his family's ancestral home. When she entered the great hall, she was captivated by the elegance and grandeur of the architecture. A servant escorted them into the drawing room where another servant brought in a tray of food and drink.

Ethan kindly told Honoria to rest while he went to find his aunt. Honoria indulged in the delicious meal on the tray before her. She admired the beautiful furnishings in the room and felt a sense of relief from the terrible laughter that had now ceased. Honoria was enjoying the tranquility of the new surroundings, but someone was surreptitiously watching her with grave disapproval.

After reconciling to the terrible fact that Charlotte and Simon were dead, the lieutenant, Dr. Greenville, and Charity made their way back to Kensington Hall to tell Mrs. Kensington that her daughter had died. During the trip, both Lieutenant Bradford and Dr. Greenville remained silent. Charity assumed that they, like all men, hid their emotions better than women did, but they were hurting as much as she was. She kept asking herself the same question again and again: *why did Charlotte have to die a horrible death.* She recalled that people have always been capable of cruelty and unspeakable acts as depicted in stories from the Bible. Cain killed his brother Abel out of jealousy; pagan tribes enslaved and killed the Israelites; and great sin caused by man made God bring a tremendous flood upon the earth. Man's inhumanity to man has existed since ancient times, and the sins of jealousy, anger, greed, envy, sloth, pride, and lust committed by mankind have tragically led to war, persecution, misery, and death. At the same time, these sinful acts claim the lives of the innocent as well, while those left behind live with pain, suffering, and shattered memories.

As the carriage approached the entrance to Kensington Hall, Charity dreaded witnessing the reaction of Mrs. Kensington to the horrific news. The death of a child is the greatest of losses; one a parent should not have to endure. Upon entering, Mrs. Kensington was sitting in the drawing room doing needlepoint. She greeted them with a smile and the silver ringlets that lined her forehead shined in the candle light, but after they informed her of Charlotte's tragic demise, the smile was replaced by a blank expression. A few seconds later, she let out a loud cry of agony and grief that was heard throughout Kensington Hall, and then all was silent.

Chapter 13

Charlotte's death cast a dreadful cloud of mourning and grief upon all of the occupants of Kensington Hall. The servants, stricken with sorrow, gathered in the kitchen to offer comfort to one another. Dr. Greenville and Lieutenant Bradford kept to themselves in solitude and checked the east wing at intervals, keeping watch on Mrs. Kensington's special guest whom Charity called the bandaged man. Charity kept a close eye on Charles, who would cry from time to time or just simply sit by her side with a sad and pitiful countenance.

Mrs. Kensington dressed in black remained complacent, solemn, and gracious while receiving friends and neighbors who came to pay their condolences. Among them were Jesse and Mrs. Andrews, Dr. Foote, Reverend Benjamin Trumbull, Mr. and Mrs. Pierpont, several members from Wallingford's high society, as well as people of both the common and privileged classes of New Haven, including Colonel and Mrs. Ridgefield. Charlotte had been a personable young woman who embraced life by keeping company with many individuals from different social circles.

Charles and Charity shared a sofa adjacent to Mrs. Kensington who sat with great propriety in a Chippendale chair in the library, receiving the mourners. Mrs. Andrews went up to Charity, gave her a hug, and proceeded to tell her that progress on the rebuilding of Andrews' Tavern was coming along nicely, and she was hoping to open for business within a month. She and her son Jesse extended an open invitation and told her not to be a stranger. Dr. Foote informed her that Grace's condition had not changed, and he and his wife were doing their best to keep her comfortable.

When Colonel and Mrs. Ridgefield entered the room, Mrs. Kensington was cordial but brief with them. In her mind, Charity could only think that her employer was harboring despicable thoughts and blame toward them for their alliance with Simon Blackwell and their indirect involvement in Charlotte's abduction and death. Mrs. Ridgefield approached Charity and gave her back her doll. She explained that Simon had had it in his possession, boasting that he stole it from Charity's room to keep as a reminder of his beloved Charlotte.

Mrs. Ridgefield expressed her sorrow and regret for what had happened to Charlotte and wished things had turned out differently. She also told Charity that her husband had asked for a transfer to train soldiers at a camp north of Philadelphia, so they would be leaving at the end of the week. Charity surmised that their departure was out of guilt but also provided a convenient escape from Mrs. Kensington's vengeful wrath.

As Colonel and Mrs. Ridgefield were taking their leave, the lieutenant entered the room, walked past them, and made no effort to acknowledge their presence. His insolent and rude behavior toward Colonel and Mrs. Ridgefield delighted Mrs. Kensington, who asked him to stay with her while she instructed Charity to take Charles out into the gardens for some fresh air.

While she was outside with Charles, Charity looked about the beautiful grounds, and then stared at the mighty and elegant structure of Kensington Hall. She considered how no one, not even the very rich, was spared from suffering and tragedy. She realized that death is not selective in its choice, and even those of the privileged class go to their graves just like the poor common folk.

As she watched Charles play, she shuddered to think that he was going to be raised as a prince by a wealthy, influential woman capable of manipulation, dominance, and unscrupulous deeds.

Dr. Greenville, who wanted to speak to her, interrupted her

train of thought. They walked over to a bench that was not far from Charles, and then he opened up to her.

"My dear Miss Charity, please forgive me for what I'm about to confess to you. I beg of you to keep an open mind. Listen carefully without interrupting," said Dr. Greenville.

He proceeded to tell her that Colonel Parker had been found unconscious in a drunken state in the woods near the Rising Sun Tavern, and in an attempt to avoid a scandal and to temporarily get him out of circulation, Mrs. Kensington discreetly used her influence and had the colonel committed to an asylum in New Haven. Dr. Greenville also confided in Charity that Mrs. Kensington was just as responsible for Charlotte's death as was Simon Blackwell and Colonel and Mrs. Ridgefield. It was all their scheming and blackmailing of one another that turned a devious plot into a tragedy.

"I must also confess that I wrote the note telling you to leave Kensington Hall for fear that something terrible might befall you. If you can muster up the courage to leave, you must get as far away from this place as possible. You must elude the misery and death that dwells here before it's too late," implored Dr. Greenville.

After he had finished speaking, he took her hand, kissed it, and then left her sight, leaving her in a state of bewilderment. She sat down on the bench, and Charles joined her, resting his head on her shoulder. She cuddled him and began to sing a song to him just like Charlotte had done. They didn't know that from the nearby bushes, the wicked Lydia Johnson had been eavesdropping while Dr. Greenville was speaking to Charity, and she was watching Charles and her.

On the outskirts of town, upstairs at the Country Squire Inn, Louise Bourget was attending to Madame Monnerat who had come out of her catatonic state and was sitting at a dressing table, looking into a mirror. She was staring at her reflection while recalling her past deeds and wondering what had become of the young, naïve, and kind-hearted girl she used to be.

"As I look into this mirror, all I see is an ugly and despicable person. I am ashamed of what I have become and the awful things I have done. Most of all, I curse the day that I married that greedy and immoral Louis Monnerat. I wish to never see him again. Now I am alone, and no one cares, or loves me," wept Madame Monnerat to Louise.

"I care for you," said Jean-Luc as he entered the room. "I saved you and Louise from the fire, fought your rogue of a husband, and injured my pride—but it was all for a noble cause. My lovely Laura, fate has brought us together again since our first encounter in Paris."

Madame Monnerat was touched deeply by Jean-Luc calling her Laura, for she was named for her mother who had died shortly after giving birth to her. Her father had blamed her for his wife's death, and had made her life miserable. She married Monsieur Monnerat for security, not for love, but her hasty and foolish decision had caused her to become a selfish and cruel person.

She recounted to Jean-Luc and Louise the horrible ordeal she had suffered at the hands of Simon Blackwell. He had seized her, puncturing her neck with his ring in retaliation for her recognizing him dressed in women's apparel. She was convinced that the brutal attack by Simon was punishment for her sins.

Jean-Luc assured Laura that she was safe and he was going to take care of her by giving her the life she had longed for since she was a little girl. Feeling grateful and safe with Jean-Luc, Laura accepted his offer, promising to denounce Monsieur Monnerat, give up her title, and return to her original name of Laura Corday.

Upon hearing this, Jean-Luc kissed her hand. Louise, taking this all in, rejoiced to herself that Jean-Luc and she now had a new companion on their side in their quest to support Robespierre and to punish the French aristocracy, including Monsieur Monnerat.

After the last of the mourners had left, Mrs. Kensington retreated to the drawing room, instructing the servants that she was not to be disturbed. Alone in the room, she studied the pieces of the chess game set up on the table. She moved one of the pawns, laughing sinisterly. Then she opened the crown jewel box containing the Winfield diamond and admired its beauty. As she studied the diamond that she cherished so much, the crafty Mrs. Kensington was formulating her next move, while an unseen and intrigued Monsieur Monnerat was spying from outside on the terrace. As he observed Mrs. Kensington, someone else was also lurking about in the shadows of Kensington Hall.

After placing the diamond back in the crown jewel box, Mrs. Kensington caught a glimpse of Monsieur Monnerat watching her. She pretended not to recognize his presence, and instead, left the room.

When Mrs. Kensington was gone, Monsieur Monnerat entered the drawing room and stealthily went to the desk, taking the crown jewel box into his hands. He opened it and was delighted to see the diamond. Then he took the diamond, slipped it into his coat pocket, and made his escape as a thief in the night. Lydia Johnson, emerging from hiding in the shadows, pursued Monsieur Monnerat.

In the meantime, Mrs. Kensington, watching Monsieur Monnerat's every move, returned to the drawing room and retrieved the crown jewel box. She opened the box and placed another diamond inside. Then Mrs. Kensington went over to the game table, moved another chess piece with great satisfaction, and spoke to herself with laughter in her voice.

"I have succeeded in deceiving that greedy, pathetic Frenchman into thinking that he has the Winfield diamond in his possession. Little does he know I have the real diamond and he has an imitation made of glass! Well done, my precious Phoebe—I am indeed still master of the game."

As Monsieur Monnerat was making his way down the road, it

began to rain so heavily that he sought shelter in a dilapidated barn. Once inside, he made a bed out of hay and soon fell asleep.

A short time later, the barn door opened, and Lydia crept quietly inside. She stood over Monnerat, and as she stared at him sleeping like a baby, she remembered the day she had a confrontation with David Cobb in the barn adjacent to Andrews' Tavern.

Lydia painfully recalled arguing with David, who had come to the barn after he had survived his fall from the bridge on Muddy River. Lydia had been very displeased with his failed attempt to kill Mr. Higgins and Charity as she had ordered him to do.

"Why didn't you kill that witch Charity and that foolish old man Higgins?" she had asked him. "Have you no respect for your dead friend Theodore or for me, the woman who has treated you like a member of the family? I demand an explanation!" she shouted angrily.

"Charity and Mr. Higgins do not deserve to die. Theodore and I wronged Mr. Higgins by murdering his daughter Elizabeth and her Redcoat boyfriend. We thought they were traitors to this country. Charity is an innocent in all of this, and she has suffered enough. Weren't Theodore's attempt on her life and your attempt to kill her in the fire at Andrews' Tavern enough? The war is over, and there is no need for further bloodshed. You are a bitter, wicked, and deranged woman who I want nothing more to do with," ranted David.

As David had turned to leave the barn, an enraged Lydia took hold of a pitchfork and viciously stabbed him in the back. David cried out in severe agony, and then fell to the ground and died. Lydia examined him to make sure he was dead, and before she left, she scrawled the word *Judas* in the dirt next to his body. In her demented mind, David was a *Judas* because he was a traitor to her and Theodore.

Lydia returned to the present moment. She searched Monsieur Monnerat's pockets for the diamond she had seen him steal from Mrs. Kensington's crown jewel box.

Monsieur Monnerat woke up to see Lydia with the diamond in her hand. But before he could react, she hit him in the head with a rock. Monnerat laid still, blood streaming down his face. After committing her heinous deed, Lydia slithered like a snake out of the barn into the pouring rain.

The next day the sun was shining, but the ground was still wet from the heavy rain the night before. A handful of townspeople, including Lieutenant Bradford and Charity attended Mr. Higgins' burial. Reverend Benjamin Trumbull presided over the service. Mr. Higgins was buried on his property under the oak tree where he had buried Elizabeth and Edmund some years before.

As the wooden coffin was lowered into the ground, Charity thought to herself that Mr. Higgins and Elizabeth, the daughter he had disowned in life, were sadly together in death. Her heart was heavy with sorrow, and she had a defeated feeling that death had been triumphant these past few days, claiming Mr. Higgins and Charlotte, two victims of tragic circumstances.

After the service, Lieutenant Bradford and Charity went to the Rising Sun Tavern to have a light meal and take a respite before returning to Kensington Hall.

Sitting at their table, the lieutenant and Charity overheard some tradesmen talking about expansion and settlement in the Ohio Valley. They mentioned that several people from New Haven as well as some farmers from North Haven and Wallingford were heading to the Valley to acquire new land and seek a new life.

When Charity hinted to the lieutenant that leaving Kensington Hall and relocating to a new place sounded like a refreshing and adventurous idea to explore, he told her adamantly to put such a ridiculous thought out of her mind. He reminded her that they were needed at their present positions, especially for Charles' sake. She did not speak another word about the matter, but she continued to listen to what the tradesmen said about the subject.

At Winchester Park, an elated Honoria Noble was running through the beautifully manicured grounds with a handsome Ethan Fairchild chasing after her in a playful manner. Honoria, not watching where she was going, tripped over a fallen branch and stumbled to the ground. They were both laughing while trying to breathe easy.

Leaning over Honoria, Ethan admired the lovely, charming young lady on the ground before him. He could not resist her sensual and luscious lips or her smooth and flawless complexion. Acting impulsively, he gently kissed her on the lips. Honoria was delighted by the kiss. But their moment of bliss was interrupted by the unexpected appearance of an older but elegantly refined looking couple staring at them with discerning eyes and shocked expressions upon their faces.

When they returned to Kensington Hall, Lieutenant Bradford and Charity found the entire household in an upheaval. The servants were frantically searching for Charles who was nowhere to be found. Mrs. Kensington begged for their assistance. The lieutenant and Charity looked at each other, both instantaneously surmising that for some reason Charles must have wandered into the east wing. They hurried to the east wing while Charity prayed that their assumption was incorrect.

There they found a stunned Dr. Greenville who informed them that Charles was in danger. They heard Charles cry for help. They followed the boy's cry, which led them to a room at the far end of the east wing. The room had a balcony, and its doors were wide open.

As they looked out at the balcony, to their horror they saw the bandaged man carrying a sobbing Charles along the ledge. Lieutenant Bradford went after them. The bandaged man had no place to go, so he stood still, setting Charles down by his side and holding his hand.

When the lieutenant caught up to them, the bandaged man

shouted for him to stay away. He began to rant that he needed his freedom, and he was taking Charles with him. As Lieutenant Bradford tried to reason with him, the bandaged man became angry and started to stomp his feet. Suddenly, the ledge gave way. The quick thinking Lieutenant Bradford grabbed hold of Charles just as the ledge crumbled from under the bandaged man, causing him to take a great fall. The lieutenant carried a frightened but unharmed Charles inside, and placed him in Charity's arms.

As Charity held Charles, trying to comfort him, all she could think about was Dr. Greenville's warning about misery and death dwelling in this place. She asked herself the inevitable question: *will this madness ever end?* In the meantime, Lieutenant Bradford and the servants went to see about the fate of the bandaged man. They searched diligently, but found no trace of him. It was like he had simply disappeared.

Chapter 14

After searching for some time, Lieutenant Bradford came to the shocking conclusion that the bandaged man had somehow miraculously survived the fall from the ledge. With the assistance of Foster and Jennings, the lieutenant stumbled upon a clue that was instrumental in solving the mystery. Alongside Kensington Hall on the east, there was a large cluster of overgrown bushes that had served as a cushion, breaking the man's fall. In one of the bushes, they found strips of white bandages entangled in the branches.

Charity had managed to calm and comfort Charles, who was still recovering from his terrifying ordeal. Mrs. Kensington entered Charles' room to inquire about his well being.

After Charles had fallen asleep, Mrs. Kensington and Charity went downstairs to the drawing room where they found Lieutenant Bradford waiting impatiently. The lieutenant explained in a worried tone of voice that he believed the bandaged man had survived the fall by landing in a cluster of bushes, and he was now roaming the countryside.

Upon hearing the disturbing news, Mrs. Kensington demanded that Lieutenant Bradford and a handful of servants go and search for him, and bring him back to Kensington Hall.

"You must find him before someone else does," she said. "He is my husband! He was trapped and burned in a horrible fire in London; he's lost his sanity and is a madman capable of harmful behavior. Please find my husband before something terrible happens. I am still grieving for my beloved Charlotte and cannot bear another loss!" begged Mrs. Kensington.

The lieutenant stared at his employer and then glanced at Charity with a frightened look in his eyes. He enlisted the help of some of the servants including Foster and Jennings, and they went on a search to locate Mr. Kensington.

Mrs. Kensington told Charity that she preferred to be alone, so she went to Charles' room to watch over him.

Mrs. Kensington's solitude was interrupted by the appearance of Dr. Greenville coming abruptly into the drawing room. He expressed his deep concern for what had happened.

Mrs. Kensington tried to dismiss the incident by telling him that her husband would be found and returned to her, and all would be right again.

Dr. Greenville was not satisfied with his friend's cavalier attitude about the situation, and he warned her that she needed to stop controlling people's lives because danger, suffering, and death were the final results. He also informed her that he was finished being her confidant and accomplice, and he was leaving for good.

At first Mrs. Kensington laughed at him, calling him a pathetic fool. Then she rudely ordered him to leave her presence and not return until he had regained his senses with an apology.

Dr. Greenville responded by telling her that he had nothing but pity and sorrow for his friend who, despite all of her worldly possessions and social position, was a lonely and miserable woman with an empty heart and only a chess game to occupy her mind.

"I am leaving for Boston and you will never see me again, my dear Phoebe. I am sorry for the loss of Charlotte and what has become of your husband. How many more innocent souls will suffer? Good-bye, my friend," said Dr. Greenville regretfully.

"Good-bye, my favorite Loyalist and dear friend. We shall meet again when you least expect it," replied Mrs. Kensington with a ghoulish grin.

Honoria Noble was enjoying a leisurely stroll about the grounds, while Ethan's parents were taking him to task. They were not pleased with what they had witnessed their son doing with a young woman they did not know. His parents demanded an explanation for his behavior.

Ethan was very calm and quietly explained the circumstances of his encounter with Honoria, saying that she was a woman of beauty, intelligence, charm, and great wit. He further informed his parents that Honoria was unlike the other women he had known before.

Their conversation was cut short by the arrival of Ethan's aunt, Evelyn Winchester, a woman of propriety and good judgment, who had a soft spot when it came to her favorite nephew. Ethan's parents, Caleb and Judith Fairchild, were delighted to see Evelyn, and they implored her to speak to their son and do her best to restore his common sense and good judgment. Realizing they were failing in their attempt to reason with him, Caleb and Judith departed, leaving Ethan in the company of his Aunt Evelyn.

"My dear nephew, what is all this fuss about? Who is this young woman who according to what I overheard your parents telling you has you under her spell?" inquired Ethan's aunt with a smile.

"We met by chance, and even though I have known her only a little while, she and I have bonded in a special way. She is like an angel. Let me introduce you to her, and you can be the judge," said Ethan, ushering his aunt outside to meet Honoria.

Honoria was enjoying the warm sunshine on the beautiful grounds while listening to the birds chirping in the trees. Suddenly, to her shocked surprise, a man wrapped in bandages came out of the bushes and hurried toward her. She screamed loudly, but the bandaged man continued toward her. As he came upon her, Ethan arrived and started to fend him off. Following the exchange of a few fists, the bandaged man ran away.

Ethan made certain Honoria was unhurt, and then Ethan

introduced her to his aunt. Upon his aunt's request, they all walked back to the house to inform Ethan's parents of what had happened. They presumed that the strange man was a thief or a mad man who was roaming about in a state of confusion.

After Dr. Greenville had gathered his belongings, he sought Charity out to say farewell, and once again he advised her to leave as well. He told her that she was a special person with a destiny that she needed to fulfill. As Dr. Greenville got into a waiting carriage, Mrs. Kensington watched from the window with vexation as her only true friend was leaving her, just like Charlotte, Elizabeth, and Mr. Kensington had. As an overriding feeling of loneliness enveloped Mrs. Kensington, she studied the pieces of the chess game before her, and then eliminated one of the pieces.

In New Haven, a scheming and lethal Lydia Johnson went to pay a visit to Colonel Parker who was languishing in an asylum cell. She managed to bribe one of the attendants into letting her see the colonel. When she found the colonel in his cell, she saw that his beard and hair had grown long. He was facing the wall, calling out the name of Elizabeth Higgins, the mother of his child. Seeing his slovenly and vanquished condition, Lydia took pity on him by whispering in his ear that she was going to care for him, and once he was restored to good health, they would embark together on their mission to find the treasure.

Lydia then showed him the diamond she had purloined from Monsieur Monnerat. When the colonel saw it, he smiled.

She wrapped him in a blanket, and with the assistance of two attendants she had bribed, they made their way to a carriage outside the asylum. Lydia instructed the coachman to take them to Boston.

Charity was in her room examining her doll, staring at its brightly painted face. Perhaps foolishly, but for a strange reason she felt that the doll was an important connection to her future. She was recalling what Grace and Patience had told her about the doll, and what Dr. Greenville had said before his departure.

She became restless so she went downstairs to wait for the lieutenant and the others to return. As she walked into the drawing room, to her horror she saw Mrs. Kensington struggling with the bandaged man who was trying to strangle her. Charity was frozen with terror and fear. Then she struggled to overcome her fear, mustering up the courage to try to help Mrs. Kensington. In her attempt to do so, the bandaged man grabbed hold of her. As she fought desperately to free herself, Mrs. Kensington hurried to the desk and took out a pistol. She shouted for Charity to get out of the way and, as Charity managed to move, she fired the pistol.

Charity screamed with fright as Mrs. Kensington fired the pistol. Right before her eyes, the bandaged man grabbed his side and collapsed to the floor. Lying on his back and bleeding from the bullet wound, he begged Charity to remove the remaining bandages from his face. Charity did as he requested and stared at the poor man's grotesque appearance as he uttered these words.

"Take good care and never trust my wife, Phoebe Kensington. Always try to be one step ahead of her. You can find the treasure that many are seeking in the mountains. It is closer than you can imagine. Now I must go meet my Maker," gasped Mr. Kensington just before he closed his eyes forever.

At that moment, Lieutenant Bradford, Foster, Jennings, and some of the other servants returned to Kensington Hall. When Lieutenant Bradford saw Charity kneeling next to the bandaged man, he gently touched her shoulder and extended his hand to help her to her feet. Mrs. Kensington put down the pistol, walked over to her husband, and stared at him. A few minutes later she spoke.

"The war has ended, and you have lost. Now you go to a far better place than here. May you rest in peace with our beloved daughter

Charlotte," cried Mrs. Kensington, with a tear streaming down her cheek.

Then she was silent, and so was all of Kensington Hall—just like when Charlotte had died. Foster and Jennings, with Mrs. Kensington's permission, removed the body while Lieutenant Bradford took Charity outside. Standing on the terrace, Charity suddenly began to weep, and the lieutenant held her by wrapping his strong, muscular arms around her. For the first time in a very long time, she finally had a calm feeling of relief that perhaps this was the end to all the chaos, secrets, and tragedies that had plagued this community for some time.

At Winchester Park, a troubled Judith Winchester Fairchild was sitting on a sofa in the drawing room, thinking about Honoria Noble who seemed to be taken with her son Ethan. The relationship was alarming to Judith, and Ethan's behavior and arrogant disregard for his parents' opinions caused great vexation and concern.

Judith's thoughts were interrupted by her sister Evelyn joining her for tea. Seeing her sister's troubled state, Evelyn poured a cup of tea and then offered some advice.

"My dear sister, there is no need to worry yourself about Ethan and his new young lady. Her heritage and place in society are a mystery to us, but she seems very fond of my nephew, and he is of her. Perhaps this is just a temporary attraction that will soon fade away, and your worry will have been for nothing," said Evelyn.

"I beg to differ with you, my sister. I believe that this girl is of inferior birth, with a past, and her attachment to my son will only lead to his ruin and downfall while putting a black mark upon the good name of Fairchild," responded Judith with a deep conviction.

After listening to her sister and recognizing her concern for her only son, Evelyn proposed a solution to the dilemma at hand. She diplomatically suggested that she would make a trip to Philadelphia, and she would invite Ethan and Honoria to accompany her so she would not have to travel alone. The excursion would provide ample opportunity for Evelyn to become better acquainted with Honoria by learning more about her while keeping a close watch on her nephew and his lovely companion.

Respecting her sister's good opinion and delighted by her plan, Judith gave her blessing for Ethan and Honoria to accompany Evelyn to Philadelphia. Judith did not tell her sister that she planned to make her own inquiries about Honoria while they were away.

When approached with the idea, both Ethan and Honoria were pleased by the invitation and accepted without reservation. By the end of the week, they were on their way to Philadelphia. Honoria was thrilled and relieved to be away from the place and the portrait that caused her unbearable torment. During the carriage ride to Philadelphia, Ethan and Honoria sat next to one another holding each other's hand and acting with great propriety while a prudent Aunt Evelyn looked on with a gracious smile.

At Kensington Hall, Mrs. Kensington had her husband buried on the property. The lieutenant, Mrs. Kensington, the servants, and Charity were the only ones in attendance, for the fact was that everyone else, with the exception of Dr. Greenville who was now in Boston, believed Mr. Kensington had died months before.

After the burial, Mrs. Kensington retreated to the conservatory, but before shutting herself into her world of solitude, she told Charity and Lieutenant Bradford to take Charles on a picnic to Indian Lookout, a high mountain on the outskirts of North Haven. She believed the outing combined with fresh air and nature's beauty would do all three of them a world of good.

After preparing a basket of food and gathering some blankets, including her doll that she carried with her for good luck, Charity, the lieutenant, and Charles embarked on their outing to Indian Lookout.

As they rode by horse and carriage through North Haven, they could see the workers diligently rebuilding Andrews' Tavern, with Mrs. Andrews and Jesse lending a helping hand. They passed the mills and the bridge over Muddy River and stopped at the abandoned home of the late Mr. Higgins to place flowers on his grave and the graves of Elizabeth and Edmund's. As they continued on their way passing the Rising Sun Tavern, they saw several tradesmen arriving at the front entrance. On the town green, they also caught a glimpse of Dr. Foote and Mr. Pierpont conversing with Reverend Trumbull.

When they arrived at the base of the mountain, Lieutenant Bradford tied the horses to a tree, and with Charles by their sides, they climbed their way to the top of the summit, which took them some time to reach. Once at the top, they stared at the majestic view in all its splendor and glory. It was a beautiful day with blue skies, a shining sun, and just a little breeze in the air.

As they stood together, the lieutenant on her right and Charles on her left, Charity felt like they were a family. They were at peace.

She quickly dismissed that notion from her mind, and instead began to recall her arrival in North Haven and all the people she had met and events she had experienced during her time there. She could still envision Grace standing at the door of Andrews' Tavern greeting her. She could see David Cobb and Theodore Norton who charmed her with their stories and tricorn hats, and Mrs. Andrews and Jesse who had offered her shelter and a place to work. She also recalled meeting the elegant Constance Singleton and attending the dances at Singleton Lodge. She thought about the encounters with the wicked Lydia Johnson and the frightening Mr. Higgins who later saved her life and became her friend, and also those scoundrels Colonel Parker, Simon Blackwell, Monsieur Monnerat, Colonel and Mrs. Ridgefield, and the formidable Mrs. Kensington and her precious Charles. She thought of kind-hearted Charlotte Parker who was taken from this life so young, and the first encounter with Lieutenant Bradford, a dashing, handsome stranger who came to her rescue, and continues to stand by her and watch over her like a guardian angel. She has these people and others etched in her memory, and she will remember her acquaintances with each and every one of them.

She had met many people from various social circles, with their sorrows and joys, stories and secrets. She had endured several toils and dangers herself. She came to America to make a new beginning after her mother's death, and she found herself always searching, learning new things about herself and the people she called patriots and scoundrels. She truly believed there was much more ahead for her with new faces to meet as well as reuniting with some of the old familiar ones, new adventures to embark on, secrets and mysteries to be revealed, and tales that had yet to be told.

As they enjoyed their picnic, Charity had a strange feeling that someone or something was lurking in the near distance. Perhaps it was the wind or her imagination, or was it something else?

Book Two

Chapter 15

Nearly two years had passed since Charity's arrival to America. It was autumn of 1792, and a cool crisp breath of air was blowing against her cheeks and the leaves from the trees were falling by her feet as she made her way to the front door of Andrews' Tavern which had recently reopened for business after a devastating fire. When she entered, Charity was greeted by the tavern's proprietor, Mary Andrews, who was delighted to see her.

"My dear Charity, I am so glad to see you. Please, come and sit with me while we converse over a cup of tea," replied Mrs. Andrews.

While sipping their tea, Mrs. Andrews and Charity talked about the proposal to create a national bank system, the prosperity of the Federalist Party, and their longing for the day when her son Jesse and Charity's friend Lieutenant Bradford would return home from the Ohio Valley. Mrs. Andrews missed Jesse and his extra pair of hands at the tavern, and Charity missed the lieutenant, especially his friendly company, his strong embrace, and bright blue eyes.

After a cheerful visit, Charity left Andrews' Tavern and the gracious Mrs. Andrews just before the afternoon crowd of traveling tradesmen had arrived. Before returning to Kensington Hall, she went to the cemetery to pay her respects at the gravesite of Grace Collins. As she stood by her tombstone, she began to recall fond memories of Grace. She took care of Charity from the time she arrived in town until the day she suffered a stroke. Although it had been several months since Grace's death, Charity's heart was still heavy with sorrow from her passing.

The wind began to blow harshly, and suddenly Charity began to feel a bit uneasy. As she looked around, she could feel that someone was watching her in the distance. She quickly hurried to the waiting carriage by the edge of the road and instructed the driver to return to Kensington Hall.

As the carriage pulled away, Charity strained her neck as she peered out the window. To her surprise, she caught a glimpse of someone dressed in a dark blue cloak moving about in the distance, but she could not identify the person. She did not realize that this person was someone she thought she would never again see in this life.

When she returned to Kensington Hall, one of the servants informed her that Mrs. Kensington and an old friend, whose name was kept from her, were waiting for her in the drawing room.

When she entered the room, Mrs. Kensington gave Charity a jovial greeting, and then she directed her attention to an elegantly dressed woman wearing a lace cap with her back towards them.

"Charity my dear, I do believe that you know my guest," said Mrs. Kensington with a smirk.

The woman rose from her chair, and as she turned to face Charity, to Charity's astonishment, she saw that it was Constance Singleton. She quickly hurried to Constance and embraced her. They were both overjoyed to see each other. Once the excitement of their reunion had ceased, they reacquainted themselves with one another.

Constance was now married to a gentleman named Alexander Caruthers. She explained that her mother had died from malaria, and she and her husband, a former slave owner, had returned to North Haven to take possession of her family's former home, Singleton Lodge. The residence had been desolate since a fire. The owner, the former Madame Monnerat, now Laura Corday, had sold Singleton Lodge to Constance and Alexander.

"We are doing some renovations, but after we are finished, my husband and I are going to host a ball in honor of our new home," replied Constance. "And you are all invited to attend."

Since they had so much to talk about, their visit lasted into the early evening. When darkness began to fill the room, Constance announced her departure.

After Constance had left, Charity went upstairs to see Charles while Mrs. Kensington returned to the drawing room. When Mrs. Kensington entered the drawing room, she noticed the terrace doors were slightly ajar, but paid no mind. Then she went over to the table that displayed the chess game, and to her dismay she noticed that the chess pieces had been deliberately rearranged in the shape of a diamond. Then, as she looked down on the floor next to the table, there were several strands of seaweed lying about.

Taken aback by her mysterious findings, Mrs. Kensington made an attempt to leave the room, but was thwarted by the frightening and abrupt appearance of an intruder dressed in a dark, blue hooded cloak standing in front of her. She bravely held a lighted candle towards the face of the uninvited stranger who first removed the hood and then spoke.

"Good evening, Mrs. Kensington. It has been a long time. Are you not dieing to see me?" inquired the stranger in a wicked tone.

To her shocking horror, Mrs. Kensington found herself staring at the face of no other than Simon Blackwell. As she tried to make her escape, Simon grabbed ahold of her arm with an iron hook that served as a substitute for his left hand.

"I don't know how you managed to survive that deadly fall off Widow's Bluff. You are inhuman and a demon from hell that must be gone from my sight and returned to the bowels of hell," ranted a frantic Mrs. Kensington.

"I am not going anywhere, because there are several things I want from you including your assistance in avenging your daughter's death. You are going to abide by my wishes or meet my wrath," laughed a demented Simon while a dreadful chill and the presence of evil filled the room.

As Simon Blackwell stared into Mrs. Kensington's crocodile eyes while holding her in his grasp, he told his formidable opponent that he was going to take advantage of her hospitality and lovely home.

"I need a place to dwell, and Kensington Hall will be most pleasing and comfortable," replied Simon. "I am certain that you will be a most gracious and cooperative hostess."

"I will not give shelter or offer hospitality to the black-hearted villain, who is responsible for my daughter's demise," said Mrs. Kensington adamantly. "You must return to the depths of hell from where you have come from. If you do not go voluntarily, I will send you there myself."

Simon became enraged by Mrs. Kensington's response. He pushed her onto the sofa, and then raised the iron hook. A terrified Mrs. Kensington covered her face. Just as Simon was about to strike his defenseless victim, he was interrupted by a loud cry from another part of the house.

Unaware of what was taking place downstairs in the drawing room, Charity hurried to Charles' room to investigate the loud cry. As she entered the room, she found a pitiful Charles sitting up in bed sobbing and shaking. Charity placed her arms around him and offered him comfort by telling him that he was safe.

After Charles had calmed down, he said that he had dreamed of Charlotte, and in his dream she was running towards him. As he reached out to her, a thick fog filled the air, and a strange man dressed in a dark cloak grabbed Charlotte from behind. Then they disappeared in the fog leaving Charles alone.

Charity told Charles that it was a bad dream and not to pay any mind to the details. After holding him in her arms for awhile, Charles became sleepy so he put his head down on the pillow, and quickly fell asleep. Charity sat in the chair by his bedside for some time, and then returned to her room, with a sense that something was terribly wrong.

Meanwhile more than three thousand miles across the Atlantic Ocean, a magnificent celebration was taking place at St. James' Court in London. King George III and his wife Queen Anne were hosting a ball for London's prominent and royal members of English society. The ballroom was filled with many men and women of nobility dressed in elegantly flowing gowns and fine tailored suits, dancing gracefully to the music played by musicians positioned at the far end of the room.

Among the guests were Lord and Lady Winfield, who were loyal subjects of the crown. As Lord Winfield engaged in a dance with the queen, Lady Winfield and King George amused themselves by partaking in pleasant conversation.

"My lovely Lady Winfield, I will be sorry to see you and your husband leave tomorrow on your excursion to America. Your charming and graceful presence as one of England's finest couples will be sadly missed at St. James' Court. We will try to endure the deprivation until your return," remarked the King.

"My dear Majesty, your compliments are always well received and deeply appreciated," exclaimed Lady Winfield. "Lord Winfield and I shall miss the gatherings at St. James' Court and your splendid company as well, but our departure will only last a short time," replied Lady Winfield. "We are returning to the former colonies to visit our dear friend Phoebe Kensington. The poor woman has endured the loss of her husband and daughter within months apart."

The King felt great sympathy for Mrs. Kensington. He remarked to Lady Winfield that Mrs. Kensington was one of England's finest women, and he implored her and Lord Winfield to try to convince Mrs. Kensington to return to England with them. Lady Winfield revealed to the King that the purpose of their trip was to do just that.

Upon hearing this, King George became elated, and then asked Lady Winfield to dance with him. While they were dancing, she smiled kindly at her partner, but her thoughts were preoccupied with a disturbing matter she had kept to herself.

At Kensington Hall, Charity was troubled by Charles' dream and felt restless. So she walked about her room. She went to the window and pulled back the lovely blue velvet drapes while staring out at the moonlit sky. All seemed calm and peaceful outside.

Then, as she glanced upon the grounds, she saw someone, wearing a dark cloak walking away from the mansion. Suddenly, this unknown person stood still, turned about while removing the hood of the cloak, and looked up at her. To her horror, she saw that it was Simon Blackwell.

Charity stood motionless and could not believe her eyes for several months ago Lieutenant Bradford, Dr. Greenville and she watched as Simon Blackwell leaped off the edge of Widow's Bluff into the sea. As Simon stared at her with a wicked smile on his face, Charity quickly closed her eyes and desperately tried to convince herself that he was not real. She kept her eyes closed for a few seconds, and when she finely mustered up the courage to open them, Simon had gone.

She gave a sigh of relief and tried to convince herself that she was creating a state of fear and panic for no reason. Nonetheless, she hurried downstairs to find Mrs. Kensington. She saw a servant carrying a tray of tea and food into the drawing room so she followed.

When they entered, the servant gasped from fright and dropped the tray she was carrying. To their surprise, the room was in a complete upheaval with the terrace doors wide open, and they found an unconscious Mrs. Kensington lying on the sofa, and she was covered with several strands of seaweed.

After recovering from the shock of viewing Mrs. Kensington, Charity tried desperately to wake her by gently shaking her shoulders and calling her name. She finally opened her eyes, but she was in a frantic state.

"What has happened to me? My dear Charity, did you see that stranger leave this room? What in heaven's name are strands of seaweed doing on me! Please, Charity, assist me in taking it off," implored Mrs. Kensington.

Charity did as Mrs. Kensington had requested, and then she asked her servant to dispose of it. The drawing room had the smell of the sea, and it reminded her when she, along with Lieutenant Bradford and Dr. Greenville, were hurrying after Simon Blackwell and Charlotte along the shore leading to Widow's Bluff. A terrible chill engulfed her as she remembered that tragic night.

It wasn't long before Mrs. Kensington had returned to her strong, formidable self, and she demanded a reply from Charity concerning her question about whether or not she saw the stranger. Charity responded by telling her that she saw no one. She did not tell her she thought she had seen someone from the window that resembled Simon Blackwell walking the grounds. Mrs. Kensington then remained silent while staring at the terrace doors. Feeling uncomfortable, Charity politely excused herself.

"If you do not need me any longer, I will take my leave and return to my room."

"Yes, you may go, and thank you for your assistance and concern. Before you leave, I must tell you not to speak a word of the condition I was in when you found me. Promise me that you will remain silent, and put this strange occurrence out of your mind," said Mrs. Kensington.

"I will abide by your wishes, Mum," Charity replied before leaving the room.

After she had left her employer's presence, she was very troubled by the entire incident. She kept asking herself what was going on, where did the seaweed come from, who was the stranger, and why did Mrs. Kensington want her to forget what she found? She had thought that all the secrets had been revealed when Mr. Kensington had died, but she was wrong.

Meanwhile in New Haven at the Peabody Tavern, a bold and arrogant Jean-Luc Tessier was entertaining a group of seamen with his tales of adventure at sea. As he drank his ale from a large mug, he had the undivided attention of his audience while an observant Louise Bourget sat quietly in a wooden chair at the other end of the room near the stone fireplace.

Jean-Luc told fascinating stories about when he served aboard a grand ship called the Unicorn that was in battle with the British navy during the Revolutionary War. Then he changed the subject of conversation by talking about a treasure that was believed to have been stolen many years ago, and buried by pirates somewhere in North America. He also mentioned that legend had it that the treasure was cursed.

"My shipmates and I searched for some time, looking for a treasure stolen from the monarchs of England and buried on this very continent. It was rumored that the treasure was cursed, and anyone who found it would meet an untimely demise," explained Jean-Luc.

Upon hearing this, several of the seamen remained silent, and then one of them accused Jean-Luc of telling a ridiculous tale. Jean-Luc walked over to the man who challenged his credibility, and stared at him with a malevolent look. The man rose from his chair. As he and Jean-Luc were about to strike one another, the tavern's proprietor, Solomon Peabody, interrupted by confirming Jean-Luc's story.

"Monsieur Tessier speaks the truth about the legend of the treasure. I can recall shortly after the war with England, three men visited my tavern while on their way to North Haven. My wife and I overheard them speaking about a treasure hidden somewhere in the mountains near the outskirts of the town. They also laughed about a curse connected to the treasure. After leaving here, we never saw them again," said Solomon Peabody. "I wonder if they found what they were looking for and what became of them."

After Solomon Peabody finished speaking, the man sat down and began to drink his ale with his companions while Jean-Luc motioned to Louise that they were leaving. Before they departed, Jean Luc pressed Solomon Peabody for further details, but he knew none. When they walked outside of the tavern, Louise held a lantern so they could see their way in the dark. Jean-Luc informed Louise that while Laura Corday, the former Madame Monnerat, was preoccupied with her charity work, they would take a trip to North Haven to seek out a special group of mountains that Solomon Peabody had mentioned.

"I am pleased by your suggestion, Jean-Luc. The sooner we find the treasure, the sooner we can assist Robespierre and the Revolution," Louise replied with satisfaction.

While Jean-Luc and Louise made their way down the street they were unaware that someone was following them carefully concealed in the shadows of the night.

At Kensington Hall, Charity was unable to sleep, so she got out of bed, wrapped a shawl around her, took hold of the candle on the table by her bed, and went downstairs to get a book from the library. As she walked through the hallway, all was silent and dark.

When she approached the library, the door was slightly open, and she saw a light coming from the opening. Her curiosity got the better of her, so she crept up quietly to the door, and carefully peeked through the crack.

To her surprise, she saw Mrs. Kensington dressed in her night gown and a lace cap, holding a crown jewel box in her hands. Charity saw her open the box, and remove what appeared to be a shiny object. As she strained her eyes in an attempt to see what the object was, Mrs. Kensington kissed the object and spoke.

"My beautiful Winfield diamond, you are all mine. If anyone tries to take you from me, I shall destroy them. After all, I am the fairest one of all and the master of the game."

Upon hearing her employer's words, Charity froze from fright while realizing that her employer was a dangerous woman with many hidden secrets.

Charity was shocked from witnessing Mrs. Kensington's actions in the library, and she quietly and quickly went to her room.

Upon returning to her room, she blew out the candle, got into bed, and burrowed under the quilt. She tossed about for some time while thinking about Mrs. Kensington and what appeared to be a diamond that she was holding in her hand.

Then a thought came to her: *the diamond Mrs. Kensington possessed could be the same one that she overheard Colonel Parker and the late Mr. Singleton arguing over the night of the ball at Singleton Lodge.*

Charity kept asking herself, *if it was the same diamond, how did Mrs. Kensington come to acquire it, and why was she so determined to prevent anyone from trying to take it from her. She remembered Colonel Parker and Mr. Singleton saying that it was called the Winfield diamond as did Mrs. Kensington, and it was stolen from the monarchs of England. She also wondered if Mrs. Kensington stole the diamond or if she had someone else to commit the crime.* Frustrated by these unanswered questions, she stayed awake for quite a long time, but then eventually fell asleep.

The next morning Charity was awakened by one of the servants who knocked on her bedroom door. The servant informed her that it was late, and Mrs. Kensington was waiting for her downstairs in the dining room. Charity quickly rose from her bed, washed her face, removed her night clothes, and dressed in a hurry. After fixing her hair and putting on a lace cap, she went downstairs to join her employer.

When she entered the dining room, Mrs. Kensington and Charles were having breakfast. One of the servants poured Charity a cup of tea. She smiled at Charles who gave her a pleasant greeting, and then returned to eating. Then she turned to Mrs. Kensington, but before she could utter a word in her defense for oversleeping, Mrs. Kensington seized the moment to speak first.

"My dear Charity, you have overslept this morning. Since you are always an early riser and have never until today kept me waiting, I shall forgive you this one time." Then she said, "I am expecting a young man by the name of Nicholas Biddle to arrive at Kensington Hall in the early afternoon. I am considering hiring him as a tutor for Charles."

She also said that Mr. Biddle came from a respectable family, and she had hoped he would have a good influence on Charles, and would fill the void of a male figure left by the absence of Colonel Parker.

After Mrs. Kensington finished speaking, Charity asked for permission to go into town, so Mrs. Kensington sent for the carriage.

"My dear, please return by early afternoon so you can meet Mr. Biddle when he arrives, and take tea with us," said Mrs. Kensington with a smile.

Charity agreed to do so, and then finished her breakfast. After breakfast, she took her leave, and the driver took her to the home of Mr. Higgins. When they arrived, the property was desolate, and the house, along with the grounds, was in a state of neglect with tall weeds and high grass surrounding the place. It made Charity sad to see the unpleasant sight.

She walked to the oak tree to visit the graves of Elizabeth Higgins, her father, and Edmund Tate. She noticed that fresh flowers had been placed on only Elizabeth's grave, and her grave had been attended to unlike the others. As she stared at the tombstones, the wind began to blow, and a nasty chill filled the air. Then she heard a voice call out to her.

"You have come to pay your respects to the dead. That is an admirable thing to do, but only one of the three rests in peace while the other two restlessly roam these parts relentlessly searching for justice," stated the voice.

Charity turned around, and standing in front of her was a tall gentleman dressed in farm attire with a shabby tricorn hat on his head and a dog by his side. After staring at him for a few moments, she remembered his name, Ebenezer Stiles, the man who Mr. Higgins and she met on the bridge by Muddy River. His dog's name was Pogo.

"Hello, Mr. Stiles. It has been a long time since our first meeting," Charity said. "What are you doing here?"

"It is good to see you Miss Charity, and under better circumstances than the last. Pogo and I walk this way every so often, and we keep an eye on the property," explained Mr. Stiles. "I see that someone has brought fresh flowers to Miss Higgins' grave again."

When Charity asked Mr. Stiles if he knew who the person was, he replied that he did not know, but he told her that every time he and Pogo walk through the property, there are always flowers on Elizabeth's grave. He continued to say that he believed the spirits of Elizabeth and Edmund were not at rest, for he could still see their apparitions moving about at night. At that moment, the tall grass in the distance began to move with the blowing wind causing Pogo to bark fiercely.

"Keep quiet Pogo. It is only the wind," he said. "But I do believe that a storm may be coming as evident in the changing appearance of the sky. We better take our leave before it begins to rain."

Charity wrapped the shawl tightly around her shoulders, and then followed Mr. Stiles and his dog. As they were walking away from the gravesite, Charity had a strange feeling that someone or something was hiding in the tall grass near the graves.

After leaving Mr. Stiles and Pogo, Charity had the driver take her to Andrews' Tavern. When she arrived, she saw Mrs. Andrews outside talking to a man and woman she did not know. When Mrs. Andrews saw Charity, she gave her a nice greeting. Then she introduced Charity to the man and woman.

"Miss Charity Chastine, this is Jean-Luc Tessier and Louise Bourget. They are friends of the former Madame Monnerat, now Laura Corday," said Mrs. Andrews.

Jean-Luc was strong and robust in appearance with long black hair neatly tied behind his neck and fine dark eyes. He tipped his hat to Charity while Louise, who was common in appearance, gave her a smile and a nod while wrapping a blue shawl around her shoulders. Mrs. Andrews politely explained that they were inquiring about the mountains near the outskirts of town. After exchanging some pleasant words, Mrs. Andrews invited them to go inside, but Jean-Luc and Louise declined the invitation, and went on their way.

As they walked away, and Mrs. Andrews and Charity were inside, Louise told Jean-Luc that Charity was the young girl who Lydia Johnson ranted about harming when she and Louise had been fighting.

Upon hearing this, Jean-Luc became very intrigued. He informed Louise that they should keep an eye on Charity and become better acquainted with her.

At Kensington Hall, Mrs. Kensington, who was waiting for Nicholas Biddle to arrive, retreated to the library and studied the chess game displayed on the table. After removing one of the pieces to the game, she went to the desk, took out the crown jewel box, opened it, and stared at the Winfield diamond.

"What do you have in the box that is so fascinating?" asked a voice.

Suddenly, a startled Mrs. Kensington frantically closed the box, and quickly turned her head. To her unwanted surprise, once again it was Simon Blackwell standing before her.

"I have returned, my dear lady. You and I have important business to discuss. Before we commence with our business at hand, I must see what you are concealing in that box. Will you show me, or shall I see for myself," uttered a fiendish Simon while pointing his hook at a defiant Mrs. Kensington.

Chapter 16

Mrs. Kensington held tightly the crown jewel box in her hands as a determined and curious Simon Blackwell made his way towards her.

"Stay away from me you foul fiend," demanded Mrs. Kensington. "There is nothing that would be of interest to you in this box."

"Let me be the judge of that. Open the box so I may see for myself," insisted Simon.

Mrs. Kensington quickly opened one of the desk drawers, placed down the box, and took hold of a pistol that she aimed at Simon. She then instructed him to leave immediately, but Simon stared at her while mocking her, and pointing his hook in a threatening manner.

At that moment, a servant knocked at the door and informed Mrs. Kensington that Nicholas Biddle had arrived. A calm, complacent, and quick thinking Mrs. Kensington told the servant to bring Mr. Biddle to the drawing room, and she would join him momentarily.

"A visitor has come to call upon the mistress of Kensington Hall. What a delightful treat! May I join you and your guest for tea?" teased Simon.

Mrs. Kensington, who desperately wanted Simon gone from her presence, cunningly came up with an excuse to have him leave without creating a disturbance. She deceivingly told Simon that she had something of importance to show him that would please him very much, but this was not the appropriate time. She told him to return later when all would be revealed to him. Overcome with curiosity, he agreed to Mrs. Kensington's request, and as he was departing, he warned her that she would suffer his wrath if she did not keep her word.

After Simon had left, Mrs. Kensington put the pistol back in the desk, and took the crown jewel box with her when she left the room.

At Andrews' Tavern, Charity was visiting with Mrs. Andrews who was taking a respite from the noon day crowd. She told her that she had heard from tradesmen and traveling merchants that settlers in the Ohio Valley were vulnerable to Indian attacks. Since her son Jesse and Lieutenant Bradford were in the valley, the news was quite upsetting to them. They both wished they had never gone there. Then Mrs. Andrews placed her hand on Charity's shoulder and informed her that they had to keep good thoughts while anticipating the day of their safe return home.

While they were talking, Jean-Luc Tessier and his friend Louise Bourget came into the tavern and sat at a table by the window. They both looked in Charity's direction while giving her a pleasant smile. Charity returned the greeting, and then continued to speak with Mrs. Andrews, but she had an odd notion that they were watching her.

After Mrs. Andrews went to check on things in the back room, Louise rose from her chair, and came over to Charity. She was gracious in initiating a conversation with her by complimenting her lace cap. Then she invited her to join her and Jean-Luc at their table.

"I thank you for your invitation, but I must decline. I am waiting for Mrs. Andrews to return," Charity said politely.

"Since Mrs. Andrews is preoccupied at the moment," said Louise, "I'm certain she would not mind if you join Jean-Luc and me. Our company will be more pleasing than sitting alone."

Since she had no further excuses and Louise was quite persistent, Charity accepted her invitation. When they approached the table, Jean-Luc stood up and pulled out a chair for Charity. Once they were seated, he began to talk about his arrival to America and said he was interested in settling down, perhaps in North Haven. Charity listened graciously, and then her attention was interrupted when she caught a glimpse of someone looking at them from outside the window. As she stared at the person, Charity suddenly realized it was Lydia Johnson. She was smiling wickedly at her. Startled by her appearance, Charity gasped while putting her hand over her mouth. Her reaction alerted Jean-Luc and Louise who looked in the same direction and saw Lydia.

Jean-Luc rose from his chair, told Louise to remain with Charity, and hurried outside to search for Lydia. A few minutes later, he returned and told them that Lydia was not to be found. It was evident by their facial expressions that seeing Lydia Johnson troubled them greatly. Then, surprisingly, they revealed to Charity that Lydia had tried to kill them and the former Madame Monnerat.

Shocked by what they had told her, Charity became agitated and decided to take her leave. She said that Mrs. Kensington was expecting her, so she had to leave at once. Jean-Luc escorted her to the carriage with Louise behind him. They waved farewell to Charity as the carriage made its way down the dusty road. But Charity was unaware that Jean-Luc and Louise had decided to follow her to Kensington Hall on horseback.

When Charity arrived at Kensington Hall, one of the male servants, Foster, helped her out of the carriage and informed her that Mrs. Kensington was waiting for her in the drawing room.

Upon entering the room, Charity expected to be greeted by Mrs. Kensington and the young gentleman Nicholas Biddle. To her shocking surprise, she found Mrs. Kensington having tea, not with the prospective tutor, but with Lydia Johnson.

"Come in my dear Charity. I do believe you are acquainted with Mrs. Johnson," replied Mrs. Kensington.

"Yes, indeed," said Lydia. "We do know each other. Hello, my dear! It is so lovely to see you again."

Charity was speechless standing while gazing upon a woman

who she did not trust, and whose presence filled the room with fear and suspicion.

Outside, and unbeknownst to those in the room, a wicked Simon Blackwell was carefully observing them from the terrace while a devious Jean-Luc and his companion Louise were stealthily wandering the grounds of Kensington Hall.

Charity quickly recovered from the shock of seeing Lydia Johnson, and she gave her a polite greeting. However, she was very concerned about Lydia's visit to Kensington Hall. Mrs. Kensington asked Charity to join them, and after pouring Charity a cup of tea, revealed the reason for Lydia's visit.

"I am in need of a housekeeper who will oversee the other servants, and Mrs. Johnson was highly recommended by my good friend Judith Fairchild. Mrs. Johnson was in the employ of Mr. and Mrs. Fairchild some years ago, and they were pleased with her work," said Mrs. Kensington.

Turning to Charity, Lydia smiled and replied, "Mrs. Kensington has made me a generous offer that I have accepted. She has informed me that you are in her employ as Charles' governess. I look forward to working with you."

Chills ran down Charity's spine, and she had an uncomfortable feeling about Lydia working at Kensington Hall. She kept her feelings concealed, and for the sake of appearances, she engaged in pleasant conversation with both women as they had their tea.

A short while later, as Lydia was about to take her leave they heard the sounds of a scuffle and shouting coming from outside on the terrace. Mrs. Kensington bravely went to investigate the disturbance. She opened the terrace doors and discovered a woman wearing a shawl standing nearby while a man with long black hair tied neatly behind his neck was making his way back towards the terrace.

"Who are you? What are you doing on my property?" demanded Mrs. Kensington. "Come inside this instant so you can explain yourselves."

As the couple entered, Lydia Johnson abruptly left the room, and

Charity was surprised to see that the people entering were Jean-Luc and Louise. Upon seeing her, they both gave her a nice greeting, and a curious Mrs. Kensington was astonished that they knew Charity.

"My dear Charity, you are acquainted with this man and woman who are responsible for making a commotion outside my drawing room? I demand an explanation at once."

After introducing themselves, Jean-Luc was very charming and explained that he and Louise came to Kensington Hall on horseback, and that when they arrived, they saw a person wearing a cloak lurking about the mansion. Their curiosity got the best of them, so they followed this person who went onto the terrace and was spying on whoever was inside. They went on to explain that when the person realized that Jean-Luc and Louise were watching him, he tried to attack them before making his escape.

To everyone's surprise, Mrs. Kensington showed little concern about the stranger, and instead, rang the bell for one of the servants to bring a fresh pot of tea. Then she graciously invited Jean-Luc and Louise to stay for a visit. Charity had surmised that she wanted to become acquainted with the mysterious couple to learn more about their connection to Charity and their uninvited arrival to her home.

At Winchester Park, an elegant Judith Winchester Fairchild was sitting alone in the library staring at a portrait of her son Ethan. Her train of thought was interrupted when her husband Caleb entered. He was not very tall, but a refined, distinguished, and well-mannered gentleman dressed in a blue coat.

"My dear Judith, what seems to be troubling you?" he inquired.

"How dare you ask me such a question? If you must know, I am thinking about our son Ethan and his foolish decision to be with that horrid girl Honoria. How could he have fallen under her spell? Has he no respect for his parents or the good name of Fairchild?" ranted an emotional Judith Fairchild.

Caleb took his wife's hand and gently ushered her to the sofa while he tried to comfort her. He told Judith that Ethan had made his decision, and they were powerless to change his mind. He also told her that they should be grateful for her sister Evelyn Winchester's assistance in watching over Ethan and Honoria.

"That is of little comfort to me. My sister promised me that the trip to Philadelphia would end Ethan's attachment to that girl of inferior birth and all would be right again," said Judith despairingly. "The trip only brought them closer, and now we have lost our only son. I am filled with sorrow and shall die of a broken heart."

As Caleb continued in his attempt to calm his wife, a servant interrupted and announced that there were visitors in the great hall waiting to see them. Caleb instructed the servant to show them in while Judith quickly composed herself.

A few moments later, Ethan Fairchild entered the room and embraced each of his parents. An overjoyed Judith hugged her son tightly and then looked in the direction of the doorway. Standing in the entrance of the room was an elegantly dressed Honoria Noble with a lace cap and a shawl wrapped around her shoulders. She was smiling at Ethan's parents. Judith stared at the lovely young girl with contempt in her eyes.

At Kensington Hall, Mrs. Kensington's little tea party came to an end when she graciously told Jean-Luc and Louise that it was a pleasure to meet them despite the circumstances, and that any friends of Charity were friends of hers. She asked Charity to show her friends to the door while she remained behind. Then Mrs. Kensington went out onto the terrace where she found an angry Simon Blackwell impatiently waiting for her.

While Charity was escorting Jean-Luc and Louise to the door, a persistent Jean-Luc whispered to her that he and Louise needed to meet with her tomorrow at Andrews' Tavern. Sensing that they were troubled by something, she agreed to his request.

After they left, Charity decided to go upstairs to her room. As she approached the stairwell, she was startled by Lydia Johnson who came out of the shadows and grabbed her arm. While she stared at Charity with a poker straight face and an evil look in her eyes, they both heard the noise of a door closing behind them. They turned their heads, and when Lydia saw who it was, she uttered some frightful words.

Chapter 17

"Black-hearted villains are not welcome in this place. Leave at once before something falls on your heads," shrieked Lydia Johnson as she held Charity's arm while staring at Jean-Luc and Louise.

"We will not leave until you release our friend Miss Charity, and let her come with us," replied an adamant Louise with her companion Jean-Luc by her side.

While Lydia was distracted and uttering hateful words at Louise and Jean-Luc, Charity had managed to free herself from Lydia's grip. Then she hurried into the drawing room to find Mrs. Kensington, who was coming in from the terrace.

"Mrs. Kensington, please come with me into the hallway. Your assistance is urgently needed."

As they were leaving, Charity thought she saw a shadow of a person from outside on the terrace, but she dismissed that image from her mind because her concentration was focused on what was taking place in the hallway.

Mrs. Kensington was at first startled, then upset to see Jean-Luc and Louise engaging in an argument with Lydia Johnson. Mrs. Kensington interrupted by raising her voice for silence. She ordered Jean-Luc and Louise to leave Kensington Hall immediately, and then instructed Lydia to accompany her into the drawing room.

After Mrs. Kensington and Lydia had retreated into the drawing room, Charity ran outside to catch up with Jean-Luc and Louise who were mounting their horses, and preparing to leave. She thanked them for their assistance with Lydia. They told her they were happy to assist and warned her to stay away from Lydia because she was dangerous. Louise informed her that they came back inside to look for Lydia, who they saw leave the room abruptly when they came in from the terrace. Then Jean-Luc inquired once again if she would meet with them in the morning at Andrews' Tavern.

The frightening encounter with Lydia and her overpowering curiosity made Charity agree to do so. She watched them as they rode away into the distance, and then she went inside. She decided to eavesdrop on Mrs. Kensington and Lydia, so she quietly tiptoed down the hallway and listened carefully to their conversation.

"My dear Mrs. Kensington, you must forbid Charity Chastine from associating with those vulgar and unscrupulous connivers. They are not to be trusted, and I fear they are plotting something. I have it on good authority from my former employer Monsieur Monnerat that they are suspected of having revolutionary connections to what is happening in Paris," replied a deceitful Lydia.

"I have my suspicions about Charity's so called new friends as well. I do not accept their explanation for their presence at my home. I will take your advice under advisement," said Mrs. Kensington.

Charity hid in the shadows of the hallway as they emerged from the drawing room. As Mrs. Kensington escorted Lydia to the door, Charity cautiously made her way upstairs. When she approached her room, she heard crying coming from Charles' bedroom. Upon entering, she found a sobbing Charles sitting up in bed.

Charity sat on his bed, gently hugged him, and then held him in her arms. He told her that he had had another dream about Charlotte. Charity began to sing softly to him in the hope of comforting him. While she was doing this, she happened to look up, and she saw Mrs. Kensington standing in the doorway watching them with her crocodile eyes.

The next morning at breakfast Charity was introduced to Charles' tutor, Nicholas Biddle. He was well mannered with a bright smile, dark brown hair, and a pair of fine eyes. He gave her a courteous bow, and as she looked at him, his appearance, along with his fine eyes reminded Charity of Lieutenant Bradford. For a moment, she thought that he could be the lieutenant's younger brother.

After finishing their meal, Nicholas took Charles into the library to begin working on his daily lessons. Mrs. Kensington was pleasant, and did not mention a word about what had taken place the night before. She did tell Charity that Lydia Johnson was arriving at the end of the week to assume her position as head housekeeper, and she expected the entire staff including her to make Lydia feel at home.

The mention of that woman's name made Charity nervous. She changed the conversation by asking for the carriage, so that she may go to visit Mrs. Andrews. Mrs. Kensington agreed and informed her that she was going to pay a call to her friend Judith Fairchild, and would take her to Andrews' Tavern which was along the way.

When they arrived at the tavern, Mrs. Kensington told Charity that the driver would return for her in a couple of hours, and then the carriage made its way down the sandy road.

Charity went inside and found Mrs. Andrews sitting at a table by the stone fireplace reading a newspaper. When she saw her, she rose from her chair, and gave her a hug.

"My dear, it is good to see you. Please, sit down, and have a cup of tea with me. I was reading an article in *The Chronicle* about Laura Corday who has purchased the old Bickford Mansion in New Haven and has made it into a dwelling for homeless women and children. She certainly has captured the attention of many with her kindness and generosity."

Charity visited with Mrs. Andrews for some time. Then she went into the back room to check on something, but she told Charity to stay. Charity started to read the newspaper when she heard the tavern door open and the sound of footsteps on the wooden plank floor, but did not look to see who it was.

Suddenly, she became startled when a hand grabbed the paper

from her. To her shocking surprise, it was the treacherous Monsieur Monnerat. Charity quickly rose from her chair, and as she tried to get away, he grabbed her, put her in a choke hold, and, whispering told her to be silent.

As she stood frozen with terror in the clutches of her captor, the tavern door swung open, and to her relief, Jean-Luc and Louise entered. Upon seeing Charity in Monsieur Monnerat's grasp, Jean-Luc demanded her release, and then he removed a pistol from under his grey coat.

"Well, if it isn't the brutish Monsieur Tessier, and my wife's devoted maid Madame Bourget, the traitor. I know you have been following me, and what good fortune on my part to take refuge in this place and to find this lovely and delicate flower sitting alone," said Monsieur Monnerat.

Jean-Luc asked Monsieur Monnerat again to release Charity, but he refused and laughed nefariously as Jean-Luc pointed a pistol in their direction.

Jean-Luc was not backing down, but Monsieur Monnerat was determined to make his escape with Charity as his prisoner. As they moved toward the back room, Charity tried desperately to free herself, but her efforts were in vain.

"For the last time, let Charity go and surrender. You cannot escape from us," replied a calm but relentless Jean-Luc.

"I will make my escape with this young and beautiful flower as my prisoner. I need to find something very valuable, and she is going to assist me. When I have found what I have been searching for, then I shall release Miss Charity unharmed if you and your companion do not pursue us," said Monsieur Monnerat in a devious voice.

As they continued to make their way to the back room, a startled Mrs. Andrews emerged and she tried to hit Monsieur Monnerat in the head with an iron skillet she held in her hands. A crafty Monsieur Monnerat moved his head, and Mrs. Andrews hit him in the arm. Feeling pain from the nasty blow, he released Charity and shoved her into Mrs. Andrews causing both of them to fall to the floor. He then made his way into the back room and out the back door of the tavern. Jean-Luc handed Louise his pistol, and after helping Mrs. Andrews and Charity to their feet, he hurried in pursuit of Monsieur Monnerat.

At that moment, Dr. Foote and Constance arrived. The good doctor came in the hope of partaking in a delicious bowl of stew while Constance's intention was to personally invite Mrs. Andrews to a ball that she and her husband were hosting at Singleton Lodge. Mrs. Andrews shouted to Dr. Foote to go and get the constable. Constance hurried to Charity's side while Louise went outside. Before Louise took her leave, she told them to remain indoors. After Charity had recovered from the ordeal, she disobeyed Louise's request, and went outside with a curious Constance behind her.

Constance and Charity gasped in fright as they watched Jean-Luc and Monsieur Monnerat fight like two wild beasts. Louise was angry at them for coming outside, and she adamantly ordered them to go back inside which they did not do. Jean-Luc had Monsieur Monnerat on the ground and was striking him in the face. After receiving a few punches, Monsieur Monnerat managed to raise his feet and shove Jean-Luc off of him. As Monsieur Monnerat rose to his feet, he picked up a dollop of sand from the ground and threw it in Jean-Luc's face. While Jean-Luc was wiping the sand from his face, a wicked Monsieur Monnerat grabbed an axe that was lying near the wood pile.

"You thought you could get the better of me by beating me to death. I am sorry to disappoint you, but you have failed just like that horrid woman Lydia Johnson failed when she struck me in the head with a rock while stealing a precious item from my coat pocket. I am still alive, and now I am going to finish you once and for all. Au revoir, Monsieur Tessier," uttered a vengeful Monsieur Monnerat.

Charity stood frozen from terror, and Constance screamed as they watched in horror as Monsieur Monnerat descended upon Jean-Luc while swinging the axe in a murderous rage. Just as Monsieur Monnerat was about to deliver a fatal blow to Jean-Luc's head, Jean-Luc miraculously managed to grab a dagger from under his coat; and with great force and contempt in his eyes, he plunged the dagger into Monsieur Monnerat's chest.

Upon receiving the deadly wound, Monsieur Monnerat took a giant gasp for air, rolled his eyes, and collapsed to the ground. Jean-Luc and Louise walked over to Monsieur Monnerat. And Constance and Charity, while holding onto one another, slowly made their way towards the dying man. As they drew near, Constance and Charity could hear Monsieur Monnerat uttering some hateful last words to Louise and Jean-Luc.

"The fight between us has ended with you as the victor, but the revolution goes on. You and Louise, Robespierre and his conspirators, and my wife Laura will not go unpunished for my death or the deaths of my fellow French aristocrats. My brother Philippe will avenge me, but until then I shall wait for you in hell," gasped a vindictive Monsieur Monnerat before closing his eyes forever.

Constance could not bear looking at the dead man any longer, so she hurried into the tavern to get Mrs. Andrews. Jean-Luc remained silent as he walked away with his back towards the dead Monsieur Monnerat. Louise stared at the body with an unholy smirk of satisfaction. Charity was terribly disturbed by the entire incident. In her heart, she knew that Jean-Luc had killed Monsieur Monnerat in self-defense, but in her mind she kept asking herself the agonizing questions of *what made these two men despise each other so immensely to result in violence and death. And what unforeseen and terrible events will transpire as a result of Monsieur Monnerat's demise?*

Charity stood speechless while pondering these thoughts that she did not reveal to Jean-Luc or Louise. Then she glanced upon the handle of the dagger that was protruding from Monsieur Monnerat's chest. She noticed that the sunlight was shining on the handle. When she stepped aside, she looked down on the ground, and not far from where Monsieur Monnerat's body laid, the dagger's handle was casting the shadow of a cross.

Chapter 18

Two weeks had passed since the deadly confrontation between Monsieur Monnerat and Jean-Luc. Charity could still see in her mind the image of a cross on the ground next to the spot where Monsieur Monnerat's body laid.

While she sat in a chair staring out the window of her room, she watched the leaves fall from the trees and cover the dying gardens of Kensington Hall. The grass was rapidly losing its rich fertile green and taking on a dry brown appearance. The falling leaves reminded her of man's fall from grace into sin and despair. She asked herself the inevitable question over and over again: *why is man capable of such evil?* Unfortunately, she could not find an answer.

Monsieur Monnerat's wife Laura gave her husband a modest burial with only a few mourners in attendance. Charity attended the service to help bring closure to what had happened. Madame Monnerat, or Laura Corday, as she was calling herself was grateful for Charity's attendance, and she was very gracious and kind. Her behavior did not match Mrs. Kensington's portrayal of her. The fact that she was an outcast from her beloved France in addition to her husband's death may have created a change in her attitude and beliefs.

Constance and Charity gave testimony to the authorities that Jean-Luc acted in self-defense when killing Monsieur Monnerat, and therefore Jean-Luc was not charged with murder. Charity had not seen Jean-Luc or his companion Louise since that awful day. Mrs. Kensington was very disturbed about the incident, and as Charity's employer, she forbade her from having any further association with them. Charity had not seen Constance, but she imagined her friend was preoccupied with preparation for the ball she and her husband were hosting at Singleton Lodge. Charity would see dear Charles at meal time in the evenings and on Sundays. During the week, he would spend most of his time with his tutor Nicholas Biddle who seemed to be winning Mrs. Kensington's approval.

Lately, Charity was feeling unwanted while loneliness and depression were her new companions. There were times when she felt herself standing at a great precipice with no place to go. How she longed for financial independence, friendship and celebration, and the return of Lieutenant Bradford.

As she sat wallowing in unhappy thoughts, she was distracted by someone knocking at her door.

"Miss Charity, you are wanted downstairs immediately. A gentleman has come to see you. He has important business to discuss with you," replied one of the servants through the door.

After telling the servant that she was on her way down, she wrapped a shawl around her shoulders while looking in the mirror to check her appearance, and then went to meet her visitor. When she entered the drawing room, she found Mrs. Kensington talking to a middle-aged gentleman dressed in a fine green suit. He rose from the sofa while Mrs. Kensington made the introductions and then revealed the purpose for the stranger's visit.

"My dear Charity, Mr. Preston is a lawyer from New Haven who is in charge of Grace Collins' estate. He has some very good news to share with you. Without further details, I will let Mr. Preston speak."

Charity sat down on the sofa next to Mr. Preston who was holding a legal document in his hand. He explained that it was Grace's will. In the will, Grace had named Charity her sole heir, and upon her death, Charity would receive the sum of 3,000 pounds. He also gave her a letter written by Grace that stated since she had no living relatives and came to think of her as a daughter, she wanted her to inherit her estate. Although the amount did not make her very rich, Mr. Preston believed that if the money was properly managed, it would sustain her for some time until she was able to marry.

Charity was taken aback by mixed feelings of joy and sadness that enveloped her. She was happy to receive the money that would be helpful and appreciated, but she was sad that Grace was no longer with her.

After reviewing some legal terms and getting her signature, Mr. Preston gave Charity Grace's letter. When she glanced at it, she noticed that the letter was written on the same day that Grace had suffered her stroke. Charity suddenly had a memory of when Jesse, David, and she found Grace slumped over in a wooden chair by the fireplace with blood coming out of her nose while clutching the doll in her hand.

Oh, my poor and beloved Grace, how I miss you, Charity thought quietly to herself.

After Mr. Preston had left, Charity went upstairs to her room. She took hold of the doll, and with the letter in her other hand she went downstairs to speak to Mrs. Kensington. Not finding her, she went outside to get a breath of fresh air and gather her thoughts. While standing out on the terrace, she was looking at the letter and asking herself what she should do now. *Should I take my inheritance and leave Kensington Hall, and where should I go?*

While she was outside pondering these questions, Lydia Johnson and Mrs. Kensington, not knowing that Charity was outside on the terrace, entered the drawing room engaging in petty and polite conversation. Lydia had taken up residence at Kensington Hall and was now head housekeeper. Her abrasive mannerism and domineering personality made her very unpopular with the household staff except for Mrs. Kensington who seemed pleased with her and her work.

As she was getting chilled to the bones by a nasty breath of cold air, Charity decided to return indoors. As she approached the terrace doors, she overheard one of the servants announce the arrival of Louise Bourget. The doors were slightly ajar, so Charity listened intently while trying to conceal her presence. From what she could observe, Lydia was not pleased to see Louise who boldly made her appearance into the room. Louise ignored Lydia by speaking directly to Mrs. Kensington, who like Lydia, was disturbed by Louise's sudden and unexpected visit.

"Mrs. Kensington, I have come to inquire about the well-being of Miss Chastine. Monsieur Tessier and I have not seen her in town or at Andrews' Tavern for some time, and we are concerned about her," inquired Louise.

"Miss Chastine is very well and has been busy tending to young Charles," answered Mrs. Kensington. "It is thoughtful of you and Monsieur Tessier to inquire, but I believe it is in Miss Chastine's best interest if she ends all connections with you and Monsieur Tessier."

"Why don't we ask Miss Chastine what she prefers," demanded Louise.

Suddenly, a vicious Lydia got in Louise's way, took hold of her arm, and tried to usher her out of the room while telling her it was time to leave. Louise broke free from Lydia's hold and pushed her out of the way while warning her to mind her own affairs. Then she turned to Mrs. Kensington and once again inquired about Charity. An uneasy Mrs. Kensington told Louise that her uncouth behavior was unacceptable and she needed to leave at once. Louise refused to leave until she saw Charity.

"My employer has requested that you take your leave, and I shall personally escort you to the front door," Lydia said in an insolent tone.

"No one gives me orders," responded Louise. "It is quite shocking that a woman of good breeding and intelligence like Mrs. Kensington would employ a vicious and dangerous woman like you."

As Lydia attempted to defend herself, Louise began to recall in detail the fight she and Lydia had the night of the fire at Singleton Lodge. She told of the frightening confession Lydia made about how she coerced her nephew Theodore and his friend David Cobb to kill Elizabeth Higgins and her Redcoat boyfriend Edmund Tate. She also expressed that Lydia ordered Theodore to kill Charity at the tavern, and when he failed, she tried to kill Mr. Higgins and Charity in the fire that she started at the tavern. When that attempt failed, she had David trap them on the bridge and try to shoot them. Louise went on to say that she caught Lydia trying to choke Laura Monnerat, and while they fought a candle fell from a night table engulfing the room in flames. Lydia managed to escape leaving Louise and her employer to perish in the fire, but they were saved by Jean-Luc.

"Take back those outrageous and despicable lies. There is no proof to these allegations. Be gone from this house, you wicked woman," shrieked Lydia.

Then Lydia slapped Louise in the face. In retaliation, Louise lunged at her attacker, knocking her to the floor. While both women began fighting like two wild animals, Mrs. Kensington went into the hall to seek assistance. A few moments later, two of the servants, Foster and Jennings, came in and interrupted the fight. As Foster held Louise, and Jennings held Lydia, both women struggled to free themselves in a desperate attempt to resume their altercation.

"This abominable behavior will end this instant. Foster, please escort Miss Bourget off the premises immediately. And Miss Bourget, do not return to Kensington Hall, and I warn you and your friend Monsieur Tessier to stay away from dear Charity. Now, away with you," shouted a vexed Mrs. Kensington.

As Foster was escorting Louise out, Louise uttered threats of retaliation against Lydia. Mrs. Kensington informed Lydia to remain behind and to take time to compose herself before resuming her duties, and said she would speak to her later. After Mrs. Kensington left the room, a flustered and disturbed Lydia sat down on the sofa, put her hands up to her face, and began to weep.

After hearing Louise's horrific account of Lydia's evil deeds, Charity was in complete shock. As she stood motionless, Charity began to process in her mind Louise's serious accusations against Lydia, and at the same time she remembered that Grace on numerous occasions warned her to stay away from Lydia. These terrible encounters were not accidents, but the deliberate actions of a deranged woman who for some unknown reason wanted Charity dead just like poor Elizabeth and Edmund. Why did Lydia despise her so much, and why did she go to extreme measures of plotting to murder her while using David and her nephew Theodore as accomplices?

Charity knew that she had to leave Kensington Hall for her own safety. She waited impatiently for Lydia to leave the room so she may enter, but she remained. Not wanting to wait any longer, she decided to return to the house through the servants' entrance by the kitchen. As she turned around, she was startled to see Jean-Luc who had crept up from behind her. He quickly grabbed hold of her, and then they fled through the dying gardens to a waiting carriage on the outskirts of Kensington Hall.

When they approached the carriage, Louise opened the carriage door and instructed Charity to get inside. Upon entering, she was greeted by Constance who was sitting to the side. She told Charity that she had nothing to fear, and she with the assistance of Jean-Luc and Louise were taking her to Singleton Lodge. Once Louise was inside, Constance gave orders to the driver to leave. Jean-Luc followed the carriage on horseback.

The carriage was drawn by four horses and had richly carved wooden sides with seats that were upholstered in a brightly colored cloth. Charity was very comfortable in the seat, and she tried to relax and collect her thoughts. As they rode along the sandy and bumpy road to Singleton Lodge, Constance and Louise began to explain the sudden and surprise plan to get Charity away from Mrs. Kensington and Kensington Hall.

"My dear friend, Louise and Jean-Luc are old acquaintances of my beloved husband Alexander," explained Constance. "They came to Alexander and me out of concern for you. They told us the terrible dealings they had had with Monsieur Monnerat and Lydia Johnson. I was very disturbed and frightened for you when Louise told us about Lydia's confession of that she plotted to harm you. With my husband's consent, we planned to rescue you, and our plan has succeeded. Do not worry my friend, for you shall remain at Singleton Lodge for as long as you wish while under my husband's protection."

Charity admitted to Constance and Louise that she overheard the conversation between Louise and Lydia in the presence of Mrs. Kensington. She also told them that she did not feel comfortable in Lydia's presence and Grace never trusted Lydia and suspected her of creating trouble between Elizabeth Higgins and her father. She thanked them for saving her from a precarious situation. Then she showed Grace's letter to Constance. After reading it, Constance informed her that Mr. Preston was in her husband's employ, and she assured her that the inheritance would be secured for future use.

After hearing Constance's comforting and encouraging words, Charity leaned her head against the soft seat of the carriage and closed her eyes while holding the doll in her hand.

She must have dozed for a short time, because the next thing she realized was Constance gently shaking her shoulder and telling her that they had arrived at Singleton Lodge. Louise descended from the carriage first, and then she held the door as a man servant greeted the carriage and assisted Constance and Charity out of the carriage. Charity followed Constance to the front door as their petticoats rustled along the ground.

When they entered, Charity's eyes were amazed by the elegant and magnificent transformation of the great hall. The furnishings and decorations were more lovely and grandeur than when Constance's father was the owner. As she looked upon her new surroundings with amazement, Constance explained that her generous husband insisted on turning Singleton Lodge into a replica of their home in Virginia.

"My loving and generous husband wanted to dispense with the old decorations and make our home a magnificent and comfortable place to live. He is always thinking of ways to please me. I am so grateful to him," Constance replied with a smile.

When Jean-Luc and Louise entered, Charity once again thanked them for their assistance and concern. They both smiled at her and told her it was their pleasure.

Then Louise motioned to Jean-Luc that they should go into the library to see Constance's husband.

Constance took Charity by the arm and led her upstairs to her new quarters. As they went up the stairs, Charity glanced over her shoulder and saw Louise and Jean-Luc enter the library and close the door behind them. A feeling of secrecy and uncertainty took a hold of her, but she quickly dismissed those feelings as she continued to follow Constance.

When she entered the bedroom, Charity was impressed by the large bed with a canopy. The room was furnished with two highboys at each end of the room as well as a desk, a dressing table and mirror, and a brightly covered sofa and matching chairs near the large window which afforded a beautiful view of the grounds. The floor was covered with colored rugs, and the windows had heavy curtains made of brocade that displayed style and elegance to the entire room. Her new bedroom was many times more attractive and elegant than the room at Kensington Hall. She knew in her heart that Constance was treating her as a friend and guest rather than a member of the hired help.

Constance told Charity that she would send a servant to Kensington Hall to fetch her belongings, and she promised to accompany her to the milliner's shop to purchase a new hat and to assist her in choosing a gown for the upcoming ball.

After helping her get settled in her new dwelling, she told Charity to rest and said she would send a servant to inform her when it was supper time.

"You shall meet my wonderful Alexander at dinner. He is anxious to make your acquaintance. But for now, please relax and enjoy your new surroundings," said Constance as she left her friend's presence.

Charity looked around the room and she settled down on the sofa and put her head on a pillow and closed her eyes. She was still recovering from all that had taken place in the past few hours, and she was still in shock from what she had learned about Lydia. She could not believe that Mrs. Kensington would hire and associate with a woman of her nature. She was worried about poor innocent Charles living under the same roof with that horrid woman. She convinced herself that Mrs. Kensington would not let any harm come to her precious Charles. She had her loyal servants, and now the assistance of the dutiful Nicholas Biddle who seemed to care for Charles. She began to think about Colonel Parker and was curious about his whereabouts. All of these thoughts exhausted her, so she decided to find solace by taking a little nap.

She soon fell asleep. However, her peaceful rest was interrupted when she was awakened by someone whispering the name Elizabeth in her ear while gently caressing her face. The voice was very soothing, kind, and familiar. As she opened her eyes to see who it was, to her astonishment, she saw that it was Colonel Parker. Startled by his appearance, she quickly rose from the sofa.

As she attempted to reach out to him, the colonel ran from the room. In her effort to chase after him, she tripped over her petticoat and fell to the floor. After rising from the clumsy fall, she hurried out into the hallway to seek out the colonel. She looked about in a flustered state, but he was nowhere to be found.

Chapter 19

After seeing no sign of the colonel or anyone in the hallway, she returned to her room and could not believe who she had just seen. To her knowledge, Colonel Parker had left Kensington Hall shortly before Charlotte's death and was not heard or seen from since then. And now he appears to her out of nowhere while she is residing at Singleton Lodge. How could this be? How did he find her and why did he run away? She stood in the middle of the room while pondering the possibility that perhaps she could have been dreaming since the colonel was on her mind before she fell asleep.

She took hold of the doll and went to look out the window. As she stared into the distance, darkness had fallen upon the grounds of Singleton Lodge. Then to her surprise, she caught a glimpse of the ghostly couple moving about among the trees. She had not seen these apparitions in quite some time. As she watched the spirits of the young couple move about, she recalled that in the past every time she would see these spirits something terrible would occur. Were these ghosts trying to send her a warning? What inevitable event was about to happen?

She closed her eyes tightly and said a prayer to maintain her sanity. When she opened her eyes and looked out the window, the apparitions were gone. She felt a sigh of relief take control of her body.

As she sat down on the sofa, she was staring at her doll, and memories of her mother and Patience began to flood her mind. She missed both of them so deeply. Her beloved mother was buried in a church graveyard while Patience was in her studio in London. Perhaps after she received her inheritance, she should embark on a journey back to England to visit Patience. She thought that she may find happiness in London while leaving behind the misery and sadness she had encountered in America. She sat quietly on the comfortable sofa in the dark and waited for a servant to call her for supper.

It wasn't long before Constance came to her room. She graciously escorted her to the dining room where they found Constance's husband patiently waiting for them.

He was well mannered and sophisticated in his appearance. He wore an outfit consisting of close-fitting silk breeches fastened with silver buckles at the knees. His shirt was white linen with lace ruffles at the neck and wrists. Over his shirt, he wore a long, brightly colored coat with wide, flowing sides decorated with gold braid and several rows of fancy buttons. Silk stockings and shoes with silver buckles completed his outfit. When Constance made the introductions, her husband gave Charity a polite greeting and kissed her hand.

"Charity Chastine, it is a pleasure to make your acquaintance. My Constance has told me many wonderful things about you. Please accept our humble and warmest welcome to Singleton Lodge. Our home is now your home," replied Alexander.

His warm and sincere greeting made Charity feel very much at ease. She thanked him for his generosity and his invitation to reside at his home. He responded by telling her that any friend of Constance's is a friend of his and is always welcome at Singleton Lodge.

The three of them sat down to a delicious meal in the elegant dining room. The furniture and decorations were imported from England and from his estate in Virginia. Many of the pieces were family heirlooms including the beautiful china dishes and crystal glasses. They engaged in polite and cheerful conversation. Both Constance and Alexander were delightful hosts.

After finishing their meal, they went into the sitting room to have tea. But their peaceful and lovely gathering was suddenly interrupted by the arrival of Mrs. Kensington who was shouting at the housekeeper, demanding to see Charity.

"I have come for Miss Charity Chastine. I demand that you get her at once. I will not be kept waiting a minute longer."

The housekeeper tried to calm Mrs. Kensington and told her to be patient while she announced her arrival. When the servant entered the sitting room, Alexander told Charity to stay calm and said he would attend to Mrs. Kensington who to everyone's surprise followed the servant and boldly made her way into the sitting room. She gave Constance and Alexander a disdainful glare, and then turned her attention to Charity.

"I do not approve of you taking lodging with the Caruthers. I was shocked when a servant from Singleton Lodge came to my home inquiring about your personal belongings. Your place is at Kensington Hall with me and my precious Charles. Please my dear, come home with me. My carriage is waiting outside," implored Mrs. Kensington.

"Charity is my friend and a guest in our home," said Constance while standing next to Charity. "She has decided to stay with my husband and me for an indefinite period of time. She needs to be in the company of people who love and respect her."

"I did not ask for your opinion," replied Mrs. Kensington. "You and your husband have no right to take Charity away from me and Kensington Hall. She was treated well at my home until you and your associates poisoned her mind against me with outrageous tales of the fabricated actions of one of my dedicated and trusted servants."

Before Mrs. Kensington could finish, Alexander asked Charity to tell her employer of her decision to stay with him and Constance. Mrs. Kensington's anger and foreboding appearance was making Charity nervous, and she was having difficulty speaking. She talked slowly and explained that it was her decision to leave Kensington Hall and take advantage of the Caruthers' hospitality. She also told Mrs. Kensington that Charles no longer needed her for he had his tutor Nicholas Biddle, and that she refused to stay under the same roof with Lydia Johnson.

"You are an ungrateful young girl. I extended generosity and kindness to you when you had no place to go after the fire destroyed

Andrews' Tavern. Charles became so fond of you especially after Charlotte's death, and now you turn your back on us. This is highly unacceptable and inexcusable," ranted Mrs. Kensington.

She turned to Alexander and Constance, and with a vile look in her eyes, uttered some idle but awful threats. A calm and complacent Alexander with the assistance of the housekeeper escorted an angry Mrs. Kensington to the main entrance.

"I am not a woman to be trifled with or made a fool of as my previous adversaries have learned. You have not seen or heard the last from me," scowled Mrs. Kensington.

After she was gone, her threatening words were echoing in Charity's ears. She sat down and began to apologize to Constance and Alexander for the upheaval and causing them to become enemies with Mrs. Kensington.

Constance put her arms around her friend and reassured her that everything would turn out well and Mrs. Kensington's idle and petty threats had no merit for concern. She then had one of the servants take Charity to her room, and she said, "I shall be up momentarily to say good night."

Charity left Alexander and Constance in the sitting room and went upstairs to her room. She felt safe at Singleton Lodge, and for the first time since Lieutenant Bradford had gone away, she was in the company of good friends.

Upon Mrs. Kensington's return home, she retreated to the library unaware that Lydia Johnson was lurking in the shadows of the first floor. Mrs. Kensington paced the floor in an agitated manner. Then her solitude was interrupted by Simon Blackwell who entered the room through the secret passage.

"I am in no mood to deal with you at this moment. Go back from wherever you came from. I will see you tomorrow," replied a disgusted Mrs. Kensington.

"My lovely matriarch, what seems to be troubling you? Has one of your pawns been seized by your opponent? How could you let such a careless move take place?" laughed Simon.

"If you must know, Charity Chastine has allowed herself to be coerced and deceived by the lies of that willful Alexander Caruthers and his pathetic wife Constance Singleton Caruthers. Charity has chosen to live with them at Singleton Lodge. I believe their friendship and alliance will prove to be trouble for me as well as for you, my horrid friend."

"Please, explain yourself woman. I am most intrigued by your statement."

"I do not wish to elaborate on the matter tonight. I am retiring for the evening and will deal with the situation in the morning. Now, I will take my leave."

When Mrs. Kensington had gone, Simon helped himself to a carafe of wine that was on the table. He drank while contemplating his next move, and unaware that Lydia Johnson was nearby, spying on him.

After saying her prayers and extinguishing the candle by the bedside, she got into bed and burrowed under the warm quilt. Charity tossed about for some time but eventually fell asleep unaware that someone was surreptitiously watching her from inside the room.

The next morning a servant brought a basin of water to her room. She opened the drapes to let the sunshine in, and then she was kind to help Charity get dressed. While the servant assisted her, Charity engaged in conversation with the young woman. The woman's name was Caroline. She said, "My parents named me after the Carolina colonies." She was a pleasant and genteel person with ash blond hair and tiny freckles on her face. After she had finished helping Charity get dressed, she politely excused herself and went down the hall.

As Charity peered from the doorway, she saw Caroline go to a room at the very end of the hall, knock at the door and utter the word "Lizzie." Charity was taken aback when she heard the name "Lizzie." She instantly thought of Elizabeth Higgins because that was what her father Mr. Higgins called his daughter. A few moments later the door opened, and a man, whose face she could not get a clear view of, let her in, and then quickly shut the door.

Overcome with curiosity, Charity tiptoed down the hall and stood by the door of the room. She placed her ear to the door in an attempt to hear voices. The voices were muffled, but it sounded like several people were in the room. As she continued to listen, suddenly the knob began to turn, so she hurried back to her room where she remained concealed with the door slightly ajar as she looked to see who was coming down the hall.

As the person got closer, she saw that it was Alexander Caruthers. His brightly colored coat with gold buttons was not difficult to notice. After he was gone, she left her room, planning to return to the door of the room down the hall when a voice called out to her.

"Good morning, my dear friend. Did you sleep well last night?" inquired Constance. "I am on my way to get you and escort you downstairs for breakfast. I see that you are going in the wrong direction."

"Good morning, Constance. Yes, I slept very well last night. Thank you for asking. I must apologize for not going in the right direction, but your lovely home is so grand that I am a bit confused."

Constance graciously accepted the explanation and said, "With the new rooms even I sometimes forget where I am going."

As they made their way downstairs, she turned her head for a moment and then glanced at the door, wondering who was in that room and why Caroline used the name "Lizzie?"

In the dining room, they were joined by Jean-Luc and Louise already seated at the table along with Alexander. Both Jean-Luc and Alexander greeted Charity while rising from their chairs. Louise smiled and then moved one seat closer to Alexander. Constance and Alexander sat at either end of the table with Jean-Luc and Charity on one side and Louise on the other. Louise was occupied admiring the beautiful chandelier hanging from the ceiling. Alexander remarked he had it brought to Singleton Lodge from his estate in Virginia. Alexander and Louise engaged in small talk over breakfast, and Jean-Luc entertained Constance and Charity with tales about his service in the French navy.

As Jean-Luc spoke, Charity found his conversation very interesting while seeing another side to his personality that was warm and sincere. His actions and manners at breakfast did not resemble the behavior she had witnessed a few weeks back when he and Monsieur Monnerat were involved in that terrible fight. After the meal, Alexander, Louise, and Jean-Luc excused themselves and went to the drawing room to discuss business, leaving Charity alone with Constance.

"That Louise is one of the men. My husband seems to be taken with her zest for adventure and her strong political beliefs. I guess she feels somewhat threatened by women and prefers conversing with the opposite sex. I do not mind her choice just as long as she keeps her hands off my husband," sneered Constance.

"Alexander seems very devoted to you, and he is quite a gentleman. I am certain that no other woman can capture his heart."

"My dear Charity, you always know the kind words to say. Thank you for putting me at ease. Now my friend, we are going to New Haven to pay a call to Laura Corday. She is doing wonderful work with the less fortunate, and we must go and see for ourselves what all the fuss is about."

Constance sent for the carriage, and within a short time they were on their way to New Haven. Charity was curious about what Alexander, Louise, and Jean-Luc were doing at Singleton Lodge and about the room down the hall from her room, but she did not reveal her thoughts to Constance who was enjoying the carriage ride.

When they arrived at Bickford Mansion where Laura Corday was residing, they saw a group of children playing outside under the watchful eyes of a handful of servants. The driver helped them out of the carriage, and Charity followed Constance to the front door. As Constance was about to knock, the door opened, and they were greeted by a tall gentleman. The tall gentleman took them down a long hallway and into a cozy sitting room where they waited for Laura. As they waited in the sitting room, a man dressed in a clergyman's outfit entered. He had dark hair and dark eyes to match. He introduced himself as Reverend Davenport, and explained that his church was down the street. He said, "The members of my congregation and I admire Laura Corday for her assistance and generosity towards the less fortunate. Miss Corday's benevolent efforts to give shelter, food, and clothing to the unwanted and misfortune souls of our society are exemplary acts of Christian kindness. The members of my congregation are very pleased to know her. She has shown that any one can find redemption and share his or her good fortune with others," said Reverend Davenport in a condescending manner.

While he talked, Charity thought it a bit odd and improper for him to be referring to Laura's actions as repentance for any of her past indiscretions. She also wondered why he was talking about Laura to Charity and Constance—two strangers whom he was unacquainted with.

His presence made them feel somewhat uneasy. Constance took the initiative by changing the conversation and talking about the possibility of a national bank and the terrible events in Paris. The Reverend seized the moment to express his opinions on both subjects.

"A national bank may succeed or it may fail. People need to take care of their own finances. Greed is the root to all evil, but sadly, money is vital for survival in this cold and cruel world. Please, let us not speak of the horrific occurrences in Paris, a city of beauty and culture now transformed into a place of corruption, violence, and death," he replied with disapproval in his voice.

They were spared from any further discussions by Reverend Davenport when Laura entered the room. She gave Constance and Charity a cheerful greeting and expressed how delighted she was to see them. Constance apologized for the unannounced visit and told Laura that she and her husband wanted to offer financial assistance with her charitable endeavor. Laura was elated by Constance's willingness to help. She graciously took them on a tour of the place and introduced them to her staff and some of the women and children residing at Bickford Mansion. Reverend Davenport accompanied them, and he seemed quite taken with Constance.

Charity saw a little boy sitting under a tree with his head between his knees. As she approached him, he raised his head, and tears were flowing down his cheeks. Laura whispered to Charity that his name was Seth and both his parents perished in a shipwreck. He had been living with an abusive uncle who drank himself to death.

"We found him wandering the streets covered in dirt from head to toe. When we took him in, he would hide in the corner like a frightened animal." explained Laura. "He does not want to play with the other children. He has finally showed some interest in eating and bathing. I cannot imagine the agonies he must have suffered."

"The boy's parents were Loyalists," said Reverend Davenport. "They were on their way to plead their case to have their confiscated property returned when their ship met with a terrible storm. It is a tragedy that this young boy has to suffer for his parents indiscretions. These Loyalists deserve no mercy for their allegiance to the monarch of England who treated the colonists in a wretched manner."

Constance and Charity stared at each other in dismay upon hearing the way Reverend Davenport was speaking. Embarrassed and irritated by the Reverend's unsympathetic words, Laura recommended that they go inside to take tea with her.

Before she left the little boy, Charity took a lace handkerchief and wiped the tears from his eyes. She told him to keep it. As she walked away, the little boy chased after her and tugged at her petticoat. As she bent down, he embraced her. Constance, Reverend Davenport, and Laura stood speechless in amazement.

"He has never responded to any of us in the way he has to you. You have a special presence about you, Miss Charity. Please feel free to visit again," said a sincere Laura.

Charity told Laura that it would be her pleasure to return for another visit.

As they made their way inside, Charity kept looking back at the little boy who had returned to his place under the tree. He reminded her so much of Charles who she cared for deeply.

After they had tea, Constance announced that it was time for them to take their leave. Laura thanked them for the visit and extended a return invitation which they promised to accept. Reverend Davenport said farewell to them but stayed behind while Laura escorted Constance and Charity to the door.

As they got into the carriage, Constance remembered leaving her purse on the chair. Charity told her not to worry for she would go back inside to retrieve it. When she went inside, she went directly to the sitting room. As she approached the room, she overheard Reverend Davenport and Laura speaking.

"Laura dearest, I know that you have only good intentions for this place and the poor souls that live here. It would be a pleasure to have Miss Chastine visit again, but you must never let her friend Mrs. Caruthers enter the doors of this place ever again. Her husband Alexander Caruthers is a sinful man in dire need of repentance," ranted the Reverend.

Upon hearing Reverend Davenport's harsh words, Charity was shocked and stood very still, but the floor she was standing on made a creaking sound revealing her presence. Both Laura and the Reverend looked up at her. At that moment, she found herself staring into the dark and mysterious eyes of a minister who had great contempt for her friend's husband.

Chapter 20

As Reverend Davenport and Laura looked up at Charity, she politely explained that she had returned to recover Constance's purse which she left on the chair. She saw the purse and quickly retrieved it, and then said farewell. She hurried to the waiting carriage, got in, and gave the purse to Constance. She did not mention what she had overheard to her friend.

As the carriage pulled away, Charity put her head out the window and stared at the building. She caught a glimpse of the Reverend standing in the window with a stern and somewhat malevolent facial expression that gave her the chills. As they traveled down the road, she was relieved to be on their way back to Singleton Lodge.

When they arrived at Singleton Lodge, Charity told Constance that she was feeling a bit tired from their morning excursion, so she excused herself and went to her room.

As she approached her bedroom door, she glanced down the hall and saw Caroline coming out of the locked room. When she saw Charity, she smiled as she walked past her and made her way downstairs. As Charity continued down the hall, a servant came out of her room.

"I have put fresh linens on the bed and filled the basin on the night table with water, Miss. Will you need anything else at the moment?" the servant asked.

"No, thank you. I am very well for now."

After the servant had left, Charity went into her room and closed the door. She removed her shoes and shawl, took a hold of the doll and rested on the bed. She was thinking about the harsh comments Reverend Davenport had made about Constance's husband. To her, Alexander had seemed to be a kind and generous man with a gentle spirit. He had been very gracious and hospitable to her, and she had noticed that he tended to go out of his way to please Constance. Could it be that Reverend Davenport dislikes Alexander because he was a former slave owner, or did the Reverend have knowledge of another sin that Alexander had committed? Finding no answers to her questions, she closed her eyes and soon fell asleep with the doll in her hand.

At Kensington Hall, Judith Fairchild had arrived to pay Mrs. Kensington a visit. Unfortunately, Judith's visit was not a social call. Lydia Johnson announced Judith's arrival and showed her to the drawing room where Mrs. Kensington was enjoying a cup of tea. Lydia pretended to leave, but she remained behind and eavesdropped from out in the hall. Judith stood tall while staring at her friend with a scornful expression.

"My friend Judith, it is so lovely to see you. Please sit and join me in a cup of tea," said Mrs. Kensington.

"I certainly will not take tea with a traitor. How dare you introduce that wretched girl Honoria Noble to my son Ethan? From what I have learned about her, she is from inferior birth and has a disdainful reputation for flirting with other men. I was told by reliable sources that you had befriended her, and it was here at Kensington Hall that Ethan, while on his way to visit you, found her lying on the ground outside your home. Are you suffering from insanity?" asked Judith angrily.

"Judith, I resent you questioning who I associate with as well as my sanity. I can assure you that my mind is fully intact; and as for

Honoria, she is a lovely young lady in need of companionship and guidance. Do not believe malicious rumors."

"Is it a rumor that she is the descendant of a Salem witch?"

Mrs. Kensington stared at her agitated friend and sipped her tea. Then she laughed, causing Judith great vexation.

"How dare you mock me? Could it be that you are you filled with grief over your daughter's death and are wishing for me to lose my son to a commoner with an unscrupulous past? Are you allowing jealousy to end a very long friendship? I implore you to assist me in getting Honoria out of my son's life. Ethan admires you and he will listen to you. Please talk to him and tell him that he needs to end his relationship with Honoria who seems to have him under her control," begged Judith.

"I shall do no such thing. Ethan is old enough to make his own decisions. I will certainly not stand in the way of his happiness. Be grateful that he has found someone who loves him. My poor daughter entered into a loveless marriage, and she died tragically without her husband by her side."

"I do not need to hear about your daughter's sad story. Since you will not assist me, I have nothing more to say to you. Our friendship is no more. Good day to you, Phoebe."

As Judith Fairchild abruptly left the room, a sly Simon Blackwell entered through the terrace doors. He had a smirk on his face from the conversation he had just overheard from outside on the terrace. He mocked Mrs. Kensington for making enemies with Mrs. Fairchild and he admitted to her that her friend's allegations were true. He then helped himself to a cup of tea and sat down on the sofa next to a poker face Mrs. Kensington.

"Forget about my affairs," said Mrs. Kensington. "I am glad you have come. I have it on good authority that certain people are searching for a treasure buried somewhere nearby. Are you interested in finding it?"

"My dear lady, you have my undivided attention, so please tell me more," said Simon.

While Mrs. Kensington and her fiendish companion conversed, an upset Judith Fairchild was making her way through the hallway when she looked up and noticed a portrait of a woman that resembled Honoria Noble. As she studied the portrait, Lydia Johnson came up from behind.

"It is a striking portrait," said Lydia. "The woman in the portrait is Rebecca Noble, a young woman from Salem who was executed for witchcraft," replied Lydia.

"Legend has it that at her execution she cursed all the residents of Salem including her own family members for abandoning her. After she died, the villagers of Salem could hear a hideous laughter every time the wind blew and her family members suffered from a severe ringing sound of laughter in their ears. Some of them were reported to have gone mad and took their own lives."

"Where did this portrait come from and how did Mrs. Kensington come to have it in her possession?" asked a curious Judith.

"After Rebecca died, a man who was secretly in love with her, painted her portrait from memory and kept it as his sole possession until his death several years later. The man's name was Samuel Bennett, an ancestor of my employer, Mrs. Kensington."

Upon hearing Lydia's story, a deviously curious Judith Fairchild pressed Lydia for more details. Lydia went on to say that Samuel did not want anything to happen to the portrait of his beloved Rebecca, so he put a curse on it. The curse was that if anyone was to destroy the portrait, suffering and death would be the fate of all Rebecca's and Samuel's descendants.

"What a very disturbing but interesting story! Who told you this incredible story?" inquired Judith who listened attentively as Lydia continued to speak.

"The other day when one of the servants was cleaning the portrait, she nearly unintentionally damaged it causing Mrs. Kensington to become frantic. I had to step in before she attacked the poor servant. After I had calmed my employer, I asked her why she became so angry, and taking me into her confidence, she told me the truth."

"And now you have told me. What a confidant you are!" remarked Judith sarcastically. "My visit here today has not been in vain after all."

Feeling satisfaction, Judith Fairchild left Kensington Hall. On the carriage ride home, she began to devise a plan to deal with her son's undesirable companion and her disloyal friend Mrs. Kensington. In the meantime, Lydia Johnson resumed eavesdropping on Mrs. Kensington and Simon discussing details about the treasure Lydia was also determined to find.

At Singleton Lodge, Charity was awakened by a knock at her door. She rose from her bed and went to open the door. It was Caroline informing her that the noon day meal was being served in the dining room, and Constance and Alexander requested her presence.

Charity told Caroline to tell them she would join them momentarily. She washed her face and looked in the mirror to fix her hair. Suddenly, she saw the reflection of Colonel Parker staring at her with an icy glare in his eyes while calling her Elizabeth. She was startled, so she screamed.

The colonel continued to stare at her. Then without warning he disappeared from her sight by abruptly leaving the room. As she went in pursuit of him, she was greeted by Constance and Alexander who had heard the scream, and came to her room.

"Miss Charity, are you in trouble? What caused you to scream?" inquired a concerned Alexander.

Charity did not feel comfortable revealing the truth, so she fibbed telling them she thought she had seen a mouse crawl under the bed. Alexander was gracious to check under the bed, but he found nothing. She confessed that perhaps she had been mistaken. Constance took her by the hand, and they went downstairs. Alexander excused himself and went down the hall to the locked room. Charity thought to herself, *Could Colonel Parker be in that room? Why is he here at Singleton Lodge and why is his presence a secret?*

At Winchester Park, Judith Fairchild arrived home to find her son Ethan and Honoria taking a stroll in the gardens. She watched them closely through the terrace doors in the drawing room. As she spied on them with grave disapproval, her sister Evelyn entered the room.

"My dear Judith, where have you been? Ethan and Honoria wanted to take a walk about the grounds with you," said Evelyn.

"I went to pay a call to Phoebe Kensington. That woman is no longer my friend, and I forbid anyone in this house to have anything to do with her," replied an irritated Judith.

Surprised by her sister's statement, Evelyn asked what had transpired during the visit, but Judith refused to elaborate. She then went outside to join Ethan and Honoria while Evelyn watched from the terrace doors with great concern.

While taking their stroll, Honoria saw a garter snake slither quickly past her feet, and she screamed from fright. Ethan reassured her that the small snake was harmless and had gone into the bushes.

While holding onto Ethan's arm, a shaken Honoria told Ethan that she feared snakes because they were scary in appearance and represented evil. Ethan hugged her and told her that she was safe.

As they continued their walk, Judith Fairchild who deliberately remained in the distance was delighted to overhear Honoria admit her fear of snakes. She then made her way towards the house while contemplating to commit a heinous deed.

At Singleton Lodge, Charity was sitting alone on a bench, embracing the tranquil surroundings. Everything seemed very peaceful for the moment.

She wrapped the shawl tightly around her as the wind gently blew.

She could not get Colonel Parker out of her mind. He had appeared to her on two occasions since her arrival, but he had vanished as quickly as he had appeared.

"Would you like some company?" asked Jean-Luc as he approached the bench.

"Oh, it is good to see you. I was just sitting here enjoying the fresh air and staring at the grounds," Charity replied. "Please, sit next to me."

Jean-Luc did not hesitate to accept her invitation. He told her that he and Louise had come to pay a call to Alexander and that Louise was inside with Alexander and Constance discussing plans for the ball. Their conversation did not interest him, so he decided to step outside and take a walk. He was glad to have stumbled upon her sitting alone. He inquired about how she was adjusting to her new home while assuring her that he and Alexander would keep her safe.

When Charity asked him to elaborate more about Lydia Johnson and her cruel acts as they pertained to her, Jean-Luc told her to dismiss Lydia from her mind and enjoy the hospitality of Mr. and Mrs. Caruthers. Then he informed her that after he and Louise had finished working on a task for Alexander, he was considering settling down in North Haven. He admitted that a small agricultural town was most agreeable to him in comparison to the large, crowded, and noisy city where he had previously resided.

Charity was enjoying their conversation, and she must admit that Jean-Luc was an interesting man to converse with. His voice was mild mannered, and he was knowledgeable in his topics. The conversation was interrupted by Louise who came to get him. She smiled at Charity while grabbing Jean-Luc's arm in an attempt to make him rise. She informed him that urgent business was causing them to take their leave.

"It has been a pleasure. Hope to see you again very soon," Jean-Luc said as he and Louise walked away.

As they left her presence, Charity stared at both of them and commented to herself that she was feeling a connection to Jean-Luc who on the past two occasions had shown her a kinder, intelligent, and gentlemanly side of his personality. Louise, however, gave her reason not to trust her. She seemed to proudly display a dangerous arrogance and tone of voice.

As daylight began to surrender to the dark of night, Charity sat in the library reading a book by candlelight. She had not finished the second page when Constance entered with two servants carrying a beautiful lace gown in their hands. Constance showed her friend the gown and asked her opinion. When Charity told her that she liked it very much, she responded, "It is yours to wear at the upcoming ball." For a moment, Charity was speechless from the surprise, and then said, "I am so grateful for your generosity. I shall be very pleased to wear such a beautiful gown." Constance then ushered Charity upstairs to her room so she could try on the gown.

At Winchester Park, Ethan and Honoria were taking a leisure stroll through the great hall. Ethan was showing Honoria the portraits of his relatives that lined the walls. He mentioned their names and told her a humorous story about each one. Honoria laughed. Her laughter enticed Ethan, and it was one of the many fine qualities that he admired about her.

A servant came to get Ethan and said his father wanted to see him. Ethan told Honoria to go to the drawing room and wait for him. Before departing, he kissed Honoria on the hand.

An elated Honoria left the great hall and made her way to the drawing room. As she approached the entrance, she heard Judith Fairchild and her sister Evelyn Winchester engaged in an intense conversation. Enticed by the conversation, Honoria listened by the door.

"My dear sister, after spending much time with Ethan and Honoria, I believe in my heart that there is genuine love and admiration between the two of them. I have never seen my nephew this happy in a very long time. He is very taken with Honoria, and she with him. In all honesty, she has never once displayed uncouth behavior or ill treatment towards my nephew or any of us. On the other hand, you, my sister, have been very disdainful in your treatment of her. Let your son be happy," implored Evelyn.

"How dare you challenge my judgment of that young girl who is from inferior birth and has a past that will bring ruin and shame to the good name of Fairchild? How could you give your blessing for this unholy relationship? Do you not care for your nephew and his place in society?"

"My sister, are you forgetting the fact that Ethan is not a Fairchild by birth, but the son of a milliner's unwed daughter? I still have not forgiven you and Dr. Greenville for what you did that night when your baby died minutes after he was born. With the assistance of Dr. Greenville who you bribed, you took a healthy baby boy from his birth mother and switched her child with your dead son," recalled a sorrowful Evelyn. "I wish to God that I was there to have foiled your sinful deed."

"I did what I had to do to secure my marriage and to ensure the survival of the Fairchild legacy. I gave a defenseless and innocent baby a chance to grow up in a household with love and unlimited advantages. The milliner's daughter went on to wed and had several children. There was no harm done," said Judith in a desperate attempt to defend her actions.

Evelyn threw up her hands and reminded her sister that her sin of the past will return to haunt her. She begged Judith to let Ethan and Honoria be together. She also warned her sister that if she interfered with their relationship, she may drive Ethan to choose between his mother and the woman he loves, leaving Judith out in the cold. Judith became angry with Evelyn and demanded that Evelyn leave her presence at once. Unable to reason further with her sister, Evelyn left the room. Honoria then made her way into the drawing room, closing the door behind her. She stood face to face with her formidable opponent. A startled and angry Judith told Honoria to leave, but she did not budge. Instead Honoria insolently revealed to Judith that she knew the truth about Ethan's parentage, and she would do everything in her power to maintain her relationship with Ethan while making certain that Judith pays for her past indiscretion.

"You are a wretched and despicable descendent of a witch. I loathe and despise you for what you are doing to my son and his family. You have no proof to your allegations, and I will do everything in my power to destroy you," threatened a vengeful Judith.

Honoria mocked Judith and said, "Ethan and I will live happily ever after without you." An enraged Judith with tears in her eyes stormed out into the hallway, leaving a triumphant Honoria alone in the drawing room.

Feeling overjoyed from her confrontation with Judith, Honoria sat down on the sofa and began to contemplate what her life would be like as Mrs. Ethan Fairchild and mistress of Winchester Park. While she was contemplating her future, she was unaware the terrace doors from behind her slowly opened, and two hands carrying a sack reached into the room and opened the sack, releasing a snake that slithered under the sofa where Honoria was sitting.

After trying on the gown and having Constance fuss over her, Charity and the servants left her alone in the room. She sat at the desk and decided to write a letter to Patience. As she began writing, she went to get the doll. She felt it only appropriate to have the doll Patience gave her on the desk while she wrote the letter. She looked about the entire room, but the doll could not be found. Instead, she found a piece of paper lying on the floor. She took it into her hands and read it. To her surprise, the words read: *Elizabeth, please help me.*

As she stared at the note, she did not know what to do. Then she came to the realization that someone needed assistance. In this case, she believed it to be Colonel Parker. She decided to wait until everyone had gone to bed, and then she would make her way to that room at the end of the hall. Hopefully, she would gain access and find out once and for all who was in there.

She put the note in a drawer of the desk and occupied the time by writing the letter to Patience. She was also concerned about the doll that seemed to be missing. Was there a connection between the disappearance of the doll and this mysterious note? She had a terrible feeling that she would soon learn the truth.

At Winchester Park, Ethan joined Honoria in the drawing room. When he entered, he sat on the sofa next to his young love. She put her arms around him and they kissed. He looked into her eyes and told her that she was beautiful. Honoria began to blush from his compliment.

Ethan rose from the sofa and went over to a table to pour a glass of water. He then turned towards Honoria and asked if she would like a glass of water. But as he looked in her direction, he saw a snake slowly moving about Honoria's feet. Ethan spoke in a soft voice warning Honoria to remain absolutely still. A terrified Honoria did not move. As the snake was about to coil itself around Honoria's ankles, a fast thinking Ethan leaped towards the sofa while trying to stomp on the snake with his boots. Honoria screamed in terror and rose from the sofa as the snake bit Ethan in the leg.

Honoria's loud screams made the snake slither back under the sofa. A few moments later, a handful of servants along with Caleb Fairchild came running into the room. Honoria frantically explained how Ethan had been bitten by a snake. Caleb instructed two of the male servants to bring Ethan into the next room. Caleb then closed the door to the drawing room and instructed another servant to bring him a knife from the kitchen and a bottle of whiskey. Caleb knew what to do from his experience assisting on the battlefield during the war. He had watched physicians treat soldiers suffering from snake bites.

"I must cut around the wound and drain the poison out before it kills my son," said Caleb in an agitated state. "We must hurry. I will not let my son die."

Honoria waited outside the room while Caleb attended to his task at hand. In the meantime, Evelyn Winchester had arrived and a tearful Honoria told her what had happened. She embraced Honoria and suggested she say a prayer and keep good thoughts.

As Evelyn and Honoria held a vigil outside the room, a very disappointed and disturbed Judith Fairchild stayed hidden in the shadows of the hallway while fretting over the fate of her son.

At Kensington Hall, Lydia Johnson was sitting in her room admiring the diamond she had stolen from Monsieur Monnerat. She recalled with delight hitting him in the head with a rock as she stole the diamond out of his coat pocket. She assumed that she had killed him, but miraculously he survived only to die at the hands of his enemy Jean-Luc Tessier.

As Lydia was trying to decide what to do with the diamond, a servant knocked at the door and informed her that Mrs. Kensington wanted to see her. Startled by the servant's knock, Lydia dropped the diamond, and when it hit the floor, it shattered into pieces. As an enraged Lydia carefully studied the broken pieces, to her surprise, she noticed that the pieces were glass.

This diamond is a fake, she exclaimed to herself. *I should have known Mrs. Kensington would not be so careless as to let that pathetic Frenchman steal the real diamond. She tricked Monsieur Monnerat into believing he had purloined the diamond while she had the real one in her possession. What a clever woman.*

After cleaning up the broken glass, Lydia went to see her employer. As she approached the library, she peered in and saw Mrs. Kensington opening up a crown jewel box. To her delightful surprise, she saw Mrs. Kensington take a diamond out of the box and hold it in her hand. Lydia was now aware of the whereabouts of the real diamond and she made plans to steal it.

After waiting a few moments, Lydia intentionally made a noise that alerted Mrs. Kensington of her presence. A sly Mrs. Kensington hastily put the diamond into the crown jewel box just before Lydia made her entrance.

"You sent for me, Mrs. Kensington?" inquired Lydia.

"Yes, I did. I would like you to join me in a cup of tea and pleasant conversation," replied Mrs. Kensington as she held onto the crown jewel box.

"What a lovely box," complimented Lydia. "Does it have sentimental value for you?"

"Yes, and so does its contents," replied Mrs. Kensington as she placed the box down next to her and poured Lydia a cup of tea.

Lydia enjoyed her tea with Mrs. Kensington. She kept one eye on the crown jewel box while scheming how she would take her employer's precious belonging from her.

As the two women sat drinking their tea and conversing, Simon Blackwell was watching them closely from outside the terrace, carefully concealed in the shadows of the night.

After successfully removing the poison from the snake bite, Caleb had his son taken upstairs to his room. He instructed Ethan to get into the bed. Caleb told his son that he would stay by his bedside the entire night to make certain that he did not have any complications.

Once Ethan was in bed, Caleb let Honoria see him. Ethan reached out to Honoria and held her hand. Honoria was sorry that Ethan had been bitten, but she was relieved and grateful for his father's swift actions. Ethan asked Honoria to stay with him until he fell asleep, which she did wholeheartedly.

Downstairs in the drawing room, two of the male servants managed to trap the snake, chop off its head, and dispose of it. The men informed Caleb that it was a poisonous black snake. Caleb commended the men for their efforts and told them to make sure the terrace doors remained closed and latched, especially at night. He then went upstairs to check on Ethan.

A relieved Evelyn went to the library where she found a calm and complacent Judith sitting in a chair doing needlepoint. Judith smiled at her sister and continued with her task at hand. Evelyn was taken aback by Judith's somber behavior and was even more disturbed that Judith did not insist on seeing Ethan. Overcome with suspicion about how the snake found its way into the house, Evelyn craftily began to talk about the incident. At first Judith did not flinch, and then she politely told her sister to change the subject or sit in silence. Before she could say another word, the male servant Hastings entered the room and asked politely if he could have a word with Judith.

"My dear sister, would you be kind as to leave for a few minutes?" asked Judith graciously.

Evelyn agreed and smiled politely as she made her way out into the hall, but she remained behind and listened to a conversation that shocked her.

"You are a pathetic and incompetent fool," said Judith. "The snake was to bite Honoria, not my son. What happened in that room?"

Hastings replied, "I waited for Miss Noble to be alone, and then I released the snake into the room from the terrace doors as you instructed me. I watched from the terrace to make sure the deed would be completed. However, Master Ethan arrived, and when he saw the snake by the girl's feet, he tried to kill it by stomping on it. His act of heroism caused him to become the victim instead of Miss Noble. I killed the snake and disposed of it. Mr. Fairchild surmised that the snake had crawled in when the terrace doors were open. No one suspects a thing."

"For your sake, that better be true. I will never let anyone or anything harm my Ethan. Honoria was very fortunate to have escaped my wrath this time, but I promise you the next time she will not be so lucky," uttered Judith. "Now leave me to my solitude."

As Hastings left the library, Evelyn hid so she would not be seen. Once he was gone, a troubled Evelyn spied on her sister Judith who was sitting very peacefully working on her needlepoint. Evelyn was shocked by her sister's malicious scheme that could have ended tragically. She realized that Honoria was in grave danger at the hands of Judith a woman capable of evil and deadly intentions.

———————————

At Singleton Lodge, Charity waited patiently until everyone had gone to sleep. Once the house became very still, she rose from her bed, lit a candle, and made her way slowly and quietly down the hall. When she came to the room, she cautiously turned the knob and slowly opened the door. When she entered, she held the candle in front of her, and she saw a man sleeping in bed. She tiptoed over to the bed and shined the candle in his face. Her suspicions were confirmed when she saw that it was Colonel Parker. As she looked down upon the bed, she noticed that he had her doll in his hand. She tried painstakingly to retrieve it, but she was interrupted by the sound of footsteps coming towards the room. She hastily took refuge in an adjoining room and closed the door while leaving a tiny opening to see through.

The door opened, and a man carrying a lantern entered the room. He went over to the bed and checked on the colonel. After a few minutes, he left. Charity had not seen his face since he had not shine the light near his face and the room was very dark. She emerged from her hiding place and quietly made her way to the door. As she was about to open the door, she heard the sound of a key turning in the keyhole and footsteps retreating down the hall. When she tried to open the door, it was locked. She was now trapped in the room with the colonel who for some strange reason was a prisoner, and she had no way out.

Chapter 21

Since the door was locked and she had no means of escape, Charity took a blanket that was on a chair and wrapped it around her and she placed a pillow behind her head while sitting on the floor with her back against the wall. From this position, she watched Colonel Parker sleeping in bed. She could not believe what was happening at Singleton Lodge. These strange occurrences along with her sudden arrival here reminded her of Mrs. Kensington keeping her deranged husband hidden in the east wing of Kensington Hall. And now Colonel Parker, Mrs. Kensington's son-in-law, who was assumed to have left town with no intentions of returning, was living in the same house with Charity. The coincidence was uncanny.

Eventually her eye lids began to feel heavy with the presence of sleep engulfing her body, so she surrendered by closing her eyes, and soon fell asleep.

The next morning she was awakened by sunlight coming through the bedroom windows. She rose from her position and went over to check on the colonel who was still asleep.

Suddenly she heard someone unlocking the door. She hastily put back the pillow and blanket on the chair, and positioned herself up against the wall near the door.

As the door opened, she hid behind it. Someone entered and went over to the colonel's bed. While this person had his back to her, she quietly and inconspicuously left the room and hurried down the hall.

When she entered her room, she closed the door and breathed a sigh of relief. Then she was startled by the unexpected appearance of Caroline who was standing by the night table.

"Good morning, Miss, and how are you?" Did you sleep well last night?" she asked.

Charity told her that she was very well and had a good night's sleep. Caroline said that she became very concerned when she came to Charity's room with a basin of fresh water and did not find her. To relieve Caroline's worry, Charity told her she was in the library reading. Caroline looked at Charity with an odd expression as if she was not satisfied with the explanation. Then she left.

Charity watched from the door as Caroline made her way to the colonel's room. She heard her knock at the door and utter the name Lizzie before she went in.

Charity went over to the window, and the warm sunlight felt good on her body. As she glanced out the window, she saw two servants carrying what appeared to be a wooden coffin into the stables. She believed it was very strange, because to her knowledge no one at Singleton Lodge had died or was at death's door. Then the frightening thought came to her that perhaps someone was going to die. *Who could it be?* Chills ran down her spine, so she got into bed and burrowed under the quilt while lying awake with unpleasant things on her mind.

Everyone was still in bed at Kensington Hall except for the servants who were busy attending to their duties in the kitchen or outside. Lydia Johnson had gone into the library and closed the door behind her. She tried to open the desk, but it was locked. Using a letter opener, she tried to pry open the lock, but her efforts were futile. Angered by her failed attempt, she threw the letter opener on the floor when suddenly someone grabbed her from behind and placed an iron hook up to her throat. Startled and frantic, she asked, "Who are you?" The person whispered into her ear instructing her to turn around slowly and remain silent. When she turned around, she came face to face with Simon Blackwell.

"Do you know who I am?" inquired Simon.

"Of course I do. Your infamous reputation is well known around here," said a harsh Lydia. "You are Simon Blackwell, the man responsible for the death of poor Charlotte Parker, the daughter of Mrs. Kensington, the woman who you seem to have a strange alliance with. How did you survive that fall off Widow's Bluff?"

"If you must know, my wicked lady, I am a good swimmer. During the war I survived a shipwreck by keeping my head above water while clinging to a piece of wood until I was rescued. When my beloved Charlotte fell off the cliff and was swallowed up unmercifully by the sea, I was devastated and jumped into the sea to join her. I managed to survive, and searched endlessly for my beloved, but I could not find her. I severed my hand on a jagged rock and now I have this hook which is very useful."

After listening to Simon's pitiful story, Lydia confessed that she saw him and Mrs. Kensington talking in the library the other night. She also revealed to him she and he wanted the same things. When Simon asked what she meant, Lydia said that she longed to get her hands on a hidden treasure and a priceless diamond.

"You may want the same things that I am seeking, but how can you be of any assistance in finding what we both are seeking," asked a curious Simon.

Lydia boldly revealed that she had the treasure map in her possession which she stole from Colonel Parker, who had stolen it from his companions Monsieur Monnerat and the Marquis de Touvere. She also said that she believed Mrs. Kensington was in possession of a priceless diamond that was stolen from the monarchs of England by her late husband and a handful of thieves.

"I believe if we work together, we will find what we are both searching for," said Lydia. "But I fear time is running out, because others are seeking what we desire. Do not fear me, dear sir. You can trust me as I did not expose your presence to the authorities when I learned that you were alive and hiding at Kensington Hall."

"What a delightful wretched woman you are," responded a sarcastic Simon. "I get the sense that we are cut from the same cloth making us very agreeable partners. My scheming Lydia, I do believe we have a deal."

Simon extended his hook to Lydia that she felt awkward shaking, and then she poured two glasses of sherry, which they drank after toasting to their new alliance.

Their little celebration was interrupted by Mrs. Kensington who was knocking at the door and demanding to know why the door was closed, and who was in the library.

An exhausted Caleb Fairchild examined his son's wound while he was sleeping. Then he quietly went into the hall where he met a concerned Honoria. Honoria inquired about Ethan, and Caleb said he made it through the night, but they had to make sure the wound would not become infected.

"Infection and disease killed more soldiers on the battlefield than bullets or bites from wild animals," said Caleb. "But do not worry, my dear. Between my novice physician's skills and your love for my son, Ethan will survive and all will be right again."

Then he and Honoria went into Ethan's room while Judith Fairchild watched from not far away.

After breakfast, Charity decided to go for a walk outside. Constance did not join her because she was meeting with the household staff to finalize plans for the ball. Alexander agreed to graciously accompany her.

As they walked about the grounds, he was very charming and genteel as he amused her with stories about when he raced horses in

Virginia with Thomas Jefferson and James Madison. He then took her to the stables to show her two of his prized horses.

When they entered, two young stable hands were putting hay in the stalls while another was brushing one of the horses. She knew very little about horses, but Alexander was very kind in telling her about them. He had a stallion and a mare that he intended to mate.

"Many farmers use their horses as work animals to plow fields and carry supplies. But for someone of the gentry class like myself, horses are for riding, racing, and admiring," boasted Alexander. "Come Charity, I invite you to pet my mare."

Charity went up to the horse and gently patted its neck. The mare seemed very calm and receptive to her. Charity complimented both horses as they were very beautiful with their shiny coats and strong legs. Her compliment made him smile, and she got the impression that he cared for his horses like they were his children.

As they walked past an empty stall, Charity noticed a wooden coffin lying next to a pile of hay. She instantly recalled the coffin she saw the servants bringing into the stables earlier this morning. Seeing the surprise look on her face, Alexander gave her an explanation.

"Don't be frightened by that thing. I know you must think it is a bit unusual to see a coffin in a stable, but I must be candid with you, my dear Charity. It is for someone at Singleton Lodge who will die very soon."

Upon hearing his words, a cold wind began to blow while a sinister presence filled the air.

Chapter 22

Returning to the mansion, Alexander told Charity that he enjoyed their little outing and he was pleased to have introduced her to his horses. He took her hand, gently kissed it, and then went into the library closing the door behind him.

Charity went to the drawing room and sat in a chair next to the fireplace trying to warm herself. She had a terrible chill from being outside. While she sat by the warm and cozy fire, she stared at the blazing flames that were very mesmerizing. She could not forget what Alexander had told me about the coffin and that someone at Singleton Lodge was going to die. She was afraid to ask him the person's name, even though she was curious to know. *Who could it be?*

Constance came into the room followed by a servant carrying a tray of tea and cookies. After the servant left, Constance graciously poured her friend and then herself a cup of tea. She seemed very pleased as evident from the elated expression on her face.

"My dear Charity, the arrangements for the ball are now complete and I must say that everyone who has been invited will be attending. Alexander and I are most honored by the wonderful response. I am certain that many of the guests are curious about the renovations we have made to our lovely home," said Constance with pride. "It will be a magnificent celebration that no one shall ever forget."

Charity looked at Constance and smiled while holding the tea cup. Then she told her about the delightful walk she had with her husband and that he introduced her to his horses. Constance remarked that Alexander loved his horses and joked how sometimes she felt she was in competition with the horses when it came to Alexander's affections.

After exchanging some pleasantries, Charity mustered up the courage to tell Constance about the coffin in the stables and what her husband had told her. At first, she stared at Charity with a blank look, and then she giggled and said her husband had a strange sense of humor that was mysterious and odd at times. Her explanation did not put Charity's mind at ease about the coffin. Realizing she was not getting an answer, she changed the subject by inquiring about details concerning the ball.

Awhile later, after discussing the ball, a servant came into the room, and he handed Charity a note. The note was from Mrs. Andrews who informed her that Jesse had just returned home. Charity was glad for Mrs. Andrews, but she was disappointed when she did not mention anything about Lieutenant Bradford. Charity became quite concerned, so she decided to go to Andrews' Tavern to see Jesse and inquire about the lieutenant. Constance sent for the carriage, and she was soon on her way.

When Charity arrived at the tavern, Reverend Trumbull and Dr. Foote were coming out of the front door. They both gave her a jovial greeting while tipping their hats to her. And Dr. Foote was kind enough to assist her out of the carriage. They told her how happy they were that Jesse Andrews had returned home safely and that Mrs. Andrews' prayers had been answered. Neither of them mentioned a word about Lieutenant Bradford. They went on their way, and Charity went inside and was greeted by an overjoyed Mrs. Andrews who gave her a great big hug.

"Jesse, my wonderful son, has come home unharmed to me and the people of North Haven. I thank the Lord for my son's safe return," rejoiced Mrs. Andrews. "I can promise you that as long as I have the breath of life in me, my Jesse will not return to that valley. His place is here at the tavern with me."

"I am so happy for you that Jesse has come home. Is he around? May I see him so I can inquire about Lieutenant Bradford?" Charity asked with anticipation.

"Yes, by all means, you can see him. Let me go up to his room and get him. Please make yourself comfortable."

While Mrs. Andrews went to get her son, Charity sat down at one of the tavern tables. She began to recall the day she spent at Indian Lookout with the lieutenant and Charles. She could still see the three of them climbing that rugged mountain, standing at the summit admiring the majestic view, enjoying a delicious picnic near one of the caves, and talking and laughing for hours.

Her train of thought was interrupted when Jesse came up to her at the table. She rose from the chair, and he bowed to her. Then they both sat down while Mrs. Andrews brought them a pot of tea.

Jesse began to ramble on about his adventure in the valley and how beautiful the lands were. He talked about the many settlers he met including families from North Haven and Wallingford who were anxious to make new lives in that frontier. He also mentioned the trouble with Indians living in the valley, but he also said reports of brutal Indian attacks were grossly exaggerated. After listening to him for quite some time, Charity interrupted by asking about Lieutenant Bradford. At first he was silent. Then he looked at his mother who bowed her head. Then he spoke.

"The lieutenant and I served as guides for the new settlers, leading them into new territories. The lieutenant seemed very accustomed to the rugged terrain and challenging mountain passes that were dangerous to cross, and he managed to get everyone in his party to safety. He also was a good hunter who provided enough game for many of the settlers. There was never a day that we went hungry thanks to his efforts. One day we came upon an Indian camp that had been massacred by soldiers, and as we went through the ruins, we found the bodies of several men, women, and children."

Then Jesse became all choked up and had difficulty continuing with his story. After taking a few sips of his tea, he continued to speak with tears in his eyes. He sadly recalled how they found a young Indian squaw lying on the ground with a small Indian boy by her side. Both had been shot and their hair cut off. As the lieutenant stared at the dead woman, she looked very familiar to him. Around her neck was a locket. The lieutenant became agitated and took the locket from the dead woman. He opened it, read the inscription inside, and then gave a painfully loud yell.

"He looked at me with devastation in his eyes, and told me that the woman lying before us was his sister Hope. The locket was a birthday present he had given to his sister before she was abducted by Indians during a raid on their town before the war. We surmised that the little boy next to her was her son," said a somber Jesse.

Mrs. Andrews made the sign of the cross after hearing her son's tragic story while Charity sat back in her chair in complete silence.

Jesse added that he helped the lieutenant bury his sister and her son. He said the lieutenant did not speak for several days, and after guiding his party to their destination, he took his belongings and left, and he has not been seen or heard from since.

Charity was very sad by the news, and her heart ached with sorrow for Lieutenant Bradford who she had come to care for and ardently admire. He was a strong, confident, and handsome man who spoke kind words and was very protective of those he cared about. At numerous times he came to her rescue and she thought of him as a guardian angel. She could only imagine the agony he must be suffering, and the fact he had no one to comfort him bothered her greatly. How she wished he would come back to North Haven so she could help him deal with his grief.

Mrs. Andrews said she would ask Reverend Trumbull and the congregation to pray for Lieutenant Bradford and his loved ones. Then she excused herself to attend to a group of customers who had just entered the tavern. Charity thanked Jesse for telling her the truth and asked him to inform her if he should hear any news about the lieutenant. He nodded his head and then proceeded to tell her that he would never leave North Haven again. After finishing her tea, Charity said farewell to Jesse and Mrs. Andrews, and then took her leave.

On the carriage ride back to Singleton Lodge, she could not stop thinking about the lieutenant. She also could not fathom the pain he must be suffering, and once again she asked herself the agonizing and unanswered question of *why is man capable of such horrible deeds against his brother?*

———

Mrs. Kensington was sitting in the library when Lydia Johnson entered the room. She instructed Lydia to close the door and join her in a game of chess. Lydia admitted that she knew nothing of the game, but a crafty Mrs. Kensington told her that she would teach her. Lydia sat down at the table and appeared to be nervous, which did not surprise Mrs. Kensington who began to explain the rules of the game to her opponent.

Then she took the queen into her hands and said: "Do not let your opponent capture your queen because she is the most powerful piece and my favorite. As long as I have my queen, I always manage to win. My challengers have given me the title of the fairest one of all, but I like to think of myself as the master of the game. I reward my friends and punish my enemies. I find this practice very effective in getting what I want and securing the Kensington legacy. Are you my friend or my enemy, Mrs. Johnson?"

Shocked by Mrs. Kensington's question, Lydia Johnson took a few moments to respond. Then she answered by telling her employer she was her friend and pledged her loyalty to her and the Kensington name. Upon hearing her reply, Mrs. Kensington got up from the table, went over to the desk, and took out the crown jewel box. She walked over to a nervous Lydia and opened the box revealing its contents. Lydia stared with greedy delight at the Winfield diamond.

"I do believe that you and Simon Blackwell desire to have this beautiful diamond for yourselves. I am sorry to inform you, but it is mine, and anyone who thinks differently shall suffer my consequences. I know that you and Simon were in this room earlier today plotting together to find a treasure and take this precious jewel from me. Don't bother to deny it, because I heard your voices from behind the door and found the letter opener that you borrowed from me on the floor."

Lydia pleaded, "Simon surprised me when I was in here and I thought he was going to kill me so I made him believe I was on his side. We hid in the secret passage way so you wouldn't find us. Please forgive me. I am on your side."

Mrs. Kensington closed the box and placed it back in the desk. Then she told Lydia that she accepted her pitiful story and apology. She said that Simon's wicked personality entices anyone to succumb to his wishes in fear for their lives.

"To prove your renewed loyalty, you are going to help me get Simon Blackwell out of my life once and for all. The key to my plan is to locate that infamous treasure he and some other adversaries of mine are desperately seeking. I want Simon and the others to become engaged in a dangerous game which I shall orchestrate with your assistance, and then I will sit back and watch them destroy each other. In the end, I shall be triumphant while maintaining my title as master of the game," said Mrs. Kensington while holding the queen in Lydia's face.

Before Lydia could speak another word, their conversation was interrupted by a servant who announced the arrival of two visitors by the name of Lord and Lady Winfield. Mrs. Kensington was startled for a moment, and then asked Lydia to leave the room. She then instructed the servant to show Lord and Lady Winfield to the drawing room. Then she returned to the desk and took out the crown jewel box. She opened it and looked at the diamond.

"My precious jewel, your rightful owners have come to Kensington Hall quite unexpectedly and uninvited. Do not worry, for they shall never find you. You are safe in this box, and you are all mine," laughed a greedy Mrs. Kensington.

Charity returned to Singleton Lodge, and a servant informed her that Alexander and Constance had gone to visit a neighbor. She politely asked if she needed anything. Charity told her that she was fine and was going to her room to write a letter.

When she went upstairs, she heard voices coming from Colonel Parker's room. She hurried down the hall and put her ear to the door, desperately trying to hear what was being said. She heard the colonel begging for assistance, and the sound of furniture being moved about the room followed by a sudden silence.

A few moments later the door began to open, so she quickly moved away and hid behind a tall statue that was in the hall not far from the room. As she peeked from behind the statue, she saw Caroline emerge from the room. She appeared a bit agitated as she made her way downstairs. Then the door opened again, and this time a man came out. He locked the door and then turned around. As he stood at the door, to Charity's astonishment, she saw that it was Lieutenant Bradford. Charity did not move from her hiding place as she watched the lieutenant standing by the door to Colonel Parker's room. His appearance was the same as the first time she met him at Kensington Hall.

She was elated to see that he was alive and well, but also surprised to see him at Singleton Lodge. From what she could gather, the lieutenant was assisting in keeping watch over Colonel Parker, which was very similar to his task at Kensington Hall when he kept watch over Mr. Kensington. She made the assumption that the colonel was being held against his will by Alexander Caruthers, and she was more curious than ever to know the reason. She also wondered if Constance had a part to play in this devious scheme.

Caroline soon returned with a tray of food. The lieutenant unlocked the door and they went inside.

As she came out from behind the statue, she went up to the door and gently tried to open it, but it was locked. She put her ear to the door in an attempt to eavesdrop, but she heard nothing. She went back to her room with her mind flooded with feelings of shock, curiosity, and dismay. Although she knew for certain Lieutenant Bradford was back in town and was safe, but the reason he was at Singleton Lodge was a mystery to her.

At Kensington Hall, Lord and Lady Winfield were waiting patiently in the drawing room for their friend Mrs. Kensington. Lady Winfield admired the beautiful furnishings and rugs that decorated the room. She commented to her husband that Mrs. Kensington's home reflected style, elegance, and grace, just like its proprietor.

When Mrs. Kensington entered, she embraced both Lord and Lady Winfield and cunningly expressed that she was delighted and surprised to see them. She invited them to be seated, and she rang the bell for tea. Then she initiated the conversation by asking what brought them to America and to her humble abode.

"My dearest Phoebe, Thurston and I were longing to see you. We were most troubled and saddened over the deaths of your husband and daughter. How are you dealing with their losses? Lord Winfield and I are here to lend our support in your time of need," replied a sincere Lady Winfield.

Mrs. Kensington smiled at her friends and said she was managing with her grief in her own way, and she filled her days by concentrating on raising Colonel Parker's nephew Charles who was residing with her. She admitted Charles had been a perfect comfort for her grieving heart.

"My precious Charles has saved my life. He has given me something to live for every day. I could deal with the loss of my spouse, but the loss of my Charlotte is too great to bear. Children are to bury their parents and not the other way around," said a tearful Mrs. Kensington.

Then she changed the subject by inquiring about the happenings in London and the gatherings at St. James' Court. Lady Winfield filled Mrs. Kensington in on the events and remarked that the royal family in particular the King, missed her very much and longed for her to return for a visit. Lord Winfield agreed with his wife by providing testimony to the fact that the King was hoping they could convince their friend to return to London with them.

Mrs. Kensington was overjoyed by the King's request and told Lord and Lady Winfield she would take the King's request into consideration. Then she dutifully poured the tea while they engaged in pleasant conversation. She did not know that Simon Blackwell was carefully observing them and listening to their conversation.

Charity was sitting at the desk in her room, trying to finish writing a letter to Patience, but she was having difficulty concentrating. She wanted to seek out the lieutenant, embrace him, and tell him how happy she was he had returned. She also wanted to find out why he was keeping guard over Colonel Parker who seemed to be a prisoner at Singleton Lodge.

After procrastinating for some time, she finally finished the letter. Then Constance came to her room. She informed her that Mrs. Kensington had refused to send her belongings to Singleton Lodge unless she went to see her.

"That woman has no right to hold your personal belongings and make demands to you. My husband will send the authorities to her home and force her legally to surrender your belongings to you. Please, Charity, just give us your permission, so my husband may act, and let the authorities deal with Mrs. Kensington," implied Constance.

Charity thanked Constance for her concern and her husband's

good intentions of assisting her with her dilemma, but she decided to confront Mrs. Kensington herself. Constance admired her tenacity and agreed to let her go as long as she and two male servants accompanied her on her visit. She admitted wholeheartedly that she did not trust Mrs. Kensington nor did she want Charity coming in contact with that horrid Lydia Johnson. Charity accepted her offer, and within the hour they were on their way to Kensington Hall.

As the carriage approached the entrance to the sprawling estate of Kensington Hall, they saw an elegantly dressed couple leaving and getting into a waiting carriage. The driver waited until the other carriage had gone, and then pulled up to the front door. Constance and Charity emerged from the carriage with the two servants behind them.

They were greeted at the door by Lydia Johnson with a malevolent look on her face. Constance was very rigid and formal in her tone when she explained the purpose to their visit. Lydia reluctantly let them in, and then made them wait in the great hall.

While they were waiting, Constance told Charity to go upstairs with the servants and gather her belongings. She would wait downstairs and deal with Mrs. Kensington. Charity did not want to see her former employer, so she did what her friend had suggested.

While Charity was upstairs with the servants, Lydia returned and showed Constance to the drawing room where Mrs. Kensington was eagerly waiting. When Constance entered alone, Mrs. Kensington was at first disappointed and then demanded to know Charity's whereabouts. Constance insolently smiled at her and then took a look about the room before making a reply, which vexed Mrs. Kensington greatly.

"Charity is upstairs gathering her entrapments with the assistance of two very strong servants. I did not feel secure in having Charity return to your home alone, especially since you employ unscrupulous and dangerous individuals," replied a sarcastic Constance.

"How dare you question and denounce the reputations of my servants. Those who have the privileged opportunity to work for me are loyal, hard working, and dedicated to my family and me except for that ungrateful Charity Chastine whose good opinion of me has been poisoned by you, your husband, and his associates," ranted Mrs. Kensington. "And speaking of unscrupulous and dangerous individuals, why don't you take a good look at Jean-Luc Tessier and his companion Louise Bourget? I would be terrified to associate with them, let alone cast my eyes upon them."

Constance laughed at Mrs. Kensington's harsh comments and said, "You have no hold on Charity any longer, and I warn you not to turn your back on Lydia Johnson."

Mrs. Kensington reminded Constance that she was not a woman to be trifled with, and those who have challenged her in the past have paid the consequences.

Constance mocked her by saying, "Your threats are the petty ramblings of a miserable and pathetic woman."

An enraged Mrs. Kensington retaliated by telling Constance the horrific truth that her mother had her beloved father murdered at the hands of Simon Blackwell. Then she sadistically made allegations that Constance's husband Alexander was a man with a past who was feared and despised by many of his fellow Virginians.

As Mrs. Kensington was about to continue, Constance raised her voice and informed her formidable adversary that she and Alexander had Colonel Parker as their very special guest, and that he was in good health but was not allowed to leave Singleton Lodge.

"What are you doing to my son-in-law?" shrieked Mrs. Kensington. "I will have you and your husband arrested for kidnapping and false imprisonment. I demand to see him at once."

"My dear lady, you are in no position to make threats or demands. When my husband and his associates get what they want from you, the dear colonel will be released to you unharmed. Remember, his fate and the fate of Charles' uncle rests in your hands."

The servants took Charity's trunk with her belongings outside to the carriage while she went downstairs to find Constance who was in the drawing room arguing with Mrs. Kensington. She had not heard the entire conversation, but what she did hear frightened her terribly.

Suddenly, she heard a noise from behind her. As she turned around, she found herself staring into the cold and malevolent eyes of Lydia Johnson.

Chapter 23

Lydia stared at Charity with a threatening appearance and shoved her against the wall. Charity became filled with fear, but her fear quickly turned to relief when the two servants came back inside. Upon seeing the men, Lydia moved away from Charity, allowing her to go into the drawing room. As she left her sight, Lydia laughed nefariously.

When Charity entered the room, Constance and Mrs. Kensington ceased their conversation. Charity told Constance that she had her belongings and the servants were waiting for them in the great hall. Constance stared at Mrs. Kensington with grave contempt, and then took Charity's hand to leave the room.

As they were leaving, Mrs. Kensington had to have the final word by telling Charity to be aware of the villains who she was residing with at Singleton Lodge.

"Take care, my lovely Charity, and always be on your guard while living in the house of sin."

The servants helped Constance and Charity into the carriage. As the carriage pulled away, Charity glanced out the window and took a last look at Kensington Hall. She saw a sad Charles staring out the window of the first floor. Her heart ached for that little boy who was in the clutches of a domineering and powerful woman, but she was convinced that Mrs. Kensington loved him, and her strange love would protect him.

On the way home, Constance reassured Charity that she would no longer be troubled by Mrs. Kensington or Lydia Johnson, and she would very soon receive the inheritance from Grace's estate, and there would be many splendid things to enjoy in the days ahead.

Charity smiled graciously at her friend, and leaned her head against the soft covering of the carriage seat and closed her eyes. In her mind, she was contemplating what she must do to escape from this gallery of scoundrels who she had unintentionally befriended. She knew she had to make contact with Lieutenant Bradford. He was her only hope, but she wondered if she could trust him or was he now one of them.

At Winchester Park, a troubled Evelyn Winchester was pacing the floor of the sitting room. She was very upset about what had happened to her nephew, and she was even more concerned about her sister Judith's behavior during the entire incident.

Evelyn's solitude was interrupted by her brother-in-law Caleb who came in to give her a report on Ethan.

"My dear Evelyn, I am happy to inform you that Ethan seems to be doing fine and there is no sign of infection. I am very optimistic that within a few days he will be up and about roaming the halls and grounds of Winchester Park," said a relieved Caleb.

Evelyn was pleased and elated by Caleb's good news. Then she asked him where Judith had gone. Caleb said his wife went to call on Mrs. Kensington, and he would be with Ethan. Then he took his leave.

After he had gone, Evelyn was joined by Honoria who gracefully entered the room and asked to speak with her. Evelyn graciously invited Honoria to sit with her on the sofa by the fireplace.

"Now my dear, please feel free to speak your mind to me," said a kind Evelyn. "I shall listen with an open mind and I will not be quick to pass judgment."

"Miss Winchester, I want to thank you for your genuine kindness and the concern you have shown for Ethan and me. You are a dutiful and loving aunt to Ethan, and he is very fortunate to have you in his life. I hope that one day I can call you my aunt," replied Honoria. "I truly love Ethan for the man that he is and not his position in society. I know that I am a commoner, but I want to prove myself and make my place in Ethan's world. But I am afraid Mrs. Fairchild wishes me long gone from her son and Winchester Park. I do not want to break Ethan's heart. Oh, Miss Winchester, can you be of some assistance or offer some advice in my dilemma?"

Evelyn took Honoria's hand while looking into her very attractive and mesmerizing eyes, and then told Honoria she believed her love for Ethan was genuine as displayed by her actions. She also promised the young woman that she would do everything in her power to support the relationship between her and Ethan.

"I have only my nephew's best interest at heart, and you make him very happy by giving him something that other young women of his acquaintance have not that being true love for him as a person and not his money," replied an adamant Evelyn. "I shall deal with my sister, and after some time she too will come to accept you as a member of this family."

Upon hearing Evelyn's words and believing she had gained a new supporter, Honoria embraced Evelyn and expressed her gratitude.

Suddenly, Honoria began to hear a strange laughter in her ears, which she did not reveal to Evelyn. She quickly and politely excused herself. She went into the hallway to recover, but the laughter continued. She hurried outside and away from the house where she screamed several times. A few moments later, the tormenting laughter had ceased. An exhausted and frightened Honoria made her way back to the house, but unbeknownst to her, the servant Hastings, who was toiling in the garden, had seen her.

Judith Fairchild was standing in the great hall at Kensington Hall staring at the portrait of Rebecca Noble. As she studied the portrait, she recalled what Lydia Johnson had told her about the artist and the curse he placed on the portrait. She was trying to convince herself that the curse was a fictitious legend rather than fact.

I do not believe in curses. How could anyone suffer and die from the destruction of a very old portrait? I must learn more about this Rebecca Noble and her artist friend Samuel Bennett, thought Judith.

Mrs. Kensington came into the great hall and demanded to know the reason for Judith's uninvited visit since Judith had denounced Phoebe Kensington as her friend the last time they were together. Judith calmly and pleasantly asked Mrs. Kensington for her forgiveness and explained that her son's undignified relationship with a girl from inferior birth and a questionable past plagued her mind with confusion and anger that unfortunately caused her to act in a bad manner.

"Please, Phoebe, forgive my uncouth and outrageous behavior the other day. I was only trying to protect my son and my family's good name. Let's not let someone like Honoria Noble destroy our very long friendship," implored Judith.

"As a mother myself, I do understand your position. We must protect our children and their legacies. I agree that we should not let anyone or anything come between us. I accept your apology. Come, my friend, join me in the drawing room for a cup of tea and pleasant conversation," said Mrs. Kensington as she made her way down the hall with Judith behind her.

At Singleton Lodge, Charity had finished unpacking her belongings, and she felt restless, so she walked over to the window. As she looked out, she saw Alexander walking the grounds with Constance, Jean-Luc, and Louise. They seemed to be engaged in deep conversation as they stood very close to one another.

Alexander turned his head and looked back towards the house. She moved away from the window so he would not see her.

Then she heard footsteps from out in the hall. She opened the door and saw Caroline going downstairs. As she glanced down the hall in the direction of the colonel's room, she noticed that his door was open. Overcome with curiosity, she went to see what was taking place. As she approached the doorway, she looked in and found Colonel Parker lying on the floor holding the doll in his hand. So she went into the room to check on him and as she examined him, she noticed a nasty cut on his forehead. She knelt down next to the helpless colonel.

As she stared at him, he opened his eyes and spoke.

"Elizabeth, please help me. Take me away from this terrible place and these bad people who mean me harm," begged a pitiful Colonel Parker.

Then he closed his eyes and was silent.

She knew she had to help this poor man, but at that moment, she didn't know what to do.

Suddenly, she heard the sound of footsteps from behind her. She stood up and found herself staring into the bright blue eyes of Lieutenant Bradford.

"You should have never entered this room and seen Colonel Parker in his present condition," he said sternly. "Now Miss Charity, what am I to do with you?"

The lieutenant's harsh words caught her by surprise. As she attempted to go near him, he abruptly moved away. Glancing out the doorway, he closed the door, grabbed her arm, and ushered her into the adjoining room.

"You need to remain here in absolute silence. I will come for you when the time is right. Do not question my actions," he said.

Before she had the chance to speak, the lieutenant closed the door in her face.

Startled by his behavior, she knelt down and peeked through the keyhole to see what was happening in the main room. She saw the lieutenant lift the colonel and place him in a chair. Then he went to the door to let Caroline in. She was carrying a tray that contained medical supplies. Caroline attended to the wound on the colonel's forehead, and with the lieutenant's assistance they neatly wrapped a bandage around his head. The colonel did not utter a word or try to move. He appeared to be completely docile.

"I will stay and keep watch over our guest while you go to have something to eat," said Lieutenant Bradford. "When you are finished with your meal, please be kind as to bring a tray for me and the colonel."

An obliging Caroline smiled contently at the lieutenant and promised to return shortly. The lieutenant told her to close the door on her way out.

After she had gone, the lieutenant came to Charity in the next room. Speaking abrasively he made it clear by his actions that he did not want to converse with her. He escorted her out, took the doll from an unconscious Colonel Parker, and gave it to her.

"I believe this is your property. Take the doll and return quietly to your room before Caroline returns. Make sure no one sees you leaving here. And for your sake and the colonel's, do not return to this room ever again," insisted the lieutenant.

Before she could respond, he escorted her to the door, opened it, looked out into the hall, and told her to leave. Realizing that she could get nowhere with the lieutenant, she left and hurried down the hall to her room.

Once she was in the room, she sat down in a chair and began to ponder about what was happening at Singleton Lodge and what had become of the kind, strong, and charming Lieutenant Bradford, the man she had known before he went to the Ohio Valley. She recalled Jesse Andrews' story about the lieutenant's sister and nephew, and she made the painful assumption that their deaths changed the lieutenant into a cold, cruel, and insensitive human being. She clutched the doll in her hands and began to cry.

Laura Corday, was sitting at a desk carefully reading the business ledger for household expenses at the Bickford Mansion. As she studied each column meticulously, she realized her income would not satisfy the large amount of money needed for yearly household expenses. She stared out the window, watching the children play, paying particular attention to the little boy Seth sitting alone under the oak tree. She knew she had to devise a plan to secure the financial survival of her charitable establishment.

After pondering for some time, she came up with a solution.

I will pay a call to Constance Singleton Caruthers and inquire whether the offer to provide financial assistance that she and her husband had made was sincere. If so, I will seriously consider accepting their generosity, she thought.

A few minutes later, she put on her overcoat and sent for the carriage. Before departing, she informed Mrs. Downey that she was going to visit Mr. and Mrs. Caruthers at Singleton Lodge. Laura and Mrs. Downey had a solid and trustworthy working relationship. Mrs. Downey was a short and chubby woman with grey hair and a fair complexion. She was very strict but fair when it came to disciplining the children. The older boys did not question her authority, because she occasionally demonstrated her strength and agility when it came to lifting and carrying trunks and heavy baskets up and down stairs.

After Laura had gone, Mrs. Downey was preparing for meal time when Reverend Davenport made a surprise visit. He entered wearing his clergyman's outfit, and a dark hat, and he carried a Bible in his hand.

Noticing Laura's absence, he asked Mrs. Downey, "Where is Miss Laura? Is she at the marketplace or another establishment taking care of business?"

"Reverend Davenport, Miss Laura has gone to pay a visit to Mr. and Mrs. Caruthers on a business matter," replied Mrs. Downey.

Upon hearing this, Reverend Davenport became quite disturbed, and he pressed Mrs. Downey for further details, but she was unable to provide them. She told the Reverend she had to prepare supper, and she politely excused herself.

Reverend Davenport decided to wait for Laura's return. He went into the sitting room, sat down on a comfortable chair, and began to read the Bible while anticipating the reason for Laura's visit to Mr. and Mrs. Caruthers, a couple he despised.

———————

At Kensington Hall, Mrs. Kensington was sitting in the drawing room watching the servants take away the tea cups and dishes following Judith Fairchild's visit. She was sitting on the sofa contemplating whether or not she should attend the ball at Singleton Lodge, considering the confrontation she had had with Constance.

After the servants had finished their tasks and had left, Mrs. Kensington was visited by Simon Blackwell who entered cautiously through the terrace doors.

"My dear mistress of Kensington Hall, you seem to be in deep thought. Do you wish to share your thoughts with an old friend?" asked a sarcastic Simon.

"You would be the last person I would share anything with," she said. "And do not call me your friend."

A cunning Simon helped himself to a glass of sherry and then sat on the sofa next to Mrs. Kensington. He stared into her crocodile eyes, and his presence greatly annoyed her. She got up from the sofa and took a turn about the room. Simon put his feet up on the sofa and relaxed while sipping his sherry. Every now and then he gave out a laugh. He was gaining satisfaction in aggravating his formidable opponent.

Finally unable to withstand Simon's behavior, Mrs. Kensington confided in him regarding her dilemma. She told him about her confrontation with Constance, that Colonel Parker was being held against his will at Singleton Lodge in exchange for the treasure and diamond, and that she was unsure if she should attend the ball.

Simon finished his sherry and then told Mrs. Kensington she should attend the ball and pretend to be gracious and sociable without letting anyone know something was wrong. He suggested she should be especially hospitable to the host and hostess, and then added that he planned to attend the ball in disguise and stealthily search for Colonel Parker while everyone was enjoying the ball.

"If I find Colonel Parker at Singleton Lodge as Constance Caruthers claims he is, then I will use my special skills to rescue him from his captors and bring him home to his mother-in-law for a family reunion," said Simon. "Think of my efforts as playing chess; I snatch the king right from under the noses of your opponents. If I succeed, you will be very grateful and generous by telling me where I can find this hidden treasure that your adversaries seek. And once I find it, I shall depart from your presence forever. Oh, you may keep your precious diamond as a gesture of good faith. Do you like my plan?"

After thinking about Simon's proposal, Mrs. Kensington became intrigued by it and she agreed to attend the ball and have Simon enact his plan. A very pleased Simon told Mrs. Kensington he needed to be on his way to take care of something, so he drank another glass of sherry and then took his leave.

As Mrs. Kensington made her way to the game table, Lydia Johnson entered the room and announced the arrival of Dr. Greenville who Mrs. Kensington was not surprised to see.

A flustered Dr. Greenville, dressed in a blue jacket with gold buttons, came into the drawing room inquiring about the health of young Charles. He had been traveling for quite some time in response to Mrs. Kensington's urgent letter.

"I came as fast as the coach would carry me," said a concerned Dr. Greenville.

"My dearest friend Mitchell, Charles is very well. He spends his days occupied studying with his tutor. I sent you that urgent and misleading letter in a desperate attempt to have you return to Kensington Hall. I need your assistance," replied a devious Mrs. Kensington. "I need you to escort me to the Singleton Ball tomorrow night, and I will not allow you to refuse me. After tomorrow night, you may feel free to be on your way back to Boston. For your trouble, I shall make a sizable donation to your hospital as a grateful gesture between friends."

Dr. Greenville was relieved that Charles was well, but very angry about his friend's deception. But he quickly forgave her and agreed to be her escort in exchange for a donation to his hospital, which was in desperate need of funds. Once their agreement was finalized, they had a glass of sherry together.

Charity must have cried herself to sleep because she was awakened by the sound of her door closing tightly. Startled by the sound, she arose from the chair and looked about the room. The room was dark so she lit a candle, wrapped a blanket around her to warm her chilled body, and sat back in the chair. Thoughts of the doll came to her. She held the candle and searched the entire place for it. She remembered holding it in her hands before she fell asleep in the chair, but it was no longer in the room.

Chapter 24

Someone must have come into my room and snatched my doll from me while I was sleeping. Why would someone want a doll that had sentimental value only to me, thought Charity. As she pondered these questions, someone knocked at the door. When she went to open it, Constance was standing in the hall with one of the servants who had the gown for the ball in her arms.

"My dear friend, we have come to deliver your lovely gown for the ball tomorrow night. I cannot wait to see you dressed in it," replied Constance. "You shall draw the attention of everyone in attendance."

After they had entered the room, the servant placed the gown on the sofa. As she stared at the beautiful outfit, Charity began to fantasize about dancing in a great ballroom with Lieutenant Bradford as her partner. They danced to the beautiful music without a worry in the world. Their dancing eliminated the drudgery and chaos of society and replaced it with peace and harmony. *If only this was not a dream*, she thought. Her fantasizing was interrupted by Constance's voice informing her that it was time for dinner.

Charity politely told her that she needed to freshen up and would join her momentarily. Constance said that she and Charity would be dining without Alexander who had been called out of town due to urgent business. She did not elaborate any further, and Charity did not press her for details.

After Constance and the servant had gone, Charity looked at the gown and the lovely surroundings, and then came to the realization that she needed to leave Singleton Lodge very soon.

At Winchester Park, Evelyn Winchester was sitting in the drawing room enjoying a hot cup of coffee when her brother-in-law Caleb came in. He poured himself a cup of coffee and sat down in the chair adjacent to his sister-in-law. He had a worried look upon his face and remained silent. Feeling compassion for poor Caleb and curious about his present state, Evelyn broke the silence by inquiring about his troubled look.

"Caleb, what seems to be troubling you? Your face reveals the sad exposure of a man who is bearing a great burden on his shoulders. Please feel free to confide in me," said a concerned Evelyn.

He sipped his coffee and stared into the distance as if he were in a fog. Then he gently placed the cup down on the serving table, rose from his chair, and went to stand by the fireplace. With his back to Evelyn, he began to speak. He expressed wholeheartedly and with grave conviction that he was worried about his wife Judith's strong disapproval of Ethan and Honoria's courtship. Caleb went as far as to say that he did not trust his wife's behavior and had a terrible suspicion that she had a part to play in Ethan getting bit by the snake.

"My wife is very angry about the present situation involving my son and Honoria," he said. "I fear that she may take extreme measures to break up their happiness. I see nothing but contempt in her eyes for that young girl who I have come to admire despite her upbringing and low connections in society."

"My beloved Caleb, I do share your feelings about your wife, my sister, and I see the disdainful manner in which she treats Honoria. I can only pray that Judith will come to accept Honoria for the sake of her son who she undoubtedly loves and adores," replied Evelyn. "You and I must make a pact to ensure Ethan's happiness and to keep an eye on our Judith."

Caleb was relieved to find that Evelyn shared his same concerns and embraced her assistance with the situation. He walked over to Evelyn sitting in her chair, reached out to her and shook her hand while they pledged an alliance to keep Ethan and Honoria together. While Caleb and Evelyn discussed their plan, they were unaware Judith, who was feeling betrayed and angry was listening from outside the room.

After dinner Constance and Charity went into the drawing room. Charity stood by the warm fireplace to rid her body of a nasty chill and Constance sat on the sofa doing needlepoint.

Their solace retreat was suddenly disturbed by the appearance of Caroline entering the room. She walked over to Constance and whispered something in her ear that Charity was unable to hear. Then Constance put down her needlepoint, and she and Caroline took their leave. As Constance was leaving, she firmly told Charity to remain in the drawing room and wait for her return.

After they had gone, Charity hurried out into the hallway. To her astonishment, she saw two of the male servants carrying a coffin upstairs. Chills had returned to engulf her body, and she fell into a state of fear and curiosity.

She quietly followed from behind. When she reached the top of the stairs, she saw them bring the coffin to Colonel Parker's room. She hurried down the hall and hid behind the statue not far from the colonel's room. After some time had passed, the servants came out of the room carrying the coffin, and they went downstairs.

The door to the colonel's room was slightly ajar, so she crept up and tried to listen to the voices coming from inside. She heard Constance tell Caroline to strip the bed and clean the room. Then Constance told Caroline that she would be in the drawing room if anyone needed her. Charity quickly went downstairs and back into the drawing room while waiting impatiently for Constance to return.

When Constance came into the room, she found Charity sitting on the sofa.

Feeling very uncomfortable in her presence, Charity told her she was tired and decided to turn in for the night. They said good night to one another and then Charity went outside rather than to her room.

Once she was outside, she made her way through the darkness with the assistance of a lantern she found by the back entrance. As she came upon the stables, she hid behind some bushes as the two male servants left the stables and returned to the house. When they were out of sight, she opened the stable door and went inside. The horses were in their stalls nibbling on some hay. Holding the lantern in front of her, she looked in each stall. When she came to the last stall, she peeked in and saw the wooden coffin.

She entered the stall, placed the lantern on the ground next to the coffin, and fearlessly removed the lid. As she glanced inside, she saw Colonel Parker lying still with the doll in his right hand. She gasped from fright, and as she rose to her feet, someone grabbed her from behind while placing a cold hand over her mouth.

As she struggled to break free from whoever had her, a familiar voice whispered to her, telling her not to be frightened. Then the voice instructed her to remain quiet while slowly turning her head. As she turned around, Lieutenant Bradford was standing in front of her with a very solemn expression upon his face.

Charity asked him what had happened to Colonel Parker. He walked over to the coffin, knelt down, and examined the colonel who Charity presumed was dead. Then the lieutenant rose to his feet and sternly explained that Colonel Parker was not dead but in a deep sleep. Then he showed her several tiny holes on the lid and sides of the coffin.

"The colonel is resting peacefully, and the small holes are allowing air to pass through. I can assure you that Colonel Parker is very much alive," said the lieutenant.

"Then what in the Good Lord's name is he doing lying in a coffin?" Charity asked with exasperation.

The lieutenant took her hand and solemnly told her it was a plot devised by the lieutenant and Alexander to make certain people believe the colonel had died, that this deceitful charade was intended to protect Colonel Parker from those who wished to do him harm, and that the coffin was a means of transporting him to a safe haven where he would remain until his would- be assassins were discovered.

When Charity asked who wanted the colonel dead, the lieutenant replied by telling her it was for her own protection that she did not know their identities. He then told her that she needed to return to the main house while he remained with the colonel.

Upon his persistence, Charity took hold of the lantern and began to take her leave when they heard a noise from outside. The lieutenant instructed her to stay in the stables, and took hold of a pitch fork and went outside to investigate the disturbance while she sat in a small pile of hay watching Colonel Parker asleep in the coffin.

Mrs. Kensington and Dr. Greenville were sipping sherry while playing a game of chess at Kensington Hall. Mrs. Kensington was delighted to have her old friend by her side playing her favorite game.

"It is wonderful to have you back at Kensington Hall. I told you that we would meet again when you left for Boston several months ago. Please consider remaining for an indefinite stay," implored Mrs. Kensington.

"My dearest Phoebe, my responsibility at the hospital urges me to return to Boston after the ball at Singleton Lodge."

As Mrs. Kensington was continuing in her attempt to change her friend's mind, Lydia Johnson entered the room and announced the arrival of Philippe and Annabelle Monnerat. When the guests came into the room, Mrs. Kensington motioned to Dr. Greenville for him to leave. After he was gone, Mrs. Kensington remained seated while moving a chess piece and rudely ignoring the Monnerats.

Annabelle Monnerat made herself comfortable by sitting on the sofa and staring with her devious green eyes at Mrs. Kensington.

Philippe stood by his wife. Unlike his brother, he was a very handsome man. He was elegantly dressed in fine attire, and his long dark hair was tied behind his neck with a ribbon.

"Philippe Monnerat, you and your Jezebel wife have come to visit me at my home. I am not impressed, so please state your purpose and then be on your way," demanded a sarcastic Mrs. Kensington.

Philippe obeyed Mrs. Kensington's request by inquiring about his brother's death. He pressed for details, but Mrs. Kensington gave little information. She did reveal that Louis Monnerat had engaged in a confrontation with a privateer named Jean-Luc Tessier, which tragically resulted in Louis' demise.

"Jean-Luc killed your brother in self-defense according to two eye witnesses. Your brother's evil dealings led to his own destruction. Let the matter of his death be done with," said Mrs. Kensington.

"What kind of a brother would I be if I let my beloved Louis' killer go unpunished? I will deal with Monsieur Tessier in my own way. I am also here to make inquiries about a treasure search my brother and your son-in-law were embarking upon. We will discuss that affair at another time. My Annabelle and I shall call upon you again very soon, and it would be appreciated if you would not defame my lovely wife's name. She and you are both English women by birth. We now will take our leave."

Mrs. Kensington did not respond about the treasure. Philippe nodded his head at Mrs. Kensington and then took his wife's hand as they made their departure. Philippe appeared to be quite angry, but Annabelle wore a delightful yet wicked smirk on her face.

After they had gone, a troubled Mrs. Kensington studied the chess game intensely as she sat quietly in her chair, unaware that Lydia Johnson was lurking out in the hall and Simon Blackwell was eavesdropping from outside on the terrace.

Charity must have dozed off while waiting for Lieutenant Bradford to return. When she awoke, she gently brushed the hay off her petticoat before rising to her feet. Then she went over to the coffin, and to her shock, it was empty.

Chapter 25

As she stared at the empty coffin, she became frightened, so she grabbed the lantern and hastily made her way outside where she was unexpectedly greeted by Alexander and Constance.

They ushered her back into the stables. Then Alexander, in a calm and gentlemanly manner, explained what was happening.

He revealed that Colonel Parker was found several weeks ago by a man named Ebenezer Stiles who was attending to the Higgins' property. The colonel was very disoriented and hugging Elizabeth's tombstone while crying profusely. During this time two strangers, who Mr. Stiles did not recognize, came upon the colonel and began attacking him. A quick thinking Mr. Stiles took out his pistol and fired two shots while his dog Pogo barked ferociously, causing both attackers to flee.

"The colonel collapsed from exhaustion, and Mr. Stiles took pity on him," explained Alexander. "It was a stroke of luck that Constance and I were traveling that road on our way to visit a neighbor when we came upon the colonel and Mr. Stiles. After hearing an account of the incident from Mr. Stiles, we decided to help Colonel Parker," added Alexander. "We took him back to Singleton Lodge where he has been residing ever since. Unfortunately, someone had learned of his whereabouts, and the other day, that person came secretly to Singleton Lodge and tried to kill the colonel. For his own protection, we staged his death and have relocated him to a safe haven. We took him away while you were asleep here in the stables."

"Where is he now?" Charity inquired.

Alexander looked at his wife, and then informed Charity that Colonel Parker was with Mr. Stiles and Lieutenant Bradford in a safe place. When Charity asked where they were, Alexander told her it was for her well-being not to know any further details. She became agitated and started to press for more information. Constance took her hand and stared into her blue eyes while informing her that everything would turn out well. She had no choice but to put her trust in them.

Then she walked Charity back to the house while Alexander remained at the stables.

When they reached the terrace, Constance gave her a hug and told her to have good thoughts about the ball that was taking place the next evening.

Realizing she could do nothing for Colonel Parker and her efforts to learn more about his predicament were futile, Charity respected her friend and her friend's husband's wishes.

She returned to her room, washed her face, put on her night clothes, and burrowed under the quilt on the bed.

As she tossed and turned in bed, her mind was focused on Colonel Parker, and then she began to think about Charlotte and Charles. *How tragic for all three of them not to be together as one family,* she thought. *Charlotte was dead, Charles was in Mrs. Kensington's care and Colonel Parker was in protective custody. Who was trying to harm him and why?*

After some time of pondering these unpleasant thoughts, she eventually closed her eyes and fell asleep.

The next day the entire household staff was preoccupied with preparing Singleton Lodge for the ball. Constance was carefully instructing the servants to carry out every detail that would make the gathering the talk of the town. There was much preparation taking place in the kitchen and in the large conservatory room that was transformed into a magnificent ballroom. Constance wanted the room to reflect the grandeur and style of the ballrooms of Europe.

Alexander had left Singleton Lodge early in the morning as a means to escape the chaos and avoid getting in the way so Charity surmised. Realizing she was not needed, she decided to go for a walk. It was a chilly day, but the cool breeze caressed her cheeks, and the exercise was delightful.

After strolling through the gardens, she made her way down to the stables. The stable door was open, so she entered. She walked over to the first stall where she saw the horses nibbling on some hay. They seemed preoccupied with eating, so she did not disturb them. Then she heard peculiar sounds coming from another stall farther down from where she was standing. Overcome with curiosity, she quietly made her way to the stall. As she approached, she saw a man and woman partially unclothed, indulging in the lustful pleasures of the flesh. As she looked closely upon them, she saw that it was Alexander Caruthers and Louise Bourget.

Charity stood still from surprise upon finding Alexander and Louise engaging in their immoral and disdainful act. They did not see her spying on them.

After recovering from the unpleasant encounter, she hurried out of the stables. As she was walking back to the main house, all she could ponder in her mind was: *why is Alexander so unfaithful to her good friend Constance who for all appearances seems to be deeply devoted to him?*

Then she recalled what her own father did to her mother before she was born. She came to the sad conclusion that men were in control, and women were mere objects to be admired, played with, and later ignored or abandoned. She had felt contempt for Alexander, just like she had for her father who she did not know. A nagging question tugged at her conscience: *should I tell Constance of her husband's indiscretion, or should I remain silent for now?*

As she made her way down the main path, she carelessly tripped on her petticoat and fell on the ground. Attempting to get up, two strong hands reached out to her and helped her to her feet. When she glanced up, she saw that it was Jean-Luc.

"Are you hurt, Miss Charity? Do you need some assistance in walking? Please feel free to lean on me," he insisted.

"I am well, thank you, but embarrassed for being clumsy. Thank you for your assistance," she replied.

Then he and Charity made their way back to Singleton Lodge. When they reached the terrace, Jean-Luc asked Charity if Alexander was at home. She became a bit agitated, but was careful not to reveal the truth. She simply responded by telling him Alexander had left Singleton Lodge earlier, most likely in an effort to avoid getting involved with preparations for tonight's ball. Satisfied with her response, he gently kissed her hand and took his leave. As she watched him fade into the distance, she began to realize that this man, who many regard as an unscrupulous and dangerous rogue has a heart and perhaps is capable of more loyalty than someone like Alexander who has a prominent position in society.

Once inside, Charity went straight to her room in order to avoid Constance. She could not face her considering what she had just witnessed in the stables. She stared at the beautiful gown before her, and realized that the very rich were more concerned with material possessions and position in society than with morals, kindness, and humanity.

Mrs. Kensington was in the library at Kensington Hall sitting in a Chippendale chair, enjoying cup of tea, when Simon Blackwell entered from the secret passage. He was in a very good mood and cheerfully told Mrs. Kensington that his luck had made a turn for the better. When she inquired about his sudden jubilant attitude, he responded by saying he was very certain to have found the location of the treasure, and he believed it to be buried in a cave somewhere on Indian Lookout.

"My lovely Mrs. Kensington, I do believe that I have pieced

together the missing parts to the map, and if my suspicions are correct, the treasure is closer than we could have ever imagined."

At first Mrs. Kensington was silent. Then she began to recall what her husband had uttered to Charity before his death. He said the treasure was closer than anyone would expect. She also remembered Elizabeth Higgins telling her about a cave at Indian Lookout where she took care of her wounded Redcoat boyfriend Edmund Tate.

"I am glad you may have finally found the treasure so many have been seeking for years. Once you find it, then I presume you will depart to somewhere far away from here," said a gleeful Mrs. Kensington.

"Indeed, I shall leave once I have my treasure and settle an old score with a longtime adversary," replied Simon.

When a curious Mrs. Kensington inquired about the identity of Simon's adversary, he arrogantly answered by saying the person was someone she had despised for a long time and would be just as pleased as he would be to have this person done away with.

Their conversation was interrupted by Dr. Greenville's voice calling out to Mrs. Kensington from the hall. Simon told Mrs. Kensington that he would see her at the ball, and then he made his escape through the secret passage.

Darkness soon came as did the guests making their arrival to Singleton Lodge. Flaming torches lined the road and the gravel driveway to the entrance of the mansion and footmen dressed in fancy outfits and white wigs helped to escort the women from their carriages.

Alexander and Constance were a dutiful host and hostess as they greeted their guests. Charity stood off to the side in her elegant blue gown watching the great room as it became crowded with finely dressed elegant ladies and gentlemen eager to dance and dine.

When the musicians began to play, several of the guests gathered in the middle of the room to dance.

As Charity looked into the crowd, there were some people like Dr. and Mrs. Foote, Mr. and Mrs. Pierpont, Reverend and Mrs. Trumbull, and others with whom she was acquainted. There were many others who she did not know. She saw Mrs. Kensington and Dr. Greenville enter, and she could tell by Constance's expression she was not delighted to see them. She did not want to confront Mrs. Kensington, so she made certain to avoid her. As Charity made her way to get a glass of punch, she had a pleasant introduction and encounter with Mr. and Mrs. Fairchild and their son Ethan who was accompanied by Honoria Noble and Mrs. Fairchild's sister, Evelyn Winchester. They all greeted her with smiles and polite manners. Mrs. Fairchild seemed preoccupied by staring into the crowd. After a few moments, she took her husband's hand, and they graciously left the others. Evelyn Winchester was very polite as she engaged in pleasant conversation. Ethan was very charming as was Honoria. As she looked upon Honoria, Charity began to recall the night she made her first appearance at Singleton Lodge at the ball hosted by Monsieur and Madame Monnerat. Her arrival shocked all the guests and greatly disturbed Mrs. Kensington. Evelyn eventually excused herself and went to join Mr. and Mrs. Fairchild.

"It is wonderful to make your acquaintance Miss Chastine," said Honoria with a sincere smile. "I hope we can become friends. Ethan and I are very soon to be engaged, and I would like to share our profound happiness with new acquaintances."

"I am very happy for you both and wish you the very best in the future," Charity replied.

"Thank you for your kind words," said Ethan. "Now, would you two lovely ladies allow me the pleasure of escorting you into the ballroom?" he asked as he extended his arms to Charity and Honoria.

As they entered the ballroom, Charity glanced at Mrs. Kensington who was watching her with her crocodile eyes. She also observed

Dr. Greenville who was in a corner having what appeared to be a serious and disturbing conversation with Mrs. Fairchild. Then she saw Dr. Greenville leave the room abruptly. Ethan and Honoria excused themselves as they went to dance, and Charity remained to the side while watching them and the other guests dance.

Suddenly, she was confronted by Mrs. Kensington who tapped her on the shoulder with her fan.

"My dear Charity, you are looking well this evening. It seems that life at Singleton Lodge is agreeing with you. How very fortunate for you! Charles misses you dearly. Perhaps one day you may call upon him and me at Kensington Hall. I can assure you that you will enjoy your visit," said a sly Mrs. Kensington.

Charity did not make any promises but thanked her former employer for her gracious invitation. Then she politely excused herself by taking leave to another part of the room.

When the dance ended, Alexander and Constance stood in the center of the room while the servants walked among the guests carrying trays of champagne glasses. After everyone received a glass, Alexander welcomed all of his guests to Singleton Lodge and then proposed a toast to his new friends and neighbors from North Haven and the surrounding communities.

While the guests were sipping their champagne, silence fell upon the entire room. Then, just before the musicians resumed playing, a terrible scream was heard from outside on the terrace. Many of the guests hurried outside while following Alexander as he led them into the gardens where they found poor Caroline standing next to the body of a man that was facedown on the ground with a sharp object in his back. As Alexander approached the dead man, he studied his face, and then regrettably announced that it was Dr. Greenville. Several women gasped from fright, some of the men whispered among themselves, and Mrs. Kensington stood absolutely still with a poker face.

As Charity looked at the many faces in the crowd, all she could fathom was the shocking revelation that someone had killed poor Dr. Greenville, just like Simon Blackwell did to Mr. Singleton at a previous ball at Singleton Lodge nearly two years earlier. Who could have committed such a vile act this time?

As the guests stood in shock around the body, the wind began to blow, filling the night air with a dreadful chill. Evil had indeed come to this grand affair as an uninvited guest accompanied by fear and death.

Chapter 26

The authorities were quickly notified of the crime and wasted little time in arriving at Singleton Lodge to investigate the murder of Dr. Mitchell Greenville. One by one they questioned all the guests, but no one was able to offer any relevant evidence toward solving the crime. Constance was very distraught and took to her room after speaking to the authorities. Alexander held himself well as he assisted the constable and his men. After each guest was questioned, they were allowed to leave. Carriages were lined up along the entrance way, and one by one they departed into the night.

When there were only a few remaining, Mrs. Kensington insisted to the constable that she would take responsibility for Dr. Greenville's body. She explained to her knowledge he had no living relatives, and therefore, as a longtime friend, she wanted to give him a proper Christian burial. The constable agreed, and said he would have the body transferred to the icehouse until the burial. Before departing, Mrs. Kensington grabbed Alexander's arm and blamed him for Dr. Greenville's death. However she was very cautious in the way she made her accusations. Charity was standing by the staircase as she left, leaving an unaffected Alexander staring into the distance. Alexander turned, faced Charity with a smirk, and then returned to the ballroom to join the authorities.

Charity hurried upstairs to see Constance, but Caroline informed her that Constance did not want to see anyone. Since she was not able to see or comfort her friend, she retreated to her room down the hall. She closed the door and went to look out the window.

As she stared into the darkness, she saw the apparitions of the young couple moving about the grounds. She clutched the drapes on the window and felt terribly chilled as she began to realize every time the ghosts appeared, a terrible tragedy took place. *What is the connection to Dr. Greenville's murder?* she wondered. This question weighed heavily on her mind the remainder of the night.

The next day after breakfast, Charity asked to see Constance, but Alexander said, "My wife will be remaining in her room for the day." Charity asked, "Is she not well?" He replied by telling her not to worry about his wife for he was taking good care of her. Charity nearly laughed in his face for his fake concern, especially after witnessing what he and Louise were doing in the stables the day before. She did not inquire any further, but she did ask for his permission to take the carriage and visit Mrs. Andrews.

"My lovely Charity, I am going to town to meet with Jean-Luc and Louise, so it would be my pleasure to take you with me," replied Alexander. "Let's be on our way."

When they arrived at Andrews' Tavern, Mrs. Andrews was sweeping the front stoop. Upon seeing Charity getting out of the carriage, she gave her a warm greeting. Charity followed Mrs. Andrews inside while Alexander waited outside for the arrival of Jean-Luc and Louise.

Jesse was repairing one of the wooden planks in the dining room. He stood up and bowed. Then he and Mrs. Andrews began to ask Charity questions about the ball. They had heard about the tragedy from Dr. Foote who had examined Dr. Greenville's body. Mrs. Andrews explained she was unable to attend the ball because at the last minute she was needed to assist a neighbor who was giving birth to her third child.

"I could not attend because Bessie needed my assistance. She gave birth to a beautiful baby boy. Both mother and son are doing well, and the father is thrilled to have another son to help around the farm. Jesse did not want to attend the ball alone, so he stayed at the tavern attending to many overdue chores," said Mrs. Andrews. "Tell us, do the authorities know or have any thoughts about who killed Dr. Greenville?"

"I do not know any details. As far as I can surmise, a servant found the good doctor dead outside while all the guests were inside. I cannot believe that another death has taken place at Singleton Lodge. Our friend Constance is grief stricken and has taken to her room," Charity said with deep sadness.

Mrs. Andrews went to get Charity a cup of tea while Jesse resumed his work repairing the floor. She could not bear listening to the banging sound, so Charity went outside and took a short walk around the tavern. As she approached the back entrance, she came upon Alexander, Jean-Luc, and Louise engaged in a serious discussion. When she got closer, she could hear them talking about a treasure they believed to be buried in a cave on Indian Lookout. Then it came to her that the cave they were talking about must be the same cave that Lieutenant Bradford, Charles, and she had explored the day they had their picnic at Indian Lookout. It was also the cave where Elizabeth Higgins hid her Redcoat boyfriend Edmund Tate when he was wounded.

While she was preoccupied with these thoughts, Louise looked in Charity's way and saw her. She pointed her finger at her as if she were a criminal. Charity quickly began to take her leave, but was thwarted by Lieutenant Bradford who came from behind her. He abrasively grabbed her arm and ushered her into the barn as Alexander, Jean-Luc, and Louise followed behind them. Once inside, they closed the barn door, and Charity was surrounded by four individuals who glanced at her with grave disapproval, especially the lieutenant who seemed to be the angriest one of all.

"Why didn't you heed my warning the first time when I told you to keep out of this affair?" asked an agitated Lieutenant Bradford. "I want an answer this instant."

The lieutenant's harsh tone of voice frightened her. He certainly was not the kind and compassionate man that she had known nearly two years ago. Even his bright blue eyes that she had always admired were very unbecoming and threatening. Before she could reply to his question, Alexander interrupted the lieutenant by saying that Charity's eavesdropping on their conversation did not put their plan in jeopardy. If anything, he was glad that it was her who overheard them speaking rather than someone else.

"We can trust Charity, and our plans will be safe with her," replied a confident Alexander.

"I must be on my way because Mrs. Andrews and Jesse are expecting my return," Charity said. "I do not want them to worry about me, or it may cast suspicion."

Jean-Luc came up with a solution by instructing her to return to the tavern and tell Mrs. Andrews and Jesse that a sudden headache has caused her to take her leave and she would visit them another day. Upon hearing his story, the others agreed, and Charity, having no choice, went along with it.

She returned to the tavern and regrettably told Mrs. Andrews and Jesse that she needed to return to Singleton Lodge due to poor health. She felt terrible about deceiving them, but they graciously understood and wished her well.

After leaving the tavern, Alexander and Louise were waiting for her in the carriage. Lieutenant Bradford and Jean-Luc had gone ahead of them on horseback. She got inside the carriage and sat across from Alexander and Louise who were sitting very close to each other. Charity remained silent as the carriage made its way down the dusty and bumpy road to a place that was unknown to her.

An elated Judith Fairchild was enjoying a cup of tea while staring out the window of the drawing room at Winchester Park. She seemed very relaxed and relieved as if a great burden had been lifted from her shoulders. As she stared outside, her peace of mind was disturbed when she saw Ethan and Honoria holding hands while taking a leisurely stroll about the grounds. A now disturbed Judith dropped her tea cup and began to utter hateful words that caught the attention of her sister Evelyn who had entered the room.

"My dear sister, what seems to be troubling you at this moment," inquired a curious Evelyn.

"That girl Honoria has my son under her spell. I have said it before and I will say it again that she will be his downfall and the ruin to this family. But perhaps the lovely Honoria will go away forever just like Dr. Greenville did last night."

Upon hearing Judith's inappropriate and alarming comment, Evelyn demanded for her sister to further explain what she had just said. Judith ignored Evelyn by pouring herself another cup of tea as she continued to stare out the window.

A frustrated Evelyn spoke directly to her sister and asked a solemn question.

"My dear Judith, did you have anything to do with the murder of Dr. Greenville? I saw you arguing with him some time before he was found dead. I did not speak a word of what I saw to the authorities, but please tell me that I have no reason to worry."

A sly Judith looked her sister in the eye, and with a calm and complacent expression replied that she had nothing to do with what had happened to Dr. Greenville. Then she politely excused herself and left the room.

Evelyn was not convinced by her sister's response and feared that Judith was hiding a terrible secret. As she looked out at her nephew and his prospective bride, Evelyn soon began to sense that their relationship was in danger and she needed to watch Judith ever so closely.

Mrs. Kensington was pacing the library at Kensington Hall while thinking about the death of her friend Dr. Greenville. Her solitude was interrupted by Simon Blackwell entering from the secret passage. Mrs. Kensington was not pleased to see him, but he was happy to see her. He revealed he had finally found the location of the treasure and he was on his way to claim it. Then he told her that he was planning to leave town and go somewhere far away to indulge in his newly found fortune. Then he insolently thanked Mrs. Kensington for her hospitality and expressed how sorry he was that he had not been able to be her son-in-law.

"My dear lady, I will now leave you forever. I do regret Charlotte's untimely demise deprived you and me the opportunity of becoming family. My beloved Charlotte shall always remain in my heart until the day I die," said Simon.

"You have no right to speak my daughter's good name. Had my Charlotte lived, I would have never allowed you two to marry. You are a deadly disease on all humanity. Be gone from my sight and never return," shrieked an enraged Mrs. Kensington.

Before he took his final leave, Simon helped himself to a glass of sherry he sipped slowly, and then he made a comment that lowered Mrs. Kensington into shock. He told her that he had attended the ball at Singleton Lodge in disguise and was lurking about outside when he saw an upset Dr. Greenville pacing the grounds. Then to his dismay, he saw a woman come up from behind and stab an unsuspecting Dr. Greenville in the back. After Dr. Greenville had collapsed from his fatal wound, the woman searched the doctor's coat pockets, removed a letter, and then fled into the night.

"As I was about to go and examine your friend, a servant came out onto the terrace and began to scream, so I left. However, I did get a look at the woman who stabbed Dr. Greenville. Do you want to know who she was?"

"Yes, who was it?" demanded Mrs. Kensington.

"It was your trusted housekeeper Lydia Johnson who killed your beloved Dr. Greenville with the letter opener bearing your initials

PK. I guess Miss Charity Chastine and the others were correct to fear Lydia. And you believed me to be a demon from hell. Good-bye Mrs. Kensington. If I were you, I would never turn my back on Lydia Johnson," said a laughing Simon as he made his departure through the secret panel.

A horrified Mrs. Kensington sat down on the sofa while desperately trying to process the shocking information that Simon had just delivered. As she began to think, she remembered that Lydia had stolen the letter opener on an earlier occasion and attempted to use it to open the desk. The authorities did reveal that a letter opener was the murder weapon. Mrs. Kensington began to worry about whether the authorities would figure out whom the initials belonged and if she would become a suspect.

As she was about to seek out and confront Lydia with Simon's accusation, a servant entered the library and announced the arrival of the constable. An agitated Mrs. Kensington desperately put on a hospitable face as she prepared to confront a situation that could lead to her downfall. Before the gentleman entered, she walked over to the chess game, took ahold of the queen and grasped it tightly in the palm of her hand.

Chapter 27

After a long and bumpy ride, the carriage finally arrived at a log cabin near the outskirts of Indian Lookout where Jean-Luc and the lieutenant were waiting. Alexander, Charity, and Louise got out of the carriage and went inside the cabin where they found Ebenezer Stiles and his dog Pogo watching a catatonic Colonel Parker sitting in a rocking chair holding the doll.

The colonel looked so pitiful sitting in the rocking chair. Charity walked over to him, and he stared at her for some time before calling her Elizabeth several times. Then he leaned back in the chair, closed his eyes, and was silent. In Charity's opinion, the colonel was a broken man with the memory of a dead woman on his mind.

"He calls out her name over and over again while clutching that doll in his hand. He is very passive and does not make any trouble," said Mr. Stiles. "Pogo has become quite fond of the colonel and stays by his side."

"Charity, you need to remain at the cabin with Mr. Stiles, and do not go anywhere until we return," replied a stern Lieutenant Bradford.

Then he, Louise, Alexander, and Jean-Luc gathered some shovels, lanterns, and an old, crumbled parchment of paper and left the cabin to make their way to a cave at Indian Lookout.

After they were gone, Mr. Stiles offered Charity food and drink, which she accepted most graciously. While the colonel was sleeping, Mr. Stiles and Charity sat at a large wooden table in the center of the two-room cabin and enjoyed a delicious meal. During the meal,

Mr. Stiles told her that he became involved with the others and their search for the treasure after he had witnessed the brutal attack of Colonel Parker by two unidentified strangers.

"The colonel must have really loved Elizabeth Higgins as her death has nearly destroyed him," said Mr. Stiles. "I found a map in his coat pocket, and I gave it to Alexander Caruthers as he and his wife were kind enough to lend assistance with the colonel. If Pogo and I hadn't come along when we did, those strangers would have killed Colonel Parker. There has been much talk and rumors for years about a hidden treasure that was stolen from Europe's monarchs and buried somewhere in this territory. I would have never suspected that it was right here in this small town. And three men have mysteriously disappeared while in search of the treasure. Perhaps after today, the treasure will be found, the colonel will be safe, and the past can finally be done with," replied Mr. Stiles.

Charity looked at Mr. Stiles' kind face and smiled. She asked him if it was ever possible to be rid of the past, for she believed it always returned to haunt us with our past sins and indiscretions. Mr. Stiles agreed with her.

At Kensington Hall, Mrs. Kensington played the hospitable hostess, but the constable made it quite clear that he was not present for a social visit. He refused a cup of tea and stated the purpose of his visit. He informed Mrs. Kensington that someone had lodged a serious accusation against her, accusing her of having Loyalist ties to England during the war and the late Dr. Greenville had proof to uphold the allegations. He also hinted Dr. Greenville's proof led to his demise while pointing an accusing finger at Mrs. Kensington.

"Dr. Mitchell Greenville was a longtime friend, and we were each other's confidants, and he was my most formidable chess partner. I would never bring harm or even wish it upon my devoted companion.

I resent these accusations and demand to know who has denounced me in this cruel and vile manner," said Mrs. Kensington.

The constable replied by saying that it was Mrs. Kensington's housekeeper Lydia Johnson, who had proclaimed herself to be a true patriot, had substantial proof to verify the accusations. Mrs. Kensington quickly retaliated by saying Lydia was a woman of questionable character and that several people had recently accused Lydia of some heinous deeds regarding which Mrs. Kensington was discreetly making inquiries. The constable was not satisfied with Mrs. Kensington's defense, so he handed her a letter written by a judge from New Haven, ordering that she be placed under house arrest pending an investigation into the allegations against her.

"You may remain in your home for the time being, but there will be guards keeping a close watch on you as well as anyone who enters or leaves this place. You are not allowed to leave Kensington Hall under any circumstances. If you fail to obey these orders, you will be arrested and taken to the prison in New Haven," stated the constable.

Mrs. Kensington sat down in a chair while clutching the queen in her hand. She was determined not to be defeated by having her Loyalist connections exposed. After regaining her train of thought, she cunningly informed the constable that she would fully cooperate with the authorities and vowed to clear her good name.

After the constable had left, Mrs. Kensington assembled Foster and Jennings, Nicholas Biddle, and two servant girls who she trusted, and she told them that they were all leaving Kensington Hall. She gave them an hour to pack personal belongings including items on a list that she had written on a piece of paper. She instructed Foster and Jennings to bring two wagons and her carriage to the outskirts of the property and to load the personal belongings onto the wagons by way of the secret passage under the mansion.

"You must be very quick, precise, and artful in carrying out this very important work. When this dreadful affair is over, I will see to it that you are very well rewarded for your efforts and loyalty. Now, be on your way to fulfill the task at hand," said a demanding Mrs. Kensington.

Then she assembled the remaining servants, gave them a hefty allowance, and dismissed them. After they were gone, she went into the great hall and glanced at the portrait of Rebecca Noble which was included among the belongings on her list.

As she stared at the mysterious portrait, a confused Charles came running down the stairs and tugged at Mrs. Kensington's petticoat while pitifully asking what was happening and where were they going. She comforted the young boy by caressing his face and telling him they were moving to a better place in a land where a person's dreams will always come true. She was very convincing, so a gullible and innocent Charles accepted her devious story and hurried to his room to gather his belongings.

After putting Charles at ease, Mrs. Kensington returned to the library to retrieve the crown jewel box containing the Winfield diamond. When she entered the room, she was confronted by a wicked Lydia Johnson who was standing in front of the desk where Mrs. Kensington kept the crown jewel box.

"Well," said Mrs. Kensington. "Look who has finally shown the right side of her face, and it is mighty ugly. How dare you betray me and try to destroy the good name of Kensington? I was told by Simon Blackwell that you were the one who killed Dr. Greenville with my letter opener. How could you be so evil? Louise Bourget and Charity Chastine were justified in their accusations against you. I took you into my home, gave you employment, and defended you against dreadful allegations, and you repay me with betrayal and treachery. I demand an explanation for your devilish deeds this instant," shrieked Mrs. Kensington.

"I despise all traitors to this country, particularly those who fought to keep this country under England's rule. I had my nephew Theodore and David Cobb kill your faithful servant Elizabeth Higgins and her Redcoat lover Edmund Tate, and I tried to kill that pathetic Charity Chastine and the former Laura Monnerat. Those women were lucky to escape my wrath," bemoaned Lydia. "You are a Loyalist who gave shelter to the man responsible for your daughter's death besides being a manipulative woman. And yes, I killed Dr. Greenville with your letter opener to indicate that you are the murderer. I got the idea the other night when I spied on Dr. Greenville in this very room, writing a letter that I happened to read when he briefly left the room. The letter contained very detailed and ruinous testimony by him regarding past indiscretions committed by you, Mrs. Fairchild, and others in this town. You are all sinners who need to pay for your sins," ranted a deranged Lydia.

Then Lydia took the letter from her apron pocket and taunted Mrs. Kensington by dangling it in her face. Mrs. Kensington desperately held her composure by walking over to the serving table. She took hold of the teapot, and then turned around and viciously threw its contents in Lydia's face. Lydia screamed in agony. With the letter in one hand, and the other hand covering her face, an angry and partially burned Lydia ran away.

Mrs. Kensington sighed with relief before returning to her desk to retrieve the crown jewel box. She opened it, took out the Winfield diamond, kissed it, and then laughed nefariously.

Unbeknownst to Mrs. Kensington, Lydia's accusations had caused an angry mob of townspeople to prepare an attack on Kensington Hall.

At the cabin, Mr. Stiles and Charity had finished eating their meal, and they were cleaning up when they heard a knock at the door. Pogo rose to his feet and began to bark. Mr. Stiles grabbed hold of his musket and slowly opened the door. To their surprise, there was no one standing in the doorway. However, Pogo began to growl. Mr. Stiles turned to Charity and said, "It must be the wind." The door was still open, and suddenly Charity saw a hand holding a large piece of wood come downward and hit Mr. Stiles on the head, and he fell unconscious to the floor. A stranger wearing a cloak and hood then grabbed Mr. Stiles' musket and shot Pogo. Charity was frozen in terror as the intruder removed the hood of his cloak, and saw that it was Simon Blackwell.

Simon laughed wickedly in her face, and she was horrified to see him alive. She began to hit him with her fists while screaming profusely. She even spit in his eye, which caused him to slap her. She fell to her knees next to Colonel Parker who sat helplessly in the rocking chair. Simon grabbed her arm and told her that she was going with him. She tried desperately to break free from his strong grip, but failed.

"If you do not come with me peacefully, I will burn this cabin to the ground with these two men in it. Do you want their deaths on your conscience?" shouted a depraved Simon.

"I will go with you. Please don't harm them," Charity pleaded.

Then Simon took her outside with a hook pressed against her throat. He pushed her along a rocky trail leading to Indian Lookout. Fearing for her life, she did what her abductor forced her to do. As they walked away from the cabin, she could hear the colonel calling out in an anguished tone for Elizabeth Higgins while Simon sneered.

Her feet began to ache from the tripping and stumbling along the rocky and unsettled trail covered with rocks and fallen branches. After some time had passed, they arrived at a cave that was carved out of the mountain. Simon pulled her into a nearby bush in order that they were not seen by Louise and Jean-Luc who were loading what appeared to be treasured objects into a wagon at the entrance to the cave.

"They have finally found the treasure so many have been seeking all these years. It truly exists, and I shall claim it all for myself. And you, my lovely Charity, will help me take it all, making me the master of the game," whispered Simon to her.

Simon waited until an unsuspecting Jean-Luc, Louise, and their accomplices Lieutenant Bradford and Alexander had finished loading up the wagon, and then they emerged from the hiding place and went into the cave.

As they entered, Simon and Charity found Lieutenant Bradford and the others taking a respite from their tedious labors. They glanced up in shock as they saw Simon holding Charity tightly with a hook to her throat. Jean-Luc quickly reacted by taking a dagger from his pocket and fearlessly throwing it at Simon's shoulder. The dagger narrowly missed Charity. Simon yelled from agony and pushed his prisoner violently into the lieutenant who grabbed her with his strong and muscular arms.

"You are safe with me," replied Lieutenant Bradford.

"I am so sorry for causing trouble. Simon came to the cabin, attacked Mr. Stiles, shot his dog, and threatened to burn the cabin with the colonel and an unconscious Mr. Stiles inside unless I went with him. He wants the treasure that you found," Charity explained excitably.

"It is not your fault, my dear. Simon Blackwell has always taken things that do not belong to him and harmed innocent victims. He is not leaving this cave with the treasure, and all of us will stop him," said Alexander adamantly.

While Alexander was speaking, Simon removed the dagger from his shoulder and threw it at Jean Luc, wounding him in the foot. Louise and Alexander grabbed Jean-Luc from collapsing as a vindictive Simon took out a pistol from under his cloak and pointed it at all of them. Then he moved towards them as they moved towards the front of the entrance. He firmly held the pistol in their direction as he came upon an empty treasure chest farther in the cave. He kicked the lid shut with his right foot.

"You have managed to find this greatly valuable and sought-after European fortune. And you have worked painstakingly to load up the wagon outside and now you are planning to depart. Unfortunately, I am the only one leaving here alive, and each of you shall receive a bullet to the head, making this your final resting place," said Simon with an evil delight.

Alexander knelt to his knees and began to beg for his life. As an insensitive Simon laughed at him, Alexander sprang like a cat and began struggling with Simon over the pistol that was pointed in the air. Charity screamed from fright as it fired once and then again.

Suddenly, a giant rumbling was heard, and sand began to fall upon them. The lieutenant shoved Charity towards the entrance, and then assisted Louise by grabbing Jean-Luc as they hurried with Charity out of the cave. As they ran outside, the sand kept falling, and they heard another shot fired.

They had made their way safely out of the cave. As they stared at the entrance, a sandy covered Alexander emerged just as the entrance collapsed, burying Simon alive.

"Is everyone all right?" inquired Alexander. "Simon did not make it out alive. We are safe from his evil clutches, and so is the treasure."

Charity stood still for a few moments while collecting her thoughts. She was grateful to be alive and for this nightmare to finally be done with. Lieutenant Bradford came up to her, stared into her eyes, and then embraced her, which she welcomed with a satisfying pleasure.

Alexander and Louise helped a wounded Jean-Luc onto the wagon, and then they made their way back to the cabin. As they were traveling on the trail, darkness began to come upon the horizon and the wind began to blow. As she turned her head in the direction of the now sealed cave, Charity saw the apparitions of the young couple moving about in the nearby distance. She thought to herself: *what are they trying to reveal and what inevitable event is yet to come?*

While on their way to Kensington Hall, Lord and Lady Winfield were sitting opposite from each other in the carriage. Lady Winfield was preoccupied with a serious matter that plagued her mind since their departure from England. Lord Winfield leaned his head back against the soft-cushioned seat, closed his eyes and thought about his hounds back at his estate in London. He missed his pets deeply, especially his two favorites Annie and Pearl who were his loyal four-legged companions. It was assumed by many of Lord Winfield's friends and acquaintances that he preferred his hounds in particular Annie and Pearl to his wife who was very overbearing at times.

As they approached Kensington Hall, the driver shouted as the carriage came to a quick and abrupt halt. Lady Winfield opened the carriage door, and as she looked in the direction of Kensington Hall, to her surprise, she saw a large crowd shouting and throwing stones while watching flames consume the beautiful mansion.

A shocked Lady Winfield emerged from the carriage with her husband behind her. When she approached the angry crowd, she asked a woman dressed in farm attire what was happening. The woman replied that the townspeople had learned that Mrs. Kensington was a Loyalist and a suspect in murdering a doctor at Singleton Lodge. She further explained that when the residents came to confront her, she did not come out, so the mob decided to force her out by setting fire to the mansion.

"My dear friend Phoebe is not guilty of these charges. There is an innocent child in that house. Please, I beg you to stop what you are doing and save them," pleaded Lady Winfield.

But her cry for mercy went unheard, and the mob shouted louder as they continued to set the mansion ablaze. A distraught Lady Winfield put her hands up to her face and wept bitterly while Lord Winfield watched in dismay at the terrible sight.

When they reached the cabin, they found Mr. Stiles sitting on the front stoop holding his dog Pogo in his arms. As Charity approached him, he was crying with tears running down his cheeks.

"My Pogo is dead. I have lost my one true friend," replied a sorrowful Mr. Stiles.

Charity sat down next to the grief stricken man and placed her hand on his shoulder and tried to offer some words of comfort.

Louise stayed with Jean-Luc in the wagon while Lieutenant Bradford and Alexander went in the cabin to check on Colonel Parker. A few seconds later, both men rushed outside, and Alexander exclaimed that the colonel was gone. A tearful Mr. Stiles informed them that when he had regained consciousness, Pogo was dead and the colonel was nowhere to be found. Lieutenant Bradford and Alexander, with lanterns in their hands, began to search the grounds. Charity prayed that the colonel was not in any danger.

Chapter 28

Mr. Stiles placed his beloved dog's body on the ground and covered it with a blanket. He took Charity's hand and stared into her soothing blue eyes and thanked her for her kindness. He also told her that she had a gentle spirit with a good heart, and she reminded him of Elizabeth Higgins.

"You are just like Elizabeth full of goodness and grace. She followed her heart but tragically it led to her death. You bear such a strong uncanny resemblance to her, and if I did not know any better, I would think you were her twin sister," said a sincere Mr. Stiles. "Stay well and keep away from danger, my dear girl."

As Mr. Stiles was speaking about Elizabeth, Charity suddenly realized where Colonel Parker could be. At that moment, Lieutenant Bradford and Alexander had returned without the colonel. Charity told them to follow her. While they went in search of the colonel, Mr. Stiles with Louise's assistance attended to Jean-Luc's wound. It was difficult finding their way through the dark with only the light from the lanterns, but they were careful in their journey. After walking for some time, they arrived at the old Higgins' place where they found Colonel Parker clinging to Elizabeth's tombstone and crying.

The colonel's pathetic and sorrowful state brought tears to Charity's eyes. For the first time, she could actually understand how much he must have loved the woman who bore his child and was later murdered. Alexander and the lieutenant showed no compassion as they stood behind the colonel shining their lanterns in his face. Charity went up to Colonel Parker and put her arms around him to comfort him. Upon feeling her embrace, he released his grip from the tombstone, turned his head, and pressed his face against her chest while crying and calling her Elizabeth.

As Charity tried to whisper comforting words, the lieutenant tapped her on the shoulder and ordered them to rise to their feet. Then he grabbed hold of a pitiful Colonel Parker and began to usher him down the path. Alexander led the group with his lantern, and Charity followed behind Lieutenant Bradford and Colonel Parker, holding the lieutenant's lantern in her hand. All the way back to Mr. Stiles' cabin, the colonel sobbed but did not try to escape. He reminded Charity of a frightened child and not the strong, charming, and dangerous man she had met some time ago.

When they reached the cabin, Jean-Luc's foot had been bandaged by Mr. Stiles, and Jean-Luc was resting in a chair. Louise and Mr. Stiles were warming themselves by the fireplace. The lieutenant placed Colonel Parker in the rocking chair where he sat in complete silence.

After seeing that they had returned safely with the colonel, Mr. Stiles went outside to bury Pogo. While the lieutenant and the others remained inside, Charity went out to offer Mr. Stiles her help. A few moments later, the lieutenant joined them and helped Mr. Stiles dig the grave.

While the two men were busy with their task at hand, Charity stared at the lieutenant while trying to figure out in her mind how to deal with his constant change of personality. She then surmised that the tragic deaths of his sister and nephew had left a terrible wound upon his heart, leaving him bitter and insensitive.

Charity was relieved and exhausted by the time they returned to Singleton Lodge. The servants had prepared a hot meal for them, and Constance greeted them expressing that she was happy to see them. She embraced and kissed her husband while a deceitful Louise looked the other way. Constance said, "You must be hungry. Let us go into the dining room and have the delicious meal that the cook and the servants have prepared."

After they had finished eating, Charity excused herself and went to her room. She took off her clothes, put on her night attire, and washed her hair to get rid of the dirt from the cave.

While she was drying her hair, Constance came to her room to see her.

"My dearest friend, how are you? My husband has just told me of the awful ordeal that you, he, and the others experienced at the hands of Simon Blackwell. Thank God all of you survived. Let's hope that we never see that evil man again," replied Constance. "Now with that said and done, Alexander and I are hoping after you receive your inheritance you will consider remaining with us. It is a pleasure to have you here at Singleton Lodge especially after what happened the other night."

Charity thanked Constance for her kind words and told her that she would consider her and Alexander's generous offer. Then Constance said good night and left the room.

Before going to bed, Charity looked out the window and saw a large cloud of smoke in the distance. Then she saw the ghostly couple moving about outside. She closed her eyes for a few seconds, and when she opened them, the couple was gone. She could take no more of this day and the events that had taken place, so she went to bed burrowing under the quilt, and she soon fell asleep.

The next morning she felt very restless, so she asked Constance if she could have the carriage to visit Mrs. Andrews who always seemed to offer her some solace. Constance wanted to get away from Singleton Lodge as well, so she accompanied her friend to Andrews' Tavern.

When they arrived at the tavern, they found a group of townspeople gathered outside talking about a terrible fire that occurred last night in Wallingford. Upon entering the dining room, Mrs. Andrews and Jesse were sitting at a table with Dr. Foote. All three of them had sadness in their eyes. Charity asked them what had happened, and they were silent for a moment. Then Jesse told Charity that an angry mob descended upon Kensington Hall and set fire to the mansion, resulting in total ruin.

Charity gasped from shock and then asked what had become of everyone residing at Kensington Hall. No one had a response to her question. Upon hearing this horrible news, Charity collapsed into a chair and fell into a state of complete silence.

Mrs. Andrews brought her a glass of water while Constance held her hand. She was very upset and then demanded to know the circumstances that led to this awful occurrence. Dr. Foote revealed that he heard from some of the locals that someone had informed the authorities that Mrs. Kensington was a Loyalist and she was involved with Dr. Greenville's murder. He said the constable visited Mrs. Kensington, and placed her under house arrest pending an investigation. When word got out to the local townspeople, an angry mob decided to deliver a brand of justice of their own.

While Dr. Foote was speaking, the tavern door opened and Lieutenant Bradford entered. Both Jesse and Mrs. Andrews were delighted to see him.

When the lieutenant saw Charity looking distressed, he inquired about what was troubling her. Constance told him of the unfortunate incident at Kensington Hall, and the lieutenant became very troubled and decided to take a ride to see for himself. Charity could not sit any longer, so Constance and she went with the lieutenant. They traveled by carriage while he followed on horseback.

Upon their arrival, the entire place was in ruins. Some soldiers and local villagers were shifting through the debris. They walked through the remains of the great mansion, and saw the remnants of a once magnificent home. The grand staircase had only a few stairs intact, and there was nothing left to the upper floors. Charity looked around, and she envisioned the beautiful family home that once stood tall in all its splendor and glory, now reduced to ashes and rubble by a violent and unruly crowd.

Constance held her friend's hand and tried to offer words of comfort. She attempted to put her mind at ease by telling her that it appeared that Mrs. Kensington, Charles, and the others did manage to escape.

When Constance mentioned Charles' name, Charity thought of the little boy whose mother was dead, whose father was in a catatonic state, and whose care was in the hands of a woman hated by her community. The lieutenant was in dismay and uttered, "Man's inhumanity to his fellow man is a very bad thing."

Finally, Charity could not bear the devastation any longer, so she urged Constance and Lieutenant Bradford for them to leave. As the carriage pulled away, Charity looked out the window of the carriage and stared at the ruins until she could see no more.

At Bickford Mansion, Laura Corday was sitting at her desk, examining the financial ledgers. She took a break from her tedious task at hand by staring out the window and watching the little boy Seth sitting alone under the tree. Laura felt very sad for the boy and pondered about how she could reach him.

Laura's train of thought was interrupted by the unexpected arrival of Reverend Davenport and two women from his congregation. Although a bit alarmed by their visit, Laura was gracious and invited them to join her in the sitting room for tea. Reverend Davenport introduced the two women as Mrs. King and Mrs. Holley who had made inquiries about Laura's establishment and her charitable work in the community.

Both Mrs. King and Mrs. Holley commended Laura for her generosity and compassion for the less fortunate, but they expressed deep concern for her association with Alexander and Constance Caruthers and Jean-Luc Tessier who killed Laura's husband. They believed that Laura's association with disdainful and immoral individuals would hurt her reputation and blacken the name of Bickford Mansion, causing those who had wished to contribute to her charitable establishment to withdraw their support.

Although upset by her guests condescending and judgmental comments, Laura refrained from making any irrational responses and smiled pleasantly at her guests and thanked them for their concern.

Then Reverend Davenport supported the women's concerns by telling Laura not to be ashamed in asking for assistance from him and members of his congregation. Mrs. King and Mrs. Holley agreed with the Reverend and reassured Laura they would personally see to it that Bickford Mansion would remain open and fully functioning for many years to come.

Before Laura could respond, Mrs. Downey entered the room and handed her a note that had just been delivered by messenger. Laura read the note quickly, and then informed Reverend Davenport and the ladies that she had to leave immediately to pay a call to a sick friend.

"I deeply apologize for my sudden and rude departure, but a dear friend is ill and has requested to see me. Please, feel free to return another day to visit me and we shall talk further," said a polite but flustered Laura.

Mrs. King and Mrs. Holley said farewell and took their leave. While Laura was preparing to leave, Reverend Davenport remained behind. He was curious to know the name of Laura's sick friend, but Laura told him it was someone with whom he was unacquainted. Then she sent for the carriage, and as the carriage drove away, a foreboding Reverend Davenport mounted his horse and followed from not very far away.

———————————

When they had returned to Singleton Lodge, Charity went for a walk around the grounds in the hopes of clearing her head with fresh air and getting some exercise. Soon her legs began to ache, so she sat down on a bench and stared at the scenery before her.

The horrific events of the last several days had left her dismayed, shocked, and very sad. Since her arrival to America, she had had the misfortune of befriending and getting involved with a gallery of unsavory and dangerous individuals capable of such sin, chaos, and destruction. Their unholy deeds stem from the seven deadly sins and were the results of secrets connected to the war for independence. That war created a free country from England's rule but caused a tremendous amount of pain, suffering, and death long after the peace treaty had been signed.

Was that war worth it and at the cost of so many lives, she wondered.

Then she reminded herself that war and sin have existed for centuries, and as long as man is capable of evil and acts upon those intentions, there will never be peace and love in any society; rather cruelty, injustice, tragedy, and heartache. At that moment, she had decided that once she had her inheritance, she would return home to London to be with her beloved Patience. Perhaps, once back home in familiar surroundings with a woman who she looked upon as a second mother, she would find peace and happiness.

As she began to make her way back to the house, Lieutenant Bradford came upon her. He seemed a bit melancholy and asked her to sit with him and allow him a chance to speak. His sincerity encouraged her to abide by his wishes. They sat down on the bench, and she listened intently as he spoke.

"My dear Charity, please forgive the manner in which I have

treated you since my return from the Ohio Valley. I have seen many terrible sights and come up against some unscrupulous characters whose actions were unspeakably horrid. I saw men kill without mercy for a piece of land, one brother against another, loved ones separated by tragedy and disease, schemers and villains always plotting to achieve power or possess material possessions belonging to others. And most tragic of all, I had the sad encounter of finding my long lost sister and her son massacred along with many other innocent men, women, and children. All these occurrences have left painful and disturbing images in my mind while turning my heart to stone. I feel like a tattered and defeated soldier marching home from war and returning to nowhere. Please, forgive me, Charity," pleaded a sorrowful Lieutenant Bradford. "Your presence has helped me find a remnant of solace during this awful and dark time in my life."

The lieutenant said he had known Alexander Caruthers briefly during the war and they met again when he had returned from his expedition in the valley, and Alexander offered him employment to guard Colonel Parker whose life was in danger. In need of money and being familiar with the colonel, Lieutenant Bradford accepted the position without knowing how things would turn out. The lieutenant also expressed his regret regarding his involvement with Mrs. Kensington, and his concern about Charles' welfare. Most of all, he admitted that their friendship was very valuable to him and he did not want it to end.

After the lieutenant had earnestly explained his feelings to her, Charity understood him better and forgave him for his ill treatment of her and was determined to preserve their friendship. With tears in his eyes, he hugged her, and his bright blue eyes and strong muscular arms reassured her that her dear friend had returned.

As they took a stroll together, a servant met them half way and informed them that their presence was required back at the house, but she gave them no details. A curious Lieutenant Bradford and Charity hurried back to the mansion. When they arrived, they saw three carriages out front and another pulling up to the front entrance of Singleton Lodge. They looked at each other in confusion and asked what could possibly be taking place.

Once inside, they were greeted by Constance who took them into the library where they were joined by several visitors including Mr. and Mrs. Fairchild, Miss Evelyn Winchester, Ethan Fairchild and Honoria Noble, Jean-Luc and Louise, and a very elegantly dressed couple who Constance introduced as Lord and Lady Winfield. As they sat down next to the others, Laura Corday entered the room, and her appearance put a giant smile on Jean-Luc's face. Louise embraced her former mistress and made room for her to sit next to Jean-Luc. Two of the servants brought a passive Colonel Parker into the room and placed him in a chair next to the lieutenant and Charity. They sat in a large circle while smiling at each other and engaging in petty conversation with the person adjacent to them. The main question on the minds of all those present was *what is going on.* Even poor Constance did not have a clue to this mysterious gathering.

After a short time had passed, Alexander came into the room with Mr. Preston, the lawyer from New Haven who was handling Grace's estate. Alexander introduced Mr. Preston and sat down next to Constance as the dutiful husband while Louise looked on. Then Mr. Preston removed a letter from the pocket of his blue coat. He put on his spectacles, opened the letter, and informed all those present that it was a letter written by his client Mrs. Phoebe Kensington. The letter was delivered to him by messenger the night Kensington Hall came under attack. And according to Mrs. Kensington's detailed instructions, it was to be read to all those gathered in this room. Curiosity and fear filled the entire room, as they all listened to hear what the letter had to reveal and how its contents would affect their lives.

Chapter 29

Mr. Preston sat in a Chippendale chair in the center of the room. He glanced quickly at all of them, and then started to read Mrs. Kensington's letter. It began with Mrs. Kensington telling everyone that she, Charles, Nicholas Biddle, and a handful of servants had safely escaped just minutes before the mob set fire to Kensington Hall, and she dismissed the rest of the household staff after they had assisted in removing certain belongings from the mansion. She boasted arrogantly that she was a devoted Loyalist and had wished that England had won the war. Then she revealed her dreadful confrontation with Lydia Johnson who admitted to Mrs. Kensington that she killed Dr. Greenville to gain possession of a scandalous letter he held in his possession.

Mrs. Kensington's letter also said that Lydia Johnson confessed to manipulating Theodore Norton and David Cobb into murdering Elizabeth Higgins and Edmund Tate as well as getting them to try to kill Mr. Higgins, Laura Corday, Louise Bourget, Jean-Luc Tessier, and Charity Chastine. Mrs. Kensington admitted to throwing hot water in Lydia's face, causing her to run away wailing and screaming in agony.

Charity was shocked by the horrible acts committed by Lydia. The lieutenant tried to comfort her by placing his strong hand on her shoulder.

After revealing Lydia Johnson's crimes, the letter then addressed all the people assembled in the room. Mrs. Kensington identified each one by name and then informed them that she possessed something each one wanted. First, she told Lord and Lady Winfield that she had a priceless item that was in the Winfield family for generations. Upon hearing this news, both Lord and Lady Winfield were dismayed and agitated as evident in their facial expressions. Second, she told Evelyn Winchester to keep a watchful eye on her sister Judith Fairchild who has dangerous intentions for Honoria Noble. Then she informed Honoria and Judith that she had the portrait of Rebecca Noble, which both women wanted for different reasons.

Judith Fairchild became irritated by Mrs. Kensington's words and demanded that Mr. Preston discontinue his reading, but her request was ignored. Mr. Preston went on reading, and Mrs. Kensington addressed Laura Corday who she praised for redeeming herself by helping the less fortunate. She then commended Jean-Luc Tessier for ridding the world of Monsieur Louis Monnerat and fighting Simon Blackwell who had survived the fall off Widow's Bluff and had returned to wreak havoc on Mrs. Kensington's life and the lives of many others. Then the letter addressed Ethan Fairchild with pity telling him that his mother was keeping a secret from him and his father Caleb. Lastly, she said that if Judith was unwilling to tell her son and husband the truth, Mrs. Kensington would include evidence to verify the truth.

A confused Ethan stared at his mother while his father got up from his chair and walked away from his wife. Honoria was taking all of this in while looking at Judith with a devious satisfaction as evident in the glare of her eyes. Mrs. Kensington addressed Louise Bourget by telling her that she was a cold-blooded revolutionist who needed to return to her beloved Paris and her fellow revolutionists. Mrs. Kensington expressed to Louise in a disdainful manner that she despised anyone who had wished harm upon his or her monarch. Lastly, she spoke to Constance and Alexander. She revealed to Constance that Simon Blackwell confessed to her that he murdered her father at the request of her mother for her father's indiscretions. Then she expressed her disapproval of Constance marrying Alexander, who she described as a womanizer, a sinner who held men in bondage to make a profit, and a dangerous man with a past. She warned Constance to always be on her guard.

"We have had enough of these ramblings of a deranged matriarch who has become an outcast in her own society," said Alexander. "I beg of you to stop reading that horrible letter," demanded Alexander.

Mr. Preston remained silent for a moment, adjusted his spectacles, and proceeded to finish reading the letter. In her final words, Mrs. Kensington wished Charity well and had wished Charity was with her and Charles and she asked Lieutenant Bradford to take care of her. She then ridiculed her son-in-law Colonel Parker by calling him inappropriate names and telling him that Charles belonged to her and that he would never see his son again. Upon hearing those hurtful words, a pitiful Colonel Parker put his hands up to his face and began to cry. Charity looked at the colonel and felt sorrow for him.

Finally, Mr. Preston read Mrs. Kensington's concluding remarks that informed all those present that if certain ones wanted what she had, they should try to seek her out, but she warned them that she was a woman who was not one but two steps ahead of her adversaries making her the master of the game. When he had finished, Mr. Preston stood up, walked over to the fireplace, and tossed the letter into the fire. He then warned everyone that the contents of Dr. Greenville's letter that Lydia Johnson had in her possession was just as lethal as Lydia herself. As those present began to move about the room while trying to gather their thoughts and react to Mrs. Kensington's letter, Constance gave out a scream as she stared at the terrace doors. Charity looked in that direction, and to her horror, she saw someone wearing a black veil standing outside and closely watching them.

Alexander and Lieutenant Bradford hurried outside after the mysterious stranger who was spying on them from the terrace. The rest of them waited indoors.

Lord and Lady Winfield came up to Constance and informed her that they were leaving. As the elegant couple was taking their leave, the thought came to Charity that their last name was the same as the name of the diamond that Mrs. Kensington had in her possession.

She wondered why Mrs. Kensington would steal from her friends and if Lord and Lady Winfield would attempt to retrieve their property; and if so, how would they find Mrs. Kensington.

While Charity silently pondered these questions, an agitated Judith Fairchild approached Mr. Preston and demanded to know of Mrs. Kensington's whereabouts, but he declined to give a response. A desperate Mrs. Fairchild pursued Mr. Preston, but was thwarted by Mr. Fairchild who took his wife's hand and insisted they leave at once. Mr. Preston smiled at both Mr. and Mrs. Fairchild before leaving their presence, and joined Charity at the other end of the room.

"Miss Chastine, I have settled the estate of the late Mrs. Collins and the papers regarding your inheritance are complete. I would like you to come to my office so we may conclude the business at hand," replied Mr. Preston. "Is tomorrow at noon a convenient time for you, my dear?"

"Tomorrow at noon will be fine for me," Charity responded with a smile.

Then Mr. Preston left Singleton Lodge with the others behind him. Jean-Luc and Louise remained with Laura Corday by their side. Constance went to the kitchen to instruct some of the servants to bring food and drink for those who had remained. While waiting for Constance to return, Charity stared out the window wondering who that mysteriously disfigured individual was and if Alexander and the lieutenant would find this person.

Suddenly Colonel Parker rose from his chair and approached Charity. He called her Elizabeth while reaching into his pocket and taking out the doll. He held the doll firmly in his grasp and attempted to speak when two male servants along with Caroline entered the room to escort the colonel back upstairs. The colonel went with them willingly while calling out Elizabeth and Charles' names.

"What a pathetic simpleton that man has become!" said an insensitive Louise. "He is a burden to Constance and Alexander while dependent upon their generosity and kindness. Perhaps it would be more merciful if he were dead like his former lover whose name he utters relentlessly."

As Charity was about to make a response on behalf of Colonel Parker's defense, Alexander and Lieutenant Bradford returned from their search that turned up nothing. Whoever it was had made a quick and effective escape and could not be found. At that moment, Constance came into the room with two servants carrying trays of food. Laura Corday politely thanked Constance for her hospitality and then took her leave. After Laura had gone, a rude Alexander ordered Constance and Charity to leave the room so he could speak to Jean-Luc, Louise, and the lieutenant privately. Without questioning her husband, Constance did as he had requested and Charity went with her.

Once they were in the hallway, Charity told Constance that she was going to her room for a brief rest, and Constance returned to the kitchen.

After she was gone, Charity tiptoed to the doorway of the library and eavesdropped on the conversation that was taking place inside. She heard an angry Alexander tell the others that while he and the lieutenant were searching the grounds for the intruder, they went to the stables, and to their chagrin, found that the coffin containing the treasure was missing. They found a note nailed to the door of the stable. It read: *I have the treasure and it is all mine. My brother Louis would want me to have it. If you are brave enough, please come and get it. But I warn you that I'll be ready and waiting, and you may very well end up like my poor brother with no treasure and in your grave.* Alexander explained that the note was signed by Louis Monnerat's brother Philippe who must have taken the opportunity to steal the treasure while they were distracted with the reading of Mrs. Kensington's letter.

"How did he know where to find it? And when did he arrive in town?" inquired Jean-Luc. "Someone had to have told him. Who was it?"

"I would wager the entire estate of Singleton Lodge on the

fact that the cunning and devious Mrs. Kensington had a hand in Philippe's carefully orchestrated plot to deceive us," said Alexander. "We risked too much for that treasure including battling the evil Simon Blackwell, to have it taken from us. I vow that we form an alliance and together seek out Philippe Monnerat and take back the treasure at all cost. Are you with me?"

Jean-Luc and Louise instantly pledged their allegiance and informed Alexander that they needed to act quickly. Then they cast their eyes upon Lieutenant Bradford who remained silent. When Alexander pressed him for an answer while telling him that his assistance was desperately needed in this matter, the lieutenant remained still and then agreed to join them. Upon hearing the lieutenant's response, an elated Alexander poured everyone a glass of sherry and then they made a toast to finding Philippe Monnerat and the treasure.

Charity was deeply troubled by what she had heard and she feared for the lieutenant's safety. Unable to listen any further, Charity decided to take her leave.

As she turned to make her way to the stairs, she was startled by Constance standing in her way and looking at her with grave disapproval.

Chapter 30

Constance put her index finger to her lips and motioned for Charity to follow her into the drawing room. Once inside, she closed the door and told her to sit down. Then she took her friend into her confidence by pouring her heart out to her. She said she was not shocked by what Mrs. Kensington had written in the letter about her mother. She explained that her mother, while struggling for her last breath of life, confessed to hiring Simon Blackwell to murder Mr. Singleton as retribution for his immoral indiscretions. She also said that she was familiar with Alexander's imperfections and married him for financial security.

"We are women, and we do not have many choices in life. But we can use our charm, good manners, unblemished reputations, and ability to bear children to make us desirable to the opposite sex, particularly those of high society and nobility," said Constance. "I admit that I married Alexander for security, not love, but I had no other choice. Both of my parents were dead, and my father had left me with a legacy of bad debts hidden by a good name. I know in my heart that I made a wrong choice, and I fear one day I shall live to regret it, but until that day arrives I will live with my decision and suffer in silence."

Then Charity spoke to Constance. "My dear friend, I am very sorry for you and the agonies you must be going through, but you must remember that the actions of your parents and your husband do not reflect the kind of person you are. I believe that the innocent and good hearted souls in this life fall victim to devious, ruthless, and

266

cold hearted scoundrels who lure their unsuspecting prey into their well concealed web of deception."

Charity continued by telling Constance that she did not condemn her for her decision to marry Alexander, and she reassured her that she was standing by her as an altruistic friend. Charity did, however, express her concern regarding the plan made by Alexander, Louise, Jean-Luc, and Lieutenant Bradford to track down Philippe Monnerat and retrieve the treasure. She feared that nothing good would come of the encounter. Constance shared her concern, but said that they were powerless in changing their minds.

The conversation was interrupted by a servant who knocked at the door, informing Constance that her husband wanted to see her. After the servant had gone, Charity told Constance that she needed to get away from Singleton Lodge and asked if she could have the carriage to go to church. Constance gave Charity a hug and told her not to worry before sending for the carriage.

Charity went upstairs to dress for the excursion. While she was coming down the stairs to get into the carriage, Lieutenant Bradford stopped her and inquired where she was going. She told him that she was going to church and invited him to join her, but he declined the offer.

The lieutenant escorted her to the carriage and waved good-bye as the carriage pulled away. Charity stared out the window watching the lieutenant as he slowly faded into the distance. On the way to church, she made up her mind that after receiving her inheritance, she would definitely return to London. She could no longer stay in a place filled with dangerous and greedy scoundrels who were determined to indulge in unscrupulous deeds; particular since to her shocking dismay, Lieutenant Bradford, a man she once regarded as her hero and guardian angel, had sold his soul to the dark side like all the others.

Upon returning to Bickford Mansion, Laura Corday found an anxious Reverend Davenport waiting for her. He was sitting at her desk reading the Bible. Laura was gracious while inquiring the intention for his visit. Reverend Davenport was shrewd in not revealing his reason. Instead he inquired about the health of Laura's so-called ill friend. Laura simply replied that her friend was doing better and thanked the Reverend for his thoughtfulness. Suddenly, Reverend Davenport slammed the Bible angrily on the desk and demanded to know why Laura did not tell him the truth. Taken aback by the Reverend's uncouth and bizarre behavior, Laura nicely asked him to calm down or to take his leave. Her comment agitated him further, causing him to raise his voice in a threatening manner.

"Do not lie to me. I followed you to that house of sin. How could you keep company with those sinners who will taint your reputation and destroy all the good work you are doing? Did you not heed the polite but solemn concerns of Mrs. King and Mrs. Holley who disapproved of the company you are keeping?" ranted Reverend Davenport. "Save yourself by staying away from those whose souls are in the hands of the devil."

Then he begged Laura to pray with him, saying that she needed spiritual guidance, and he would assist her. He folded his hands and began to pray in front of a startled Laura who found herself trapped in the presence of a religious fanatic. In an effort to appease and calm the Reverend, Laura sat down in a chair, bowed her head, folded her hands, and began to pray.

Mrs. Downey, who overheard the Reverend shouting, entered the room and interrupted the prayer by informing him that his wife needed him home immediately. Reluctantly, the Reverend composed himself, took his Bible into his hands, and told Laura he would see her tomorrow.

After he had left, Laura gave a sigh of relief and thanked Mrs. Downey for her interference. Then both women made their way upstairs to see the mothers and their children.

After arriving at St. John's Episcopal Church, Charity went inside and sat in a pew close to the altar. She stared at the gold cross on the altar. Sunlight from outside was shining through the stained glass windows leaving beautiful images on the stone floor. She bowed her head and began to pray silently. The church was empty and very peaceful. She knew she had come to the right place to find solace.

After meditating in prayer for a while, her solitude was interrupted by the sound of footsteps coming down the aisle, which became silent. As she stood up to leave the pew, she was confronted by a woman wearing a long gown and hat with a veil that concealed her face. Before she could speak a word, the woman raised her right hand and tried to strike her with a candlestick holder.

Charity was stricken with horror which prevented her from screaming for help. She desperately tried to fight off the attacker by raising her hands to protect her face. Then, with a mighty shove, she pushed the woman away from her. As the woman stumbled against another pew, Charity hurried out of her pew and ran frantically down the aisle without looking back. When she came to the wooden doors of the church, she opened them, and to her surprise and relief, Lieutenant Bradford was standing in the entrance. She reached out to him and collapsed in his arms from fright and exhaustion.

"Charity, what is the matter? Why are you trembling and so frightened?" asked the lieutenant with genuine concern.

She explained to him a woman wearing a veil tried to strike her with a candlestick holder while she was praying in the pew and she had to fight her off. The lieutenant went inside and looked around the church, but he found no one. Then they heard the side door of the church shut loudly. They assumed the woman had escaped through the side door.

The lieutenant told Charity that shortly after she had left Singleton Lodge, he reconsidered her offer to come to church so he came. Once again the lieutenant had come to her rescue, and she was most grateful.

They left St. John's and returned to Singleton Lodge where Charity informed Constance and the others about the encounter. After hearing the story, Alexander suspected the attacker to be Lydia Johnson, and he was certain that she was the mysterious person Constance saw spying on them from the terrace. Lieutenant Bradford agreed and told Charity not to leave Singleton Lodge without an escort.

Exhausted from the occurrence at church, Charity had supper and went to her room for the night. While getting undressed, her mind was focused on the meeting she was to have with Mr. Preston the next day. She was hoping that Grace's kindness would afford her passage back home to London and to her beloved Patience.

Before going to bed, she wrote a letter to Patience, telling her she would be returning to London very soon, and that she longed to see her smiling and benevolent face.

When she finished the letter, she blew out the candle and got into bed. When she closed her eyes, all she could envision was the woman wearing the veil trying to strike her with a candlestick holder. That horrible memory forced her to recall the time when she saw Colonel Parker strike Mr. Singleton with a similar object. To rid her mind of such terrible thoughts, she convinced herself that after the meeting tomorrow with Mr. Preston, she would be able to leave this place and the evil that dwells here.

At Winchester Park, Judith Fairchild was sitting alone in the drawing room enjoying a cup of tea when her sister Evelyn entered. Judith ignored her sister, but Evelyn began a conversation inquiring about Caleb. As Evelyn continued, Judith got up from her chair and threw her tea cup on the floor.

"I am not my husband's keeper!" exclaimed Judith. "But I can assure you, my dear sister, that he is taking a stroll about the grounds with my loving Ethan and that wretched Honoria. I wish she would leave Ethan and go far away from him. She will be his downfall. Why won't you and Caleb believe me?" she cried out.

"My foolish sister, it is in my good opinion that Honoria is the best thing to happen for Ethan," said Evelyn. "I truly believe that their unexpected encounter is a blessing that must be embraced. And you should be the last person to cast judgment after what you have done. "I am afraid that Phoebe's letter has cast grave suspicion upon you, and that your hidden sin from the past is about to be exposed, and then you will be Ethan's ruin, not Honoria."

"You are a traitor just like Phoebe Kensington. I do not wish to speak to you any longer," shrieked Judith. "Remember one thing, my loving sister. You are just as guilty of harboring my secret of the baby switch as I am for committing the unspeakable act. I will take care of my Ethan, and I vow to stop anyone who proposes a threat to my son and the Fairchild legacy." Judith abruptly left the room. Troubled by her sister's behavior, Evelyn decided to find Caleb and Ethan to tell them the truth before they learned it from someone else. She wrapped her shawl around her shoulders, and left the drawing room in search of Ethan and Caleb. Then Honoria emerged from the shadows of the hallway and followed an unsuspecting Evelyn. In the meantime, Judith was secretively meeting with the male servant Hastings, and she enlisted his help in finding Lydia Johnson and retrieving from Lydia the scandalous letter written by the late Dr. Greenville.

The next day Charity went to see Mr. Preston at his office. Lieutenant Bradford accompanied her, but waited outside while she went in. Mr. Preston was very professional and gracious. His office was nicely decorated with comfortable chairs. After being seated, he began to explain the details of Grace's will. As Mr. Preston was going through the papers, his clerk interrupted and informed him that his immediate attention was needed in the next room. Mr. Preston apologized for the inconvenience and promised that he would return quickly. Charity sat back in the comfortable chair while admiring the beautiful furnishings and portraits hanging on the wall.

A few moments later, she heard someone enter the room. She assumed it was Mr. Preston, but as she looked up, to her horror, she saw the woman in the black veil. Charity tried to get away, but she lunged at her placing her hands on her throat and choking her. She fought profusely, and she tried to scream a couple of times.

The commotion alerted Mr. Preston and his clerk who hurried into the room. As they tried to get the woman off of Charity, Lieutenant Bradford entered and grabbed hold of her. Holding her in his grasp, he pulled off the veil, and they saw that it was Lydia Johnson with a badly burned face.

"Please let me hide my face. Mrs. Kensington threw hot water in my face, and I've been in agony ever since," bemoaned Lydia who slumped to the floor.

Lydia wailed and begged for mercy. She expressed her hatred for Charity, because she reminded her of Elizabeth Higgins. Then Lydia looked out the window and began to shout the names of Elizabeth and Edmund.

"They are outside and they're coming to get me. Don't you see those traitors Elizabeth and Edmund like I do right now? Why can't they stay dead?" shrieked a deranged Lydia.

As the lieutenant attempted to lift Lydia to her feet, she pushed Mr. Preston into Charity and kicked the lieutenant in the leg. Then she ran out the front door, and they chased after her as she ran into the path of an oncoming coach. The driver shouted for Lydia to get out of the way, but she froze from fright, standing still like a statue while screaming in anguish as she was trampled by the galloping horses. The sight was too horrible to witness so Charity covered her eyes with her hands.

After the coach had passed, Lydia's crushed and distorted body was lying on the ground. As the lieutenant and bystanders hurried to her side, a tall gentleman went up to Lydia, took something out of her pocket, and quickly fled into the crowd.

Lydia's tragic demise reminded Charity of how the evil queen Jezebel died from being trampled to death by wild horses as punishment for her sins. Charity thought *perhaps now the spirits of Elizabeth Higgins and Edmund Tate can finally rest in peace.*

Chapter 31

Lydia Johnson was now dead, and Elizabeth and Edmund had been avenged. The authorities recorded Lydia's death as a tragic accident, and no charges were filed against the driver of the coach.

Mr. Preston and his clerk were apologetic regarding the incident in the office. The clerk said that Lydia had tricked him into believing she needed immediate assistance, but it had been her way of luring Mr. Preston away, and leaving Charity alone and vulnerable.

Since Lydia's first encounter with Charity, she was determined to harm her, because she reminded her of Elizabeth Higgins, the girl she had killed. The lieutenant said it was Lydia's guilty conscience that made her become obsessed with Charity. Charity got chills when she thought of her manipulation of Theodore and David getting them to carry out her evil deeds, which ended in their own demises. Lydia's wicked actions caused great pain, suffering, and death to many innocent people. Perhaps peace and tranquility would reign in North Haven for a long time.

The lieutenant and Charity left New Haven and he took her to Andrews' Tavern for a light meal, as he thought seeing Mrs. Andrews and Jesse would help to raise her spirits. Mrs. Andrews was delighted as always to see them. They sat down and told her what had happened. After they had finished speaking, she looked at the lieutenant and Charity with a solemn expression and reminded them that Grace never trusted Lydia and suspected her of somehow being responsible for the murders of Elizabeth and Edmund.

"Lydia was always lurking around the tavern and hovering over

Mr. Higgins," said Mrs. Andrews. "Grace expressed, on numerous occasions, that Lydia's behavior warranted suspicion. I wished that I had listened to Grace. She was a wise woman and a good friend. "Oh, how I miss her."

Charity reached over and gave Mrs. Andrews a hug as her eyes filled with tears and she tried to refrain from crying. Charity told her that although there has been great pain and loss, it is now time for healing and comfort. Mrs. Andrews shook her head in agreement, and then went into the back room to get their meal while the lieutenant and Charity sat in silence.

Then Jesse entered the tavern, and upon seeing them, came up to their table. He had some exciting news that he wanted to share. After waiting for his mother to join them, he said that he had just heard from Mr. Pierpont and Reverend Trumbull that the selectman had signed a legal contract allowing for the construction and expansion of public roads and bridges in North Haven.

"The building of roads and bridges will attract workers to our town, and with better roads, more tradesmen and travelers will come which will help our town to prosper financially. I imagine that we will be busy here at the tavern," replied an elated Jesse. "North Haven may even become a booming city like Boston and Philadelphia, or like New Haven."

Mrs. Andrews smiled at her son and told him not to be over zealous about North Haven's future, but she expressed her interest in the news as did the lieutenant and Charity. Jesse was too excited to sit and visit with them, so he went to share the news with his friends. Lieutenant Bradford and Charity enjoyed their meal while visiting with Mrs. Andrews and then they returned to Singleton Lodge.

In their quarters at lodging in New Haven, Lord and Lady Winfield were enjoying their afternoon tea. Lady Winfield had Mrs. Kensington's letter on her mind. She was thinking about Mrs.

Kensington's comment about possessing a priceless item belonging to the Winfield family. Then it came to Lady Winfield that it had to be the Winfield diamond. She recalled that her friend had always talked about the diamond in an obsessive way, especially when they attended the gatherings at St. James' Court.

Lady Winfield took a turn about the room while flashbacks of past conversations with Mrs. Kensington regarding the diamond flooded her memory. Then Lady Winfield recalled that the diamond was stolen after the war when Mr. and Mrs. Kensington were in London visiting the King, and that their visit was cut short by a terrible fire at one of London's taverns which claimed several lives including Mr. Kensington's.

"Why would Mr. Kensington, a man of his position, patronize a public establishment with a disreputable reputation, and why did Phoebe leave her beloved England and return to a country she despised instead of staying with the people who loved her during her time of mourning?" asked Lady Winfield.

Then she came to the surprising realization that perhaps her dear friend left England to hide a secret that had nothing to do with her husband's death, but rather with the theft of the Winfield diamond with which Mr. Kensington and his companions were involved. She also recalled that Mrs. Kensington was upset with her husband for keeping company with Monsieur Monnerat, the Marquis de Touvere, Mr. Singleton, and Colonel Parker during their stay in London. She also recalled that Mrs. Kensington had harbored feelings of contempt for these men as evident in her correspondence with Lady Winfield following the fire.

She must have the diamond or knows who does, thought Lady Winfield while clenching her hands into a fist. *How convenient of her to suddenly disappear to somewhere unknown and to have the colossal and devious nerve to arouse my curiosity in her farewell letter that Mr. Preston read at Singleton Lodge.*

Lady Winfield abruptly informed Lord Winfield that they were leaving for London immediately. She sent for the servants and told them to pack their trunks. Lord Winfield was delighted by his wife's news, for he had longed to return home to be with his hounds, especially his precious Annie and Pearl who he missed terribly.

Lady Winfield had a strong suspicion that Mrs. Kensington had returned to London; and if her assumption was correct, she was determined to find her deceitful friend and reclaim what rightfully belonged to the Winfield family and the English monarchy.

When the lieutenant and Charity returned to Singleton Lodge from their visit to Andrews' Tavern, they found that Alexander and Constance were waiting for them. Mr. Preston had sent word by messenger what had happened. Constance embraced her friend and told her that she was now safe. Alexander expressed his relief that Lydia Johnson had paid for her crimes, and he complimented the lieutenant for being with her.

"Lieutenant Bradford is a good man to have around during a crisis, and also a good man to have on your side at any time," commented Alexander. "I'm glad to have him on my side. Don't you agree, Miss Charity?"

Charity nodded her head with a smile. As in the past, she was very grateful to the lieutenant for his assistance. She regarded him as her guardian angel from the very first time they met, when he came to her rescue during a confrontation with Colonel Parker.

Alexander poured all of them a glass of sherry and asked them to be seated. While they sipped their sherry, he informed them that he and Constance were planning a trip to London, and they invited them to join them. He said that he had business in London and decided to make the excursion both business and pleasure.

"I believe that we all need some time away after these past several weeks. Christmas will soon be here, and London is a beautiful place during the holidays. I will make the arrangements and take care of the travel expenses," said Alexander. "Constance and I will not take no for an answer, so it is off to London with all of us."

The lieutenant and Charity were taken aback by the generous and surprising invitation. They looked at each other in amazement, and then the lieutenant inquired about Jean-Luc, Louise, and Colonel Parker. Alexander said that Jean-Luc and Louise would return to Paris for a short time, and then would join them in London, and Colonel Parker would join them as well under the supervision of Caroline and two trusted male servants. Alexander believed that the trip may help restore the colonel's mental health. Charity knew that Alexander's purpose for this excursion was in connection with the treasure and it was that reason that Jean-Luc and Louise would meet up with them at a later time. Although she did not trust Alexander, Constance had her heart set on the trip and on Charity joining them. She did not want to disappoint her friend, and she thought it would be the perfect opportunity for her to return to London and to her Patience who she longed to see again.

The lieutenant accepted, which did not surprise Charity. Before she could respond, Lieutenant Bradford reminded her that she would be a fool to refuse Alexander's offer. She made everyone happy, especially, Constance when she said yes. Upon hearing Charity's reply, Alexander excused himself and went to make preparations for the trip.

Constance told Charity that tomorrow they would go shopping to buy new clothes for the trip. She then went to the kitchen to speak to the cook about supper. The lieutenant smiled at Charity and reassured her that the trip would be well deserved and perhaps unforgettable. He asked her to join him for a walk about the grounds, but she declined and went upstairs to her room to rest before supper.

As she approached her room, she glanced down the hall at the door to the colonel's room. While she was day dreaming, Caroline came out of the colonel's room, and when she saw Charity, she came up to her and returned the doll to her.

"The doll is yours and belongs with you. Take good care of it. It is unique and special," she replied with sincerity.

After thanking Caroline for returning the doll, she entered her room. She sat down at the desk and began to reflect on the last two years of her life. She could not believe all that she had endured while trying to find her place in America. She tried to focus on the good people and the good memories, but she found her mind recalling the not so nice people and painful experiences. She closed her eyes and made a promise that she would survive and within days she would be returning home to Patience who she loved as a mother.

While everyone at Singleton Lodge was anticipating the impending trip, the residents of Winchester Park were experiencing an upheaval. Caleb Fairchild could not be found, and Ethan Fairchild was in his room pondering over what secret was his mother keeping from him.

Judith Fairchild was elated when her servant Hastings returned home with a special gift for his employer. He handed Dr. Greenville's letter to Judith, which he took from a dead Lydia's pocket. Judith held the letter in her hands while kissing it and praising Hastings for a job well done. As she praised her servant and relished in her triumph, she was unaware that Honoria Noble was lurking in the shadows and watching her very closely, and that an unconscious Evelyn Winchester was lying at the bottom of the stairs.

After instructing Hastings to take his leave, Judith opened Dr. Greenville's letter and began to read it. She was shocked by its contents, but was relieved to have it in her possession. As she continued to read the letter, Honoria quietly entered the room and crept up behind Judith. Sensing that someone was behind her, a startled Judith crumbled up the letter and turned around to find Honoria staring at her.

"How dare you creep up on me in an inappropriate and disdainful manner? Have you no respect for a person's solitude or privacy?" asked an angry Judith.

Honoria looked directly at Judith and mocked her for her hypocritical remarks. Then Honoria made reference to the snake that had slithered out from the sofa and bitten Ethan. Honoria revealed to Judith that she suspected that the snake found its way into the mansion with a little help from her and her trusted servant Hastings who does whatever his employer instructs him to do. Judith remained silent for a moment, and then she slapped Honoria and uttered some hurtful words.

An unaffected Honoria touched the cheek that Judith slapped, remained still for a moment, and then reached forcefully to grab the letter. In retaliation, Judith shoved Honoria who returned an even more forceful push causing Judith to fall to her knees while clutching the letter in her hand.

"That's where you belong, on your knees and at my mercy," shrieked an angry Honoria. "I know that you intended for the snake to bite me, but your son became the victim during his attempt to save me. I will not let you destroy my relationship with Ethan. Your friend Mrs. Kensington has put doubt in your husband's mind about you, and Ethan now doubts you as well. The sin from your past is about to be revealed, destroying you and your precious Fairchild legacy."

"You are an evil witch just like your ancestor Rebecca Noble. I will not let you have my Ethan. I will destroy you and I have the means to do it," retaliated a vengeful Judith.

Honoria was not intimidated by Judith's threats and continued to harass her. Then Honoria took her hands and placed them on Judith's throat while demanding she give her the letter.

As both women began to struggle, a servant hurried into the room and frantically announced that Evelyn Winchester was not well. Honoria left Judith and went to find Ethan, leaving an agitated Judith to rise to her feet and regain her composure. Then Judith told the servant to be on her way. Once the servant was gone, Judith took a book that was on the table, put the letter inside it, hid the book, and left the room to inquire about her sister.

On a passenger ship traveling across the Atlantic Ocean, Jean-Luc and Louise were standing on the deck enjoying the fresh sea air and watching the waves hit against the side of the ship. They were on their way to England and then to Paris to give their leader Robespierre a report on their latest activities. Both Jean-Luc and Louise were upset that Philippe had stolen the treasure from them, and they knew that Robespierre would not be pleased when he heard the news.

After discussing the matter discreetly, they decided not to return to Paris, but to stay in London, wait for Alexander to arrive, and then search for Philippe and the treasure. Louise was relieved and agreed with their plan for she feared that Robespierre might send them to the Bastille or even the guillotine for failing him.

Jean-Luc told Louise that he preferred to be alone, so he moved about the ship's deck singularly. As he stared into the rolling gray-green sea, he envisioned the beautiful face of his beloved Laura. The image of Laura's face upon the ocean waves brought comfort to this lonely man who longed for the day that he would be done with the awful business of revolution and piracy, and he and Laura would be together. As Jean-Luc meditated and fantasized about his Laura, a sly Louise was intensely watching her revolutionary companion.

At Winchester Park, the servants had managed to bring Evelyn Winchester to her room and place her in bed while one of the servants went to get the doctor. In a state, a worried Ethan and Honoria waited outside Evelyn's door. When Judith came upon them, she asked what had happened to her sister. Ethan told his mother that one of the servants had found Evelyn unconscious at the bottom of the stairs and was assumed that Evelyn had fallen down the stairs.

Judith told Ethan to go and help the servants locate Caleb. At first, Ethan did not want to go, but Honoria cunningly convinced him to honor his mother's request so she could be alone with Judith.

After Ethan had left, a servant came out of Evelyn's room and told Judith that her sister requested to see her alone. The servant went downstairs to wait for the doctor while Judith went in to see her sister. After making certain no one was in the hallway, Honoria cautiously opened the door slightly and eavesdropped on Judith and Evelyn.

Judith walked over to Evelyn's bedside. Evelyn opened her eyes, stared at her sister with a discerning look, and then spoke.

"I have walked up and down that staircase for many years and never lost my footing until today when someone gave me a push. I felt this person's hands upon my shoulders. Was it you my loving sister?" inquired Evelyn. "No, wait a moment I do not want to hear your response. I will tell you this: I believe there is no reason to destroy Ethan and Caleb's lives by exposing the truth about Ethan's parentage. As far as we are concerned, he is a Fairchild and heir to the Fairchild fortune. I will keep your secret and carry it to my grave as long as you, my sister, swear to me that you will not interfere with Ethan and Honoria's relationship. I want your word as a God fearing Christian woman and as my sister that you will leave those two young people alone."

Judith knew she had to appease her sister, for she needed her as her confidant. She also realized that she had much to lose if the truth about Ethan was made public. As much as she despised Honoria, Judith agreed to Evelyn's request while convincing herself to wait patiently for the day when she could rid herself of the woman who had her son under her spell.

Feeling relieved by her sister's response, a tired Evelyn closed her eyes and drifted off to sleep as Judith sat vigil by her bedside.

The next day, Constance and Charity went to New Haven to visit the local shops and warehouses in preparation for the trip. First, they made a stop at Bickford Mansion to see Laura Corday who was delighted to see them. Constance told her that they were leaving for London by the end of the week. She also told her that Jean-Luc and Louise had left for Paris, and Constance gave Laura a sack of coins with a note which Jean-Luc had asked Constance to give to Laura. The gift was a donation from Jean-Luc to Laura and her charitable home. Laura became emotional and thanked Constance and Charity for bringing the donation to her. She wanted them to stay for tea, but they said had to be on their way. Before they left, she wished them a safe journey and told them to return home safely. She also gave them an open invitation to visit her place upon their return.

As they were getting into the carriage, Charity caught a glimpse of the little boy sitting under the tree. He reminded her so much of young Charles. She made a promise to herself that if she should ever return to America, she would volunteer her time at Bickford Mansion and become better acquainted with the little boy sitting under the tree.

Constance kept Charity busy as they went from shop to shop. Her feet were begging for a rest when Constance agreed to end the excursion after a final stop at the milliner's shop. When they went in, the milliner was very pleasant and gracious in showing them the latest fashions in bonnets and lace caps. While browsing through the collection, the door to the shop opened and a terrible chill blew in. Charity turned her head, and to her horror, standing in the doorway was a woman wearing a long gown and a black veil. Charity froze from fright as she imagined the woman to be Lydia Johnson.

Chapter 32

As Charity stood speechless and frozen from fear thinking the woman in front of her was Lydia Johnson, the milliner greeted the woman by calling her Mrs. Applegate. She was pleasant as she apologized for startling Charity. She said that she was in deep mourning for her husband who had died a few weeks ago. She had come to the milliner's shop to purchase a bonnet as a gift for her daughter. Charity quickly began to relax after learning Mrs. Applegate was not Lydia Johnson. After making their selection of several bonnets and lace caps, Constance and Charity left and headed back to Singleton Lodge.

Sitting in the drawing room at Winchester Park, Caleb Fairchild was reading the newspaper and was intrigued by an article pertaining to the expansion of roads and bridges in the area. As a businessman, he knew that road improvements would attract more travelers to the town and thought it would be beneficial to be involved in such a venture.

While about this, Ethan came into the room and expressed to Caleb with the knowledge that his Aunt Evelyn would make a full recovery from the fall she had taken. Ethan became quiet for a few moments. And then he told his father that he was going to make a formal proposal of marriage to Honoria. He expressed wholeheartedly that Honoria was the woman he wanted to spend the rest of his life with, and he wanted the blessing of his father and mother.

Caleb put down the newspaper and told his son to sit next to him. He looked into Ethan's eyes and gave his blessing and said that he knew Honoria would make him a perfect wife, and he was not concerned about her family background and low connections. He explained that as long as Honoria stood by Ethan and the good name of Fairchild, he would be pleased to have her as a member of the family. After receiving his father's blessing, an elated Ethan shook his father's hand and then went to find Honoria to make his proposal.

After Ethan had left, Caleb sent for his wife. Although she was not pleased by her husband's news, she remembered her promise to Evelyn concerning Ethan and Honoria, so a calculating Judith smiled and pretended to be happy while concealing her true feelings about the marriage. Caleb told his wife that he wanted Ethan and Honoria to get married in church and then host a reception at Winchester Park. And as a wedding present, he wanted to send them to England for their honeymoon. Judith became irritated by her husband's plans but once again kept her thoughts to herself.

When Caleb had finished speaking to his wife, he left for an appointment he had in town, leaving Judith alone in the room. As she sat alone in the drawing room, she stared at the elegant furnishings and admired the grandeur of her home. She was very distraught in thinking that her son's future wife, a young woman she despised, would one day be mistress of Winchester Park. Judith was determined that one way or another she would not let that happen, but for the moment she vowed to bide her time.

In the afternoon, the lieutenant and Charity went to see Ebenezer Stiles. They went to his cabin, but he was not there, so they went to the old Higgins' place on a hunch that he might be there. When they arrived at the Higgins' property, they found Mr. Stiles tending to the graves of Elizabeth, Edmund, and Mr. Higgins. He was clearing away the fallen leaves. As they approached, a large brown dog came up to them wagging his tail and rubbing against their legs. When

Mr. Stiles saw them, he gave them a nice greeting and introduced them to his dog.

"This is my new companion. I named him Ishmael after the wandering prophet from the Old Testament, because I found him wandering around the docks begging, for food and attention," explained Mr. Stiles. "He cannot replace my beloved Pogo, but I welcome his company and loyalty. It is not good for anyone to live alone, and I believe animals, when treated properly, offer more respect and love than human beings."

The lieutenant and Charity told Mr. Stiles about Lydia and the letter Mrs. Kensington left before she was driven out of her home by an angry mob. Mr. Stiles shook his head in dismay, and then looked at the tombstones in front of them, and uttered, "May all three of you finally rest in peace."

Charity's eyes began to fill with tears and the lieutenant put his strong arms around her to offer her comfort.

Then the wind began to blow and a chill filled the air. As she looked in the distance, Charity saw the ghostly couple. To her astonishment, they were holding hands and smiling at her. Then they slowly disappeared into the horizon.

For the first time since she saw their images, she believed these spirits were Elizabeth and Edmund embarking together on their spiritual journey and finally at peace. And so was she.

Chapter 33

Preparations for the trip to England were finalized, and the day for the departure had arrived. The servants had been very helpful in packing the belongings, especially in arranging the women's gowns in a neat fashion. Constance made certain that they had everything possible to make the voyage comfortable. Alexander was very attentive and accommodating to his wife's requests.

As she watched Alexander's attentions to Constance, Charity could not help but to have disapproval and an utter dislike for him and his infidelity. She could still picture him and Louise in the stables. She did not want to be the cause for a broken marriage, so she kept what she knew as a secret for the time being. She hoped and prayed Alexander would never hurt Constance by being unfaithful again.

To everyone's chagrin, Colonel Parker's mind seemed to be improving. His speech was more coherent and he was no longer uttering Elizabeth's name. He did not seem to need the doll in his possession, and on occasion even smiled at Charity. Lieutenant Bradford seemed a bit distant; however, he was more talkative than when he first returned from the Ohio Valley. Charity assumed he was working through his grief in his own way. She was relieved and no longer felt lonely, uncertain, and afraid that something terrible was going to happen.

Mr. Stiles had adopted a four-legged companion, and both master and dog seemed fond of each other.

Jesse and Mrs. Andrews as well as their fellow tavern owners and shopkeepers were busy with the arrival of large numbers of workers coming to town to work on roads and bridges.

Reverend Benjamin Trumbull was pleased with the influx of new faces in the hope of expanding his congregation.

Dr. Foote and his wife opened up additional rooms in their home for boarders.

Mr. Pierpont and other mill proprietors were busy filling orders for lumber and other building materials.

The small agricultural town of North Haven was slowly but surely coming alive with people and activity. The promise of hope and prosperity had taken control, replacing the mystery, fear, death, and misery that held their grip on this community ever since the end of the war. Charity began to have reservations about leaving North Haven. If she ever grew tired of London, perhaps she would return to North Haven to set down permanent roots and establish her place in American society.

———————————

At Winchester Park, Evelyn was delighted with Ethan and Honoria's upcoming marriage, but she was keeping a watchful eye on her sister Judith who spent most of her time alone.

Caleb and Ethan seemed closer than ever, and Caleb was seeing to it that his son's wedding would be a gala affair. Honoria spent her days in elated bliss with a fixed smile upon her face. She no longer suffered from hideous laughter that had plagued her head. She believed that her life would be wonderful as the wife of Ethan Fairchild.

While the occupants and household staff were busy preparing for the wedding, Judith spent the majority of her time sitting in the drawing room in solitude with Dr. Greenville's letter close at hand. She read it over and over again while rejoicing to have the letter in her possession. But one afternoon Judith's solitude was interrupted by Honoria who entered without knocking. Judith hid the letter behind her and then demanded an explanation for the rude disturbance. A cunning Honoria seized the opportunity to irritate Judith by recalling Evelyn's unfortunate fall. But Judith was curious about Honoria's interest in the incident, so she listened intently and suspiciously.

"I am grateful Miss Winchester will make a full recovery. It would have been most tragic if something terrible had happened to her, and I know Ethan would have been devastated as she is his favorite aunt. It is very difficult for one to see who is behind another in the dark," replied Honoria. "It could have been anyone, but you are the most likely suspect and your sister seems to be in agreement with that."

"It was you who pushed my sister down the stairs, and now you're trying to put the blame on me. You are certainly the devil's disciple just like your ancestor Rebecca Noble," said Judith.

Honoria gave Judith an icy glare and told her to keep her wild accusations to herself for no one would listen to her. Then she mocked Judith, informing her that they would soon be one big family residing under the same roof while partaking in the glory and advantages of the Fairchild legacy. Before Judith could retaliate, Honoria left the room, laughing nefariously, leaving Judith alone to wallow in misery.

Judith stood up and took the letter in her hand. She walked about the drawing room several times, and then she stared out the terrace doors catching a glimpse of Ethan and Honoria standing under a tree kissing. An unvanquished Judith smiled deviously and vowed that she would soon have the last laugh.

Suddenly, she was startled by her husband who came from behind and grabbed the letter from her hand.

"Caleb, what do you think you are doing? That is my letter. Give it to me this instant," demanded Judith.

Caleb ignored his wife's request and calmly sat down on the sofa and began to read the letter. An upset and flustered Judith could not thwart him. When he was finished, he rose from the sofa and walked towards the terrace doors. Peering through the glass, he saw Ethan and Honoria enjoying each other's company. He smiled while shaking his head. Then he turned to his deceitful wife and spoke.

"I finally know the truth after all these years. I love Ethan as if he was my own flesh and blood. As far as I am concerned, Ethan is my son and my rightful heir. He and Honoria will marry and live here at Winchester Park with us. And you, my dear wife, will be very kind to them, and perhaps one day I shall find it in my heart to forgive you," replied a solemn Caleb.

Then he placed the letter in his pocket and left the room in grim solace. Judith remained standing and raised her hands to her face, and began to weep.

At the palace in London, King George III was joyfully anticipating the ball that he and the Queen were hosting at St. James' Court to welcome some new friends and celebrate the return of an old friend. Waiting outside the King's chambers, Philippe Monnerat was standing next to his wife Annabelle who was fussing with herself.

They were interrupted by Mrs. Kensington who walked past them. She was dressed in an elegant gown and wore a large, shiny diamond necklace.

Upon seeing Philippe and Annabelle, a coy Mrs. Kensington stopped to acknowledge the couple. She expressed cunningly how delighted she was to see them. Both Philippe and Annabelle looked with amazement while complimenting the diamond necklace. Mrs. Kensington told them that it was a gift from her late husband shortly before he died. She then changed the subject by reminding Philippe how fortunate he was in marrying an Englishwoman giving him the protection of the English monarchy from those in his country of France who wished him and his fellow aristocrats harm.

Philippe politely and gently took hold of Mrs. Kensington's arm while they walked to another end of the great hall. He whispered to her that he knew the Winfield diamond was carefully crafted into the necklace, and he was not going to reveal the truth in gratitude to her for aiding him in stealing the treasure from Alexander Caruthers and his companions. He also informed her that he had strong suspicions Alexander and others may come to London to seek him out, and that he was ready and waiting.

"You are more clever than I give you credit for, my dear Philippe. I cannot wait to see the look on the faces of Alexander and company when they see me dancing with His Royal Majesty and showing off my diamond necklace, and keeping company with you and your wife," laughed Mrs. Kensington.

A very pleased Philippe smiled at Mrs. Kensington and then escorted her and Annabelle into the King's chambers. As they entered, the King gave his guests a proper greeting and complimented Mrs. Kensington on her diamond necklace without suspecting a thing. He had the servants pour glasses of champagne and distribute them to his guests, and then he proposed a toast to the meeting of new friends and the reunion of old ones.

As they sipped their champagne, Mrs. Kensington and Philippe smiled at each other with ghoulish grins. While Annabelle was speaking to the King, Philippe and Mrs. Kensington had a private toast between themselves, declaring each other to be masters of the game. Mrs. Kensington graciously agreed with Philippe, but to herself, she mocked him and all her other adversaries proclaiming herself to be the one true master of the game.

———————————

The carriages and wagons were filled with many trunks and personal belongings. As they rode to the docks, Charity was happy to finally be on their journey. Constance and Alexander rode in the same carriage as the lieutenant and Charity. Caroline and two male servants rode in another carriage with Colonel Parker. The horses galloped along the bumpy and dusty roads.

Alexander entertained them with stories about his visit to England before the war. He talked about many interesting places to see and things to do in London. Charity sat back in her seat listening politely but laughing to herself about how much Alexander loved himself and his travels abroad. She also did not pay close attention to the details of his stories, because she was very well acquainted with London since she was born and raised there. While Alexander rambled on, Charity held onto the doll which she forgot to pack in her trunk, and she thought of her reunion with Patience.

When they arrived at the docks, Alexander instructed the waiting seamen to unload the belongings. He paid the men quite handsomely as they placed the trunks on the wooden planks prior to taking them aboard the ship.

As they waited to go aboard, at the far end of the docks, a group of men and women were performing a play that enticed an intrigued crowd. Constance wanted them to see the performance, so with the colonel who was behaving very properly in tow, they went on their way, leaving one of the seamen to watch the belongings. Charity got tired of carrying the doll, so she left it on the top of one of her trunks.

As they walked the docks, she had a strange feeling that someone was watching them. She turned her head a couple of times and glanced in the direction of where the ship was, but saw many people with unfamiliar faces walking about.

Lieutenant Bradford noticed her agitation and asked if she was feeling all right. She told him that she was fine but a bit anxious about the voyage. He reassured her that they would have a safe passage to England. She agreed with him and then became distracted by the performance.

After the performance had ended, they walked back to the ship. The captain was announcing that all passengers should come aboard. Constance and Alexander went first, followed by Colonel Parker who was using a walking stick with a dutiful Caroline, and the two male servants escorting him. Then the lieutenant and Charity were next to go aboard. Charity suddenly remembered the doll which she had left on the trunk. She told the lieutenant to go ahead and that she would be right back. He told her to hurry and he would wait for her.

She quickly made her way through the crowd. As she approached the place where they had left their belongings, she had that strange feeling again that someone was watching her. She turned her head and glanced over her shoulder. In doing so, she wasn't watching where she was going, and consequently bumped into someone wearing a dark blue cloak. She could not see the stranger's face and he did not speak as he continued to walk down the wharf in the opposite direction. She paid no mind, for her concentration was on retrieving the doll and rejoining the lieutenant. When she reached her destination, the crewmen had already taken some of the trunks aboard. She looked intensely, and then found that her trunks were still on the docks. Feeling relieved, she went over to her trunk, but as she stared at the lid, she saw that the doll was gone. She looked about frantically in hopes of finding the doll. Finally, she looked down by her shoes, and leaning against the bottom trunk in an upright position was the doll. She reached down to take hold of it, and to her strange surprise, the doll smelled like the sea and had a strand of seaweed tied around its neck. As she stood holding the doll, she stared into the crowd and heard an eerie but familiar laughter in the distance.

Preview for

Destiny
— and —
Deceit

Chapter 1

It was a windswept, raw December morning and the city of London looked bleak and dreary under the overcast sky. But the woman who stood at the window of the large drawing room in the house on Dover Street did not hear the rattling of the wind against the panes or even feel the persistent draft that penetrated between the window frame and sill. She was staring unseeingly into the street. In her mind she was thousands of miles away and just arriving at Kensington Hall. Eagerly she pictured the last few minutes of that journey. The carriage would gather speed as the horses galloped up the winding road. Then they would round the bend and it would be there—the great house, gleaming and white in the afternoon sun. It was a grand house with many rooms filled with beautiful and ornate furnishings. The pillars in the front stood tall representing strength and the high position the name Kensington held in society. But now the magnificent home was a pile of rubble and ashes due to the revenge of an angry mob.

The woman was so absorbed in her thoughts that she didn't hear the light tap on the drawing room, nor did she note when the door opened. For a long moment Mrs. Kensington stood surveying the servant and the tall, distinguished and handsome gentleman who had entered the room. The servant announced the gentleman as Lieutenant Michael Bradford. After announcing the lieutenant, the servant left the room closing the doors behind her. The lieutenant walked over to Mrs. Kensington who was stationary on the sofa. He gently placed his hand on her shoulder. Then an elated Mrs. Kensington extended her left hand, which the lieutenant kissed. "It is so good to see you,

Lieutenant Bradford. I've been expecting you," said Mrs. Kensington. "You have done a magnificent task in assisting Monsieur Philippe Monnerat and I in stealing the treasure from that pig headed fool Alexander Caruthers and his wretched band of revolutionaries that dreadful Louise Bourget and her devilish companion Jean-Luc Tessier. And now you have guided Alexander and his companions to London and right into my path. My compliments to you on a job well carried out, my son. Now, come and sit next to me so that I can look at your handsome face."

At the house on Market Street, Charity Chastine was standing by the front door putting on her bonnet. She was very anxious to be on her way to see her beloved Patience. She could not wait to see the expression on Patience's face when she walked through the door of her shop. As Charity fussed with her bonnet, Constance Caruthers descended the staircase and approached Charity. "My dear friend, I am glad that you are still here. I have sent for the carriage and if you please, I would like to accompany you to your friend's shop," said Constance.

"I welcome the company and I know that Patience would be pleased to make your acquaintance as I am certain you will be of her," said Charity. "Now let us be on our way."

As Charity and Constance went to the front door, Constance noticed a note that had been slipped under the door. She picked the note up and read it. Suddenly, a look of fright engulfed her face. She then showed the note to Charity. The message read: *Leave London immediately and never return. You are in terrible danger.*

At Baxter Lodge, an estate several miles outside of London, Margaret Ann Thatcher was returning from her afternoon ride. She led her chestnut mare into the stables. She bid the dogs, two

Irish wolfhounds, to remain outside. Jupiter and Apollo sank to the ground, whining softly, their large heads resting on their paws. The horses in the stalls nibbled at their straw bedding. Margaret Ann swung open a stall door, murmuring encouragement to her reluctant mare. Suddenly, her task at hand was interrupted by a voice. "Do not move or I shall shoot," a deep masculine voice growled from the depths of the stall.

His clipped, gentlemanly tones conflicted with his harsh words. Dropping the reins, Margaret Ann turned very slowly to face him. Grunting, a dark-haired man levered himself up from a sitting position against the wall, his face had an ugly expression of pain. He slumped against the rear wall, a hand pressed to his side. His dirty and wet shirt stuck to him in a way that revealed the athletic muscles beneath. Judging by his fine linen shirt and cravat, he was a gentleman.

"You are no stable boy," his voice laced with pain. "Who the devil are you?"

"My name is Margaret Ann Thatcher. These stables are the property of Victor and Irene Kent."

The stranger grunted. "I suggest you turn around and leave, woman. Let me die in peace." Margaret Ann saw the smudge on his shirt was not dirt, but blood. "You are hurt. Let me help you," she implored.

The stranger shook his head, looking dazed, "No I am not worth it." Margaret Ann refused to leave and she told the stranger that he was a human being and any human life was worth saving including his. But the stranger continued to beg her to let him die.

She ignored his request and stepped forward as she noticed a pistol slip from his grasp and into the straw. Then the man toppled to the ground and became unconscious. She rushed forward, bending to touch the pulse of his sweaty neck. She felt the beat of his heart. The stranger was bleeding and he was burning up with fever. As she studied his face, he seemed very familiar. Then she recalled who he was. It was Jean-Luc Tessier. To be continued …